Henry Plummer:
A Novel

FRANK BIRD LINDERMAN

Foreword by Sarah Waller Hatfield

University of Nebraska Press : Lincoln & London

Library of Congress Cataloging in Publication Data
Linderman, Frank Bird, 1869–1938.
Henry Plummer : a novel / Frank Bird Linderman;
foreword by Sarah Waller Hatfield   p.   cm.
ISBN 0-8032-7989-2 (paperback : alkaline paper)
1. Plummer, Henry Amos, d. 1864 Fiction.   1. Title.
PS3523.I535H46 2000 813'.52–dc21 99-42663 CIP

Contents

FOREWORD

Frank Bird Linderman was born in Ohio in 1869 and from boyhood was interested in learning, before daylight, habits of birds and animals in the woods near his Elyria home. A deep concern that the West of his dreams would fade before he could reach it and become a trapper drove him to study maps of the western states and territories, searching for an unspoiled wilderness.

In 1885, when he was only sixteen, he went directly to the Flathead Lake country in northwestern Montana Territory, the area that seemed yet to be the farthest removed from contaminating civilization. Hunting and trapping there for the next seven years, he became friend and confidant of Indians, mountain men, and prospectors. As Linderman learned tribal customs and stories of creation from the Blackfeet, Cree, Chippewa, Flathead and Kootenai Indians, who so impressed him, he mastered Indian sign language. His skill cemented his relationship with the great Crow chief Plenty-coups, whom he first met in 1892.

Plenty-coups named Linderman "Sign-talker" when he recorded his autobiography in the 1930 classic *American: The Life Story of Plenty-coups, Chief of the Crows*. Two years later Linderman wrote Crow medicine woman Pretty-shield's autobiography in *Red Mother*. Both books, originally published by the John Day Company, are now available from the University of Nebraska Press in Bison Books editions, titled *Plenty-coups: Chief of the Crows* and *Pretty-shield: Medicine Woman of the Crows*.

In his 1930 memoirs, "My Camp Kettle Career," edited posthumously by Dr. H. G. Merriam and published as *Montana Adventure: Recollections of Frank Bird Linderman* (University of Nebraska Press, 1968), Linderman described events that took place when he was twenty-one and that changed his destiny. Territorial governor Sam Hauser (1885–97), an organizer of banks in Virginia City and Helena, was a member of the group of prominent pioneers that Linderman was asked to guide on a hunting party. Included in the group were Judge Woody and G. A. Wolf, prominent in banking and the development of Missoula, and Sterne Blake, a rancher and part owner of the Curlew Mine in Victor, Montana. When Governor Hauser misquoted Shakespeare around a campfire and Linderman corrected him and completed the quotation, the men all urged him to leave the wilderness because he didn't belong there. When he left, he should look up any of them for help in finding work.

Linderman did leave the wilderness life behind him in 1892, to find other work and to marry Minnie Johns the following year. He again guided a Blake-Hauser hunting party before he started as watchman at Blake's Curlew Mine. At that time Hauser and Blake were the only living members of the 1863 Yellowstone expedition, in which two groups, failing to meet at an appointed rendezvous, were attacked by Crow Indians. "Ugly" men had ridden in those groups, including George Ives of the infamous road agents gang that operated in the gold rush days near Bannack and Virginia City when Henry Plummer was sheriff. In the other group had been Henry Edgar and Bill Fairweather, who discovered gold near present Virginia City. Edgar gave the name Alder Gulch to the area.

When the Curlew mining operations were cut back, Linderman became the mine's self-taught bookkeeper and assayer. He later became assayer for the Butte and Boston Mine in Butte, leaving there in 1896 to become an assayer for the owner of the old Toledo Mine in Brandon, near Sheridan, Madison County, Montana.

For twenty-five years after leaving the wilderness, Linderman followed his self-taught careers of miner, assayer, newspaperman, writer, and sculptor. He was a member of the Eighth and Ninth Montana Legislatures (1903–7), assistant secretary of state in 1907, and Montana general manager for Germania Life of New York.

Linderman's first book, *Indian Why Stories: Sparks from War Eagle's Lodge-Fire,* illustrated by Charles M. Russell, was published by Charles Scribner's Sons in 1915. He retired in 1917 to Flathead Lake to preserve in writing and sculpture the Old West—especially Montana—history he had come to know so well. Scribner's published his next seven books: *Indian Lodge-Fire Stories* (a school reader, 1918), *On a Passing Frontier: Sketches from the Northwest* (1920), *Indian Old-Man Stories: More Sparks from War Eagle's Lodge-Fire* (illustrated by Russell, 1920), *How It Came About Stories* (illustrated by Carle M. Boog, 1921), *Bunch-Grass and Blue-Joint* (verse, 1921), *Lige Mounts, Free Trapper* (illustrated by Joe DeYong, 1922), and *Kootenai Why Stories* (illustrated by C. L. Bull, 1926).

Linderman had long been collecting the known scattered facts of Henry Plummer's life from men like Governor Hauser and Sterne Blake, from old-timers who had known him, and from the Masons who finally hanged him. Living in the Bannack and Virginia City areas, the Masons became known as the Vigilantes who brought law and order to Montana Territory. Linderman had become a member of the Sheridan Masonic Lodge in 1899 and later an Honorary Thirty-Third Degree Mason. While a member of the Montana Ninth Legislature, 1905–7, he introduced a bill to commemorate the services of James Williams as leader of the Vigilantes. House Bill 49, passed February 13, 1907, appropriated money for a bronze tablet to be placed in the rotunda of the Montana State Capitol building. The commemorative statement and poem were written by Linderman, as verified in his introduction to *Henry Plummer*. As the twentieth century closes, Linderman is being honored as an Outstanding Montanan in the same rotunda.

Early research for *Henry Plummer* included recollections by C. L. Bristol, postmaster at Babb, Montana. On December 6, 1909, Bristol wrote to Linderman:

But as to the subject of your inquiries I will say it is a delicate matter. At the time I suppose I knew every one of the fourteen men who pulled the ropes (seven to each victim) but years afterward stories began to circulate that another I had never suspected was involved. This man was one of the most prominent in the county and he and I had worked together in republican politics often assisting each other. I never admitted nor believed that he was involved and the only circumstance that indicated that such might be the case was that he and the arch leader of the mob (who never did agree before) became very friendly and seemed to work together to keep the "Birch creek hanging" from becoming a political issue. (One of these men was a republican, the other now dead, was the democrat leader in the county). On account of my known hostility, then and always, to all kinds of violence and lawlessness, I would be held responsible for any published account of that horrible hanging, especially if the account were full and accurate. The survivors among the guilty and the public generally would lay the publication to me and I hardly feel as tho I could afford it. If I could see you I would tell you how the affair was suppressed at the time (suppressed to a great extent). I will say this. That, leaving out some of the early work of the vigilantes in

Virginia City, Bannack and a few other places, nothing has ever happened in Montana which, properly written up, would be more sensational than the account of this affair. . . .

Very truly, C. L. Bristol

Five years later, Linderman was still gathering material. On March 10, 1914, from Dillon, Montana, he expressed his thoughts to Charles M. Russell:

Dear Charley

I left Butte day before yesterday on the Oregon Short Line. . . . Then we struck the Beaverhead and turning down the river, skirted its rim for miles. . . . Once we came to some low country and away off I could see a wonderful range. I think they were the Rubies. You know how they looked, Charley, —all black and blue and white with just a suggestion of a haze to purple them and dull the sharper outline. . . . It was a pretty trip and sharp contrasts kept me busy from the time we left Butte far enough behind until we sighted Dillon. From Dillon I see the country I am best acquainted with, and over it, in the old days, roamed the best and the worst lot of men the world ever knew. . . . From here I can see the Beaverhead. . . . Up in old Virginia City the only graves in the old cemetery that are kept up are those of Club-foot George, Boone Helm, Jack Gallagher, Jack Parish and the rest of the gang and one is reminded that monuments are most always built to rascals. However I am glad they have not destroyed them for they belong to the days of the pioneer and there is little left of any sort.

Your friend

By 1919 Linderman was steeped in his subject. On April 21 he told Charley Russell that he was "starting a long story . . . about Henry Plummer and the bunch." Another letter to the artist followed on May 11: "There's plenty to make a story of Plummer and maybe I can do it. I can make as fine a start as anybody, but I hate to lie like a hound, especially in print. But I'm doing the Plummer yarn slowly and so far I haven't had much lying to do. Nice man, Plummer."

Russell's reply, with typical original spelling, followed on May 19:

Friend Frank

You say you have started a new novel that Plumer gang aught to make good stuff for a book but don't stay to close to the truth and be shure and stick in a lady and a hero. You like straight goods but the world dont and they are the folks that buy books. . . . with best whishes to you and yours from all of us

   your friend C M Russell

On November 17 Russell wrote that the Plummer book "ought to bee a winner."

   Like all writers, Linderman needed reassurance. That year (1919) he confided to his youngest daughter, Norma, a student at the university in Missoula, Montana:

Dear Babe:

   Just now I feel sure that Plummer is a rotten story. Day before yesterday, I knew it was bully—so it goes with our brand of humans. . . . I'm typing Plummer now. I wish it were done. I hate awfully to run a machine.

   Dad

Linderman was firming up the character of Plummer, still collecting information about his life prior to the events in the novel. Lew L. Callaway, his friend and fellow Mason and a partner in the law offices of Pray and Callaway in Great Falls, wrote to Linderman on November 27, 1919, about Plummer's 1858 murder trial in Nevada County, California, which led to a prison term in San Quentin. Through trickery and political pull, he was pardoned in 1859, "whereupon he started upon his pursuit of women, in which he was wonderfully successful, and of unlawful gain, ending up at Bannack on a cold day of January 10, 1864." Primary sources like Callaway confirmed the cunning of Plummer's character.

   Linderman was not oblivious to the irony of Plummer's physical fate, as an undated handwritten research note in his files suggests:

To paint a moral and adorn a tale: This gay debauchee, who had for so many years enjoyed the favors of the fair sex, was laid away in the sandy soil of a gulch near Bannack. A cloudburst sent its torrents down and these swept away the soil and the bones of Henry Plummer; no trace remains of the burial place; the bones were scattered far and wide and were trampled in the dust. A far cry was that transistory rocky-bed from the scented couches of the hours!

   On January 10, 1920, Linderman advised his friend, Dr. H. D. Rossiter of Sheridan, Montana, that his novel about Henry Plummer was completed. He continued to solicit details that might enrich the work. Writing to Lew Callaway, he asked the meaning of the numbers 3-7-77 that the Vigilantes had printed on cards bearing skulls and crossbones. Linderman had a copy of what he thought was an original card, pasted in a 1900 scrapbook. Callaway replied on February 5:

I suspect the joke is on you, for I doubt if there is any photograph of one of the original cabalistic warnings 3-7-77. This was written with charcoal, or some similar substances, on the door of the house where the undesirable was residing, or upon his tent, or it may have been handed to him written on a sheet of paper. Sometimes the writing was 3-7-77 and sometimes it was 3-11-77. I think the latter was used more often than the former. I used to ask the old vigilantes what it meant, and every one said it meant that the recipient had three hours, seven (or eleven) minutes, and seventy-seven seconds to make himself scarce, and it is not recorded that anybody ever took his full time. This was what Williams told me, and the way he expressed it.

Callaway thought that the 3-7-77 card in Linderman's possession was printed not in Plummer's time but in the latter 1890s by Bill Chealy of Virginia City, when citizens there were trying to ward off riffraff who had been run out of Butte. (In 1956, as a tribute to the Vigilantes, the first law enforcement group in Montana Territory, the Montana Highway Patrol adopted a new uniform shoulder emblem —the patrol star with the state seal above the numbers 3-7-77.)

Henry Plummer was rejected by Scribner's. The turndown was the first for Linderman, who on November 23, 1920, wrote to Dr. Rossiter: "My Henry Plummer ran against a snag, so I don't know what to do with it, but my Lige Mounts [a historical novel] is coming along again." Linderman clarified the publishing snag in a letter to Charley Haire, of Link & Haire Architects, on January 1, 1921:

I am mighty busy and I'll tell you why. I've written two novels. One of them is altogether historical, and Scribners have rejected it because it's too close to the facts to be a novel. They have suggested changes that I'd like to make, and am working on them. . . .

You see I've made a success as far as establishing my name goes and I've four books that they say will be selling when I'm dead. Now I want to get out a pot-boiler, and believe I've got it—two of them, for that matter. But they need work yet.

3-7-77. In an early 1900 scrapbook he titled "Buffalo," Frank Bird Linderman identified this rare photograph as "Photo from an original Vigilante Notice," which was the warning from the Vigilantes to road agents around the Virginia City and Bannack, Montana Territory areas. The origin of the notice is explained in a February 5, 1920, letter from Lew L. Callaway to Frank Linderman as "a notice printed by Bill Chealy in Virginia City in the latter 1890's." Courtesy of the Frank Linderman heirs and the Frank Bird Linderman Collection, K. Ross Toole Archives, Maureen and Mike Mansfield Library, University of Montana, Missoula MT.

In a letter to Charles Scribner's Sons on January 30, 1922, about their rejection of *Henry Plummer*, Linderman admitted that the first draft was a "poor piece of work" and he was "ashamed of it." But it *was* "a splendid story" and worth rewriting. "Someday Henry Plummer again will make his bow to you, and I hope you will let him in," he wrote.

Family friends were supportive of the disappointed author. One of them, Joe DeYong, a young protégé of Montana's cowboy artist, Charles M. Russell, corresponded in May 1922 with Frank Linderman's daughter Verne: "May Henry Plummer continue on his wicked way. The old timers here say he married a very nice girl who lived at Sun River Crossing, and that he was a good looking likeable man himself."

Although the reading public's changing taste for dimestore Westerns hurt sales of Linderman's books and created financial hardships, his commitment as a western historian is touchingly revealed in his June 28, 1922, letter to Harry R. Cunningham of Helena:

I have not thought of lessening my literary efforts, for I am getting along fairly well and my books are being well received. I found long ago, that I could not write books and Life Insurance and while I am sure that I could earn more money at the latter game I have long ago determined that there are more worth while things than dollars.

It is hard for some of my friends to believe that I feel it a duty to, in some way, preserve the old West, especially Montana, in printers ink and if I can only accomplish a small part of that duty I shall die contented. I have written six books and am half done with the seventh, besides finishing a dozen stories of old Marysville times since I came here and I am not half through. So, you see, if I can live comfortable and complete my work I shall be doing what I believe I was intended to accomplish. I suppose it sounds foolish but as Mark Twain has said, "I know I am a fool but I am God Almighty's fool and his works must be respected".

Nobody can tell what an author or his books can do until time has juggled both. Everybody knows that some of the best things have begged and some of the worst have known worship for a limited time.

I want to do my work and I had rather do it well and up to the standard of the West itself as I know it than get money for flimsy or cheap literature. I am going to stick for a while, Harry, and play the string out or until I see that I am in financial danger.

DeYong had illustrated Linderman's book *Lige Mounts: Free Trapper* and on November 25, 1922, Linderman wrote him from his winter Santa Barbara retreat, where he was revising *Henry Plummer*: "Dear Joe: The [news] paper has given 'Lige Mounts' big boosts, Joe, awful big. I am sure you must have a copy by now. . . . Henry Plummer is nearly done again; I hope for good."

He hoped in vain. Scribner's sent a disappointing and yet complimentary letter to him on April 19, 1923:

Dear Mr. Linderman:

We have read your novel "Henry Plummer" but I am very sorry indeed to say that we have not been able to feel that we could successfully cooperate in its publication. The difficulty seems to us to be inherent in the nature of the subject. There is, perhaps, no literary feat more difficult than that of making a novel out of actual material with an actual man for the hero. It is much easier to present a real character of a compelling sort in a novel in which at least the hero, and perhaps most of the other characters are fictional, but in which the real character may play a part of great importance. This is partly due to the mental attitude (at that time) of the reader of a novel, according to which a man like Henry Plummer is not satisfactory as a hero, whereas his career might be followed in a chronicle with much more interest. There is much to admire in your narrative. It has the breath of reality in it and so have all the characters. It does form a splendid picture of the time and places, but we cannot think that we could successfully publish it, much as we regret having to come to such a conclusion in the case of any manuscript by you.

Sincerely yours, Maurys Perkins

Did Perkins think that readers would object to an *attractive* badman as "hero"? His letter suggested the difficult choices facing the author in delineating the lead character. A close friend and fellow Mason and legislator, Dr. O. M. Lanstrum of Helena, advised Linderman to stick to his guns. He wrote on July 2, 1923:

My dear Frank:

I cannot tell you how sorry I am about the Henry Plummer business, because I have always looked forward to its publication in order that certain facts in the early history of Montana might be nailed down.

I do not think I would alter it from a historical standpoint if I never published it, because I do not think you can afford, with credit to your name, to alter a detail of what happened in Alder Gulch unless it absolutely sticks to the facts, because a large number of people in this State would accept your novel as history, knowing you as they do, and it would be quoted for a long time as an accurate statement of the facts of the early days.

I still feel that it is your duty to write the early history of Montana that some absolute record may be left that is dependable and that is not filled up with a lot of nonsenses.

As I have often said, each year is making it increasingly difficult to assemble the data necessary to get out the exact truth. With the passing of Granville Stewart and Jim Sanders and many other old timers, I do not know of anyone left who can even lamely do this. I have always felt that you were the one to do it because you could do it better than anyone else, but I now feel that you are the only one who could do it at all.

With love to Mrs. Linderman and the girls, I am
Yours very sincerely, "Doc" O. M. Lanstrum, M.D.

Nearly four years passed, and Linderman approached another publisher. On May 8, 1927, he wrote to Winfield Shiras at Putnam:

I have two or three unpublished manuscripts. One, "Henry Plummer," is the story of his life and death which I gathered from men who hanged him. Remember that it has been rejected by Scribner's. . . . However, it is only fair to say that the rejection of "Plummer" seemed based upon the fact that he was the "hero" and the villain—was hanged, and so made a "bad ending" to the story. . . . If you are in the market for sketches of the Northwest (from real life) I can furnish many. I should like, above all things, to write them, because they ought to be written before it is too late.

Shiras replied on August 10, 1927:

I hope you do not think that your manuscript has been lost or mislaid. . . . Four or five of us in this office have given it a very careful reading. All of us liked the story for one reason or another, and read it through with interest to the very end. The consensus of opinion, however, is that the difficulty of your theme, which necessarily must blend biography with fiction, weakens the story . . . and falls short of publication.

Henry Plummer, although he stands out in the story strongly and [is] nicely portrayed, falls between the fictional and the biographical treatment. I do not believe that the unhappy ending in any way hurts the story. I feel that it is the strongest portion of the whole book. The hanging scene is exceptionally fine.

The dialogue I think could be improved. . . . At all events you have a great story here and I hope you will have the patience to do something more with it and that you will eventually place it.

Linderman's daughter Norma Linderman Waller, who worked with her father in preparing his manuscripts during the last ten years of his life, said that he continued to make the suggested changes to his Henry Plummer story but *did not alter historical facts* he had learned. A much improved *Henry Plummer* was finally put aside for a future generation of readers to discover as he continued to publish works with the John Day Company in New York. He had much yet to write. In 1932 *Old Man Coyote* (Crow legends illustrated by Herbert M. Stoops) followed *American* (1930) and *Red Mother* (1932). *Beyond Law* (1933), a sequel to *Lige Mounts: Free Trapper* (1922), was his second published novel based on historical fact, and *Stumpy* (1933, illustrated by H. M. Stoops), a children's story about a chipmunk living at Goose Bay, Flathead Lake, that has enchanted generations since, completed his association with the John Day Company.

Discouraging book sales during the Great Depression did not deter Frank Linderman. He wrote the text "Out of the North" in *Blackfeet Indians* (1935, illustrated by Winold Reiss) and continued to write books that have been published posthumously by the University of Oklahoma Press (*Recollections of Charley Russell*, 1962, and *Wolf and the Winds*, 1986) and by Mountain Press Publishing Company of Missoula, Montana (*Quartzville*, 1985, a historical novel of true Marysville, Montana, mining stories told to Linderman by early-day Dr. O. M. Lanstrum and edited by Larry Barsness; illustrated by Newman Myrah). Many unpublished works remain in the Linderman family archives since his death in 1938.

Frank Linderman surely died very contented. He did accomplish his dream by presenting and preserving a wealth of stories about the Old West as he knew it. He introduced future generations to the way it was when Montana was young and wild.

Henry Plummer again makes his bow.

SARAH WALLER HATFIELD
Granddaughter of Frank Bird Linderman

INTRODUCTION

To this land from all creation
Fortune beckoned every kind:
They were best and worst who answered;
Averages were left behind.

It was greed that led the white man to the Northwest. He did not come primarily to build or to settle but to enrich himself and go away. It was an enchanted land where treasure was unguarded. Its unexplored vastness bewildered him till, wandering, he met the three Genii: Adventure, Danger, and Hardship, who cast their spells and held him in his youth and strength.

No man who has not lived in virgin wilderness can know the subtlety of its charm. The trapper fell easily under it, for he loved solitude, and so long as there was wilderness he wandered. The trader built rude posts or forts to protect his life and his goods during his stay near his red patrons. In taking their harvests of fur, both the trapper and trader fought unrecorded battles, braved every hardship, performed the noblest of deeds, and committed nearly every crime before they passed, leaving little to testify to their occupancy and almost nothing of their history, for they were nomads, not builders.

It was not until the booted miners followed the moccasined trappers to the Northwest that settlement was made on any of the tributaries of the five great rivers which rise in the vicinity of Yellowstone National Park. They came, however, to gut the land of gold, not actually to settle. Most of the mining camps which burst into being at the discoveries of pay gravel along these rivers' courses thrived, waned, and died, leaving scantiest skeletons to mark the spots where wealth and poverty, vice and virtue met and were more intimate than any otherwhere on earth. But in their time the bearded miners were gregarious, and in the deep fastnesses on unexplored mountain gulches they prowled in pairs or parties, prospecting, picking, panning, prying into nature's treasure vaults for *pay*. When they struck it they beckoned, and immediately the tramp of thousands was upon the heels of the discoverers. A city was born almost overnight—a city of flimsy structure and of heterogeneous population, including men of learning, men of means, and men who lived and left their names as giants among their kind.

I

When the camps were struck, the Civil War was raging. There were those who had emigrated to the wilderness to escape service in the great contending armies, and there were discharged soldiers from the Union and Confederate forces, all of whom were more or less bitter in their expressions of sentiment, so that far from the scene of the regular war, battles were fought over that question which had divided the nation. At times the American flag was torn from its staff and trampled in the dirt. Regular soldiers stationed in the wilderness to protect miners and settlers were assaulted and murdered because of the uniform they wore; and, although punishment usually followed such acts, the excitement of the times, the great war of the sections, the lack of government control in the new and remote Northwest made crime abundant and license free.

Miners from California, gamblers famed the world over, and desperate ones from every nook and cranny came there to better their condition, or to escape justice. There were good women and bad, but the bad far outnumbered the good, for life in a new mining camp is hard. There was no law and few questions were asked. Prosperity, the universal excuse for license, was rampant, and so no man made note of another's shortcomings. Only the good in his fellows, like the gold in the gravel, attracted his attention.

There was a time when murderers and highwaymen were believed by honest folk to be in the majority, when even to whisper of suspicion meant death to the whisperer. No trail was safe. Men mysteriously disappeared. Miners, with their hard-earned wealth, left the camps for their homes and were never heard of again. Robberies were a daily occurrence, and stagecoaches escorted by armed guards were held up and plundered in open day on the public highways. Whole freight outfits, long trains of wagons with their attendants, were looted and the freighters murdered in their beds. Pack trains, laden with goods for the camps, were waylaid in the mountains and their owners killed; even the horses and mules were slaughtered sometimes, in order to hide the greater crime. Men rode into stores and saloons on horseback, and tossing buckskin pouches upon the counter or bar, ordered them filled with gold dust, and it was done. There was no help for it, no law, and no man dared to raise his hand or his voice in protest. It was the *bal masque* of civilization where decency fiddled—an orgy which for a time threatened to engulf the infant mining camps and to forbid the establishment of peace and industry there. Fortunately, its hour was short; but in its time, while deliberately burning its candle at both ends, it presented unbelievable characters.

Of them all, Henry Plummer was most remarkable. His story has always fascinated me. Having lived most of my years among men who knew and finally hanged him, I have gathered whatever I could of his life's history, piecing together the bits and striving to imagine the forces and motives that set him off the course which his birth and early environment should have fashioned for him; for it is known that he was gentle-born. Indeed, when he was dead, his misinformed relatives in an eastern city were bent upon avenging his taking off, and were only prevented from entering upon such folly when, in kindness, two Montanans, Nathaniel P. Langford and Edwin R. Purple, presented to them the established proofs of their kinsman's infamy. Mr. Langford and Mr. Purple have testified as to the gentility and culture of Henry Plummer's family.

Where I could do so and tell my story, I have followed facts in sequence. When it was necessary to employ fancy to build a connected tale from the scattered bits of fact, I have done it grudgingly. Be it known there are men yet alive [in 1920] who knew Henry Plummer, and while it is not strange after so many years, there are differences of opinion concerning his movements even among them. They are the critics whom I most fear. Still, while this story of mine does not pretend to be a true history of Henry Plummer's life in Montana, it is not likely that a truer one will be written from the meager history of his time.

That Henry Plummer could so long have escaped and carried on as he did seems altogether unbelievable, especially when the only explanation offered for such license, aside from his own cool ability, is the absence of confidence among the men of the mines, their lack of acquaintanceship and community organization. Yet he did carry on —did dominate not only the outlaws of his band, but others whom he made, by his masterful will, to believe in him. And, of all who knew him and finally judged him, there was none who knew him as he knew himself; for Henry Plummer held a secret belief in his own unavoidable destiny which controlled his life and which at his death he revealed.

3

Following are variations from history I have chosen for this novel: (a) Of the main characters, only three names have been substituted —those of Elizabeth Bryman and Jane and Seth Bailey. (b) There is nothing to show that Henry Plummer was in any way responsible for the quarrel between Pinkham and Patterson, and he may not have been in the vicinity when it occurred. I have used the story of the quarrel to show the conditions in the mining camps during the period of the Civil War. (c) I have changed the time of the hangings at Virginia City of Gallagher, Club-Foot George, and the others, which occurred three days after, instead of before, the execution of Henry Plummer. (d) I have no proof that James Williams himself hanged Henry Plummer, but Williams was the leader of the Vigilantes, and it is probable that he would have insisted upon hanging the archcriminal of them all. His name has been withheld from all written histories and stories of the times, but I have succeeded in having a bronze tablet to his memory placed in the Capitol at Helena, Montana. It bears this inscription:

TO COMMEMORATE
THE NAME AND DEEDS OF
JAMES WILLIAMS
CAPTAIN OF THE VIGILANTES

Through whose untiring efforts and intrepid daring, law
and order were established in Montana, and who,
with his associates, brought to justice the most desperate
criminals in the Northwest.

*The sluice was left unguarded when Williams' task was done,
And trails were safe for honest men through victories he won.*

The Masonic funeral played the part I attribute to it, and it was the brotherhood of that fraternity which led men to insist upon the establishment of law and order in the mining camps.

It is generally believed that the woman I have called Elizabeth Bryman did not know Plummer's real character until after his death. She never returned to the mines.

The graves of Gallagher and the rest who were interred on Cemetery Hill at Virginia City are well marked and undisturbed, save that of Club-Foot George, which was once opened to prove the order in which the outlaws were buried. The deformed foot of George Lane (Club-Foot George) was taken as proof that no mistake had been made in marking the headboards, and has long been displayed in the courthouse in Virginia City. But the elements, as if to prove to the world what must be his fate beyond the grave, refused to let Henry Plummer rest. His bones were washed from their shallow grave in Bannack by a cloudburst and scattered over the rocky bottom of a dry gulch near the Grasshopper diggings.

I am indebted to Chief Justice Lew L. Callaway for the story of the encounter between Williams and Slade, which in this book I attribute to Bill Thompson in his speech to the Masons in the Masterson cabin, and to *Vigilante Days and Ways* (Nathaniel P. Langford, 1890), as well as *Vigilantes of Montana* (Thomas J. Dimsdale, 1866), and many men who have lived in Bannack, Virginia City, and Helena.

FRANK BIRD LINDERMAN, 1920

1

Two hours after the sun had set on a May day in the early sixties, the Walla Walla stagecoach reached the Snake River. Shadows were creeping out of the willows that grew on the banks of the stream, and as though fearful of them, the driver popped the long lash of his whip over the ears of the leaders to urge them on toward the journey's end. The coach, rocking on its leather thorough-brace, chucked and joggled over the rutty road and tossed the passengers about uncomfortably.

"Most there now, lady," said a voice in the growing dusk of the coach.

"I am so very thankful." It was a young woman who answered softly above the rattle of the wheels. "Not that the journey has been at all unpleasant. Indeed, everybody has been so considerate of my welfare I feel as though I have been a nuisance," she added, as if in apology for her presence in so rough a country.

"A good woman—a lady—is never in nobody's way," said the man.

The flush which spread over her face was hidden in the dusk, and the man continued, "We can tell 'em. They're so different from the others; and they're scarce enough here, God knows. Beggin' your pardon . . . there's Lewiston!" The coach had rounded a sharp turn and was crossing the river when more than two thousand lighted tents burst into view.

In the soft night air of spring, and under the sky of lowered clouds that threatened showers of rain, they resembled strings of giant Japanese lanterns hung by magic in the land of dreams. They winked and flickered in groups while, a little apart from the conventional multitude, like bawds in a ballroom, larger, brighter tents glowed in the darkness, extending their welcome to the tired passengers in the coach, as did the more fraternal strings that reached merrily to the outermost parts of the town.

"Oh, how enchanting, Henry," whispered the young woman to the young man beside her.

"Yes, it's pretty enough," he answered indifferently. Then, as though he had felt her shrink at his lack of enthusiasm, he added, "I'm glad we're here. I'm tired."

She pressed his hand secretly. "I, too, am tired, Henry," she whispered appealingly. And then, startled by the welcoming shouts and shots as the stage swung in between the long rows of lighted tents, she clutched his arm. "Ah, here we are," she said. She winced at the sharp cracks of the driver's whip and the reports of six-shooters which announced the arrival of the coach in the main street. Up the street it dashed amid cheering citizens, seemingly all men, dressed in slouch hats and red or blue flannel shirts, and with trousers tucked into heavy boots.

Flimsy dance halls where dancers whirled to loud music, their shadowy forms showing plainly through the cotton walls, flashed by the passengers in the coach, and now and then a log building standing darkly among its neighbors with an air of greater substantiality. Men called their greetings to the driver. Bits of conversation, cut short by the speed of the coach, flung themselves at the passengers under its canvas cover. "Look at him!" cried a man astride a boney horse as the stage swung up and stopped at the Palace Hotel. "Gimme a hundred! Ain't a blemish on him. Gimme a hundred!" he went on, literally carried away by the crowd, for the street was packed with men and, like an ant hill, seemed to move with life.

"Good night, lady; good night, sir," said the other passengers as the young couple alighted from the coach before it should whirl away to the express office just beyond. The young woman bowed pleasantly and, mindful of their kindness and respect, waved her hand. Then, holding her palm upward, she laughed lightly, but as if with determination. "Why, Henry, it's sprinkling. Do they have electrical storms here, I wonder?"

He did not reply but, stooping, gathered up their two carpetbags and turned to the doorway, where the bowing clerk stood ready to take them from his hands. "I'll show you to your room, sir," he said. "Supper's all ready. You'll want to wash up. But it's nearly closing time," he added, his pudgy, perfumed form shuffling down the hallway over the flimsy, creaking floor to a door which he threw open. There, setting the bags just inside as though glad to be relieved of their weight, he struck a match and lighted a candle on the bureau, lingering to admire his black hair plastered low on his forehead and shining with oil. "Number nine sir," he said. "I'll hold places for you in the dining room." And he turned a moment at the door and bowed.

"We shall require but a moment," said the young woman, beginning to remove the veil which she wore pinned over a modish bonnet.

Then, while the clerk's footsteps creaked back along the hallway and she folded the veil, her eyes scanned the bare, unpapered walls and the single window. "It's very close in here, Henry," she sighed, removing her bonnet.

He strode to the window and threw up the sash, propping it with a stick that was on the sill for the purpose. "Get ready for supper," he said coldly.

After perhaps ten minutes, they entered the dining room, a long, narrow hall with bare log walls, windowed only on one side, and with but two doors, one opening into the office, the other into the kitchen. Its ceiling was very low, not over seven feet, and was, in reality, merely the rough board floor of rooms above that was supported by round, peeled logs crosswise of the dining hall. The rooms above were occupied. The tread of heavy cowhide boots on the boards so near the young woman's head was disconcerting, but only for a moment. After a half-startled upward glance, she smiled amusedly and her hand sought the young man's arm. A Chinaman was serving a dozen men scattered at the several tables in the light of tallow candles, and as the new guests entered every eye in the room turned toward them. They were a striking pair. The same young man who had been at the door as the stage drove in studied them intently, as if trying to place them.

The woman, alone, would have appeared to be considerably above the average height of women, but with her escort did not seem to be overly tall. She was dressed in a traveling dress of stone-colored merino ornamented with blue silk and black velvet, with a wide-sweeping skirt and a close-fitting bodice, and she moved with perfect grace across the room. As she smiled acknowledgement of his courtesy in seating her, her large blue eyes swept the room, and although the glance appeared casual, it somehow left every man with the uncomfortable feeling that he had been appraised.

Her escort was nearly six feet tall, fair, and as straight as an Indian. He was slender, even delicate, moving with a swift grace that so often characterizes people born to place and influence. He had a firm mouth that was finely cut and a chin that was strong and suggestive of daring. His slender shapely hands, white and almost as soft as those of a woman, were quick and sure in their movements, as though nature had fashioned them for some peculiar deftness.

A thoughtful person might have observed that his clear gray eyes were not only inscrutable but steely cold, and the attractive woman by his side strove with her charm to soften them. But if she had ever possessed the power to set those eyes aglow with passion it was now hopelessly lost, for while searching and seeing all with comprehension, they never changed their expression of heedless indifference—never offered her a morsel of devotion, though he attended her with studied courtesy. His voice, in addressing her, was not unpleasant, but pitched in a low monotone that in a long continued conversation might prove tiresome. One would not, at least at first, have associated the man with his voice. Moreover, his hair was out of keeping with his otherwise neat person and correct appearance. It was badly dishevelled and fell over his forehead in a rumpled pile. Still, he was handsome, and in spite of the fact that he was evidently but a boy in years, there was that about him which commanded attention and held it.

As soon as these late guests were served, the Chinaman closed and bolted the door. As one by one the patrons left their places at the tables, he followed to let them out and to prevent others from coming in.

Alone, even the desultory conversation that had been maintained in the presence of others ended, and the handsome pair finished their meal in silence. At last they also rose, the shuffling Chinaman accompanying them to the door and saying "Goo'-bye" as he closed it behind them.

"I'm likely to be out late," said the young man when they were back in their room, and picking up his black slouch hat from the bed, he crossed to the window and closed it against the damp west wind that stirred the crumpled curtain.

She shifted the candlestick on the bureau. "The fresh air smells good," she said, guarding her voice against a tone of disappointment. "Of course, I shan't mind your going out if you need to go, Henry. If I feel lonesome, I shall sleep."

He offered her no explanation. Deftly brushing back the tumbled lock of hair from his forehead, he put on his hat, pulling the wide brim down well over his eyes. Striding back along the hallway to the office, with a nod to the clerk, he went out of doors.

"Who is that fellow, Billy?" a miner asked of the hotel clerk.

"I don't know," the clerk replied. "He came in on the coach. His name's Plummer. That's all I know."

"Salt Lake City, hey?" muttered the other, peering at the register. "Further east, further east, I bet."

2

Leaving the hotel, Henry Plummer turned down the main street of Lewiston, which, despite the pitchy darkness and gently falling rain, was crowded with roughly garbed miners and prospectors from the hills. Here, indeed, was a new country, a new mining country; and as a wolf's blood is quickened at sight of his quarry so Henry Plummer's stirred with the thought. But there was no hint of his mind's work in his eyes under the dark hat brim, as his tall figure clad in fashionable clothes—dark frock coat, fancy brocaded vest, and gray trousers over well-polished boots—picked its way with quick, springy steps to the far end of the street. There he turned and, crossing over, came more than halfway back on the other side, his eyes measuring each lighted tent wherein there was gaming until he reached the Combination Gambling House, at the door of which he turned in.

The Combination was the most pretentious of all gambling houses in Lewiston, its sturdy log walls reaching fifteen feet from a floor of fifty by seventy feet. There was no ceiling, and, under the pole rafters set thick beneath a steep-pitched shake roof, the smoke from scores of cigars and pipes hung like a gray cloud throughout the year. On the right of the front door, leaving but a narrow passageway between it and the building's end, was a long bar, behind which three and at times six bartenders waited on the patrons who stood before it or sat at the many card tables in the room. Three faro layouts, always attracting crowds of players, occupied spaces near the wall on the opposite side from the bar, the chairs of their dealers and lookouts touching the hewed logs. The remaining floor space was plentifully furnished with fixed round tables and accompanying hickory chairs arranged so that a passageway reached from up near the front to the back of the room.

The place was always well patronized. Tonight, perhaps because of the rain, every chair was occupied, every table full. Men stood four and even six deep about the faro layouts, watching the deals and the luck of the men at play. Now and then an onlooker, who with neck craned from the outermost row had been anxiously following the turn of the cards, would cry, "Hold the deal!" and, elbowing his way to the layout, glance quickly at the cases there to reassure himself, then make a bet. "All down?" the dealer would ask disinterestedly, and again the deal would go on.

Now there was no disorder, no conversation, save an occasional short comment on the run of the cards. The games held every man tense, anxious, expectant; and many were perspiring, though the room was not warm. The dealers seldom spoke, but quickly and surely paid bets or deftly swept chips, money or gold dust to themselves as winnings. They were marvels of speed and efficiency. Even though layouts were strewn with bets great and small, some cards played to win, others to lose, and still others to win and lose, they made no mistakes, gave no man cause for complaint. Seated a little above them, the lookouts, with faces like graven images, never took their eyes from the game. Witnesses they were, and not a play escaped their studied notice, no bet but what they knew, though their countenances remained as expressionless and vacant as those of the Sphinx of old Egypt, and as hard—like the fates themselves who watch men's lives with seemingly cold indifference. Good and bad luck as evidenced in the games before them provoked neither smile nor frown; though they firmly believed in both goddesses, worshiping one and fearing the other with a wholeheartedness that would have shamed the superstitious Indian.

Stopping at the bar, Henry Plummer bought cigars and, lighting one, stood for a moment watching the scene with deep satisfaction. The constant clicking of chips and the hum and babble of voices about the card tables were music to him. When at last a man arose from a chair at a table well back in the room, he at once began to move towards the vacant seat, slipping through the crowd of watchers with the ease of one well accustomed to such places and their patrons. Slowly, and as opportunity offered a way through the jam, he approached the table at which four men were playing poker and from a vantage point near the vacant chair began to watch the game, intently and in silence.

Two of the players were professional gamblers, clean-shaven save for luxuriant mustaches and goatees, wearing the dark frock coats, black or blue neck scarfs, and fancy waistcoats which distinguished the more respectable among them; for already in the new Northwest clothes were affected to differentiate picturesquely between callings, and professional gamblers were the most fashionable of men. The others were full-bearded placer miners clad in the conventional red shirt of California. Their trousers were stuffed into heavy boots and on their belts hung holsters containing long navy six-shooters.

Plummer, standing there, must have watched the play for an hour, when at last one of the miners winning a pot of considerable size looked up, nodded pleasantly to him, and smiled.

"I beg your pardon, gentlemen," said Plummer, "but I have been watching your game and I should like to beg a part in it."

The four men surveyed him appraisingly. "I'm agreeable," said one of the gamblers, shuffling the cards.

"Suits me," said the other, brushing the cigar ashes from his lap.

Plummer seated himself in the vacant chair and, together with the others, was instantly lost in the game. Only at long intervals did any man at that table order a drink, and as the hours passed there was no apparent slacking in their absorption. Once after midnight one of the miners stood up to stretch his legs, being unaccustomed to sitting so long; but withal they endured close attention to the game as hour after hour slipped by and one by one the other tables were forsaken.

Dawn came with its mountain chill. The crowd had thinned to a few gamblers about the poker tables and to four or five men and a woman who still played at the faro layouts. The babble of voices was gone. There were not twenty people in the room. The bartenders dozed behind the bar, and several drunken men, snoring loudly while they slept, were on chairs ranged along the wall at the back of the room. A Chinaman began cautiously to ply a broom about their feet. Morning was coming. The floor of the Combination must be swept.

At last one of the gamblers at Plummer's table looked at his watch. "Oh, Dick!" he called, "Fetch us a round of drinks. Then I'll go to breakfast."

Fortune had been unusually fickle at that table and had favored first one and then another of the players. "I had intended retiring early," remarked Plummer, as he began to stack his chips, "but I've enjoyed the game. Let me compliment you all. You are poker play-ers." He gave no reality to the low-spoken words other than their mere pronunciation, and his expression did not change, for he kept himself always under vigilant control; yet the men, perhaps against their own wills, felt distinctly flattered. Thus do fashion, good looks, and an air of authority influence us. Bending over the table, he pushed his stack of chips to the banker, and then, straightening in his chair, drew a fresh cigar from his pocket, lighting it at one of the candles which still burned beside him. "Pardon me, gentlemen," he said as he made use of the light.

An Indian had been standing for some time up by the door with his back against the wall near the bar. As Plummer replaced the candle on the table, the red man made quick movements with his fingers as though tying a neck scarf. Plummer's eyes gave no hint that he had noticed, but turning back to his companions at the table, he coolly counted the money paid him for his chips before he said, "Good morning, gentlemen." He bowed to each as he rose from his chair and turned towards the door, from which the Indian had already van-ished.

Outside, he glanced up and down the street in the early light of day as though undecided which way he would go. The Indian was only a short distance up the street. He started in that direction but turned and for a time walked leisurely opposite. At last, however, he faced about and, without attempting to overtake him, kept the Indian in sight until he saw him enter a lodge by the river on the out-skirts of the town. People were already stirring on the streets. Plum-mer made a wide detour before he finally slipped into the lodge.

The Indian was kindling a fire. Plummer dropped the lodge door behind him noiselessly and stood still, watching him intently. The Indian, on his knees, bent low and blew on his infant blaze. "Pretty good rig, ain't it, Henry?" he boasted, without changing his posi-tion.

"Yes, it is. I took for you an Indian. But I shall know you in a minute. Look at me!"

The Indian turned his face, hard and with a low, narrow forehead and black, beady eyes. "I am innocent," he said with a whimpering chuckle, mouthing the three words as a child would a lump of sugar.

Plummer watched him closely, though his gray eyes seemed to look through him and beyond him without consciously seeing him.

14

"Yes, I know you are innocent. I saw your sign." And before the man could speak he added coolly, "What are you doing here, Bill Bunton?"

"You called a turn, Henry!" The Indian pulled a wig from his head revealing a crop of short, coarse black hair. "I didn't guess my rig was so good," he exulted, squatting beside his fire. "But I was dead sure *you'd* spot me mighty quick—an' you did, too," he said approvingly.

He was a square-built fellow with a short bull neck and dark skin, a brute in nature, if face and form spoke truthfully. Squatting there, he worshiped Henry Plummer with his shifty eyes.

"How long have you been here, Bill?" Plummer asked, sitting down on a blanket near the lodge door.

"Not long—only five days. I had to run for it. They was crowdin' me mightly close in Nevada, an' I made up as an Injin an' fooled 'em. Cherokee Bob, Jack Cleveland and Club-Foot George are here, too. They was in on the racket with me, but nobody knows it but me. Bob made a mess in Walla Walla a little while ago."

"Club-Foot George, you said? I thought he was killed in San Francisco."

"Well, he ain't dead, or wasn't yesterday. He was drunk as a lord an' lookin' fer trouble. I saw *you* early last night, Henry, but I couldn't get yer eye. You win anything?"

"No," said Plummer, handing Bunton a cigar. "Where do the boys hang out, Bill?"

"I'll have 'em here any time you say, Henry. They'll be mighty glad to see you. We need the chief. Nothin' goes right when you're gone."

Plummer thought for a moment. A whole year had passed since he had been in close touch with Bill Bunton and other members of the gang of road agents that had recognized him as its chief. High-handed brigandage in California and Nevada had at last reaped a whirlwind of wrath. The miners of the southern country had turned. The gang had scattered. Even he had found it the part of wisdom to leave San Francisco, after a jury there, packed it was claimed, had acquitted him of murder. Drifting aimlessly eastward, he had visited the larger cities between San Francisco and Boston, gambling successfully wherever he had found gaming to his liking. Now he had come to the new Northwest where another strike of gold had been made, feeling certain that those of his scattered gang who had escaped the vengeance of California and Nevada camps would find their way also to the new diggings.

"Make it eight o'clock tonight," he said shortly. "I'll be here."

"Good! The boys'll be here, too. An' Henry, the roads out of here are rich as milk gravy. They ain't been worked, neither. Hardly a day goes by that the stages don't carry a stake in gold dust an' we're a-lettin' 'em git clean away."

"Well, we'll see," said Plummer, rising. "I'll be here at eight o'clock. Don't have any light here or any fire. How long are you going to continue masquerading as an Indian?"

"Till eight o'clock, Henry. Not a damned minute after you take hold. God! It's good to have you back handlin' things. The boys ain't no good without you. Where you been?"

Plummer raised the lodge door. "I'll be here at eight o'clock sharp," he said again, ignoring Bunton's question and hurrying away.

Already his thoughts were busy with vivid plans for the future. He did not note that the sun was rising, that the morning was fair, or see the green grass and wildflowers he crushed with his feet as he cut across to the main street which would lead him to the Palace Hotel.

3

At room number nine he knocked gently on the door, and it opened at once. "Good morning, Catherine," he said easily.

His eyes swept the bare room in a flash, reading the story of its occupant's sleepless night, noting, too, that the carpet bags had been unpacked and her garments and his own cared for. "I wondered if you would be up," he added, stepping past her to pour water from the pitcher into the wash bowl. Removing his coat, he unbuttoned his soft shirt that he might wash his face and hands and thus freshen himself for a new day.

"Oh, I've been up more than an hour," she answered cheerfully, consulting the watch which hung by a long chain of gold about her neck. "And Henry, I'm so ravenously hungry! It must be the change of air. I could hardly wait until you came," she said, handing him a towel.

"I'm sorry you waited," he said, accepting the towel and burying his wet face in it. "I can't breakfast with you. You will have to excuse me. I came only to tell you."

She could hardly believe she had heard him right. Pulling at her watch chain as if to steady herself, she asked in a voice that trembled in spite of her effort to hold it, "Is it—is it only because of your—your unexplainable prejudice against removing your hat? Or what is it, Henry? What is it? Tell me, dear? Is it only because you dislike to be bareheaded?" She hoped, oh, how she hoped it was only that!

He glanced swiftly into the mirror. "Let's not discuss it," he said as he dried his hands. "I dislike argument. I cannot be with you today. I have work to do. Go to your breakfast."

He had not spoken sharply or above his accustomed tone, but there was a finality in his word that dazed and crushed her. She sank back on the bed, burying her face in a pillow. The door of the room opened and closed quietly. Then when his footsteps had set the hallway floor a-creak, her sobs shut the sound from her ears.

In ten minutes he was seated at a table in a Chinese restaurant, where, with his hat upon his head, he ate a hurried breakfast. Then he went back to the Combination Gambling House. As he entered he saw the Indian leaning against the wall near the door, but without appearing to notice him, he went on to a card table, picked up a newspaper, and feigned examination of its pages.

He was thinking about the proposed meeting at the Indian's lodge, however, and the old lust was upon him. If Cherokee Bob, Bill Bunton, Cleveland and Club-Foot George were in Lewiston, others were sure to drift into the camp too. He would organize them as he had done in California and Nevada. He would secure the confidence of the better citizens of Lewiston, and holding himself aloof from the companionship of the outlaws, he would be able to know when the merchants, miners, gamblers and other men possessed money in sufficient quantities to be worth plundering. This information he could transmit to the highwaymen and, as their chief, share handsomely in the spoils. Some of the most respected citizens were gamblers; as a gambler he could keep in close touch with the life and affairs of Lewiston. He had seen no familiar face since arriving and there were few who had cause to suspect him. He knew he had been too cunning in his operations. In San Francisco he had cultivated acquaintance with the influential men, and when finally he had needed them, they

17

had responded, honestly believing in his good character and in his plea of self-defense. The test had come suddenly. He had killed a man marked for slaughter by the gang, and when obliged to stand trial for murder, the prosecution was unable to establish any connection between him and the highwaymen, although, in reality, he was their chief. There had been veiled talk, mutterings, it is true; but after acquittal he had left the scene of the trial with the friendship and sympathy of many honest men. He could do it again—win the men of Lewiston and operate as he had in California.

He laid the paper aside and picked up a deck of cards that was on the table. Almost without his bidding, his fingers began to shuffle them, swiftly and with ease. Then in a preoccupied way he began to lay out a game of solitaire. One by one he turned the cards, and as though by magic, the card most desirable appeared. He became interested, intent, fascinated by his run of luck. His fingers moved even more swiftly. Card by card, the game was being beaten. It was nearly done. Not a card had been against him. His luck was phenomenal. It held him as one hypnotized. His eyes gleamed and his breath came fast between his white teeth—until suddenly a disappointing card changed success into failure. He laid the remaining cards face downward and, glancing towards the bar as though to discover whether anybody had been watching him, met the gaze of a prospector. The man, dressed roughly in the garb of the hills, was standing in front of the bar waiting for the barkeeper to fill a two-gallon keg, and his sharp blue eyes were looking straight at him. Plummer quickly turned his attention back to the cards on the table. He was sure there had been recognition in the gaze of the prospector, and he was trying hard to place him.

In another moment the man had picked up the keg and left the place. Plummer rose and, going to the door, watched him put it in a sack and tie it fast to the outside of a pack on a Spanish mule, then swing onto a roan saddle mare and ride out of Lewiston, followed by three loaded mules.

"Who is the gentleman that had his keg filled?" inquired Plummer of one of the barkeepers.

"I'm sure I don't know," replied the barkeeper, leaning forward to see out of the door. "I've seen him before, but I don't know his name. He's a quartz miner from the east side of the range. Mighty nice man."

Plummer returned to the table and picked up the cards again, but the prospector would not be driven from his thoughts. "Where have I seen that man?" he pondered. "He knew me. I'm certain of that. I don't like his looks."

4

When at eight o'clock in the evening he entered the lodge near the Snake River he found only three men waiting for him. They were Bill Bunton, Club-Foot George Lane and Jack Cleveland.

"Jack," he said, dropping the lodge door behind him and shaking the hand of a young man who had risen in the dim interior, "I'm glad to see you. You're a high card in any game. And George, too," he added with less enthusiasm, "I'm glad you're here; seems like old times to see you. Make a light, Bill."

Bunton at once began to lay a small fire. "I'd a-had one, only you said not to," he muttered, setting fire to the twigs.

Plummer made no explanation regarding his former orders, but seating himself by the door, watched the blaze grow and illumine the lodge. He asked no questions concerning their doings of late and they knew he would answer none touching his own since leaving California. Yet there was a certain friendship between them, not a sentiment born of honest fellowship but only the brittle bond which makes wolves to run in packs, hating common enemies, and fearing most of all the wrath of their fellows.

"You're drinking altogether too much, George," Plummer said abruptly in the firelight.

Club-Foot glanced suspiciously at Bunton, who sat by his chief's side across the fire.

"No, no—you're entirely wrong." Plummer spoke impatiently, noting the cripple's accusing look. "Bill has said nothing about you. I can see by your face and general appearance that you've been drinking again, and heavily. You've got to stop it."

Club-Foot tossed his hat behind him. "All right," he grumbled. "Now you're with us again, I will. But mebby it's because I need a shave that I look like I do."

A grin spread over his coarse face, revealing uneven yellow teeth.

The mouth, partially hidden by a thin blonde moustache, was cruel, and his pale blue eyes were set close together under bushy brows that nearly joined. His nose, heavy and flat, was of the pronounced negro type, and his forehead, though not so narrow as Bunton's, sloped suddenly above his heavy brows into a shock of unparted, curly reddish hair.

Looking at the grinning face, one would have thought instinctively of a wolf. But when the smiling lips were closed there was something clownish there. He was heavier than the others, and older in years; not so tall as Plummer. Had it not been for the deformity of his right foot, which was clubbed, requiring a curiously fashioned boot, George Lane would have been a perfectly built man, though never neat in appearance or pleasant to look upon. By trade he was a shoemaker, having learned while yet a boy, "so's he could always be dead sure of havin' somethin' to fit his right foot," Bill Bunton declared.

"Where is Cherokee Bob?" Plummer asked, lighting a cigar.

"I couldn't find him, Henry," Bunton said. "He's here somewhere though—or was the other day."

"Cherokee and Bill Mayfield are courting," laughed Cleveland, putting wood on the fire. "I think they are over in Oro Fino. Both of them are infatuated with a woman—a Cynthia Ames from down Walla Walla way. But Bill seems to have the edge on Cherokee. He's the better looking of the two, you see."

"I'll find him soon, an' Bill Mayfield, too," promised Bunton. "They'll be with us all right enough, Henry."

"We shall have to build us a shebang somewhere so that we can keep horses and have a headquarters," said Plummer musingly. "Where would you suggest building a ranch house, Jack?"

Cleveland gazed thoughtfully at the fire. He was tall as Plummer and as fair, his black slouch hat, tilted backward on his well-formed head, revealing thick yellow hair. He was boyish in appearance and neat in person. In his blue eyes there was only daring, and his clean-shaven face, though willful, showed no trace of the life he had led. He looked even younger than his chief, although he was in reality nearly a year older—twenty-six. Mischief had early led him into bad company along the wharves and among the byways off an eastern city, where, finding that he could live by his wits, he had turned to gambling. Then a quarrel over cards had made him a murderer in a second, and before the law could take him he had fled to the mines of California. There, discovering many whose lives had likewise been forfeited, he had associated himself with the roughs, and was nearer to Henry Plummer than any member of the gang, knowing more of his past life than any of them.

"I think Craig Mountain would be the best place, Henry," he replied after a time. "You see the trails fork there—or the pack trail crosses the stage road there to go into Oro Fino, and we could work both the road and the trail from a place at Craig Mountain. And Alpwai Creek is another good place. I think we could establish ourselves at both Craig Mountain and Alpwai Creek."

"Say, Henry," interrupted Club-Foot, "that Dutchman Hiltebrant's got a lot of dust an' money. He keeps it in his saloon here—sleeps with it—him an' two more Dutchmen. Let's take 'em in, hey?"

"That sounds attractive, Jack," Plummer said, ignoring George. "We'll have a look at both places, you and I. Be at Craig Mountain between one and two o'clock tomorrow, Jack. I'll meet you."

"It's the boss pick, Craig Mountain, Henry, an' Alpwai, too," agreed Bill Bunton. "An' both the road an' the trail is rich as milk gravy."

"Boone Helm is in Oro Fino. I saw him a week ago," said Cleveland, still talking to Plummer while ignoring Bunton, as men who count themselves in authority will talk above those who they feel to be inferior, but whose devotion they do not doubt. "He says the camp is flourishing and that the mines are paying big. I'll send him word to come over if you say so, Henry."

"Yes, by all means do so," agreed Plummer. "Boone is a valuable man. I'm glad he's in the country." He searched his pocket for a match. "Do you happen to know any quartz miners or prospectors from the east side of the range—I mean do you know any of them who have been in Lewiston lately—today?" he asked.

"No. Why?"

"I saw a man today, and they told me he was from the east side. He knew me, I'm sure. He had a roan saddle mare and three pack mules—young man of medium size with whiskers and sharp blue eyes. I wish I knew who he was, or where he knew me."

"What of it?" laughed Cleveland lightly.

21

Plummer lit another cigar. "Oh, I didn't like the way he looked at me, that's all," he said. "If I knew who he was—"

"Oh, hell, it was some half-crazy prospector, no doubt. You just imagined he knew you," interrupted Cleveland, looking sharply at him.

"No, that man wasn't crazy and he wouldn't be afraid of forked lightning. I'm glad he is on the other side of the mountains. We couldn't both live in the same community, that man and I."

Cleveland laughed. "I didn't know you were superstitious, Henry," he said wonderingly.

"I don't think I'm superstitious, Jack," replied Plummer, rising. "But I know a dead game man when I look into his eyes, and I only hope I was mistaken in thinking the prospector from the other side recognized me. That's all. I'll be going now. Meet me at Craig Mountain between one and two tomorrow afternoon. Good-night, boys."

He slipped silently from Bunton's camp and turned his steps toward the Combination Gambling House. At the edge of the town he looked back and saw that the fire in the lodge was brighter. "They're visiting," he thought. "I'll find a place and set up housekeeping. It will have a better appearance and give me a higher standing in the community—make me a stronger citizen." He turned a corner and entered the throng of men that moved up and down between the tents and buildings. His eyes took note of the appearances of men and women, and he thrilled with his own cleverness. "Wealth and poverty," he mused. "Wealth and poverty, and the roads just marked ways in the wilderness. Without the knowledge that it is my business to acquire, who could distinguish between them by outward appearance?"

5

Bannack City, eastward from Lewiston, was hardly a year old. Gold in the Grasshopper diggings that had occasioned the camp was paying its miners handsomely. The climate, more rigorous than on the western slope of the Rockies, shortened the mining season, it is true, but with the discovery of placer gold, a few prospectors had found gold-bearing quartz veins in the mountains about Bannack. These could be mined at any season of the year, provided supplies could be brought to the claims before the earlier storms set in. So one or two men, because of that advantage and the limited number of claims available on the Grasshopper, had turned to quartz mining. "Hard-rock" mining was new as the country itself, and the methods of treating the ores mined for gold were adopted from the Mexicans or early Spaniards in Mexico and California. Crude machines fashioned with few tools, the Spanish arastras, when operated by a master of the art, saved most of the free gold; and as they were set on the banks of mountain streams flowing near to the mines, water furnished the power to turn their large over-shot or hurdy-gurdy wheels. Back, and yet farther back from the infant civilization of Bannack City, and into the vast surrounding wilderness, these few men pressed their way, uncovering the quartz veins, building their arastras, and packing in their supplies either from Lewiston on the western slope of the great mountain range or from Fort Benton, established by the American Fur Company years before, three hundred miles away on the Missouri River. The steamboats brought freight to Fort Benton from St. Louis and other cities, so that supplies were to be had at a lower price there than at Lewiston, where goods came only by the more costly pack or wagon trains. The distance to Lewiston from the Montana mines was shorter and there was less danger of encountering hostile Indians in the mountains than on the plains. The only merchants at Fort Benton were the American Fur Company and the firm of Labarge, Harkness and Jallard, essentially fur traders, not dispensers of merchandise to miners. Both might at any time, if their stocks were low, refuse to part with their goods intended for the more lucrative Indian trade, so that, purse permitting, men from the eastern slope of the Bitterroots often outfitted in Lewiston.

The May sun was yet an hour above the wooded tops of the Rubies when a man leading a roan saddle mare, followed closely by three heavily laden Spanish mules, stopped to rest from the fatiguing climb up a steep gulch in the Tobacco Root Mountains, two days' ride eastward from Bannack City. Looking across the dreamlike valley below and to the Rubies purpling under the setting sun, he could trace the shining course of the Stinking Water, winding through groves of green cottonwoods and alders, flashing across stretches of plains to its junction with the Beaverhead; and could plainly see the point of curiously fashioned rock—like the head of a swimming beaver—which gave the larger stream its name.

Wilderness all, and beautiful. The rivers, receiving their tributes from the white-capped mountains that walled the sister valleys, grew larger and more majestic with each contribution. And no wonder, for soon the waters could meet others from the same district that, flowing by different routes, would join them at Three Forks to make the great Missouri, the river of Lewis and Clark.

The man could also see the white-capped Trappers and Bloody Dicks clearcut against the blue of the northwest sky, and even the blue foothills where Bannack City nestled. Though as he reluctantly turned his eyes away and glanced upward at the sunset-reddened peaks to resume his climb, he did not guess that nearer to him than Bannack City, nearer even than the Beaverhead rock, was an undiscovered gulch which within less than a year would stir the world with its wealth—a gulch richer in placer gold than any discovered unto this day.

"Come, Kit," he said, at length.

The climbing was sharp just here. The scrambling hoofs of the pack mules loosened stones that went pitching down into the gulch below, striking the fir trees and rattling through bushes on the steep hillside. Suddenly, routed from his hiding place, a blacktail buck bounded from a clump of small firs and then, blacktail fashion, stopped in an open spot to look back and listen to the rolling stones that had startled him. In an instant the man's rifle cracked. The deer bounded blindly down the hillside with his tail crimped tightly to his rump. For a moment the man stood listening to the echoes his shot had wakened as, back and forth, growing fainter and farther away, they played with the sound until at last it was tossed beyond hearing.

"Meat, Kit—good fat meat," said the man as the echoes faded. "You wait here a bit."

The mare began contentedly to crop the grass on the hillside and the mules, edging closer, nibbled here and there, restless under their burdens, until the man, after perhaps ten minutes, reappeared. "Got him, Kit," he laughed, taking up the lead rope.

The mare, smelling the blood on his hands, snorted suspiciously. "Come, come, no foolishness," he said. "I got to have meat and that was handy. You're mighty lucky I didn't take you along to fetch it in, you good-for-nothing."

For half an hour they continued their climb, the man revelling in each change of light on the white peaks above him as a child delights in a picture book of fairies. He loved the mountains, loved his life, loved his mine, with the love of youth that has turned to the wilderness with its whole heart and with something of the spirit of the true miner who spends his life in the quest of gold. And, as they climbed, he more than once spoke encouragingly to the mare when the way was especially difficult.

The shadows of night were creeping down the gulch, growing deeper as the red light faded from the peaks above him, when at last he turned downward to enter a park-like meadow beside a rushing creek that foamed here and there over boulders in its bed. Following the roaring water a little way, he came upon a small log cabin, its stick and mud chimney barely clearing the almost flat dirt-covered pole roof. As he came abreast of it, he dropped the mare's lead rope and walked around to the south side of the cabin to bend over a luxuriantly growing peony. "It's budded, Kit," he said, returning. "Our peony's budded." Then with practiced hands he began to relieve the mules of their packs by the cabin door.

This beautiful spot was typical of the camps of quartz miners. On the hillside, above the cabin, the man had opened up a vein of gold-bearing ore, a red dump marking the mouth of his workings from the hills for miles around, while down by the creek stood his arastra with its hurdy-gurdy wheel, idle for the time.

"Now, Kit, it's your turn," the man said when the mules had been unsaddled and turned loose to roll on the green meadow. "Come, come, hurry," he urged. "I got to fetch in that meat yet, remember."

The mare, ready enough though slow—relying upon the favoritism that was hers—came up to him dragging her rope and bridle reins, and even after her saddle and bridle were hanging on a peg by the cabin door she did not offer to go away, nickering gently and poking her soft muzzle against her master's arm.

"Uh-hmn. You no-account little beggar," he laughed happily. "It's sugar you want, hey? And me packin' it a couple of hundred miles. Huh!" He picked up a sack from among his supplies piled near the cabin and opened the door and went inside.

The mare nickered again, looking through the door.

"Stop that racket," scolded the young man in play anger. "Want to advertise? Think I want to feed *mules* with sugar, hey? It's too far to be packin' sugar for a band of mules, hear me? Now, take this and git out of here, or I'll—" He did not finish his threat, but handed the mare a lump of brown sugar and stood watching as she turned contentedly towards the grazing mules.

"Now," he said to himself—for always men who are long alone talk to themselves—"I'll go and fetch in that meat. If the way was fit I'd take a mule, but 'tain't fit, nor 'tain't far, and that's lucky."

An hour later a fire was burning in the cabin fireplace and there arose the savory odor of coffee and drying venison. As the man squatted before the fire attending his cooking, the shadow of his head covered almost as much space on the cabin wall as did the rest of his body. Although square-built and sturdy, with stout shoulders and rounded chest, the body appeared dwarfed by the manner in which the shadows emphasized the large, well-poised head, its broad, high forehead and heavy shock of tumbled black hair parted low and carelessly tossed so that it hid his ears.

His blue eyes twinkled in the firelight with the silent good nature of a man satisfied with his lot. They were small eyes, but bright, minutely searching eyes that would not shrink from looking into the muzzle of a threatening gun. Men knew this at a glance. Hot temper had no record in his face, but instead a sluggish nature that would brook much before it protested. Even then the eyes would warn tormentors—perhaps in time. His mouth also, not being finely cut and having rather thick lips, gave his face a serious, moody look. "That man never laughs," one would have declared, not seeing his eyes. There was something compelling in those eyes—a look of honest, searching appeal, and an element of daring which amounted almost to defiance, as if they sought it outright and rested on its authority. Like the majority of the men in the new country he was young—twenty-nine—although his rough garb made him appear somewhat older. Asked as to his height, most men could not have answered, though it was average. But nobody would have forgotten his eyes.

Placing the hot frying pan on the table, he lighted a candle, poured a tin cup of coffee, and sat down to his supper. He ate slowly—and if one had observed him at his cooking he would have expected all of his movements to be slow. At a noise near the open door, he turned expectantly and the mare looked within and nickered.

"Beggin' again!" He set down his tin cup in mimic disgust. "You no-account Injin Cayuse! Well, you can't have any more this time," he said, glancing at a tin cup of sugar on the table.

A louder nicker.

"Condemn you! Listen, Kit. I can't afford it. And there's something on my mind besides sugar. This country's filling up with bad men. They're drifting in here from the lower country. You and your mules had better stick right close to the cabin or they'll get you sure's a butterfly's pretty. Hear me?"

Whereupon he reached for the sugar cup and, selecting a generous lump, got up and went over to the door, outside which the mare stood in a streak of light from within. "Here," he said, "take this and don't get any more—not tonight. And remember what I've told you. The bad ones are coming in. I saw one of them in Lewiston—the very worst of them all. I knew him as soon's I set eyes on him, dad burn him. And he knew I knew him, too."

6

"Mrs. Plummer! Mrs. Plummer, look! Mrs. Plummer! Look at *me*!"

Startled by the excitement in the child's shrill voice, the young woman called for ran to her open door. A little boy, hardly six years old, his eyes shining with the thrill of his own daring, was balancing a half-dead snake on a stick held at arm's length. "Look at *me*!" he cried, both tiny hands clutching the stick around which the snake's mottled body writhed in hideous contortions. A cry of horror rose to her lips, but she smothered it there lest she frighten the child. The instinctive fear of serpents, common to the human family, was on her.

"Archie, drop the stick quickly and run to me, dear," she said, as evenly as she could. "Quick, Archie!"

"Ah-h! It's a killed snake. Ah-h!" the child protested, revelling in her terror. "It's a killed snake," he repeated sarcastically, "an' I wanta keep it."

He changed his position. Now his elbows rested against his chubby sides, as intently he turned the stick to keep the twisting snake from falling.

"If you'll drop it and run to me before I count ten, I'll give you a great big piece of cake," she trembled.

He cast the stick from him, but, still fascinated, walked a step nearer to the snake to watch the effect of the fall.

"Archie!" In terror of his next move, she ran and snatched him into her arms and fled to the house.

"It might be a rattlesnake," she panted, setting him down inside. "It might have bitten you, child. What would your mamma say when she came home and found her little boy" her voice grew suddenly husky—"bitten by a snake," she finished. She cut a generous slice from a chocolate cake on the kitchen table, and nervously glancing out the door where the snake lay squirming in the grass, said, "There, dear, eat your cake."

The boy noted her glance. "Harry Needler give it to me," he told her, his mouth full of cake. "Harry said it was the poisonest snake they is; an' he's more'n nine," he added impressively, his eyes grave with thoughts of his friend's advanced years.

She closed the door and secretly turned the key. "Let's play at guessing riddles, Archie—just you and I," she proposed, determined to keep the youngster in the cabin until his mother, who had gone to the new schoolhouse to see an older daughter take part in exercises, should come for him. She gave herself to the task with her whole heart and, fearing sudden rebellion, cleverly suggested clues to answers for the simple riddles she propounded, assuming surprise whenever the boy followed them successfully and always feigning deep perplexity over the riddles offered by him, fashioned often in his own romantic mind.

Perhaps it was art that gave the little home the distinctive touch so noticeable to women callers. Its neatness had much to do with its charm, for it was neat without affiliation with the chill sometimes found with extreme order. Its spotless floor, its shining windows and polished cookstove bespoke the housekeeper; but the touch given to curtains, a picture, a book or two, and to the arrangement of the furniture in the rooms was different from other homes around it— was of the woman's self. Everything seemed to be of more worth, the furnishings almost ample, although nobody could have much of household goods in Lewiston.

In the flame of a passion—whether noble or ignoble—we are able to live amidst hardships without so much as feeling discomfort; and she could have been happy here if only the secret fear of losing Henry

Plummer's love would cease its torment. She tried to believe he was fond of the little home in spite of the irregularity of the hours he spent there—for a gambler could not choose his hours.

This profession of gambling did not impair his standing in Lewiston, be it known. The country was new. Men, anxious to get a start—to make money quickly and go away—were engrossed in their personal affairs, and their wives, lonesome for the company of their own sex, could not afford to be snippy where all were adventuring, so that individual worth was generally recognized as the only requirement in Lewiston's meager society. She had made friends among her neighbors, none of whom had known the early advantages which had been hers. They were good, honest, home-loving young womenfolk who shared their husbands' ambitions to get a start, and go back to the homes of their childhood.

For nearly an hour she kept Archie interested, when at last the cries of homecoming schoolchildren stirred him and he became restless. Only the charm of another generous piece of cake held him within bounds till from the open window he called, "Here comes mamma an' that ol' Miss Fancher. She's sister's teacher. An' mean! Gosh! Harry Needler says so."

His borrowed dislike for Miss Fancher did not deter him, however, from running with a glad cry to meet his mother and sister; while within the little cabin the fire was being hastily kindled for the brewing of tea, the maker's hands trembling not only with the zeal of the hostess but with an almost feverish desire to please. For if there was one avenue through which she was sure she won Plummer's approval, it was in this making his home attractive and popular.

While she served the tea and cake she recounted the snake story, interrupted with exclamations of "Mercy, Archie!" and "Why, Archie Murray!" which so delighted the youngster that the combined efforts of the ladies were necessary to restrain him from intruding the serpent to the tea party.

"Miss Fancher, won't you please sing that little song again? The one you sang for the children this afternoon?" begged Mrs. Murray when they had finished their tea. "Just for Mrs. Plummer?"

"Why, of course," laughed the teacher. "It's just a little thing I've picked up," she explained, apologetically, reaching for her accordion. "I call it 'The Laugh of the Light.'"

Having heard Archie's disparaging remarks concerning the teacher, Miss Fancher, one would have wondered how such a little lady could have acquired the reputation thus ascribed her. She was beautiful to look at—a fresh blond with exquisite features, and a voice so soft and sweet that it charmed. A mere girl she was, whose father was part owner of a claim in Oro Fino.

Her song so pleased the two ladies that another and yet another was asked for, until having thoroughly entered into the spirit with the little teacher, they all sang popular songs in chorus while Archie slipped away unnoticed to find his oracle, Harry Needler.

They were singing when Henry Plummer, coming rapidly toward the cabin, stopped to listen by the open door. On the way from the Combination Gambling House where he had spent the day at cards, he had been pridefully conscious of approving glances, occasioned he knew by his faultless attire; and as he walked along he was carefully measuring his chances in the more desperate game he had secretly set out to play. Just now there was occasion for satisfaction. Things were moving smoothly and profitably for him. Already the stage from Lewiston to Walla Walla had been held up and robbed on a day when it carried a gratifying amount of gold dust. Four days ago two miners had been relieved of their cleanups, and the day before a wagon train had been robbed—all without bloodshed—and all at his orders. His popularity in town was growing every day and he congratulated himself upon setting up housekeeping. It had, as he intended, strengthened his position in Lewiston. And now, standing in the shade of his own roof, he smiled in deep satisfaction. His home was popular. Suspicion would be long in pointing its finger at him. Just as the song was ending, he playfully knocked on the frame of the open door, bowing low at the confusion his alarm occasioned.

"Is Mrs. Plummer in?" he asked in mock seriousness.

"Yes, indeed, Henry dear! Come in and meet Miss Fancher. You already know Mrs. Murray. We've been having such a pleasant time, Henry."

"Of course I know Mrs. Murray," he said, advancing into the room and bowing over that lady's hand. "And Miss Fancher, I am delighted to meet you."

The girl's eyes were smiling when they looked into his, but at the young man's boldness they fell to the accordion under her arm. Her cheeks reddened.

"Won't you continue singing?" he asked them, vainly conscious of the disturbance his look had created in her mind. "I shall blame myself for breaking up your party unless I can prevail upon you to go on with it as though I had not come."

"Oh, Mr. Plummer, we must be going now," laughed Mrs. Murray. "I had no idea it was so very late. You see, Miss Fancher has accepted my invitation to sup with us, and the fire isn't even started."

"A very pretty excuse, I am sure," said Plummer with a bow.

Mrs. Murray laughed and Miss Fancher blushed. "We'll see you again tomorrow, Mrs. Plummer," said Mrs. Murray at the door. "And thank you so much for caring for Archie."

"You have made some nice friends here, Catherine," Plummer said, when she had closed the door and he had taken up a cedar pail to go for fresh water from a cold spring near the cabin, noticing as he turned it in his hands how the brass hoops that held its staves together were polished bright as gold. He smiled to himself. His scheme was working even better than he had hoped. Catherine, innocent of any knowledge of the real part she was playing in his secret game, was a great help.

"Yes, Henry, I like them very much," she answered evenly, though her heart was like lead because of the look he had so easily bestowed upon Miss Fancher. And catching her breath to keep back the tears, she made the inevitable effort of a desperate one for at least temporary respite, like the loser at cards who tries again because his better sense is stifled with desire.

"Do you like my hair done this way, Henry?" she asked, her head poised gracefully, hopefully, to show the coils of her hair done low on her neck and confined in a net, in place of the curls of the period.

"Yes, Catherine," he said, turning his cool gray eyes upon her from the door. "Yes, your hair is always beautiful."

7

In June, when the mountain slopes were velvety green and only the far-off peaks stubbornly refused to accept the young summer, Jim Bent brought his wife and two children to Lewiston from California. Inquisitive, anxious, feverishly active to little purpose, Bent had followed up every discovery of gold since his twenty-fifth year, and now he was thirty-five. He was always late, but ever expecting good fortune to be with him the next time. His quest had come to live in every line of his face, marked by the winds and privations in inhospitable gulches where men had but little to divide with the luckless and where fortune played pranks beyond their ken. His money was gone, and as usual Mrs. Bent had been obliged to move her washtubs from the old wagon and take in washing to feed herself and the children.

"Never you mind, Ma," Jim said encouragingly while he built a rough bench for the tubs, "we'll strike it yit. Then you'll see, Ma." And straightaway, to be of help and yet keep at his quest, he began delivering the bundles of clean clothes—he and the little boy—listening to whatever was said by men in the street or women at their back doors. "Don't you worry, Ma," Jim told his tired wife at the end of every harrowing day. "We'll strike it. I know it, doggone it. We gotta!"

At last the woman fell sick, and the household, thus crippled, sank to despair—all save Jim. Nothing could daunt his faith in his fortune, and he clung to his hope of finding a claim that would pay, even when his wife had been forced to take to her bed.

Far down from the Palace Hotel in an obscure portion of the town a hot wind shook the tent that sheltered a miserable couch where the sick woman lay watching the clock on a box in the corner. Over a cracked stove, one corner of which was propped with a chunk of white quartz and the broken door of which was held shut with a stick that leaned against it, a boy and a little girl were cooking a grouse.

"Ain't they no salt, Ma?" asked the boy hopefully.

"I think there's a little in that small can in the cupboard, but don't use too much, Willie dear. Your grouse smells good. I'm glad you got it," said the woman, turning her tired face to the wall.

"I killed it with a stone, Ma. An' when we eat it, I'm goin' out ag'in. Mebby I kin kill another. Sis scared 'em or I'd a-killed another, anyway."

"Didn't neither."

"You did, too."

"Oh, children, don't quarrel. Eat your grouse," sighed the woman, straightening the blankets upon the tumbled cot.

At that moment the door opened and Jim Bent rushed in and seized a blanket from the bed. "They've struck it rich in Florence!" he cried, and bolted from the tent with the blanket in his arms.

"Jim! Jim!" called Mrs. Bent, but there was no answer. He was on his way to Florence with nothing in his pockets and hungry as a bear.

So they went, the rich and the poor, the good and the bad, the capable and the incapable. Fortune dealt the game for them all and knew and recognized her favorites with a free hand, regardless of their worth in the eyes of other men. "They've struck it rich in Florence!" The magic words spread as the winds. Overnight they robbed Lewiston, Oro Fino, and other prosperous camps of more than half their population, and the stampede was wild. Men and women rode in stagecoaches, upon saddle horses, or walked to the new diggings in breathless haste that they might arrive in time to secure a claim. Many —most all—failed utterly and were forgotten. Some succeeded. But there was a force at work against them also—the Highwaymen.

Two hours after the sun sank behind the hills, Henry Plummer rode a winded horse up to the shebang on the ranch at Alpwai Creek. The house already wore an air of settled substantiality, and the meadows about it were sweet with the evening song of birds, as if the shebang were some lover's cottage rather than the hangout of cutthroats soon to terrorize the whole community. Plummer walked rapidly toward it and entered. The last of daylight came in at the window and across the floor to the fireplace where Bill Bunton was frying meat. Jack Cleveland, stretched upon a bunk in a corner, was reading an old newspaper in the fading light, and Tom Ridgely, lately arrived from Nevada, was cleaning a rifle, whistling softly as he worked.

"Well, Henry, you're jest in time," smiled Bunton, who had risen with the frying pan in his hand.

"No, I haven't time to eat, Bill," said Plummer. "Catch me a good fast horse, one of you. Mine's played out. You go, Ridgely. I'll tell the boys the news while you're gone. And hurry, Tom!"

"What's the game, Henry?" Cleveland swung his feet to the floor.

"Easy job, Jack." Plummer's voice was low as usual, but eager. "Two men and a woman—strangers—have left Lewiston for Florence. They have with them close to seven thousand dollars, mostly in treasury notes. I'd meet them down the road a good piece so as to keep suspicion from the shebang as long as possible. Make a good

33

job of it, boys. The people are strangers—easterners. And the stage, day after tomorrow, I've found out, will carry a crowd that is well worthwhile; but you will have to be extremely careful at that job, if you attempt it."

"What do these two men look like—these two that are with the woman?" inquired Cleveland. "How are they traveling?"

"One of the men is nearly six feet tall. The other is considerably shorter, and is younger. Both are total strangers. The woman is the wife of the younger man and she is tall and a blonde. They are traveling horseback."

"The road's plumb full now days," said Bunton, glancing out of the window and setting the frying pan on the hearth. "We've been right busy 'tendin' to 'em. Ridgely's comin' with your hoss. I'll saddle him fer you, Henry."

"Thanks, Bill," said Plummer, following Bunton out of the door and still talking to Cleveland. "Well, good luck, boys," he added, as Bunton, working swiftly, cinched the saddle. And swinging easily onto the horse, he was off.

Anxious to pass the victims of the intended robbery as near to Lewiston as possible in order that suspicion might be diverted from himself, he rode at a furious gait. The dusk had deepened when, just as he was about to enter the water in a small creek that crossed the road ten miles from the shebang, his horse suddenly shied, so that, good horseman though he was, he nearly lost his seat. With a muttered curse he struck the animal's sides with his spurs and the horse jumped to the opposite bank and was away again.

"That feller's in a hell of a hurry," said a voice in the willows not far from the crossing.

"Must be," replied another voice, and two men, followed by a woman, came into the road from the brush, each leading a saddled horse.

Even though at the creek Plummer had been within a few feet of them, the men had not recognized their chief, so swiftly had he passed. The one ahead was an outlaw by the name of Bill Mayfield, young, fair-haired, and tall. He turned suddenly in the road, and with his right hand resting on the butt of his six-shooter, faced the other man, Cherokee Bob, a swarthy mixed-blood giant of thirty years.

"Bob, you know me," he said, looking into the man's black eyes in the gloom.

34

"I sure do, Bill, I sure do," answered the other with his hand on his own gun. "An' you know *me*, so we're both acquainted."

"Are we going to make fools of ourselves over a woman, Bob?"

"I don't know, Bill. It's up to you. I'll play my hand in any game you start, an' it's your ante."

The woman, fair to look upon even in the dusk, spoke soothingly. "Now boys, don't quarrel, please. I'm a friend to both of you. Have done with this."

"Cynthia," said Mayfield impatiently, "I can't stand it to see you flirting with Bob, and now you've got to choose between us—right here and right now."

"Oh, Bill why are you so particular?"

"You know why. If you belong to me, no other man is going to come between us. But if you don't belong to me, I want to know it now. Choose, Cynthia." He made his demand with the assurance born of a certainty that she would not choose Cherokee before him, for, though he knew her history, he did not guess that her cupidity would influence her choice.

She struck her skirt with her riding whip. "Bill, dear," she cooed, "don't you think that Bob is better able to take care of me just now than you are? Bob has a good deal of money, and it's hard for a woman to forget comfort. I've been square with you, Bill—"

"You win, Bob," said Bill disgustedly, breaking off her speech. "I'll ride a way with you, an' then you can go on. I'll stop at a ranch I know near Alpwai Creek. Heigh-ho!"

The cloud of a quarrel so threatening but a moment before had vanished, and they mounted their horses, turning them in the direction of Florence. They were silent, and the horses, being fresh after a long rest near the creek, broke into a winging lope.

There was no moon. The night was still and comfortably cool. They were riding abreast, each busy with his own thoughts, when upon turning a sharp bend in the road, a voice from the darkness commanded, "Hands up!"

Instantly three pairs of hands were raised. "Don't move!" warned the voice, and a man with a black handkerchief tied below his eyes rode out from the shadows close to Mayfield. When he reached for the gun in Bill's belt the latter said, "I'm innocent, and so is Cherokee Bob."

The robber stopped, shoved his own gun back into its holster, and said, "Wrong party. Go on."

Mayfield, spurring his horse, cried, "Come on, Bob! It's a joke, I guess."

"A pretty joke," said Cynthia, spurring her horse to follow. "I'm nearly scared to death."

"Well, you needn't be. It's a joke, all right," declared Cherokee Bob. "Those men are out to scare somebody. Most likely they didn't see *you* at all." And he began to sing, a signal the gang had adopted as a means of recognition. "What do you think of that, Jack?" demanded Bill Bunton, as Cherokee Bob and Mayfield rode away with the woman between them.

Cleveland was bent over his saddle, his sides shaking with suppressed laughter. "It's Mayfield," he gasped. "Mayfield and Cherokee Bob and the Walla Walla woman."

"Sh-h-h!" Bunton held up his hand. Horses were coming. The two drew back into deeper shadows, where intermittently over the rustling of the leaves above their heads the sound of iron shod hoofs came to them from the stony road. Suddenly Bunton, who was leaning forward in his saddle, straightened his body, his hand feeling of the fastening knot on the black handkerchief that masked his face below his eyes. "It's them," he whispered. "Three of 'em."

The unsuspecting riders, strangers in the country, came on—a man, a woman, and a man in single file, the leader a tall thin person of middle age, as plainly unused to their present mode of traveling as the others; the woman, a girl in years, the bride of the young man who rode close behind her. They talked but little and then in low tones, for a spell of the strange new land was upon them, and in the darkness the creaking of their saddles took on a rhythm, cadenced by their horses' steps, that, together with the mystery all about, held them silent.

Suddenly there was a stir in the bushes, a rattle of hoofs in the road ahead.

"Hands up!"

Cleveland, spurring his horse close to the leader whose hands were obediently uplifted, grabbed his bridle reins.

But the young woman's horse had whirled, bumping violently against her husband's, and would have bolted had not the young man caught hold on his cheek-piece. "Whoa, boy, whoa," he trembled, while both horses milled excitedly into the brush. The screaming woman's hands locked in her horse's mane, her long riding skirt catching and threatening to pull her from the saddle.

"Hands up, damn ye!" Bunton, spurring after them, angrily caught the reins from the young man's hand, but the frantic horse was breaking his hold. "Hands up!" he repeated, and fired.

The young man fell lifeless from his saddle; and relieved of the hold on his cheek-piece, the woman's horse stopped and stood trembling in the road.

"Oh! Oh! Uncle John! Uncle John!" screamed the now hysterical woman, her fingers still clutching her horse's mane, her eyes wide with terror.

"Stop that noise, or I'll have to kill you, too," threatened Bunton, dismounting to take the saddlebags from the dead man's saddle, after which, tying the loose horse to a sapling, he searched the man's pockets and came up beside her. "Give me the money you got," he growled. "I don't like to kill women."

"It's—it's all in the cantinas—all I have. Oh, my husband, my husband."

"Shut up that noise," advised Cleveland, threateningly.

"All right, pardner," said Bunton, as he took the cantinas from her saddle.

"Now ride on, and don't stop," ordered Cleveland, letting go the bridle reins of the older man's horse. "Hurry on."

"Oh, but we cannot go and leave him—my husband!" sobbed the young woman. "Oh, Uncle John, what shall I do?"

"Go; and go quickly," said Cleveland, leveling his six- shooter. "We'll take care of him."

"Come, Mary dear," urged the tall man, huskily. "We *must* go to save ourselves. Don't you see?" And picking up her trailing reins, he began to lead her horse away.

"How was it, Bill?" asked Cleveland, as the slow hoof beats of the departing horses grew faint in the distance.

"Fine, Jack! Them cantinas is heavy. I'll go through the buck that wanted to fight, and then we'll be moving. I've got his horse safe. He's a beauty."

He stooped over the dead man and took from his pockets everything of value. Then, catching hold of an arm, said, "Grab on, Jack. We'll drag him into the brush a ways."

8

Among the passengers on the stagecoach to Florence, which on the day after the holdup and murder near Alpwai Creek carried the crowd that Plummer called "well worth- while," was a man who because of drink talked a great deal. His good-natured conversation included everybody within hearing. He rode with the driver and kept the party of passengers merry with his yarns, which he told in a loud voice and with great bravado. He had come from California, but there was a twang to his words that branded him a Yankee.

On the outskirts of Lewiston some citizen had set up a flag-staff, and from its top there fluttered a small American flag. The big man on the driver's seat saluted it soberly. "That little old flag looks mighty pretty and awful good, don't it, boys?" he called down to the other passengers.

"No," asserted a voice in the coach beneath him. "I hate that damned rag, and the Union and Abe—"

"Whoa, driver—whoa!" said the man on the driver's seat, laying a hand on the reins. "Whoa!—stop her!"

"What's wrong?" inquired the driver, setting his foot on the brake.

"Stop her. Little matter that needs attention—won't take us but a minute."

Curious, the driver complied. In a jiffy the big man was on the ground beside the coach and poking his head inside. "Which one of you made that speech about the flag an' Abe Lincoln?" he demanded. His voice was low now. There was nothing of the bravado in it—no bluster or coarseness, as his keen gray eyes glanced from face to face seeking guilt among the silent passengers. "Hurry up! Who was it?" he insisted.

"I said it," admitted a small dark-eyed man defiantly, "and I—"

"Now don't let interest accumulate on the principal mister. Come out o' there, or I'll drag you out, you rebel whelp!"

The man did not move. His black eyes looked sullenly at his challenger.

"My name is Pinkham—Old Pink they call me," said the Yankee, slowly, glancing at the other passengers. "I hope I'm not disturbing you gentlemen?" And he grabbed the fellow by the collar and dragged him from the coach to the ground. "Now, stand up and salute that flag, or I'll kill you," he commanded.

The man saluted.

"Now, say Lincoln is president of the United States, and I pray that the Union army may win the war."

"I *won't.*"

"You *will!* And you'll say it *twice* now," declared Old Pink.

"Lincoln is president of the North," began the man.

"Whoa! Back up! Ye're flirtin' with death, my rebel child. Begin again, and if you don't say it right, I'll pay your fare to Florence but your seat won't be occupied. Now, say it."

"Lincoln is president of the United States, and I—I pray that the Union army may win the war," stammered the man.

"Good," applauded Pinkham. "Now say her again, and say it real slow and distinct."

The man obeyed.

"Now," said Old Pink, "get aboard, an don't never use such talk when you don't mean it strong enough to fight."

Climbing back to the driver's seat, he said, "Here we go! All good Union men again.

> *We'll hang Jeff Davis on a sour apple tree,*
> *We'll hang Jeff Davis on a sour apple tree,*

he sang loudly, and the driver chuckled, for he, too, was a Union man, though not of the fighting sort. Verse after verse of "John Brown's Body" rolled from the throat of the big Yankee. Then he shouted out, "Now, all together on the chorus! 'Glory, glory, halle-lujah! Glory, glory'—Whoa! driver. Stop her again, please. My rebel friend has lost something and I think it's his voice. I'll help him to find it. It's too damned sweet to lose, and we need it. Hello, hello! What's all this?"

Quick as a flash, Pinkham drew two six-shooters and fired; and so sudden was his assault and so wholly unexpected that three masked men who had ridden into the road ahead of the coach turned and fled. Bang! Bang! Bang! went the guns of Old Pink, though the bullets flew wild of their mark. The driver sat in his seat as though para-lyzed, mechanically holding the startled horses. "Well, well," said Pinkham impatiently, "let's be movin'. This game is out. Whip up."

The driver, obediently starting his team, turned a frightened face to his seat mate. "You saved us from being held up and robbed," he said, "mebby murdered. You got more nerve than any man I ever see—too much for me to want to travel with you often."

Pinkham laughed merrily. "Let's all take a little drink," he sug-gested, "and then we'll have another verse of 'Old John Brown's Body.'"

He furnished the liquor, and everybody partook. "Now, here we go! All good Union men together.

We'll hang Jeff Davis on a sour apple tree,
We'll hang Jeff Davis on a sour apple tree.

"Good. Not a voice missin'. All good Union men an' friends. I don't think them fellers will try to hold us up again, but keep your shootin' irons ready for use in case they should. I'll promise you I'll start the ball rollin' if they come at us."

And everybody knew that he would. Somehow they liked him; even the man whom he had made to salute the flag could not help but admire him for his fearlessness.

The driver, however, dreaded meeting the road agents a second time, for he knew that this time Old Pink would force a fight, and he would rather have had the coach robbed than to chance a battle. But with no further interference they reached Florence in safety, where the passengers went their ways without loss of time, and Pinkham opened a gambling house which became known for its square dealing far and wide.

Florence was overflowing and wild with the excitement of new gold discoveries, and believed in itself in spite of the fickleness of fortune that between suns depopulated camps and peopled name-less gulches. Buildings were already in every state of construction, for always those who live by barter are with the pioneers, and ever the catch-penny is among the first of civilizations's establishments wherever the pioneer builds his fire.

On the next morning at the rear of a large tent, from which the odor of frying meat pervaded the air, Jim Bent, safe in Florence, was industriously swinging an axe at a wood pile for his breakfast. The sun had moved perceptibly since he had commenced to pay in advance for an opportunity of satisfying his hunger, when at length a Chinaman opened the door of the tent. "Yo' ketchup blekfus' now," he called, and slammed the door as though to shut in the grease-laden smoke from the cookstove. Jim stuck the axe in a log and spat a chew of tobacco from his mouth preparatory to enjoying his well-earned meal; but the Chinaman's head again popped in the doorway. "Blingum axe," he cried. "Mebby some fella stealum." For, having heard of robbery after robbery on the road, the Chinaman no doubt felt that nothing was safe. Only two nights ago a sluicebox not far from the restaurant had been rifled, and this morning a man had ordered and eaten a hearty breakfast for which he boastfully refused to pay "a damned heathen."

After delivering the axe at the kitchen door, Bent went around the tent to enter the dining room and sat down at a table across from two men who were conversing in low tones. Their attitude of secrecy attracted him — an eavesdropper by nature who listened whenever he could, not as a scandal-monger to gather thorns with which to torment others but in the hope that someday he might learn of a chance to locate a claim on pay gravel. He caught bits of their conversation, and ravenously hungry though he was, he pieced together broken sentences that he could manage to hear, even adding to them from what he knew must be a part of the story he was sharing, until the Chinaman set his breakfast before him. Even then he delayed his eating, arranging the dishes and sugaring his coffee slowly that no word should escape his fox-like ears, until the men, who had finished their breakfast, arose and left the tent. He wished he knew their names and where they came from.

He was bolting his food, eagerly anxious to be on his quest, and wishing with his whole heart that there was somebody he knew upon whom he could unburden his mind of the load the stolen conversation had placed upon it, when the door opened and a big jolly man greeted the Chinaman with, "Good mornin, John. Cook me a steak an' some fried potatoes. Lots of people here, John. Lots of people."

Bent, sitting with his back toward the door, jumped as though a pin had pricked him, and his pale blue eyes shone with hope as he spun around in his chair. One glance at the newcomer and he was on his feet, his little body quivering with excitement. "Mr. Pinkham! Mr. Pinkham!" he called, pointing eagerly at the vacant chairs by his table.

"Hello, Jim! Well, well!" The big man strode up and shook hands warmly. "What are you doin' here, Jim, prospectin'?"

"Yes, sir. I'm tryin' to find me a claim. My wife's over in Lewiston. An' say, Mr. Pinkham, set down. Jimminy crickets I want to tell you somethin'!"

The big fellow smiled, and brushing away some bread crumbs, sat down across from Bent, resting his heavy hands on the table. "Let her go, Jim—let her go. What's on yer mind?"

Bent swallowed the last of his coffee and, brushing back his drooping moustache, whispered, "I overheered a conversation in here this mornin'—only a few minutes ago. Two men was talkin'. One of 'em was settin' right where you be now." He glanced over his shoulder towards an occupied table in a corner, his nervous fingers clawing his moustache that persisted in covering his lips. "They was talkin' about a holdup an' murder near Alpwai Creek. An' by Jimminy crickets! I bet I know who done it, or had a hand in it."

Pinkham, interested, got up and moved to Bent's side. "Now, go on Jim," he said. "an' talk careful."

"Well," resumed Bent, gratified to have the big man's attention, "when I come in here this mornin' I didn't know about it, but after I heered them men I begun to put things together, like, an' now I know who done that job."

"Evening before last on my way here from Lewiston Henry Plummer passed me goin' towards Alpwai Creek. He was ridin' a blood bay with a black mane an' tail. Before I got to Alpwai Creek he passed me again but goin' the *other* way—towards Lewiston—an' he was on a gray gelding. Both times he was ridin' lickety-split.

"Now he couldn't have reached a point farther from Lewiston than Alpwai Creek *noway;* an' he couldn't possibly have spent any time with anybody anywhere. That holdup wasn't far from Alpwai Creek, an' there's a ranch house at the Creek. I don't know whose place it is; it was dark when I passed it. But Henry Plummer went to that ranch house, an' no farther." Bent was tapping the table in his earnestness and leaning closer and closer. "I was afoot," he whispered. "A good many men passed me. I didn't pay no attention to them nor them to me; but not very far from Alpwai Creek I heered horses comin'. It wa'nt anything new, but by Jimminy crickets, Mr. Pinkham, I hid. I don't know why, but I did it like it was the thing I'd ought to do. It was pretty dark, but Mr. Pinkham, when them horsemen come along by me, I knowed them. They was Bill Bunton and Jack Cleveland. By Jimminy crickets, yes, sir, Mr. Pinkham! You know 'em both, an' so do I. That there ranch house at Alpwai Creek is nothin' but their shebang, an' the same gang is here that was—"

Pinkham nudged him. John was coming with his steak and potatoes. "'Course you're right, Jim," he whispered when the Chinaman had gone back to the kitchen, "but don't talk—Don't say a word fer a spell. They'd kill you like a dog."

"Oh, I know it well enough," Bent whispered. "But I wanted to let you know, Mr. Pinkham, that's all."

"'Course. Somebody tried to hold up the coach I come in on, an' 'twas close to the Alpwai place, now I remember. But I cut loose an' run 'em off. I'd been drinkin or I'd a-got one of 'em."

"Somebody *will*."

"You bet, Jim. Somebody will. I'm expectin' to be appointed United States Marshal, an' if I am, *I'll* give 'em a game."

"Oh, Lord, Mr. Pinkham!" said Jim Bent fervently. "I hope you get it."

"I hope I do, Jim. I'd deal that gang a card or two from the bottom," smiled Pinkham, cutting his steak.

"I bet they're all here," continued Bent. "Plummer's gang, I mean —all that's alive. Boone Helm's over in Oro Fino."

"Yes, I know that," said Pinkham. "But I didn't know Henry Plummer was here, nor Jack Cleveland, nor that devil Bill Bunton." He drained his coffee cup and tapped loudly upon it with his spoon. "More coffee, John," he said, as the Chinaman shuffled up to the table. Then he resumed, "Cherokee Bob's here in Florence. He's a saloon keeper now, him and a woman he's picked up. He stole a saloon, tent, stock, an' all, in broad daylight."

"Stole it! How Mr. Pinkham?"

"Why, two fellers come here to Florence with a stock of liquor, an' the minute they landed a gambler shot one of 'em. Mr. Cherokee hears of it—if he didn't rib it up—an' goes to the dead man's pardner claimin' the dead man owed him a thousand dollars. He demands payment an' bluffs the poor fool into givin' up the tent and stock of liquor to square the account. Cherokee, the poor devil, gave two hundred to boot, I hear. Anyhow, he's got the saloon an' he only landed here yesterday. It don't sound possible, but it's true!"

"Are you minin', Mr. Pinkham—got a claim?" asked Bent, returning to the subject nearest his heart.

"Nope. Openin' up a gamblin' joint. It'll be open tonight. Come around an' see me, Jim, when I get fixed. I'm mighty busy today."

"I will, Mr. Pinkham. I'll come around, an' we'll have a talk." And Jim Bent, happy in the knowledge that he had a friend in Florence, left Pinkham to finish his breakfast.

Outside, he looked up and down the gulch where red-shirted men were at work opening up their claims. "There must be a chance here," he thought, turning up the gulch where the largest number of miners were at work. "Maybe," he thought, "Old Pink would stake me." Though not for the best claim in Florence would he have addressed the big Yankee as Old Pink.

9

A few settlers, who were not attracted by gold mining but who sought to establish themselves in the new country, had turned to stock raising instead. Squatting on meadows where wild hay might be cut and wide range afforded their cattle and horses, they built their houses and corrals near the road which crossed the country when possible. Food or shelter was never denied to wayfarers coming in to the mines or going out to civilization, so that their establishments were generally respected as stations where help might be had in time of need.

The shebang at Alpwai Creek had every appearance of the ranch houses of the day. Backed by mountains and built of logs, it stood on a rise of ground near the road and close to where the trail and road crossed the creek. Its barn and corral were ample, and in the fenced pasture embracing the green meadowlands along the stream, thickets of willows and alders afforded shelter and concealment for stolen horses.

Henry Plummer, riding through a driving rain that had come suddenly from the west, slipped out of Lewiston with the fading daylight, intent upon a visit to the shebang at Alpwai Creek. There was booty to divide and he wished to be there for his share. News of the holdup and murder on the road the night before had created the usual flutter of protest in town, but he felt no fear that it would endure. He knew too well that public opinion, though all-powerful in itself, is as impotent and aimless without a trusted leader as a pack train of mules without a bell mare. And public opinion had no leader in Lewiston. He bent over in his saddle, his horse keeping to the lonely road on a swinging lope, while he busied his mind with more important troubles than Lewiston's temporary excitement.

There had been rumors that the appointment of a United States Marshal, whose territory would embrace the mines in the new Northwest, was soon to be made, and so sure had he become of his popularity and high standing in Lewiston that he had at once set about securing that appointment for himself. He had been tactfully cautious in seeking out endorsers of his candidacy, approaching only those who he knew would be considered in Washington. He had not allowed his ambition to become generally known, however, fearing that somewhere in the surrounding country there might be men who knew his past. But young as he was, he had so cleverly handled his campaign among his fellow citizens in Lewiston that he felt they had grown to look to him for leadership in community affairs because of his evident ability and the closer relations afforded by a common interest. He had been quick to see and use his advantage; but lately someone somehow had got the news that another man would be named United States Marshal. It was this story that was troubling him, not so much because he coveted the office or its emoluments but because the man named in the rumor was known to him—and in California. Somehow, against his will, he believed the story, and his thoughts were all bent on ways and means to evade the trouble the rumored appointment would bring.

He was glad to see a light in the house. Its fraternal glow streaking into the night touched and warmed him while he quickly dismounted, turned his horse into the barn, and ran through the driving rain to the house.

Cleveland, Bunton, Ridgely and Bill Mayfield, engaged in a game of cards, sprang to their feet when the door burst open, admitting Plummer.

"Never heered you till this minute!" cried Bunton, following his chief to the fireplace. "No sir, never heered you come, by God!" he said again admiringly, while he hastily put wood on the fire.

Plummer turned his back to the blaze. "What luck?" he asked, looking at Jack Cleveland.

"Good and bad, Henry," playfully punching Mayfield. "You see, we first held up our friend Bill here, and Cherokee Bob. They had a woman with them so they answered the description of the party we were after. Then a little later on we nabbed the right outfit, but had to kill one of the men."

Plummer turned about, his back already steaming. "Good haul?" he asked, looking into the fire.

"Bully, Henry, bully," Bill Bunton laid a burly hand on Plummer's arm. "Take off that coat, Henry," he urged. "You'll catch a cold. Yes sir, Henry, over seven thousand we got—over seven thousand," he repeated, "an' then, by God—"

"The next day we tackled that stagecoach job you spoke of," interrupted Jack Cleveland. "There was a fighting rooster on the box with the driver, and he went to war at the drop of the hat. I got a good look at him. And who do you suppose it was, Henry?" Cleveland got up and strolled over to Plummer's side, his hands in his pockets, a quizzical look on his face.

"Pinkham." Plummer spoke to the fire. His face showed no change, although he felt his blood leap at the name. "Pinkham, Jack," he said turning to Cleveland. "I seem to smell him."

"Well, your smeller's a good one all right, Henry. You hit it— made a bull's-eye. Ain't he a wonder, boys?" Bunton asked admiringly of Ridgely and Mayfield at the table listening. "Smelt him. By God, I bet he *did,* too."

"Yes," Cleveland spoke again, "it was Pinkham, Old Pink himself, and on the fight as usual." Whistling softly, he dragged two rude stools to the fire.

Plummer leaned over to feel his coat which Bill Bunton was carefully drying, and then turned his face to the fire again. He hated Pinkham—would gladly quarrel with him and kill him. But in his role of respected citizen of Lewiston he dared not seek the quarrel. As the thought of his place in society crossed his mind he glanced at the window, and Cleveland, guessing what was in his mind, went to his bed and pulled an army blanket from it, which he hung on two wooden pegs so that it completely covered the glass. His booted feet made little sound on the dirt floor as he moved across the room, bare of furniture save for the bunks, a few stools, and the table at which Ridgely and Mayfield had begun a game of cards. Saddles and riding rigs, clothing and many weapons hung plentifully about the walls, together with a few cooking utensils near a Dutch oven just beyond the fireplace. But the place was inhospitable looking—hard in the flickering candlelight, made weird by the wallowing flames of the fire before which Bunton squatted with the coat.

"It's still raining," said Cleveland as he returned to the fire and sat down. "By morning the roads will be good and muddy."

"Pinkham's bad medicine, Jack," said Plummer. "And the worst of it is that he's liable to be appointed United States Marshal."

"Who says so?" Bunton bristled, standing up with the coat.

Plummer did not answer, but drew the other stool closer to the fire and sat down. A plan, already formed in his mind, might be useful, might turn away trouble.

"Ferd Patterson is in Florence, too, or should be by now," he began, turning to Cleveland. "Ferd is our one best bet against Pinkham, Jack."

"Looks like they all was all comin', damn 'em," growled Bunton, squatting again by Plummer's side.

"Old Pink's a Union man to the marrow of his bones," Plummer went on, "and Ferd is a rebel bred and born. Both will fight at the drop of the hat any time or any way. Get them together. There's our chance for a clear trail, boys. Get them at it." He rose and began walking up and down before the fireplace. "The majority of people here seem to favor the South. Keep that in mind, boys," he said, turning to the table where Ridgely and Mayfield were playing pitch. "Keep that always in mind and start a fight on that ground between Patterson and Pinkham. One of them is sure to be killed—maybe both. We ought to *arrange* it for both. Some of you are sure to be in the crowd, and an extra shot can't be traced. Get them both." He stopped before Bunton, and stood looking down at his coat.

"'Tain't quite dry, Henry," Bunton said. "Wait a spell."

Plummer turned back to Cleveland. "Where's Club-Foot?" he asked suddenly, his eyes darting from face to face in accusation.

"Gone to Florence. Left this afternoon," answered Cleveland.

"Cherokee's got a saloon there now, Henry," Bunton offered. "Bluffed a feller out of it, tent an' stock an' all. Soon's Club-Foot got the news he lit out to call on Cherokee. Ha, he, he! The feller couldn't a-been more'n set up in business till—"

"What are you talking about?" Plummer asked ungraciously, and Bunton, with a glance at Cleveland, subsided.

"Why, we heard this afternoon that Cherokee had acquired a saloon in Florence," explained Cleveland, "and Club-Foot rode in to find out if the story was true. He hasn't been drinking any more than the rest of us lately."

Cleveland was fond of Club-Foot George, and Plummer, seeing that Jack was protecting him, dropped the subject. "How many horses have we in the pasture now?" he asked.

"Eighteen new ones," answered Cleveland. "Boone Helm will take them to Oro Fino the first of the week. He thinks he can sell them there. Some good ones among them, too."

"There's a buckskin gelding that can run, Henry," said Ridgely, laying down his cards. "He's a Nez Perce hoss."

"How fast is he?" Interested at once, Plummer moved over to the table. "Have you timed him?"

"No, but he'd make a fast quarter hoss. I'll bet he can skin anything in Lewiston."

"Try him out," urged Plummer. "I could use him if he's good." And seating himself at the table, he fell to talking of horses he had known, more as if musing to himself. His voice was in low monotone, but evincing. A little glow in his eyes showed real admiration for these animals he had known. The card game ceased, and Bunton and Cleveland listened from the fire. At last in a silence Bunton looked at his watch. "Two o'clock," he yawned. "Your coat's dry. Hungry, Henry?"

"No. I'll be going. I had no idea I'd been here three hours." He stood up and Bill brought his coat and held it for him, while Cleveland went to his bed and drew out a package from beneath the blankets, handing it to Plummer. "There was just seven thousand twenty-five in that job, Henry," he said.

Plummer took that package without examining it and walked towards the door with his hand on Cleveland's arm. "Jack," he said, "you can find a way to start a quarrel between Pinkham and Patterson. Do it as soon as you can."

"I'll try, Henry," promised Cleveland. "They'll quarrel easily enough if excuse is furnished, especially on the question of the North and South."

"Don't put if off," urged Plummer. "We can't afford to lose time."

"I'll git your hoss fer you, Henry," Bunton offered, pushing past them in the doorway.

They waited there until he brought the horse up from the barn. "It's pretty nigh let up stormin'," he said, as he handed the reins to his chief, who, mounting, turned his face towards the sky.

"I guess it *has* quit," Plummer said, wheeling his horse out of the streak of light from the doorway. "Did you bury that man?"

"No," said Bunton, with his hand on Plummer's knee. "We jest dragged him back into the brush a piece."

"They will come for the body," warned Plummer, sitting straight on his horse in the sweet damp darkness. "If they do, and should ask you boys for help, give it freely. And don't forget Pinkham and Patterson. I'll be out again as soon as anything worthwhile turns up. Good night."

10

The appointment of a United States Marshal was delayed. The government at Washington, busied with the Civil War, again forgot the Northwest and left it to shift for itself. Crime was increasing, the roughs pouring into the country from the south grew bolder each day, while the stolen saloon known as Cherokee's Place became their hangout and Bob and Cynthia lived in style on the proceeds of its bar and card tables. But the stampede, which like a giant wave had filled Florence to overflowing, now subsided, leaving many a man strapped and stranded in the gulches and in the camp itself. Broken and heartless, with all the valuable ground staked, these luckless adventurers seemed unable to better their condition or even to go away where chance might show them favor, until the magic tocsin, "They've struck it on the other side," lashed them to life. Able as any, they moved, wild with excitement to find the rainbow's end.

49

Florence at once gave of her citizens more than half. Only the miners who were working their claims and those engaged in business were unaffected by the new discovery. And these considered themselves somewhat superior to the transient, excitable majority that at the first whisper of a new gold discovery folded its tent (if it had one) and stole away.

Thus, suddenly stripped of all save stable citizens, Florence began to examine itself. As closer acquaintance bared facts that had been overlooked in the whirl and whelm of hurried organization, the standard of social requirements was raised. The Who is Who committee, self-appointed judge of pedigree and character, included members who, with loud protestations or professions of personal holiness, stripped aspirants for social recognition of all declared decency in order that, by comparison, they might shine the brighter in the light of contrast. Its decree made a muss in Florence.

There was to be a ball in the camp—a public ball it is true, but it had been projected by Mrs. Tell Hastings and Mrs. Jed Caruthers. Tell Hastings was a gambler, and Jed owned the Nugget Saloon. Their wives were the social lights on the very peak of perfection in Florence. They had conceived the idea of the grand ball, and therefore constituted themselves a managing committee to handle the affair. Tell and Jed, free-hearted and anxious to please, indulged them in their every wish, and spared no expense or pains that would make the ball a success.

When the hall was to be decorated, willing hands lent their services and almost everyone came to look in at the work of the artists. A special orchestra was hired and the coming ball was the talk of the town, especially among the women.

Cherokee Bob had given no thought to the party until Cynthia, with tears in her eyes, cuddled in his lap at supper time. "Bob, dear, I do wish I could go to the ball," she whispered.

"Well, you *shall* go if you want to," blustered Bob, kissing her quivering lips. "Indeed you'll go, girl, and you'll be treated like a lady, too."

"But," began Cynthia with misgivings, "Mrs. Hastings and Mrs.—"

"Oh, hell," broke in Bob impatiently, "didn't I know them two women before them fellers got 'em? Humph! They ain't got no patent on decency, them two ain't."

"Well, I'd like to go," whimpered Cynthia, with her arms about his neck.

"You're goin', Cynthia," he told her, "or I'll know the reason why you ain't."

He was quick to assure her that she could go to the ball; but as quickly he foresaw that their going would be liable to cause a row. He had no notion of giving them the opportunity to object to his own presence. He would not deliberately go that far to find trouble. But they would have to accept Cynthia. He would enlist Bill Willoughby, he decided. Bill was his closest friend—his shadow—and besides he was a good dancer. He would ask Bill to take her, and Bill would jump at the chance.

"Yes siree, old girl," he said finally, "You're goin', and Bill Willoughby'll take you."

"Why, Bob, dear—"

"Whoa—see here girl, I ain't never ducked a mess o' trouble when it was cooked up for me, never. But I ain't goin' to make no bid fer a fight, now we've got the saloon an' are doin' well. They can't buck agin Bill Willoughby none at all. An' by God, they've got to associate with you this one time without no funny business, or I'll go to war, me, Cherokee Bob."

"Mind, Bill, you ain't to make no ante," he explained to his friend. "But if they don't treat her like a decent woman, you come away with her. Then I'll take the deal off your hands."

Willoughby agreed readily to the proposal and Cynthia began hurried preparations for the occasion. When at last the evening came and she was adorned for the party, Bob admiringly told her she was a queen. "You'll put 'em all in the shade, old girl. You've got 'em best three ways from the deuce."

So she went radiantly away to the ball, and Bob turned back to his saloon to await developments.

The music of the grand march had just died away and the couples were idly promenading towards their seats when, leaning upon Bill Willoughby's arm, Cynthia made her appearance. The men bowed politely and made way for her and her escort, but Mrs. Hastings, with her nose in the air, sought her co-sponsor of the ball, and with their heads together these two made their decision.

"Tell, come here," ordered Mrs. Hastings of her husband, who was already engaged in friendly conversation with Bill Willoughby.

"Jed, can I speak to you a moment?" sweetly called Mrs. Caruthers to her better half, who was busy scattering wax on the floor by scraping a wax candle with the blade of his jackknife.

The two men thus summoned joined their ladies.

"What is it, my dear?" asked Hastings, half suspecting what it was.

"Tell Hastings, what *can* you be thinking of!" she sputtered.

"Thinkin' of? Nothin' that I know of. What's the matter now? What have I done, damnit?"

"Done? Done! Listen to the man! Why, you welcome that—that woman with that man to *our* ball. I'm—I'm—well, they've got to go. You've just got to tell them that they can't stay here."

"Oh, now Nell, don't be foolish. They won't hurt nobody."

"Hurt us! The idea! You know who she *is*."

"Yes, yes, but it won't rub off onto nobody, will it? We don't have to make a steady chum of her, do we?"

"Tell Hastings, you have *got* to tell those people they must leave," declared Mrs. Hastings, stamping her foot for emphasis.

The same dialogue, substantially, was being repeated between Mrs. Caruthers and Jed. And the two men finally confronted each other miserably.

"Well, Tell," growled Jed. "I'd sooner take a lickin'."

"So would I, a damn sight," agreed Tell. "The woman's all fixed for the dance an—"

"Come, you men must act at once," broke in Mrs. Hastings, observing their reluctance and fearing rebellion.

"Yes, Jed, dear," seconded Mrs. Caruthers, "they must be put out, that's all."

Appeal was useless. The sudden gathering in the corner was attracting attention and, of course, its cause was suspected. The two luckless husbands marched towards the undesirables, where Cynthia, still holding Willoughby's arm, was sweeping her flashing eyes over the assembled guests as though she would impress upon her memory every person there. Her head was high and her delicate nostrils quivered with wrath, but her poise was perfect, nevertheless, as she deftly spread a feathered fan and waved it to and fro. Not a glance did she deign to give the commissioned pair until, embarrassed, they stood directly before her. Then her eyes blazed. "Well?" she sneered. "Have those whose ways are mended cast a stone?"

Tell Hastings blushed a deep red. "I—that is—" he stammered and stalled.

"You see—. Oh, hell, Bill, we've got to ask you not to stay here," blurted Caruthers. "I'm sorry. So is Tell, but—"

"Indeed?" Cynthia's voice was stagey in the extreme. "Very well, Mr. Willoughby, we will go," she said. But before leaving the hall she looked witheringly a moment at the committee of two, and in her eyes was promise of retribution. Then, her bosom heaving in excitement and anger, she turned and left the ballroom on Bill Willoughby's arm.

"The very idea!" exclaimed Mrs. Hastings, as the angry Cynthia departed with her escort. "The brazen effrontery of that pair is beyond me," she finished somewhat nervously.

Tell and Jed, after a moment's conversation with several other men, had pulled down the shades over the windows and had barred and bolted the door.

The spirit of the evening was broken. A cloud had fallen and dimmed the long-planned pleasure. Groups had gathered here and there and they were so absorbed in whispered conversation that they interfered with the dancers. Couples began preparing to leave, hurrying on their wraps and calling their good nights at the door. "We're so sorry, ladies," said one woman as she approached the committee of two, "but Mr. Gibbons is obliged to be in Lewiston in the morning early. We have had a delightful time—"

"Oh, going so soon?" exclaimed both Mrs. Hastings and Mrs. Caruthers. "Why, it's just begun."

But the Gibbonses had to go. So did many more. In twenty minutes the hall was nearly empty, and Mrs. Hastings was in tears.

"It's suffocating in here," said Mrs. Caruthers. "Can't we open those windows, Jed, dear?"

"If it's too hot for you here, you'd better go home," growled Caruthers, now touchy as a porcupine.

And an hour afterward the music was still, the lights were out, the ball was over.

The dawn of morning found Cherokee Bob and Bill Willoughby waiting for it. Behind the closed doors of the stolen saloon the two were watching for those who had been prominent in the social affair of the night before. When the light had grown so that the buildings and tents along the street were discernible, Bob spoke. "Bill," he said, "we've got to get Jakey Williams first, if we can. He's the fightin' man of that nasty-nice gang. Better open the back door just a crack an' watch from there. I'll stay here. Kill the first one that shows, but get Jakey first if you can."

Willoughby walked to the back door and opened it as Bob had ordered. Hardly had he taken his stand there when he beheld Jakey coming and whispered, "Bob, he's comin'."

Cherokee tip-toed back to him. "Let me have him, Bill," he whispered, opening the door a little wider. "It's my quarrel."

Williams was on his way to his own saloon, which to reach he must pass close to Bob's place. But suddenly, as though he scented trouble, he turned and headed in another direction. Instantly Cherokee Bob stepped from the door and fired, whereupon Williams whirled about, ripped out a six-shooter and returned the shot, then ran towards his own saloon, pursued by Bob and Bill.

The shots had already wakened the sleeping camp, for there were many who had expected them, and men began to appear in the street, guns in hand. Jakey, flying before his pursuers, tore into his saloon and reappeared with a double-barreled shotgun with which he faced them, firing both barrels. Cherokee Bob stumbled and fell but, staggering to his feet, emptied his six-shooter at Williams at close range.

Men now appeared in windows and began firing at the two in the street, each shot bringing reinforcements to Williams, until fifty or more were engaged against Bob and Willoughby. Both were sorely wounded and began to retire, fighting desperately; but then, half-blinded by blood, Bob discovered Tell Hastings among his enemies. He dropped his empty six-shooter, and steadying the hand that held its mate, aimed and fired.

Hastings fell. "I got him, Bill, damn him!" he yelled. "An' Jakey, too. He's down. Whoopee!"

Then, his clothing soaked with blood, he sank to the ground. "Pull off my boots," he gasped to the men who crowded about him with smoking guns in their hands. "Pull 'em off. I'd do it fer you."

Someone did him that service. "Tell my brother," he faltered, "that I got my man an' have took the long trail." Eleven bullets had passed through his body, and eight had found their mark in Bill Willoughby.

And so both branches of society were satisfied in Florence. But

Cynthia and Mrs. Hastings were without supporters as a result. The despised one joined her old lover Bill Mayfield and, beginning life anew, was happy until a bullet robbed her a second time. Then she joined Mrs. Hastings in oblivion, for the years had scarred her past the possibility of further conquests.

11

When the fight occurred Pinkham was in San Francisco, and it was more than two weeks before he returned. The camp had cooled down by then, and the fight had dwindled into the past along with other outbursts of lawlessness which it had countenanced.

But nothing could have contributed more to make easy the plot which Henry Plummer had hatched against Pinkham. The killing of Jakey Williams, who had been Pinkham's closest friend in Florence, so stirred him that he threw caution to the winds, and not only did he openly denounce and defy the outlaws but he included in his denunciations all sympathizers with the Southern cause. Every lawless person was a rebel to Pinkham, and he believed without reason that every member of Plummer's gang was a supporter of secession and the South. "They are all of one feather—outlaws," he declared bitterly, "for those who are against law and order are against our government, and a man that fires on the Stars and Stripes ain't one damned bit better'n the fellow that holds up the United States mail."

He determined at once to call a meeting of the men of Florence, to plead before it the cause of law and the Union. Stuffing an American flag into his coat pocket so that its colors could be seen without mistake, he went about the camp posting notices "To the citizens of Florence" and personally inviting his friends to attend a mass meeting that night in his gambling house, a large log building.

Most of the men invited had promised to come, and the notices had been read by all the friends and foes of Pinkham, but it was as though each individual had received a secret invitation to the meeting. It was not discussed, unless among the members of the gang of outlaws.

The night fell sultry. Pinkham's place, draped plentifully with Union flags and lighted beyond its usual brilliancy, filled up with miners, merchants and gamblers. Men whose personal interest had anchored in Florence, crowded before its bar where the sweating bartenders served them at the proprietor's expense. They scarcely knew each other—never had visited. Now they were talking and laughing as neighbors—guests of Pinkham. They did not intend to quarrel among themselves. They were remote from the national strife, news of which reached them only in garbled fragments, and they hoped for its end and peace, and to reap the harvest before them unhindered. They had not dared to speak out against the outlaws—would not even now; but Pinkham was honest; he could be trusted; and they had come to listen to him—to drink with him.

Below the draped picture of Lincoln back of the bar, and arranged on the wide-spreading antlers of an elk fastened to the rough logs of the wall, with due regard for their importance in Pinkham's mind, were the uniformed likenesses of many Union generals illuminated by candles fastened to each prong of the antlers. These decorating lights, together with the heat of human bodies, made the air almost unbearable. The room was ovenlike when Pinkham climbed to the top of his bar and held up his hand, his eyes scanning quickly the bearded faces before him as though he would sort them as friends or foes.

"Men," he began, "this camp is a hell; an' we, who ought to be fightin' for the flag, are afraid to even take a stand against a gang of cowardly thugs that not only defy us but our government."

"Meaow!" He was interrupted with a deriding catcall from near the door. Old Pink whirled, his six-shooter in his hand. "Point him out!" he thundered, leaning forward tense and ready as a crouching tiger. But there was only a shuffling of feet.

"I say we're cowards!" he repeated, his heavy six-shooter poised—waiting, hoping for a challenge, which did not come. "Our country is suffering," he continued, disdainfully stuffing his gun back into its holster, "an' it can't establish law here. Its hands are tied. But *we can an' must* put a stop to lawlessness in this community. *Damn* a man that sneaks an' cowers before such a scum! I know 'em an' *you* know 'em—by *name,* some of 'em. An' they've got to get out an' stay out. Ain't they?" he demanded, his hand outstretched.

"You bet!" The men were beginning to be stirred.

"They think that by breaking down law and order they will be helpin' secession," he went on. "They are too cowardly to put on a suit of rebel clothes and face government guns. This is *North* country, not *South*. It belongs to the *United States of America,* and there never was a slave owned in it. Its flag is the Stars an' Stripes, because it never adopted any *other*. It's time we come out of the brush, men, you an' me! Is it right for able bodied Americans to be dodgin' their country's fight here, an' at the front, too? Don't it make you feel small an' sneakin'?"

Finally, at the mention of Lincoln's name, the men cheered. Then Pinkham, snatching a flag from a rafter above his head, marched to the middle of the bar and held the banner aloft. "Three cheers for Abe Lincoln, the Union, an' law an' order!" he shouted.

"Hip, hip, hurrah! Hurrah! Hurrah!" It had needed but a touch. The cheers were deafening. Men with tears in their eyes waved their hats and shouted themselves hoarse, till Pinkham, his whole attitude changing suddenly from accusation and defiance to supplication, hushed them with uplifted hands. "Men," he implored, and his voice accused himself with them, "let's brace up, an' punish the very next outrage in this camp. Everybody have something on me. Boys," turning to his bartenders, "set 'em up lively!"

The meeting lost its order and became a social affair. Men talked more freely to those they knew or had seen at work in the diggings than ever before since coming to Florence. They were glad they had attended the meeting. It would result in good, for the citizens favored law and order, that was plain.

But when, after midnight, they drifted away alone or in pairs as partners to their camps or cabins, they suddenly ceased to talk of the meeting, and began to feel that they had foolishly taken part in an open demonstration against a power which might in retaliation smite them with a heavy hand. Their sympathies suffered no real change for the most part. Because they left the meeting as they came, alone or with the partner who shared their beds, their enthusiasm for the right, borrowed for the moment from another but overshadowed by their fear of the unknown, ebbed before they slept. Though always there are a few—and they are best—who with the urge of their own enthusiasm upon them are quick to catch the promise of sincerity in the light of another's eyes, and acknowledging the bond, somehow seek out and cling to them until their cause is won.

The time was plainly ripe for Plummer's plan. Pinkham would quarrel easily enough, but despite the rumor of his earlier arrival, Ferd Patterson had not yet reached Florence. He had stopped in Idaho City. Plummer, impatient for the removal of both Patterson and Pinkham, was delighted when two days after the meeting in Florence, Jack Cleveland, on July first, brought him the news that Pinkham had been drinking to excess and would spend the Fourth of July at the hot springs just out of Idaho City.

There was no time to waste. Plummer summoned all of his men who were within reach to meet him the next night at the shebang at Alpwai Creek. Twelve answered the summons. Many of them were burly, coarse-looking fellows with loose, cunning faces, a few of them young and gentlemen born, the wild streak in whose natures the life in the camps had fostered. Such was their leader, standing straight and slim before them in the candlelight, his quick, beautiful fingers toying with a piece of rope, his cold, gray eyes now upon one of his men, now on another as he talked. His voice, though still low and guarded, was alive with eager authority. "Now is the time to act," he said. "Go to Idaho City and tout the rebels there to show the Southern flag. Get Ferd Patterson interested in suppressing any attempt to celebrate the Fourth in camp, and when Old Pink lands he'll go to war, sure. Get somebody else to go to Patterson and stir him up. He knows most of us and we must not show ourselves to be mixed up in the affair. Find someone else."

The meeting was of deep interest to these men. Both Pinkham and Patterson, having come north from California, knew every one of them, and their presence in the camps was a menace to their success, and especially to Plummer's since they knew he was the arch criminal of them all. There in the candlelight, by the look in those men's faces and the atmosphere which so many minds bent upon evil had woven, it was plainly not the gang that need fear.

"Terry's in Idaho City. We'll get Jim Terry," said Bill Bunton eagerly. "Patterson made him beg for his life—made him get down on his knees and beg like a dog a year ago in Frisco. Since that time Terry's been like a slave to him whenever he was near, but I know he hates him an' would do anything to get him killed. Terry's our man, boys."

The man Terry was himself a low rowdy, too weak in character to be associated with Plummer's men. Posing as a gambler, he frequented gambling houses, but when unable to maintain that coveted position, turned to the dance halls and hurdy-gurdy houses where he acted as roustabout for his food and drink, and was known as "Red the Swamper."

Rat-faced and shifty of eye, his narrow chest resting against the edge of a card table over which he leaned, Terry was the picture of infamy as he listened to Plummer's plan, outlined by Jack Cleveland who had come to Idaho City to see him.

"Show me yer ante," he whispered greedily, "if I'm t' git them two mixed." And for fifty dollars he agreed to bring about a quarrel between Patterson and Pinkham, his hate for the former spurred to new life by the bribe money.

Fate itself had appeared to foster the plan from the beginning, for the fight in Florence had aroused Pinkham to rashness. Bad news just come to Idaho City concerning the Southern army had so weighed upon Patterson that he was drinking more than his wont and was quarrelsome. But, although circumstance had contributed so much to shape the moods of both victims of the proposed plot, the quarrel was not easy to bring about. Having hoisted the rebel flag at Terry's suggestion, or dare, Patterson forgot to guard it, and turned back to finish his spree, so that when at two o'clock on the Fourth of July the stagecoach from Florence reached Idaho City, he was not in the crowd which gathered to greet it.

Pinkham, from the driver's seat, was quick to see the offending flag and, raging at the insult to the nation's birthday, could scarcely wait until the coach stopped at the express office. Springing down, he bolted into a store, purchased a double-barreled shotgun, loaded it with buckshot, marched to the flagpole and hauled down the rebel flag. With his hat on the ground, he drew from his pocket the Stars and Stripes, fastened the Union banner to the halyard, ran it up to the pole's peak, stepped back, fired a salute with one barrel of his gun, and reloaded it. Not a hand was raised against him, even when, standing bareheaded in the hot sun beneath his flag, he sang a verse of "John Brown's Body" with the chorus, "We'll hang Jeff Davis on a sour apple tree." Not a voice was heard, save, as he marched back to take the coach to the hot springs, a cry of "nigger-lover," at which Pinkham stopped and cocked his gun. "Where's the white-livered copperhead that called me a nigger-lover?" he demanded, walking defiantly closer. The crowd fell back silently, and as no challenge was offered, Pinkham took the coach to the hot springs.

The golden opportunity was gone. Patterson, a fearless man, too deep in liquor to care what was going on around him, had not shown himself. The plan had miscarried, and Terry was upbraided.

"I'll take him to the hot springs. I'll fix it yit," he promised when Cleveland demanded the return of the fifty dollars.

But Patterson was stubborn, and not until late in the afternoon could Terry and his accomplices prevail upon him to go to the hot springs. Even then he insisted upon making straight for the bath-house, while Terry, knowing that Pinkham was in the barroom, endeavored to lead his victim there, though to no purpose. Patterson went to the bathhouse, and reluctantly Terry followed him, repeating his invitation to join him in taking one more drink before entering the hot water. At last Patterson, half undressed but tired of Terry's pleading, said, "All right—just one more, mind you. Then we'll boil it out of us."

As they emerged from the bathhouse Pinkham came out onto the porch of the saloon and, leaning against a post which supported the roof, watched their approach without interest until Terry suddenly thrust a six-shooter into Patterson's hand, whispering, "There he is, Ferd. He says he'll git ye. Kill him, Ferd."

Patterson, not having been aware that Pinkham was at the springs, stopped in his tracks, the gun in his hand, and Terry's plotters stepped expectantly aside.

"Draw, will you?" Patterson's challenge came in deadly earnest.

Pinkham's hand fell to his holster. "You know damned well I will, Ferd," he said.

Patterson fired, and his bullet broke Pinkham's shoulder. Staggering backward from the shock, Old Pink returned the fire, but missed. Before he could shoot again, a bullet tore its way into his heart and he fell, his weakened thumb trying in vain to cock his six-shooter until the breath left his body.

Patterson was arrested, hastily tried for murder, and acquitted. Fearing Pinkham's friends, he fled to Walla Walla, where he was shot down by one of Plummer's men.

And so, as was then so often true, it was the gang's meeting which bore fruit, while whatever enthusiasm poor Pinkham's meeting had aroused for law and order died with him at Idaho Hot Springs.

12

Lewiston, now more stable than the other camps, her citizenship having been sifted again and again by the stampedes, had nevertheless grown rapidly. The rush had passed her but, still holding her own, she strove to be a center, a distributing point for the surrounding camps. Tents had given way to more substantial buildings and her merchants, having settled down to deal with a profitable business, kept regular hours so that no longer lights shone all night in the streets, save in dance halls, gambling houses and saloons. And there was an exception among the saloons, for Hiltebrant the Dutchman, an eccentric old German who held the patronage of his countrymen in Lewiston, closed his door at midnight and opened it again at daylight.

On the night of July 8th the lights from the Combination Gambling House, mingling with the reflections from other places of its kind, shimmered upon pools of ruffled water in the streets of Lewiston, for rain had been steadily falling all the day before, and now wind from the west was driving it in fitful sheets against the window-panes. The crowd in the Combination was small. Men waited for lulls in the storm and then bolted into the night to gain their homes and beds before the arrival of another downpour.

Henry Plummer had, since his first night in Lewiston, sat at the same table at the back of the room whenever he could do so. He felt lucky there, and tonight he was occupying his favorite place. The front door was open and gusts of the damp wind fluttered the candles.

"Bad storm," remarked the miner opposite Plummer, as he dealt the cards.

"Yes," agreed Plummer.

"Two more holdups today and a murder. It's high time that something was done to put a stop to such doings," went on the miner.

Plummer picked up his cards, his slender fingers working rapidly as he sorted them. Then he shoved a stack of chips to the center of the table. "Two cards please," he said. "All new countries are much alike I guess." He looked at his watch. "Two o'clock," he observed with a yawn.

Outside, the rain continued to fall in the black darkness of the western slope of the mountains, soaking the ground and swelling the dangerous Snake River at Lewiston's edge. At two o'clock four horsemen turned into the rainswept street not far from the Combination, and three of the riders dismounted in the darkness beside Hiltebrant's place, handing over their bridle reins to the fourth. "Now remember, Bill," said that man as he leaned over in his saddle to take the proffered reins, "there'll be three of 'em, and they all sleep in that corner. I'll be here when you git back. Good luck, an' hurry. I'm soakin' wet an' cold as a snake's belly in the bottom of the sea."

Hastily tying black silk handkerchiefs under their eyes, the three men were ready. "Here, Bill, take the shotgun. She's loaded with buckshot. I've kept her dry all the way," whispered the man on the horse.

The three turned away and the darkness hid them. Club-Foot George, the man on the horse, bent his head and the water poured in a little stream from his hat. Once he saw his three friends cross a patch of light that penetrated the blackness from the windows of a dance hall. Then they were gone.

Hiltebrant's saloon was dark. The old German had retired early as was his custom. The patter of the rain upon the flimsy roof lulled him and his two companions within, its monotony added to the liquor they had taken, making their slumber deep—so deep that they did not hear the growl of the little dog that had been adopted by the proprietor as the three robbers stopped before the place.

Two of them threw their weight against the door, and as the frail wood smashed inward, Bill Bunton, pointing the shotgun at the corner where he knew the bed was located, pulled both triggers. Two men sprang up from it and fled through the back door of the place. Bunton calmly lighted a candle and, together with his fellows, approached the bed where Hiltebrant was dying, dragged him to the floor, and then searched the bed and the room for the gold.

A dozen men had gathered outside the door when finally Bunton blew out the candle, whispering, "It's gone. Them two that got away must have took it. Damn 'em. Let's be gittin' out of here, boys." And in the face of all the men gathered before it, he opened the battered door and walked out of the place, followed by the others.

The group at the door parted, allowing them to pass as though held silent by a terror that froze their blood. No one spoke a word, until from down the muddy street they heard the splash of departing hoofs. "God *Al-mighty!*" an awed voice husked, and the spell was broken. Some of the men went into the saloon; others ran to tell the news of the murder to the various houses and dance halls. One rushed into the Combination. "Hiltebrant's been murdered and his place robbed!" he cried.

There was a scraping of chairs, as men, startled at the nearness of the crime, moved from the card tables; and a mumble of voices arose. Plummer brushed the ashes from his cigar and relighted it. "I thought I heard a shot," he said quietly. "It's your ante, Mr. Brice."

"No," declared Brice emphatically. "I've played enough. Something has got to be done to stop this thing. The people will have to get together, Mr. Plummer. I am going to see Mr. Ford and some other good citizens before daylight. We can depend on you, I know, Mr. Plummer?" He rose and gave Plummer a searching look.

"Certainly, Mr. Brice," smiled Plummer, running his cards together and tapping them once or twice on the table. "I am willing to do anything I can do. We must enforce the law. Our officers are lax and cowardly, I'm afraid. I'll see you tomorrow."

The two other men who had been playing at the table with Plummer followed Brice, and, shoving his chair back from the table, Plummer watched Brice walk out of the place before he rose and sauntered up to the bar. He did not look for more play, but bought cigars and, after listening to the bartender's account of the murder, started for his home.

Brice was part owner of a stage line, a man of importance, and he had spoken with a determination quite unusual. He would be liable to stir up trouble, and Henry Plummer, knowing men, was more disturbed than ordinarily, though not once did he feel that he, himself, was in any danger.

He found a crowd of men at the Combination Gambling House the next morning. He had expected as much; but aware of the lack of real intimacy among the men there, he still felt no actual alarm. Curiosity was uppermost in his mind, and nothing that was said or done escaped his quick notice. When he entered, Ford, a saloon keeper who bore the reputation of being a fighting man, was speaking.

"We're a lot of cowards!" he was shouting. "We have let murder and robbery go unpunished too long. I'm not afraid of any or *all* of the murdering rascals! I s'pose there's some of 'em here right now, listening. Well, let 'em listen! I say that we must organize a vigilance committee and *hang* a dozen or two of these fellows! We know some of 'em, don't we?"

"You bet!" cried a voice near Plummer, who secretly marked the man for punishment.

"Well then," continued Ford, "let's go after 'em! I'm ready right now. That's all I've got to say," and he jumped from the bar to the floor where men crowded about him with congratulations.

"Mr. Johnson! Mr. Johnson!" someone called. "Let's hear from Mr. Johnson!"

A fat man in shirtsleeves, one of the leading merchants of Lewiston, being pushed towards the bar, reluctantly climbed to its top and held up his hand for silence, after which, in tones that trembled with fear and embarrassment, he began: "I don't much believe in violence myself. We might get into a lot of trouble. It takes a lot of men to do as Mr. Ford suggests, and we don't know who we can trust here. We might make matters a lot worse by forming a vigilance committee. I want to do something to stop the murders, of course, but I don't want to—"

"Oh, hell, fatty, you've said a-plenty!" cried a man in the crowd. And Mr. Johnson, glad of an opportunity, got down from the bar.

"Let's hear Plummer! Let Plummer talk. That's the boy!" called Ford, who had formed a good opinion of the handsome young gambler. He was quiet and rather reserved, but Ford felt he could be counted on.

"Plummer! Plummer!" the crowd took up the cry.

"Come on, Plummer," urged Ford. "Tell us what you think we ought to do."

Plummer had hoped to be asked to speak, even after Ford's words had found supporters, because he knew the fickleness of the hastily formed composite mind and believed that he could turn these men away from vengeance on his gang more easily than Ford had set them on. Self-interest, excused, does nothing gratis for the public weal, and apathy makes no sacrifice.

Smilingly sure of himself, and young as the youngest there, he placed his hands on the bar and vaulted lightly to its top, regaining his poise with easy grace and looking calmly down into the faces before him, his own suddenly sobering to seriousness, as though he felt their confidence and acknowledged it with humility. "Gentlemen," he began, going directly to the point, "a vigilance committee is a good thing—"

"That's the talk, Plummer!" interrupted Ford, slapping the bar at the speaker's feet.

"I was about to say that a vigilance committee is a good thing when men are well acquainted with one another," continued Plummer, smiling down at Ford, his attitude boldly that of good-natured chiding.

There was a snicker, a laugh, and a low murmuring of approval; the amiable affront to Ford was so confident of support and so plainly challenged debate that the meeting forgot its expressions of a moment before. "Go on, Plummer!" it cried. Ford was non-plussed and, backing away from the bar, looked his disgust.

"Where men are strangers to each other there is always danger in such organizations," Plummer went on, "for how can they *know* that a vigilance committee formed under such conditions is free from criminals? And if such a vigilance committee were formed, its membership, peppered with enemies of the law, could not of course be kept secret. In that case there would be sure to be reprisal at the hands of those whom the committee sought to punish, for no move it might contemplate or make would be secret from the outlaws themselves. There lies the great trouble in such organizations in new countries, I think, gentlemen." He was not smiling now. His voice had lowered so that men leaned forward to catch the words his thin lips seemed to begrudge as useless expressions of self-evident truths. "Lewiston is young," he said. She has a bright future before her. Men are coming here from the states and these men read the newspapers. If we could succeed in catching these criminals—all of them—then it might be different. But suppose that we make a fizzle of it? What will be the result? More murders. Fires will be frequent as well, for the bandits are certain to retaliate if we proceed against them and fail. The newspapers everywhere will tell readers to shun our city if we call down the wrath of these criminals upon us by a blundering attempt to punish them. If we were sure of our own citizens, if we were old acquaintances, we might then with safety take the law into our own hands. But we should stop to think before we call the vengeance of every desperado in the whole section against Lewiston. Instead let us insist that our officers enforce the law. We can do this if we have to turn them out and elect others that will do it."

"That's the talk! That's the truth!" shouted a man close to the bar.

"The history of vigilance committees," continued Plummer, ignoring the interruption, "is not such as would attract men who are engaged in building a city in a new country, but let me assure you that I am willing to abide by the will of the majority here. Let us not be hasty of action, however. Let us think matters over before we act."

There was a moment of silence after Plummer had finished. "I guess mebby we'd better wait a spell before we organize a vigilance committee, boys," advised Jed Caruthers, who after the fight in Florence had moved to Lewiston.

"Yes! We'll wait till we're all murdered in our beds," cried Ford in anger. "I'm through trying to make fighters out of a bunch of old women!" Thrusting his hands deep into his pockets, he flung out of the door.

Ten days later Ford was killed in a fight with the road agents in his own place of business. "There, you see," said the weak-hearted in Lewiston, "that's what he got for his talk about organizing a vigilance committee."

And so the sentiment in favor of such an organization was dulled and seemed to die. But Lewiston awoke one morning to find three dead men hanging in an unfinished building and many determined citizens busily looked for Club-Foot George and other members of the gang. A vigilance committee had been born in spite of the protests of the weak-hearted in Lewiston.

13

Near noon the day after the hanging of the three men, Henry Plummer, riding toward Craig Mountain, met Jack Cleveland on his way to Lewiston. "You are the man I want to see, Jack," he greeted. "They have hanged Bill Peoples, Dave English and poor old Nels Scott."

"Who have?" inquired Cleveland, startled.

"The vigilantes, that's who, Jack," said Plummer, holding his beautiful, restless horse near to Cleveland's, "and you and I better move before it's too late. I can't tell where the lead is coming from, but there's a wheel within the wheel in Lewiston. That's plain."

"Where'll we go, Henry?" asked Cleveland, pushing his hat back on his boyish head.

"Let's go to Deer Lodge; and if that doesn't suit us, *I'm* going to Fort Benton, and then down the river to New Orleans. I'll take the Mullan Trail. I believe it's shorter."

"I'm with you," agreed Cleveland.

"Good! Meet me an hour's ride out of Lewiston tomorrow at daybreak. I'll be waiting for you along the trail. Don't say a word of our intentions to anyone." He turned his horse. "You've saved me a long ride," he said. "But we'd better not go into Lewiston together."

"All right. Go ahead, Henry. I'll come in a little later," agreed Cleveland.

In Lewiston there was much excitement. The whispered news of the hangings had spread like a prairie fire. Half of the town, tiptoeing in the gray light of morning, went to see for itself; and half of that half recounted its own past hastily and secretly, in dread of the unknown avengers of lawlessness that must be among Lewiston's own citizens.

A sense of this same undercurrent made it obvious to Plummer that he had not been so entirely in the confidence of the better citizens as he had proudly believed; and he was uneasy enough to be well on the trail out of Lewiston while the daylight of the next morning was still hours away. Yet he rode slowly, for Cleveland would not start until nearly dawn. He planned to unsaddle and wait for him when he had traveled what he considered an hour's ride from town. Once out of sight of the scattered lights that still twinkled in Lewiston, he was conscious of relief and quite at ease under the stars. His face was turned towards a new territory. He had no tormenting thought for the woman whom the town had come to know as Mrs. Plummer and whom he was leaving for all time, the poor victim of blind infatuation.

But this secretly organized vigilance committee in Lewiston puzzled him. How had it been accomplished without his knowing of the movement? He ran over carefully in his mind the names and characters of the men he knew there, but found none among them who he felt could possibly be the leader. Had they captured Club-Foot George? Could they connect *him* in any way with Club-Foot, or the three dead men? No. He had never been seen with any of them, he was certain. But he felt that he had been wise in leaving. Many of his men had already crossed to the east side, enough to make a fresh start, anyhow, if he decided to stay there himself.

Suddenly his horse pricked his ears forward. Somebody was coming. He drew up to the side of the road in the shadow of a fir tree and slid one of his six-shooters forward on his belt. Then he waited. A lone horseman was approaching at a slow gait. Plummer drew his gun from his holster. The wind gave the approaching horse no hint of his presence, so that the oncoming rider was within ten paces from him when his horse stopped short in the trail. Plummer fired. The man fell, and, springing from his saddle, Plummer secured the other animal, unsaddled him, pulled off his bridle, and turned him loose. He dragged the dead man into the brush where he took a poke of gold dust and some treasury notes from his pockets, carefully hid the saddle and bridle, and rode on. It would be days, perhaps weeks, before the man would be missed, and then he himself would be far away and unsuspected.

A sunbeam, pricking its way through the treetops and falling like a streak of gold upon the trail before him, stopped him. "I've ridden too far," he muttered, and dismounted.

He found a spring of clear water bubbling from beneath a great rock on the hillside and forming a pool before it crossed the trail on its way to join the Snake River. Under a bush close to it in a grove of quaking aspens, he sat down to wait for Jack Cleveland. Presently he removed his hat and kneeling, bathed his hands and face in the water, brushing the hair back from his forehead. The shallow bottom of the pool, disturbed by his fingers, became roiled and, while he dried his hands with his black silk handkerchief, he watched the muddy streaks in the water creep away until the pool had become crystal clear. Stuffing the dampened handkerchief into his pocket, he bent to drink.

As his face came close to the water, he started, gazed a second at his features reflected there, and then struck at them with his clenched fist. A snarled oath came from between his white teeth, and he seized his hat and pulled it down savagely upon his forehead. His eyes were strange with the light of mingled fear and hate. He glared at the pool his blow had rendered murky. "Damn you! Curse you, you—" he hissed.

But the busy, bubbling source beneath the rock wiped out the proof of his temper, and when Henry Plummer stooped to drink from the pool that was clear once more he gazed long, and not without admiration, at the face he saw reflected there.

Suddenly he sat erect and pulled his hat yet lower over his forehead, turning his head to listen. A horse was coming up the trail. He pulled a boot from his foot and was feigning an examination of its interior when Jack Cleveland rode into view.

"Your hour's ride is a long one, Henry," said Cleveland, dismounting to drink from the spring.

"Yes, I know it," laughed Plummer. "I got to thinking and didn't wake up until I saw the sunlight on the trail ahead of me."

"I passed a loose horse headed for Lewiston," said Cleveland, wiping his mouth with the back of his hand. "Somebody's afoot, I guess."

"Yes, I passed that horse, too. Let's be moving."

14

From the Bitterroot Mountains eastward to the main range of the Rockies and beyond, the change is great to one who has grown accustomed to the climate and country of the western slope. The skies are bluer, sunshine brighter and more constant, and air drier and clearer on the eastern side. There is more in the atmosphere that imparts zest to man and beast than on the western side, until one passes the plains and comes out of the west altogether. Indeed, nearing either ocean, east or west from the Rockies, is to leave behind that magic elixir for which Ponce de Leon so earnestly sought.

Not abruptly, but gradually, as though cautiously leading one away from accustomed satisfaction, the trail crosses the Bitterroot Mountains and descends to a moderately timbered valley. There it follows the windings of a crystal river's course through green groves of cottonwoods and bits of pine forest that soon leave the stream to claim only the hillsides reaching back to barer, bolder, higher moun-taintops beneath the brighter sky until at last it has led one to the plains. By then, one's allegiance will have been shaken, and if one tar-ries by the way, it will soon be transferred to the kingdom of the sun.

The Deer Lodge diggings on the eastern side were not extensive. The flood of gold seekers, like a swarm of bees attracted by a field of flowers, had come, made its hurried search for claims or business chances, and leaving a few lucky ones to grow fat, had gone to Ban-nack or Virginia City. And so, the camp was not to the liking of Henry Plummer and Jack Cleveland, who, after a day in Deer Lodge, decided to go to Bear Gulch, where a new strike had recently been made. But so utterly without set purpose was their plan to visit Bear Gulch that it was changed before they had ridden five miles. They met a miner, old and grizzled, driving a packed burro ahead of him, and Plummer, reining his horse, drew a flask from his cantinas and proffered the old fellow a drink.

"What are the prospects in Bear Gulch, partner?" he asked, as the miner returned the flask after a deep draught.

"Well," said the old man, stroking his whiskers, "I wouldn't want to undermine nobody's claim in Bear nor no place else. I w'n't there but two days noway, an' I might be mistaken, like as not. But I took a good look around the camp and the diggin's, an' I noticed that the gamblers was a-sawin' their own wood, an' that the dance hall gals was a-doin' their own washin', so I figured there wa'n't a hell's mint o' pay in the gravel there. Goin' in?"

Plummer laughed with youthful and unfeigned delight. "No, partner," he said. "You've saved us a ride. Have another!"

The old miner took a second hearty drink, and, pleased to have such an appreciative audience, added, as he wiped his mouth with the back of his hand, "The Chinymen are beginnin' to work over the ground in Bear, an' them's the vultures that picks the ribs of a gold camp's carcass. She's had her day, Bear Gulch has, I reckon. I'm goin' to Virginny City."

Plummer and Cleveland turned back to Deer Lodge. "Jack," laughed Plummer, with a departing glance over his shoulder at the old man and his burro, "I've heard reports on mining camps before—reports which dealt with bedrock, and gravel, and water, and fall, and formation, and folderol; but, with simple logic a fool could understand, that old fellow back there sized up a situation and, without sticking a pick into the ground or panning a shovel of gravel, prospected a gulch. Wait!"

He pulled up impulsively and, once more drawing the whisky flask from his cantinas, waved it over his head, chuckling to himself as he swung down from his saddle to place it in the middle of the trail. "His burro'll spot it if *he* doesn't," he laughed. "And I want him to have it—what's left—the sharp old cuss."

From his saddle he waved another farewell, and the old man, evidently understanding, snatched off his hat and answered enthusiastically.

There was hint of fall in the air when, after supper, Plummer and Cleveland sat on the porch of the Deer Lodge Hotel, where they had registered for the night. The windows behind them were dark, for within the office there were no lights, patronage having dwindled with the rush of gold seekers. Those who labored in the diggings lived in tents or cabins now, and the hostelry had fallen into careless ways.

The moon rose over the mountains and its light crept slantwise across the porch at their feet. "Henry," said Cleveland, "let's have a look at Bannack before we go down the river."

"I've been thinking of that, Jack. We'll decide in the morning. But I am inclined to believe my course will be down the river. I'm not satisfied here."

Cleveland tilted back in his chair against the wall. A cool breeze was stirring the willows by the creek in the moonlight where crickets were singing in contented monotony. "I think we ought to," he said, taking off his hat to rest the back of his head against the logs. "We won't be likely to come this way again."

Plummer caught the tone of dissatisfaction in Cleveland's voice. Why *not* go to Bannack? A week or two was nothing to him. He was still carefree. And Jack wanted to go there. It was yet August. There was plenty of time—nearly all of September—to go south after seeing Bannack. What was it that made him disinclined? It was the secret desire to get away from the Northwest that had come to him in Lewiston, but which he would not own or consciously give a place in his reasoning. He would go to Bannack.

Even as he opened his lips to speak, a man stepped upon the porch, pausing near him to strike a match on a post supporting the roof. The sulphur match spluttered a moment, then flared into a clear, yellow flame. As the man's hands cupped themselves to shield the match from the breeze, his eyes met Plummer's. In a trice he had tossed the match away and, puffing at his pipe, turned deliberately and entered the hotel.

"Who is that man, Jack?" asked Plummer in his low tone.

"I'm sure I don't know, Henry. Why?"

"I saw him in Lewiston one morning. I'm sure he knows me. He's from California, most likely; I don't like the way he looks at me. But I think I told you of seeing him before." He turned his head, listening to the man's footsteps within, which suddenly stopped; and a match flared in the darkness there. He stirred nervously in his chair. "It annoys me," he uttered. Rising, he stepped through the open door of the office. The match was instantly extinguished and the man disappeared through another door which closed sharply in a gust of the evening's breeze. Plummer crossed to the desk and struck a light. The hotel register was turned outward and a burnt match was lying upon his own name there.

"Let's take a walk, Jack," said Plummer in a troubled voice, returning to the porch. "That prospector's got on my nerves."

Wondering, Cleveland followed his chief beside the creek. Henry Plummer afraid of another man? Henry Plummer who ruled over more than fifty outlaws who would dare anything but his anger? He scoffed at the idea. There was a secret here, he thought. And there *was* a secret there which neither he nor Henry Plummer understood—the overwhelming power of a clean, fearless mind directed at evil.

When they returned to their room after perhaps half an hour by the creek and opened the door, a sheet of paper was brushed within. Stooping, Jack Cleveland picked it up, glanced at it, and handing it to Plummer, saw his face change slightly as he read. "The People of California vs Plummer" was written on it.

"This settles it for me, Jack," said Plummer, crushing the paper in his hand. "That man is a California miner. I'm going down the river. If I see him again, I'll kill him."

"He's the fellow, no doubt, that put the paper under our door," said Cleveland. "You were foolish, Henry. You'll have to change your name like the rest of the bad ones."

"Perhaps I was foolish, Jack, but that man would have known me anywhere, name or no name. There's something about him that makes me want to move, and no man ever made me feel that way before." He sat down on the bed and slipped a gun under his pillow. Then he got up and walked to the window and looked up at the moon. He felt strangely at sea. He had known fear of punishment, of death even, and fled before it. But he had never before faced the fear of another man. He felt as though he had been swung out into space. Was it possible that his once unbounded confidence in himself had somehow weakened in a brief meeting with another man? Where were the things he had trusted—the speed with which he could draw his gun, his amazing good luck, his power over other men? He had no power over this man.

"Well, if you go down the river, I'll go with you," Cleveland was saying. "Let's go to bed. We'll get up early and make a start. While you undress I'll slip out and see if that fellow is registered here."

"No," he said, upon returning, "nobody has registered after us. He can't be stopping here. He's camped down by the river, most likely. Shall I blow out the candle?"

"Yes, and if you wake early, call me."

But Plummer lay awake all night. He watched the shadows of a leafy bough dance on the wall in the moonlight, saw and marked with impatience the line of shadow climb higher until the papered ceiling alone told him that the moon was yet above the mountaintops. Would it never set and let the daylight come? Almost angrily, he listened to Jack Cleveland's measured breathing, and three times looked at his watch before the moonlight faded in the room. Then he fell asleep, to waken with a start. He struck a match and looked at his watch.

"Come, Jack," he said, springing from the bed to pull on his trousers and boots.

"What time is it, Henry?"

"Nearly five o'clock. I'll go out to the barn and feed the horses and rustle out the cook, if I can."

Cleveland was not yet dressed when Plummer returned to the room and announced that they could get breakfast, and he would go and saddle up while the cook was getting it. Cleveland, left alone again, sat on the bed to pull on his boots. "Losing his nerve," he muttered. "That bit of paper has scared him. I'd like to see Bannack, myself, but I'll go wherever he goes, I guess."

Smoke was beginning to climb from the miners' chimneys along the creek as they rode out of Deer Lodge; and as they faced the east, where soon the sun would appear above the hills, Plummer's spirits rose with the brightness of the morning. "I hope we'll be lucky enough to catch a boat at Fort Benton that is bound down the river," he said after they had been riding for a time in silence. "Day after tomorrow's the first of September. It won't be long before winter will be here. But if we are lucky, it won't catch us in this country. We'll be in the sunny south somewhere, Jack."

15

In a bend of the Sun River, fifty or sixty miles west from Fort Benton, the United States government maintained a ranch. Beautifully situated by the stream that empties its waters into the Missouri some miles below, the place was a garden in the wilderness. Groves of giant cottonwood trees adorned the banks on either side, and distant snowy peaks, glimpsed through their rustling tops, were misty white against the blue sky. Closer at hand, like monuments to bound its level bottomlands, were set strange flat-topped cliffs of clay and grassy knolls that now in the sunlight of late summer were brown and sere, in contrast with the rich green about the log ranch house. There, broad, well-fenced pastures harbored horses and mules of travelers, and hospitable doors were open to all wayfarers.

Along one side of this comfortable house, which stood at the edge of a grove of trees near the river, a broad porch extended, and from its low ceiling a canvas hammock was hung, spread amply by the use of forked sticks. The afternoon was warm. The lonely heated plains reaching away to the mountains on one side and to the horizon on the other offered nothing of interest to a girl who reclined in the hammock, listlessly turning the leaves of an old volume of *Pilgrim's Progress* that she held in her hands. Now and then her eyes strayed from the book to scan the trail over which all travel passed but, seeing no living thing, they reluctantly turned back to the printed pages. "Oh dear," she yawned, covering her mouth with her hand, "I do wish that something would happen." Then her head sought the pillow and the book rested upon her breast.

At the sound of her voice, a wolfhound, wakened from light slumber in the porch's cooling shade, arose, stretched his great length and, as though regretting the necessity of attention, lumbered towards her, his toenails scratching on the boards of the porch floor. He poked his long nose close to her face on the pillow. His soft brown eyes expressed sympathy, which he emphasized with a plaintive whine.

The girl languidly placed a hand on his head. "Yes, Badger, you're a fine fellow," she said. "My! but you're a big dog. You can kill a wolf, can't you?"

Badger's tail gave assent; but the next moment he had raised his lips, baring his sharp white fangs, and a growl, deep and fierce, caused the girl to turn her head anxiously. Chief, Badger's wolf-killing companion, had stepped upon the porch to seek recognition, and it was denied by the present recipient of the young lady's attentions. "Now, now, you Badger! Be good," she scolded. But Badger, jealous of momentary favor, continued to growl, and his eyes took on a dangerous light. "Stop it, I say! Shame on you!"

Badger hung his head and slouched away to the far end of the porch, where he lay down with a sigh that brought a smile to the girl's lips. Chief, not wishing to chance a rupture for so slight a cause, turned back to the shade of a tree. And the girl, relieved of both, closed her eyes.

A soft breeze came down the river to cool the plains and coulee places where the wolves were waiting for the night. It brushed her cheek, stirred her hair, and as the leaves on the tall cottonwoods whispered their lullaby, she slept.

The breeze grew stronger and began to swing the hammock perceptibly, but the sleeper did not waken, sleeping only the deeper because of it. Her face was fair with the bloom of eighteen summers. The sun had not left a mark upon it, nor had her reclining position in any way disturbed the careful arrangement of her soft light brown curls or the freshness of her blue muslin gown. A small stockinged foot hung over the side of the hammock as it swung in the breeze, its slipper having fallen to the floor unheeded, and one delicate hand was tucked under her rosy cheek, the other resting idly upon the book on her bosom, which lifted and fell gently with her regular breathing.

"Betty! Betty! Where ah you, Betty?"

A little girl in pantalettes and with her hair tightly curled came around the corner of the house, fresh from her nap. As she approached the sleeper, she paused with one moccasined foot upon the porch, and a look of deep mischief lighted her little face. Stealing up to the hammock, she stood a moment with a finger in her mouth, then gingerly reached and began pulling the pins from the sleeper's hair with her chubby fingers, taking care to avoid the swaying hammock lest it strike her tiny body and the jar waken its occupant. One by one the child removed the pins until the curls fell loose upon the pillow about the girl's face. Then, having accomplished her purpose, the mischievous one tiptoed away, looking backward at her handiwork with doubtful anticipation.

Out on the plains a cloud of dust rose and began to sweep eastward of the wind. Then in plain sight from the ranch a herd of buffalo covered a knoll so completely that the earth beneath them seemed to be a huge anthill. Badger's keen ears had distinguished the rumble of the distant hoofs, and half inclined to chase, he rose and gazed at the moving herd; but laziness was upon him, and he returned to his nap.

Once or twice the child's curly head peeped around the corner in order that she might enjoy the mischief she had done, but the form in the hammock had not stirred, and dispraisingly the child finally went to play with Chief in the corral near the river. A flock of sage hens, evidently flushed by the buffalo herd, flew over the stream and settled down among the bullberry bushes near the water on the far side just as the ranch gate opened on its creaking wooden hinges and two horsemen entered the enclosure. The taller of the two had opened the gate and, leading a limping horse, was approaching the porch. He was dressed in a black slouch hat, a tight-fitting vest, a pearl gray flannel shirt against which a blue silk scarf was carefully knotted, and gray trousers tucked neatly into elaborately stitched boot tops. On his heels were silvered Spanish spurs. Badger growled ominously, his displeasure deepening at every step the stranger advanced, until he rose with a sharp bark that stopped the young man, about to step upon the porch, in his tracks.

"Badger!" cried the girl, starting up in the hammock.

Her sudden movement completely loosed her unpinned hair and it fell about her shoulders bewitchingly. Embarrassed, she sought to catch and stop it but in vain, and a deep blush reddened her face and neck.

The wolfhound, baring his white fangs, advanced towards the stranger threateningly, his hair bristled.

"Why, Badger!" the girl cried again, clutching his collar and holding him with all her strength.

"Good afternoon." The young man bowed, admiration leaping into his eyes. He was now apparently unconcerned with the dog's attitude. "I'm truly sorry that I have disturbed you."

Still holding fast to the wolfhound, the girl stooped to pick up her slipper and, as she put her foot into it, inquired, "Did you want to see my uncle?" Her face was rosier; her curls were cascading about it.

"My friend and I are on our way to Fort Benton," explained the young man in a low, courteous voice, "but my horse blundered into a badger hole and has crippled himself so that I cannot go farther. If we could arrange to stop here for the night, or until I can procure another saddle horse, the favor would be greatly appreciated. Do you suppose we might be permitted?"

A light laugh rippled from the girl's lips with the gaiety of youth released from loneliness. "Of course," she replied. "We'd—they'd be glad to have you stay." The stranger was young and handsome. "Just a second. I'll tell Aunt Jane," she said, rising, while her free hand reached to confine her loosened curls.

At that moment a short, stout woman in a starched calico dress appeared in the door. "What is it, Betty?" she asked, and then seeing the stranger while Badger growled and bristled, bowed graciously and reprimanded Badger. "Shame on you!" she said sternly. "Go lie down on the back porch."

"I have asked the young lady if we might stop with you for the night. My horse had been crippled," explained the young man, himself bowing deeply.

"Why, certainly. You are welcome. The men are out on the range, but if you will turn your horses into that pasture near the barn they'll be looked after later."

"I am deeply thankful, madam." And turning, he called to his companion at the gate. "It's all right, Jack!"

"Just come right in as soon as you are ready, please," said the woman. "Make yourselves perfectly at home while you stay with us, for we like to be of help to travelers. I am baking bread, and I'm sure you'll excuse me, but Betty can entertain you, can't you, dear?"

But Betty had disappeared.

"Don't trouble yourself further, I beg you," said the young man. "We will turn our horses into the pasture at once." And with his companion he turned away towards that enclosure.

"Jack, I've seen a wonderful woman," said Henry Plummer seriously while spreading his saddle blanket upon the fence to dry.

"Again, Henry?" laughed Jack Cleveland, slapping his hat against the barn to free it from dust.

"I've never seen one before, Jack," he said sharply, his gray eyes cold in an instant. "I mean it, and I don't want you to make light of it."

Cleveland turned and surveyed the crippled horse that was hobbling after the other. "That's a bad sprain," he remarked. "You'd better get another mount, Henry. That one won't be worth much for a long time."

"I'm afraid you are right, Jack," agreed Plummer, in better nature. "I'll see what can be done when the men come in. Isn't that a fine place?"

"That river looks good to me," observed Cleveland. "I think I'll take a swim. Better join me."

"No, go on if you want to. I'm going back to the porch and rest a while."

16

Elizabeth Bryman, niece of Mrs. Jane Bailey, had fled from the porch as soon as her aunt had relieved her, and in her room had begun to rearrange her hair. The grinning child who had done the mischief stood on a chair beside her at the bureau and watched with deep interest the replacing of the pins.

"Oh, you naughty girl to pick the pins from my hair! Just think, that gentleman saw me with my hair all undone," chided Elizabeth. "Naughty Margaret!"

"Ith nither muthed, lots nither, Betty," lisped the child in all seriousness.

"Is it?" asked Betty with a hairpin between her lips and a little smile in her eyes. "But you must not do such things, dear," she said, touching her hair, now carefully done, with her fingers, after which she surveyed herself in a hand mirror and, satisfied, laid it upon the bureau. "Come, dear," she said, stealing a last glimpse in the mirror. "Mama is busy. You and I will talk to the gentlemen until Papa comes."

Henry Plummer was waiting. He had hoped she would come. He stood up as they came through the door. "Won't you come and see me?" he coaxed, addressing little Margaret, while Elizabeth seated herself in the hammock. "Come." But the child shook her head and clung to her cousin's skirt.

"Have you traveled far?" Elizabeth asked conventionally.

"From Deer Lodge," answered Plummer.

"Do you live in Deer Lodge?"

"No, my home is in Connecticut; but do you live here, Miss—"

"My name is Elizabeth Bryman," she supplied prettily. "No, sir, I do not live here. I am visiting my aunt and uncle, Mr. and Mrs. Bailey, for this year. My home is in Illinois."

"Oh, then you are not a rebel," laughed Plummer, drawing a chair ever so slightly nearer the hammock and seating himself.

"No, indeed. We are all Union folks here; even this little desperado, aren't you Margaret?" and she lifted the child to her lap.

"Yeth," whispered the little one, turning her face up to Betty's, "an' my papa ith Union, too."

"Of course he is," agreed Plummer. Then addressing the girl carefully, he announced, "It is refreshing and helpful to find a home of Union people here in this wilderness. It has seemed to me that nearly all of the people in the mining camps are rebels. I have been persecuted to some extent because of my sympathies for the Union. In fact I warned my parents and my brothers and sisters and friends in the East that I may—well I may be missing some day—accused of almost anything that will give countenance to a death sentence. I wanted to prepare them, so that they would understand."

"Oh, is it so bad as that!" and she leaned forward, her dark blue eyes wide with surprise. "How can such things be? Have they actually attempted your life—tried to—to harm you?"

79

"Oh, yes, at times," smiled Plummer. "I do not fear them in that way. What I most fear is their underhanded methods of first staining a man's reputation, and then, with hastily constructed legal machinery, making away with him because of his sympathies for the North. Most of the officials—local, I mean—are rebels, and I have known some monstrous outrages to be perpetrated in the name of the law."

"My! I wouldn't stay here if I were you," advised Elizabeth. "I'd go away."

"I was on my way to"—he checked himself—"to the states," he finished, "but it seems cowardly to run away. I may go to Bannack. I haven't seen the camp, and I may be missing a great opportunity. Mr. Cleveland, my companion, is much in favor of returning to the mines, and since leaving Deer Lodge, I have been half inclined to listen to him, and turn back."

While he talked, he allowed himself only fleeting glances at her, resting his gaze elsewhere on the distant mountains, the river, the green pasture—anywhere other than the place they most wished to dwell. When she turned the full blue innocence of her regard upon him, he forced himself to turn away, for he felt that the least expression of what that sweet look aroused in him might frighten her away.

"Where is Mr. Cleveland, your companion?" she asked, looking about.

"He has gone swimming in the river," replied Plummer.

A little silence fell, broken finally by a joyful bark from Badger, around a corner of the porch. Elizabeth rose. "You haven't told me your name, and I shall need to know it now, for here comes Uncle Seth and Mr. Parker."

"My name is Henry Plummer, Miss Bryman. At your service always," he answered, himself rising, as two horsemen rode in through the gate.

"Uncle Seth! Uncle Seth!" called Elizabeth, waving her hand, and a tall man with a rifle across his saddle before him wheeled his horse towards the porch and dismounted. "Mr. Plummer, this is my uncle, Mr. Bailey," said the girl in a half-shy introduction.

Mr. Bailey shook his visitor's hand warmly, the good nature of an honest man manifested in the appraising glance of his sharp hazel eyes. "I'm glad to see you, sir," he said.

"And I am more than delighted to have met you, Mr. Bailey," returned Plummer. "I am an intruder here, but my horse stepped into a badger hole and so crippled himself that I was obliged to stop."

"Well, well, I'm sure we're sorry your horse went and did that, but we're glad to have you with us. I hope they're making you feel at home."

"Mr. Plummer is a very pronounced Union man, Uncle Seth," put in Elizabeth, as though she would strengthen his position as a visitor at the ranch.

"Glad to hear it," said Bailey, shoving his hat backwards on his head. "I guess the country is filling up with rebels. What's your native state, Mr. Plummer?"

"Connecticut, sir."

"You're safe," laughed Bailey, patting his horse's neck, "perfectly safe. I'm from New York, myself, so we're both well north of the Mason-Dixon line; but it's a terrible struggle, and the pity of it is that it's between Americans. I've felt like I ought to enlist—although I'm serving the government here, this being a government ranch."

"I, too, have wanted to join the army," said Plummer, "but I have been so far from home since the war began that I have put it off hoping the end would come. However, I have tried to be of some service even out here."

Mrs. Bailey had appeared upon the porch. "Seth," she said, as Plummer finished, "supper will be ready in a very few minutes. You'd better put up your horse and get ready for it."

"All right, Jane," complied the ranchman turning to his horse. "Come on, Peggy, and we'll ride old Buck to the barn." He lifted little Margaret and led his horse away with the laughing child clinging tightly to the horn of the saddle. Plummer and Elizabeth and Margaret's proud mother watched from the porch.

Cleveland, looking fresh from his swim, had meanwhile come around to the porch, and Plummer presented him to Mrs. Bailey and to Elizabeth.

"If you gentlemen would like to wash, I'll show you to your room," said Mrs. Bailey, mindful of her supper and leading the men to the neat bedroom with bare floor and high four-poster bed that opened upon the porch.

"Jack," said Plummer in a whisper when Mrs. Bailey had left them, "isn't she beautiful?"

"Yes, Henry, but—"

"No buts, Jack. I'm in love with her and I am going to win her. If I do, I shall be a different man. I believe I shall go back to Bannack and turn over a new leaf."

"I suppose some of the gang are in Bannack by this time," whispered Cleveland, ignoring what Plummer had said.

"I suppose so; but I'm to be left out of whatever they do after this," declared Plummer, impulsively brushing his hair so that it covered his forehead. "I'm going to settle down, Jack. I'm not too old."

There came a knock on the door, and Plummer opened it. Little Margaret stood in the doorway. "Mama seth thupper ith weady," she announced. Plummer tried to seize her, and she ran laughing excitedly into the dining room where the family awaited the guests.

The conversation at the table drifted from the mines to the war, and at length to the boldness of the criminals in the mining camps. "The officers of the law are either in league with the highwaymen and murderers, or they are too cowardly to do their duty," declared Mr. Bailey positively.

"I am inclined to believe it is the latter, Mr. Bailey," said Plummer, touching his lips with his napkin. "They believe the robbers are closely organized and fear the consequences of an attempt to punish them."

"I'd rather believe it that way, Mr. Plummer; but it would seem like somewhere a man could be found that wasn't afraid. Of course, the communities are new, and men don't know each other. Their politics and their sympathies in the fuss between the North and South are known only to themselves, and not till something makes them talk out does anybody know where they stand."

"If a good brave man would enter the race for sheriff, I am sure he would be elected, or selected by the miners' courts, whichever way they follow in such matters," Mrs. Bailey offered. "I know the law and order element is in the majority everywhere, if only it had a leader," she finished, filling little Margaret's glass with milk.

"In that I am sure you are quite right, Mrs. Bailey," Plummer assented. "If the criminals were in the majority there would be little hope; but, as you say, they cannot be."

"There'll be an election at Bannack in November," said Mr. Bailey, leaning his fork against his plate and passing his coffee cup to his wife. "Some organized effort should be made to get a sheriff that would enforce the law. Any man that would do it would be serving his country, for the government is a sight too busy just now to give much attention to our local affairs."

Plummer glanced involuntarily at Elizabeth. An idea had leaped into his mind, and from his to hers. She colored vividly, but returned his gaze with her wide blue eyes. "That is your opportunity, Mr. Plummer," she said, remembering what he had told her on the porch.

"But I am a stranger," he laughed, as if inviting her to go on.

"Everybody is a stranger in the mining camps," she reminded him. "That is the cause for so much distrust there, Uncle Seth always says. The election is almost two months away, and sixty days—why, a citizen is actually an old timer in sixty days, they say."

"Men move about a great deal, it is true," he replied, "but—"

"Why, you might try for it," said Mrs. Bailey. "It wouldn't be so bad to fail. You would at least have tried to serve the decent people in those communities, Mr. Plummer."

"Yes, Henry," smiled Cleveland, a boyish twinkle in his eyes. "We'll all help to elect you. You are the making of a splendid sheriff."

Plummer's enthusiasms suffered a sudden check. Beneath the table his hands clenched in anger at Cleveland's unguessed sarcasm. But, pushing it defiantly aside, his quick mind began to measure his chances.

"I'd think of it, Mr. Plummer," advised Seth Bailey. "The camps are in a bad way. I think your personality will go a long way in making friends and supporters in sixty days. You're a good Union man and believe in law and order. You would have as good a chance as any other candidate, surely; and your appearance is in your favor."

"Thank you, Mr. Bailey," said Plummer, bowing. "I *will* think of it."

"You've talked like a parrot tonight, Henry," whispered Cleveland, when they had gone to their room.

"I have need to talk, Jack, and I mean what I have said. Do you believe that I could be elected sheriff?" he asked pausing before the mirror.

"Maybe," answered Cleveland from his seat on the bed. "The boys would leg hard no doubt. They'd come a long way to work and vote. I could do a little something towards it, myself," and he smiled.

"I know—I know; but I—well, they would help, of course," he answered, checking upon his lips the words which his resolution to reform had offered. He would have need of help. Then, when he had succeeded—"I believe I will do it. I'll run for sheriff, Jack," he said. "We'll go back and go to Bannack and set up in business."

17

Cleveland fell asleep almost immediately, but Plummer was wakeful. Pictures of Elizabeth marched through his mind repeatedly. Never before had he known the regard for womankind that the very innocence of her deep blue eyes had wakened in an instant. It was not only her physical charm, her soft girlish beauty with its promise of womanhood that set his pulses throbbing—it was also the romantic trust with which she looked at him—as if he were the Sir Galahad that he knew he was not. Sitting up on the bed, he compared her with the women he had cared for—women who, knowing the world, had loved him even after they had learned something of his life. Each would have spurned protection against any man, and measuring glance with glance, had finally followed him, only to be discarded at last, when he had tired of their charms. A sudden distrust of his intentions towards Elizabeth stung him to thoughts of his heartless desertion of Catherine in Lewiston until, as though standing accused before the innocent girl asleep under the same roof with him, he got up restlessly. Hearing Badger bark, he went over to the window to look out over the moonlit plains where a wolf was howling. He saw the two hounds race to the gate, leap high over it, and away under the moon, their long gray bodies resembling hoops that opened and closed as they ran like the wind, eager to chase their self-supporting wild relation to his death.

"Outcast!" he whispered under his breath, his fingers against the window sash.

The howling ceased, and the great peace of the unmeasured expanse was again undisturbed. It oppressed him. The seeming peace was not for all. The wolf—the outcast—was running for his life. And why? The Creator had made him a wolf; gave him his nature. Why should man complain, much less his kindred, the kept dogs? Hatred for the wolfhounds surged up within him. Well, the Creator had fashioned them, too. Ah, but had he? *Man* had bred the wolfhound. He was not natural, but a hybrid with the blood of the wolf in his veins. So the blood of the outcast was needed to make the dogs fit—to give them courage and to fight the wolf—it was needed by men.

The clock in the sitting room struck two, its chime faint and musical in the still night. Glancing at the sleeping head on the pillow, he turned from the window to the bureau, whose mirror was damascened by cottonwood leaves that stirred in shadow. Pushing back his hair, he gazed a moment at his dimly reflected face, leaning nearer and nearer until with a sigh he turned away and crept back into bed, the wolf still in his thoughts. Only a little—ever so little was between the wolf and conventional decency. Was it choice or chance that kept it there? Even wolves had changed their ways and become companions of men. Given an opportunity to live a different life, even a wolf could prove himself worthy. He would drop his acquaintances. They were nothing to him; coarse, uneducated low outcasts—wolves. He would begin again. There was time. His associates would not dare to interfere—and he was a stranger. Ah, that was the secret of his opportunity. And then, besides, there was his luck.

A breeze came up from the plains and stirred the curtains. He heard the rustling of the leaves on the cottonwoods outside the moonlight. At length he slept.

When he awoke the sun was shining on the porch floor outside the bedroom window, and for a moment he wondered where he was. He sat up in bed, staring sleepily at Cleveland. Cows and calves were bawling about the weaning pasture near the barn, and as he listened a hen began to cackle vociferously under the porch. He shook Cleveland. "Hear that, Jack?" he laughed. "Get up and we'll go get that egg." He jumped out of bed and stretched his arms. The odor of coffee stole in from the kitchen. "I'm hungry as a bear," he told Cleveland as they both began dressing.

Used to outdoor life, they dressed quickly but they found that Mr. Bailey had gone out on the range with Mr. Parker an hour before they appeared for breakfast. "Mrs. Bailey," said Plummer after greeting her, "we are ashamed of ourselves. We slept so soundly we did not hear you stirring, and I ask your pardon."

"Oh, we wanted you to sleep and rest. That's the reason we didn't call you," replied the good woman, setting a plate of honey on the table. "Your breakfast is all ready, and when you've finished it you will find that the porch is comfortable. Sit right down, gentlemen, and I will bring in your breakfast.

"The men have gone out on the range, and Betty's washing the dishes," she explained as she brought in the breakfast with short quick steps and seated herself a trifle breathlessly at the table with her guests.

"And little Margaret, where is she this morning?" asked Plummer, unfolding his napkin.

"Oh, she is helping Betty," laughed Mrs. Bailey, her good face revealing her fondness, "but her help is of rather a questionable character, although she believes she is doing her full duty as assistant housekeeper."

After a time, during which Plummer and Cleveland obviously enjoyed Mrs. Bailey's breakfast, the kitchen door opened and Elizabeth, leading little Margaret, came in. "Good morning, gentlemen," she greeted. "Say good morning, Margaret," and she bent over the little girl, placing a hand upon her curls.

"Dood mornin'," murmured Margaret, bobbing her head.

"I trust you slept well, gentlemen?" continued Elizabeth.

"So well that we are ashamed of ourselves," assured Plummer, who had risen, together with Cleveland.

Mrs. Bailey left the table as soon as the two girls appeared. "I'll have to leave you to these two young ladies," she said. "I have some churning to do this morning."

Elizabeth led the way to the porch, and Plummer, moving a chair near the hammock, invited her to be seated. She took the hammock with Margaret beside her, and he sat in the chair. Cleveland, having chosen the porch rail, tapped it uneasily with his foot. He was not blind to the girl's charms, but he felt himself to be in the way. "I think I'll go out and have a look at your horse, Henry," he said presently— "if you will excuse me, Miss Bryman?"

"Certainly, Mr. Cleveland," answered Elizabeth, and Plummer smiled.

"This is a beautiful place, Miss Bryman," he said, after Cleveland had gone. "And your uncle and aunt are hospitable people."

"They are dears, both of them, Mr. Plummer—so good to me and everybody."

"Do you know you have put an idea in my head, Miss Bryman?"

"I?" she laughed, her cheeks rosy.

"I am going to Bannack and run for sheriff."

"You are?"

"Yes. I shall make the effort to be elected, and if I am successful it will be because you inspired me to do it." He was speaking seriously and his gray eyes glanced at her face quickly.

She did not answer. Her fingers toyed with the ribbon in Margaret's hair.

"May I call—that is, may I come here to—" he began, taking courage.

"Oh, yes," she interrupted him, "we shall be glad to have you call at any time, I'm sure."

"We?" he asked. "Does 'we' include yourself?"

"Why, of course," she told him, the blood mounting to her cheeks. "I, too, want you to come."

"Then I *will* come," he said and was silent. His eyes wandered to the plains, and in them there was a faraway look. What would he not have given at that moment to be able to wipe out the past in his life—to have lived as she had lived! He loved her and wanted her. He believed that he could have her; but if she knew—. His heart bounded with fear at the thought. It seemed that fear was becoming his constant companion now. He told himself that its torturing presence was proof of his honest love for Elizabeth Bryman. He believed that he could leave it behind him with his old life of crime. There would be nothing to hide in the life he now intended to lead, and she need not learn of any other.

"Sthwing, Betty?"

"What, dear?"

"Sthwing the hammock," begged Margaret, and Elizabeth, pushing with her slipper upon the porch, swung the hammock to and fro.

Plummer did not return to their conversation but continued to gaze fixedly across the plains in the distance. Elizabeth studied the sharp profile of his handsome face, bronzed by exposure, until she dared to look no longer lest he turn suddenly and sense her thoughts. The silence became embarrassing, even for little Margaret, who snuggled close to her cousin with impatience. "Talk, an' sthwing, Betty," she lisped.

Plummer sighed and turned back to Elizabeth. She was quick to detect sadness in his eyes.

"Oh, you restless little mortal," she said, lifting Margaret to the porch. "Go and get your dolly."

"Dolly's athleep," declared Margaret, with a knowing air, and climbed back onto the hammock.

"I hope your horse is better," said Elizabeth, addressing Plummer.

"I am afraid I shall have to buy another horse. I wonder if your uncle has any horses to sell?"

"Oh, I guess he has," she told him. "There are ever so many horses about the place, and he doesn't use nearly all of them. Here comes Mr. Cleveland now. How is Mr. Plummer's horse?" she asked, as Cleveland came up to the porch.

"Worse, if anything, Miss Bryman," answered Cleveland, smiling. "He's stiffer anyhow, but that doesn't necessarily mean he is really worse." Then to Plummer, "I flushed a big covey of chickens in the pasture, Henry, must have been fifty. Been feeding on the bull-berries."

"They ought to be fine and fat now," said Plummer, looking towards the pasture.

"If you gentlemen would like to go hunting, there are two shot-guns in the house, and there are plenty of prairie chickens in the field above the pasture. I saw them there yesterday," offered Elizabeth, desiring to revive Plummer's former lightness.

"Want to go, Jack?" asked Plummer.

"Sure, I'll go."

"Then I'll get the guns for you," volunteered Elizabeth, and she went into the house.

"That horse won't be able to travel within a month," said Cleveland to Plummer when they were alone. "Have you decided to go on to Fort Benton, or is it Bannack?"

"I'm going to Bannack," declared Plummer quickly.

Elizabeth, having brought the guns gingerly to her guests, watched them until they had climbed the pasture fence and then sat down in the hammock. "Run and play, dear," she said to Margaret; and, with the day having seemingly settled down to the commonplace, the child left her to romp with Badger.

Elizabeth picked up her book but, though her eyes were on its pages, she did not read. Her thoughts poised quaveringly about Henry Plummer like a hummingbird above flowers. She liked him more than any man she had even known. His polished manners, his way with her which had been so gently bold, fascinated her. She knew he would court her, and the thought thrilled her with its romance. She closed her book and opened it again, as if to read. She had never seen a handsomer, manlier man. She did not misunderstand his request to revisit the ranch. She wished now she had not proposed the hunting trip.

Mrs. Bailey came to the door. "Betty, will you help me plan my new dress?" she asked, her eyes twinkling with ready admission that she was old-fashioned and behind the times.

"Oh, I'd be glad to, Aunt Jane," eager for any sort of action, and together they went into the house.

It was afternoon when Plummer and Cleveland returned with their chickens, both of them dusty and warm but as pleased as boys. "I never saw so many birds in my life before," Plummer marveled, as he displayed the bag. "Why, we could have loaded a wagon with them. They are fat as butter, too."

"I am going to give you a cold lunch," apologized Mrs. Bailey, as the men hung up their hats. "It's so near supper time."

"That will be fine, Mrs. Bailey—just a piece of bread and butter," suggested Plummer, but Mrs. Bailey set out a hearty lunch.

"Now I will help you pluck the chickens," offered Elizabeth, picking up the two heavy game bags, with a pretty coquettish glance at the young man.

"Here, here," protested Cleveland, taking them from her with a quick look of admiration which he hid from Plummer. "Gentlemen for packs always," he laughed.

Elizabeth laughed lightly, and led the young men through the kitchen where a daughter of the Parkers, who occupied a comfortable cabin near the ranch house, was helping Mrs. Bailey with supper, and onto the back porch. And the three turned to the task of plucking the chickens—all in a happy mood.

Elizabeth did not return to the front porch afterward, or again during the afternoon. Plummer and Cleveland walked about the ranch and, when Mr. Bailey returned opened negotiations with him for a horse which Plummer finally bought from among a number

Mr. Bailey showed him, arranging to keep his own in pasture there. At supper he looked anxiously across the table at Elizabeth, for he had noticed that she kept away from the porch and he feared he had offended her by his manner of the morning. He felt greatly relieved when she greeted him with her smile.

"I met a man from Fort Benton this afternoon," said Mr. Bailey, passing a piece of bread to Plummer. "He told me the Union army's been successful in every fight of late, and that the end of the war's in sight. He also said the diggings in Alder Gulch were rich and other strikes have been made in the gulches north of Alder."

"I have much faith in General Grant," declared Plummer. "He is a fighter; also a great general—Mrs. Bailey, I have never known prairie chickens, or any other chickens, to be cooked so perfectly as these."

Mrs. Bailey was pleased and looked it. She urged her visitors to eat heartily. "Nothing makes a cook as happy as to see the food she has prepared disappear at the table," she said. "Mr. Plummer, won't you let me help you to some of this jelly?"

"When I find a wife I trust she will prove to be of the same school as yourself, Mrs. Bailey," he smiled, after tasting the jelly. "Mr. Bailey, sir, you are a most fortunate man."

"Yes, I know that," laughed Bailey, "but please don't make my trail rough by too many compliments to my wife. She may remember them and remind that I'm stingy with my praise now and then."

"Mr. Plummer is going to run for sheriff, Uncle Seth," put in Elizabeth, with a shy glance at Plummer.

"Good," applauded the host. "Good! I'll do what I can for you, even at this distance from the camps, Mr. Plummer. You have determined to go to Bannack then, and settle down?"

"Yes, sir. Perhaps it is a foolish undertaking, and it never entered my mind until last night here in your home. If I'm successful, I shall give you people the credit for it."

Bailey looked long and earnestly at him, but Plummer's eyes, though they wore their habitual veil and seemed to look at Mr. Bailey and yet beyond, did not falter. His clean-cut mouth and firm chin were set with determination. "Excuse me," murmured the ranchman, suddenly realizing that he was staring at his guest. "I believe you'll make a real sheriff, Mr. Plummer."

"I thank you, sir," said Plummer, bowing, and it was as though a tightened string had been cut. Elizabeth laughed aloud.

"Let's go into the sitting room," proposed Bailey, and, with the exception of Mrs. Bailey and little Margaret, they followed him in, where Cleveland, who before supper had been telling Bailey how the Mexicans in California fashioned hondas for their reatas, began relating to him some feats of roping he had seen in the Southwest. Plummer picked up an album from the table and began turning over some pages.

Elizabeth crossed the room and, seating herself on a low stool beside him, began to tell about members of the family and their friends, Plummer commenting on them now and then. If he discovered any unpleasing characteristic, he kept it to himself, but so accurately did he describe their individual character that it seemed to Elizabeth nothing short of marvelous. She was puzzled and astonished. "Wait!" she said, diving at the back of the album. "Tell me what you see in *this* man's face."

The photograph was of a man of middle age, partially bald and dressed in an ill-fitting suit of clothes that gave him a clumsy appearance, but rather striking and handsome. Plummer studied the picture a moment. "Who is the gentleman?" he asked.

"Never mind his name, Mr. Plummer, please," she said knowingly. "Tell me just what you see in his face, won't you?"

"Well," said Plummer, thus urged, "I should say that he would be easily led into almost anything."

"Do you think he is a *bad* man?" she asked, brushing the picture with her handkerchief.

"Perhaps he *has* been, not from the actual desire to be bad but because he drifted into bad ways through associations. He doesn't possess enough character to be a bad man, by himself," he said hesitatingly.

"I think that is wonderful, Mr. Plummer," marvelled Elizabeth. "That is a second cousin of Uncle Seth's, and he is a black sheep. He went to prison for stealing a horse. You haven't once failed in telling the true character of any of these people. I'm actually afraid of you," and she moved away in mock alarm. He laughed but, turning back to the page marked by his finger, looked for a moment earnestly at a picture there. It was of a man, evidently a miner, young, but much older than himself, although he wore a beard in the fashion of the time. He was dressed in a slouch hat, and a flannel shirt and trousers tucked into his boots.

"That's a friend of Uncle Seth's," she said. "His name is James Williams—'Uncle Jim' everybody calls him here, although he's not a real relation of any of us. He's a dear, and we are all so fond of him. I've only seen him once, but I'll always remember him."

"Where does he live?" asked Plummer, turning the page.

"In the mountains, somewhere near Virginia City," said Elizabeth. "He is mining there. He came from California, but I think his old home was in Pennsylvania."

It was the picture of the man whom he had seen in Lewiston, the man who had put the paper under his door in the hotel at Deer Lodge. "Good strong face," murmured Plummer, and closed the album.

18

Plummer could not have planned a more auspicious entrance into Bannack. Fortune, turning incident to account, brought him at once before the eyes of the citizens there as a champion of law. His cool fearlessness commanded recognition that months of clever plotting could not have attained.

Only a little time had passed since the camp, an irregular line of cabins, tents and covered wagons occupied by men from every section of the States and even the world, had been thoroughly stirred by wanton murder. Moore and Reeves, two members of the gang of road agents, had willfully emptied their six-shooters into an Indian's lodge pitched on the bank of the Grasshopper and without provocation had killed, in cold blood, an aged and friendly chief, his woman, and daughter, a small child, and a Frenchman who at the moment happened to be a visitor in the Indian's lodge.

The utter wantonness of the hideous crime had brought to all honest men a quick resolve for vengeance, and the ages-old spirit of mob violence stirred in their blood. Like a scourge, it found its way from tent to tent, from wagon to wagon, and cabin to cabin, until by community impulse a mass meeting was called to consider the murder. Groups of men, not unmixed with friends of the murderers but on the whole honest men burning with a determination to punish the perpetrators of the frightful deed, armed themselves and hurried to the cabin which had been selected as a meeting place; and amid the confusion of heated arguments, fights, and shots, organized a miners' court, that dread instrument of justice of the early days in Montana. Volunteers were immediately dispatched to bring in the murderers. It was found that Moore and Reeves had fled, but nothing daunted, the court had sent for horses on which the volunteers might pursue the fugitives; and while it waited it had elected a judge, J. F. Hoyt, and a sheriff, Hank Crawford, to serve it.

Someone then suggested a platform. "A platform! Make the judge a platform!" And the cry being taken up, the sheriff, assisted by two or three miners, constructed a rough platform from boards which had been brought to Bannack for sluice boxes. Several other miners with guns in their hands guarded the workers, for the friends of Moore and Reeves objected to the platform and caused interruptions whenever possible.

When someone by the door gave the word that the volunteers were coming with the prisoners, the crowd in the close, log-walled room had stirred as one man. Sentiment was all for a hasty trial— hot for judgment upon the two criminals. "Try 'em, Judge! Try 'em quick!" the men had cried, crowding upon each other in their eagerness.

But one of the four volunteers who had taken the prisoners and brought them back to Bannack had climbed upon the platform and held up his hand. "Wait!" he had shouted. "These fellows surrendered conditionally. We found them in the brush and couldn't have taken them without some of us being killed; so we promised them a trial by a jury of twelve men and not a trial by whole miners' court. We must not go back on our word, even to them."

An angry growl arose in the cabin. "No, you don't!" They weren't going to be cheated out of justice this time. They wouldn't allow it. A jury of twelve men wouldn't *dare* to convict, for if it did, each man would be marked for slaughter. The miners' court, on the contrary, *would* dare, for in a chorus of voices no man could testify that another had been guilty of voting for conviction.

But already several were crying, "A jury, a jury! Give them a jury!"

"Shut up! Who'll serve on a jury?" demanded a big man who towered about the heads of his fellows. "I say, who's damn fool enough to serve on a jury?"

"*I* will!" Some hot-headed, bearded miner with a navy six shooter in his belt and the buttonless collar of his red flannel shirt gaping wide, sprang upon the platform.

His friends admonished him with, "Get down, get down, you fool!" Great confusion had followed, but finally, in spite of all opposition, in full justice to a pair of cutthroats, a jury was elected.

In thirty-five minutes the trial had ended and the jury had retired alone to deliberate. Then it was that consequence had bared its awful form to the jurors, and in terror they had stood or sat without speaking for a time. No man cared to voice his sentiments to eleven strangers. Hardly a man there but had a family left behind in the States. They owed everything to *them*, nothing to all the barren hills, the deep-cut gulches, or the snow-topped mountains of this wilderness, and they could not know how soon they would die for their part in bringing the law to this land where it had never been. Who was in the next tent to their own? Who in the nearest covered wagon or cabin? Perhaps an outlaw. Perhaps some of the jurors themselves were outlaws. No one of the jury could answer for any save himself.

And so nothing had come of it all. For the jury, long after midnight, standing eleven for acquittal and one for guilty, had brought in its verdict of acquittal, recommending banishment to the disgusted court, which dissolved into individual miners in the twinkling of an eye.

Only weeks had passed but already several of the men who had spoken against the outlaws at the trial of Moore and Reeves had been killed by the outlaws or fled the country. And so Bannack, intimidated, betrayed, had settled back without faith in its citizens, its court, or its sheriff.

The camp was now idle, too, for work had been suspended for the winter, though the gloom of a winter far from civilization had not yet settled upon the men. They were happy in the bright, crisp days, and with money to spend were enjoying the little that Bannack had to offer in the way of amusement.

It was at this time that Henry Plummer made his appearance there. It was the middle of September and a sunny Sunday morning. Already new snow had powdered the peaks of the Trappers, and in the early sunlight the deep gulches back of Bannack City were dimmed in a purple haze. The straggling camp, consisting of scores of miners' cabins and tents, skirted the course of Grasshopper Creek, with here and there more pretentious store buildings or warehouses. All bore the evidence of hasty construction. The topsy-turvy piles of tailings and litter had a look of vandalism along the murmuring creek which—low after the dry months of summer—wound its way as though bewildered at the sudden changes in its ancient bed. Placer miners, freighters, and men with no occupation at all were in town to trade or to gamble, since nearly all work in the diggings had been suspended for the winter season.

Suddenly a shot was fired in Goodrich's Saloon not far from the City Livery Stable, and a man, desperately wounded, staggered out through the open door, making his way towards the stable, where he fell in the doorway. A half dozen miners rushed to assist him, but a man appeared in the door of the saloon, flourishing a Navy six-shooter, and ordered them to go about their business. "Hear me? Damn you!" he shouted. "Get away from that man!"

The miners wavered. "Git!" yelled the ruffian, sending a bullet into the ground at their feet. It spattered the dirt, and a flying pebble struck one man's hand and drew blood. So they fell back.

Just then two horsemen turned into the street, and scattering the men as they passed, rode straight to the door of the stable. They were Henry Plummer and Jack Cleveland. Plummer swung lightly down from his horse and bent over the wounded man in the doorway. His alert mind had already seized the situation and the advantage to himself of appearing to enforce law and order before the men of Bannack. He was intending to settle here and run for sheriff. "What is the man's name?" he demanded of those who began edging up.

For a minute there was no answer. Reluctance born of long distrust and fear of the lawless element in the camps held the men silent. Cleveland, knowing that his chief had started something, quietly led Plummer's horse and his own to the rear of the stable and began to unsaddle them. Finally a miner who had just entered elbowed his way to a view of the wounded man and said his name was Keeley. "But that's all I know about him," he added hastily, spitting to one side upon the ground.

"He's dying," declared Plummer, with his hand over the fellow's heart. "Who did the shooting?" His gray eyes scanned their faces swiftly.

"Horan," said a dozen voices.

"Jack Horan shot him. Jack is on a spree and he's a mighty bad man," supplied the miner who had given the victim's name.

"Where's the sheriff?" next inquired Plummer. "Have you no sheriff, or is he sleeping?"

"Sheriff, hell," someone growled under his breath, and many more laughed.

"Crawford is sheriff," said a man near Plummer, but there won't be anything done about this. There never is."

That was all Plummer wanted. He assumed authority on the instant. At a wave of his hand, men hastened to carry poor Keeley into the barn and stretch him carefully upon the floor. Plummer again bent over him and declared him dead in a quiet voice as he stood up.

"It's just one more to plant, that's all, stranger. Nobody dies in his bed here, an' nobody's punished for killin'." A miner muttered the words as he bent over Keeley's body.

Just then Plummer's quick ear caught the sound of boot heels on the gravelly ground outside. "Get out of there!" cried an angry voice at the door. "Get away from that man! He's my meat, damn you!"

The men fell away from Plummer and sought to hide in the stalls or behind the harnesses that hung from pegs along the walls, as Jack Horan, gun in hand, entered the stable. "Get out, I say!" he cried with an oath.

Plummer, left alone by the side of the dead man, did not move. Horan began walking towards him menacingly with his gun cocked and ready. A smile came to Plummer's lips, and his voice took on the low monotony of the purring of a cat. "Did you want something, stranger?" he asked.

Horan stopped.

"I say, were you looking for something, stranger?" repeated Plummer, his words cold as blue ice.

The eyes of the ruffian blazed. "Damn you!" he muttered. "I'll—"

"Drop it, quick!" came the purring voice of Plummer, in whose hand a cocked six-shooter had appeared as if by magic.

Horan's gun hand sank to his side, and his gun fell to the floor and went off. The shot frightened the horses in the stalls and powder smoke filled the barn. There was much confusion. When at last the excitement subsided, those in the stable beheld the stranger with one hand on Horan's shoulder and his other hand empty.

"Get the sheriff, men," he ordered, and a dozen messengers scurried away to spread the news of the stranger's daring and, incidentally, to find the sheriff if they could.

"Just tie his hands behind him," commanded Plummer. "I have some business to attend to, and I wish you men would take the prisoner off my hands. I can't be bothered further."

The men reluctantly took charge of Horan, who, having been delivered to the proper authorities, was subsequently tried and condemned to death, perhaps more because the sheriff wished to compare favorably with the daring stranger than for any other reason.

As Plummer and Cleveland entered the hotel across the street, the arrest was already being discussed excitedly, and men craned their necks to see Plummer's name on the page as he registered and whispered, "That's him. That's the man that done it."

"Cool!" said a miner who from behind a harness had seen the arrest and considered himself something of a hero. "Why, he's ice, that's all, jest ice. He never batted an eye when Jack Horan come at him. He talked low as a woman, too—and where in hell he got his gun from so damned quick, I can't tell nor even guess. I didn't think he had any gun, till Bingo! there it was. Horan was lookin' right into that man's six-shooter quicker'n hell'd scorch a feather, an' it was as steady as a clock. Horan had the drop—way the best of it; but 'Drop it, quick' was all that feller said, an' he said it like butter wouldn't melt in his mouth. There was somethin' awful nasty in the way he said them words, an' so low I couldn't hardly hear 'em, an' I wasn't ten feet away, neither. 'Drop it, quick,' he says, like that, an' Horan dropped his gun. God, 'twas awful."

Plummer and Cleveland meanwhile had been having supper in the adjoining room. When they had finished they again passed the staring men in the office, and leaving the hotel wandered to a gambling house where they began to play cards with two miners. One of them had sold his claim on Grasshopper and was to leave on the morning coach. This man was unlucky and in a jackpot with Plummer offered to wager his log cabin, which the other miner had already offered to buy for two hundred dollars. It was well furnished for the times, and situated on the only real street, which was called Main Street, across from and a little below Crawford's butcher shop.

Plummer fairly won the cabin, and the next day he and Cleveland

97

moved into it. Both began to follow their vocation as professional gamblers.

Plummer's boldness became the subject of talk in Bannack; and while he himself appeared to underrate it, he at the same time did not miss an opportunity to point out the worth of a good sheriff, and Cleveland began to hint that if pressed Plummer might become a candidate for the office.

Crawford, the present sheriff, kept the meat market in Bannack. Broad-shouldered, good-natured, and willing to wink at wrong-doing, he had tried to win favor by being hail-fellow-well-met to good and bad men alike, until, driven by public sentiment, he had been forced to take a stand against Moore and Reeves. During the trial of these criminals, which as we have seen only resulted in their banishment, Crawford had incurred the hatred of the roughs, and so weak and faltering had been his decisions before the miners' court that many of the miners also condemned him.

Knowing that Moore and Reeves were members of the organized gang of outlaws which had so long defied California, Nevada, and Idaho Territory, Crawford was secretly aware that his life was in danger because of his part in their arrest and trial. And, on the other hand, he feared that he could never wholly regain favor among the miners. This double fear outweighed his jealousy of Plummer's sudden popularity. He avoided Plummer. And men began to talk. "He's afraid of Plummer," said the miners, who, largely because of his arrest of Horan, believed in Plummer. "Fine sheriff we've got; and he's going to run again. Well, we'll see about that."

Plummer had not yet declared himself a candidate for the sheriff's office, but he was already eliminating Crawford from the coming race. Miners sought his advice in their private affairs and found his counsel always impartial, fearless, and just, even when the decision was between two men who were both admirers of his. He had ordered his men, many of whom were known as bad men in Bannack, to treat him as a stranger. But though he thus avoided them and intended to drop them when he should begin right as sheriff of Bannack, he also counted upon their aid. And so Club-Foot George, Dutch John, George Ives, Hayes Lyons, Jack Gallagher, Frank Parish, Boone Helm, Bob Zachary, and many others equally infamous had begun to espouse his cause among their own kind; and Henry Plummer was acknowledged leader among good men and among thieves.

98

He began to allow himself to dream. This would be his future home. When the race was won he would have an assured standing in the community and he would begin right.

Near two o'clock in the afternoon of his second day in Bannack, and while he was shaving in his cabin, luck, this time in the form of a visitor, again favored him. There was a knock on the door. Scrubbing his face with a towel till his skin glowed with the young blood beneath it, giving him the appearance of a boy in his teens, he called cordially, "Come in!" and meanwhile hastened to arrange a necktie and glance into the mirror.

The door was opened by a spare old gentleman wearing a frock coat and a snow-white mustache and goatee. "My name, sah, is Lovejoy," he said, bowing low, "and I have called to pay my respects to bravery, sah—bravery in upholdin' the law."

"Won't you sit down, Mr. Lovejoy?" asked Plummer, returning the bow, and placing a chair for his visitor, the dignity so easy for him apparent in every movement.

"Thank you, Mr. Plummer, sah." Mr. Lovejoy sat down, his gold-headed cane between his spare knees, his boney fingers clasped tightly about it.

As though he would prevent his visitor from again referring to the arrest of Jack Horan, Plummer inquired, as he seated himself opposite him, how long he had been in the camp.

"Two months, sah—two miserable months. Came heah hopin' to find the murderers of my son; to invoke the law; but there is nothin' of the so't heah—no law, sah!" He got up and walked the length of the cabin, his cane pounding upon the floor. "Pardon me, sah," he said, coming back to his chair. "My boy was all to me—me and my wife, sah. She insisted on comin' 'way out heah with me as mothers will—and she's heah."

Then, as though he had broken an embarrassing barrier between them, "You're a Yankee, I reckon—but no mattah. I'll come to the point, sah. Will you consent to run for sheriff if I promise you to remain heah and help you with all means in my powah, sah?"

Plummer saw at a glance that his visitor, however vain, was an aristocrat, and no doubt a man of means. Here was offered help that would go far among the better class of people in Bannack. As a gambler crowds success while luck is smiling, Plummer affected to consider. "I'll tell you what I am willing to do, Mr. Lovejoy," he said slowly, offering the old gentleman a cigar. "I will help you to find a good man for sheriff, and together we will try to elect him."

"No, no, Mr. Plummer, sah. That won't do. My son had a claim heah and I can sell it. I will sell it and go away if you will not consent to make the race. Can you not see that it is your duty, your bounden duty, sah? Now what I would like to have you do, sah, is to come have suppah with Mrs. Lovejoy and me. I told hah I would fetch you to hah, sah—promised to do it. I hope you will help me to keep my word. Will you, sah?"

"With pleasure," agreed Plummer gallantly, rising with his visitor. "At what time?"

"We'll say at five, sah—promptly at five. I'll call for you. Thank you, sah." And the old gentleman left the cabin.

Plummer watched him from the door as he would have watched the turning of a lucky card. There was in his mind nothing of admiration or thanks for the individual who so graciously had proffered aid in the project nearest his heart, but only a secret hilarity over this latest manifestation of his own abiding good fortune, the luck which he believed belonged to him and to him alone.

When he returned home from the bare little Lovejoy cabin, he had with feigned reluctance promised to run for sheriff, and the resolve to reform was again uppermost in his mind. For he had not been able to accept without some inward shame the praise which the sweet-faced, white-haired old lady had poured out to him as an honest man who in the face of great odds had upheld the law. And he had listened, not without sympathy, to the recital of the murder which had led the old couple to journey out to the Northwest. He had stayed to supper, and had talked of his mother and sister and had even mentioned Elizabeth Bryman whom he hoped to make his bride. Looking often across the table at the gentlewoman whose sorrow touched him, he pictured Elizabeth in her place and himself, softened by the years, by her side. He *could* live such a life, and he *would*.

He determined to visit Elizabeth as soon as he felt he could leave his interest in Bannack for perhaps a week. It was in the morning of the first of October when he decided to leave, and not having seen Cleveland for several days, he went in search of him. The bartender in the Pioneer Gambling House had not seen him either for several days, he said, and Plummer, going next to the livery stable, discovered, as he had suspected, that Cleveland's horse was gone. The liveryman could tell him nothing of Cleveland's whereabouts, and he decided to postpone his journey until morning. But Cleveland had not returned when morning came, and Plummer wrote a note telling in confidence where he had gone and gave it to the stableman for delivery to Cleveland upon his return. Then, after saddling his horse, he rode away towards the government ranch on the Sun River, a distance of one hundred seventy miles.

His thoughts were of Elizabeth, the one woman in the world to him. He would soon see her, talk to her, and propose marriage to her. The thought set his heart to beating faster, and unconsciously he urged his horse to greater speed. Then fear seized him. What if that miner—that friend of her uncle's whose photograph was in the family album, had called at the ranch since his own visit there? A cold sweat of fear broke out upon his forehead. He gritted his teeth. "By God, it can't be," he almost groaned. "It must not be. I love her so."

His spoken words startled him, and he turned in his saddle as though he were followed, but there was nobody in sight, and he shook off his fear—that thing once so strange to him—and again began to think longingly of Elizabeth. He crossed the Beaverhead and turned down the stream. The miles were long before him but at the journey's end was Elizabeth, his sweetheart, and he could scarcely withhold the spur. He would tell her of his marvelous success in winning the confidence of the people in Bannack, of his certainty of gaining the election in November. How delighted she would be with it all! Then he would tell her that he loved her; and his heart bounded anew with the joy of it. He began to choose his words—the words he would use to express his love for her. Was there another woman in the world so beautiful, so innocent and sweet as she? Henry Plummer, like any other lover, thought not.

He saw a wagon in the road ahead and coming up with it, turned aside to pass the two miserable horses that were struggling with its weight. It was loaded with household goods as racked and mean as itself. A torn canvas cover that flapped in the breeze, partially shielded a man, a woman, a boy and a girl. The man's face was eager, expectant, but that of the woman on the rough seat beside him, was depressed, beaten, miserable and hopeless.

Plummer turned his head to glance back at them and as though anxious to leave so decrepit an outfit behind, touched his horse with his silver spurs. The man in the wagon beside the woman suddenly straightened in his seat. "By God, Jennie, that's ———— " He stopped short and spat over the side of the wagon.

"That's who?" asked the sad-eyed woman, rousing herself.

"Oh, a feller I knowed on the other side," replied the man, and struck the footsore horses with the stick that was in his hand. "Gitap, Joe! Pete! go 'long."

It was Jim Bent and his family on their way to Alder Gulch; but Plummer had not recognized him and rode on with his thoughts of Elizabeth. He had banished his fear and was happy.

19

Henry Plummer crossed the Jefferson River, and soon afterward the way he followed, leading up to the sage-covered benchlands, joined the now well-marked road from Fort Benton to Virginia City. Between the river and the beautiful Tobacco Root range and along it over a plain cut out here and there by dry coulees, there was not one mark of civilization, only the road that disappeared among the hills in the distance—no human being in sight. Turning in his saddle, he scanned the almost straight course of the road over the plain towards the mouth of Alder Gulch, the sunlit peaks of the mountains marking its way. But upon facing about he beheld the overland stagecoach coming rapidly towards him against a thin film of dust that followed behind it. Instinctively, he straightened in his saddle, pulling his hat lower over his forehead and hastily arranging his tie, which was fastened in the peculiar knot the robbers had adopted. His horse, at the touch of the spurs, broke into a swinging lope which showed his rider's grace to advantage. As the Concord coach, bright and new, for the route was just established, swept rocking by, drawn by six spirited horses, the driver waved his whip to the lone rider and then sent its long plaited lash popping smartly over the leader's ears.

Plummer answered with a flourish of his hand, smiling pleasantly as the weary passengers called their greetings, and, turning in his saddle, he watched the coach speed away towards the placer diggings in Alder Gulch.

"What a handsome young man," said a woman in the coach, looking backward through the thin cloud of dust. "I wonder who he is?"

"His name is Henry Plummer, lady," volunteered a man who had been a miner in Bannack and now held a claim in Alder Gulch. "He's to be our next sheriff, I hope." And he went on to relate the story of the arrest of Jack Horan, embellishing it to suit the occasion, while the passengers listened with the interest of newcomers in a land of romance.

At ten o'clock, tired by an extremely long ride, Plummer stopped for the night at the new stage station on the Whitetail, established when the steamboats first began to bring gold seekers to the mines in Bannack and Alder Gulch. A fire crackled in a great box stove, and after a hearty meal he sat near it to smoke before retiring. Outside, the night was clear and cool. The fire felt good, and he nodded more than once before he rose to go to his room. "I'll bid you good night, sir," he said to the station keeper, at last.

He had undressed and was turning the bedding down to get into bed when he heard a hard-ridden horse stop outside the door. He could even hear its heaving and the jingle of spurs as a man dismounted and hurried into the station.

"The coach has been held up!" panted a voice.

"Where?" asked another, which he recognized as that of the station keeper.

"This side of Wisconsin Creek. Two men did the job."

"Anybody killed?"

"No, they just shelled out; but Billy, the driver, knows one of the robbers."

Plummer bent forward eagerly to listen.

"Who does he say 'twas?"

"He won't say. Just says he knows, that's all. Gimme another horse."

The men went outside, and Plummer heard them leading the jaded horse to the barn. Then he got into bed; but the absence of Jack Cleveland from Bannack set him to thinking.

It was three days afterward, at about five in the afternoon, when he came to the Sun River and turned in at the government ranch. He walked and led his horse from the gate towards the house. He was tired. Moreover, the fear had again gripped his heart—fear that

Elizabeth might have learned of his life. The thought chilled him and his knees weakened under him. "If she has," he muttered, "what shall I do? I've never been like this before. I'm—" He stopped short. A man and a woman were walking beside the river in the cottonwood grove not far from the house, but almost as soon as he saw them they were hidden by the ranch buildings. A jealous rage, coupled with the deep-seated fear that had seized him but a moment before, urged him forward and, dropping the bridle reins, he ran around the corner of the house, where with a muttered oath he stopped. Elizabeth and Jack Cleveland were coming towards him so engrossed in their conversation that they had not yet seen him. The wind blew Elizabeth's wide pink dimity skirt, which with dainty hand she held from brushing the ground, and her curls, loosed in the breeze, fluttered about her ears bewitchingly.

"Good afternoon," said Plummer.

Cleveland started guiltily, and his hand dropped swiftly to his belt.

"Too late, Jack," Plummer's voice purred, his own hand at his waistband. "Too late in the afternoon to be so far away from the supper table," he added, the light in his eyes changing as Cleveland's hand fell to his side.

Meanwhile, Elizabeth, not having noticed the challenge in Plummer's tone, nor having seen her startled escort reach for his weapon, stood with her little hands clasped. "Oh, Mr. Plummer! I'm delighted," she beamed.

Plummer bowed low over her hand. "I told you I would surely come," he said, "and I have been anxiously waiting for a time when I could get away. The minute it appeared, I came as fast as my horse could carry me."

"I'm so glad. Aunt Jane and Uncle Seth will be happy, too, to see you again. Come, let's go into the house, for after the sun goes down it grows chilly so soon now," she laughed with a little shiver of her thinly clad shoulders. And with no suspicion of an impending quarrel between her guests, she led the way into the sitting room, where a cottonwood fire burned cheerily in the open fireplace.

"Well, Mr. Plummer," exclaimed Mrs. Bailey, who was busy mending tiny stockings in the short time before supper, "I have been hoping you hadn't forgotten us." Hastily gathering her work from her lap, she placed it in a basket by her side and arose to greet him.

As she did so, a pair of small scissors fell from the folds of her full, hooped skirt. Plummer instantly stooped to recover them, and the heavy six-shooter that he carried in the waistband of his trousers beneath his vest slipped from its place to the floor beside the scissors. Both women sprang backward with a startled cry.

"Your weapon and mine are bent on attracting attention today, Mrs. Bailey," laughed Plummer, swiftly replacing the offending gun and handing her the scissors with a bow. "Mine, I will agree, is the more warlike," he smiled, "but a man must go armed in these times, you know."

"Yes, I know," returned the good woman, regaining her usual composure, "and I should be used to it by now. Supper will be ready just as soon as Mr. Bailey comes in. And your horse must be cared for. I'll tell Mr. Parker." And she stepped to the door to call him.

Outside, the leaves on the trees were changing from green to gold, and from every bush along the Sun River red and yellow foliage fell with the chill gusts of wind. These, together with the odor of spiced bullberries which floated in from the kitchen, were constant reminders that the summer was gone.

But it seemed just budding in Elizabeth's heart. She was very happy. She at once engaged Plummer in conversation, including Cleveland not to seem a careless hostess, although Plummer, from his very nature, demanded the more attention. "Mr. Cleveland has told me all about it," she chatted gaily, seating herself in the rocker which her aunt had abandoned for the kitchen, and motioning the young men to be seated.

At this beginning Plummer felt the fear again at his heart and his face paled ever so slightly; but the innocent girl continued, "He says that all the people respect you, and that you have established yourself in Bannack. I am so glad. It must have been thrilling to have arrested that dreadful man. Oh, he has told me about it, and how you accomplished it. It frightened me. How could you do it, Mr. Plummer?"

Some of Plummer's anger at finding Cleveland with Elizabeth faded. "I had no trouble in arresting Horan," he protested. "He was a common bully—a coward at heart, that was all," he said.

"But he might have shot you," she reminded him.

"I doubt it," he said with a deprecatory smile and a glance at Cleveland.

105

"You must be expert in the use of a pistol. Mr. Cleveland said that no one saw you draw your gun until it was pointing straight at that man. They did not even suspect you had one. It must have been thrilling."

Plummer was puzzled. His friend had evidently stolen away from Bannack with the intention of courting Elizabeth, but with her his conversation had dealt fairly with him. He could not understand it. When Cleveland, who had been an unwilling listener to the conversation between Elizabeth and Plummer, made excuse to visit his horse, Plummer, excusing himself also with the explanation that he had forgotten to take some money from the cantinas on his saddle, followed. Catching up with Cleveland as he turned the corner of the smokehouse out of sight from the windows of the sitting room, he demanded, "Jack, why are you here?"

"I came to visit the folks, that's all," answered Cleveland, backing away.

"Wait! Did you come to court Elizabeth?"

Cleveland did not answer, and his face darkened with a frown.

"Speak, damn you!" growled Plummer. "I told you like a man that I loved her, and you—you—" his voice was heavy with anger. Never before had any one of his men heard his words when they actually shook with wrath. "Answer me, you coward!"

"I don't see why I haven't as good a right to be here as you have," wavered Cleveland, stepping slowly backward.

"You lie!"

Cleveland's hand moved nervously, and a sneer curled Plummer's lips. "That's right, damn you, *draw!*" he whispered, and his voice had lost its anger in its eagerness. "I *beg* you to draw. I will give you time to draw and cock your gun before I go for my own. Will you *draw?*"

"No," said Cleveland. "I won't."

"Gentlemen! Mr. Plummer and Mr. Cleveland!" called Elizabeth, running around the smokehouse. "Uncle Seth has come and supper is waiting. Boo! It's cold, isn't it?"

"Coming right away, Miss Bryman!" Plummer whirled around and began to walk rapidly towards her, followed by Cleveland. "We were talking horse trade, and when we get to discussing that subject we forget time and place," he explained, as they came up to the porch.

"Well, come into the dining room and trade," she laughed. "We are ready for supper, and I know that you must be hungry."

She led the way happily to the dining room. "I found them, Aunt Jane," she said, laying her hands daintily on the knobs of her chair, "and they were trading horse. Think of it! And supper all ready!"

"Well, I never could blame men for horse trading," sympathized Mrs. Bailey, her good-natured face still flushed from the heat of her kitchen fire. "I'm fat, and—well, nearly thirty," she smiled, with a glance at her husband, "but there's such a lot of room for surprises in horse trades, such odd developments that—"

"She's shooting at *me* now," grinned Seth Bailey, seating himself at the table on which were roast venison, roast sagehens with bullberry jelly, potatoes mashed and beaten until they were white as snow, hot biscuits and butter, pickled peaches all the way from St. Louis, raisin pie, coconut cake, and coffee.

"I'd willingly stand and allow such a cook to shoot at me all day long," vowed Henry Plummer, dividing a glance between Mrs. Bailey and Elizabeth.

"I *did* get bamboozled in a horse trade last spring," admitted Bailey, as he picked up the carving knife, "and Jane never will forget it, I guess."

"Tell it, Uncle Seth," urged Elizabeth. "It's so clever, I think. I mean—"

"Yes," the ranchman broke in, "I know what you mean. You see," he smiled, turning to his guests, "I traded horses with a Frenchman who is living with the Piegans over at the Agency. I don't speak French, and the Frenchman said he couldn't speak English. But he hooked me with what he *did* know of it.

"I never saw a prettier pony than he had. Snow white and well made. Of course he was a little thin, his coat long, just in off the winter range, you see. But just the same he was a fine looking pony, and gentle. I saw him from the door of the Agency." Here Bailey paused in his story to carve and serve, passing the plates between sentences. "I liked the horse. Hunted for the owner. Didn't take long. He was this Frenchman. Asked him how he'd trade for a bay gelding I'd ridden over there. 'Twas Jane's horse. Good enough, but lazy as thunder. Figured she'd like the white pony better. The Frenchman said he couldn't speak English, but made me understand he'd trade easy enough. 'She don' look veree good dat 'orse,' he says, leading the white pony around in a ring so I could look him over. But pshaw!

107

No horse looks good when he's just in off a winter range, long hair, you know, and thin. So I traded, tickled to death, too." He stopped to pass the gravy bowl. "I forgot this in my excitement," he smiled. And then continued, "I rode the new pony home. I thought once or twice he acted queer, but he was gentle and kind. I was sure Jane would like him better'n the bay. But when I got him in the stable and unsaddled him I found that he was almost *stone-blind*. The poor little devil couldn't see a foot from his nose.

"Well, I didn't squeal nor try to back out; but the next time I saw Mr. Frenchman I accused him of trading me a blind horse. 'Oui,' he says, as innocent looking as a sucking pig. 'Oui,' he says, 'me, hi'm say dat w'ite 'orse, she han't *look* veree good.' Then I remembered he *had* used those same words. But nothing can make me believe that he didn't butcher me with his butchered English, or that he didn't do it with perfect understanding. There, I've confessed. I do it quite often—when we have company."

Cleveland laughed heartily. "It's a good story," he said. "I'll bet you look at a horse's eyes when you trade now days."

"Indeed he *does*," laughed Mrs. Bailey. "He was *so* taken back."

"I am told your chances of election are good," said Mr. Bailey, turning the conversation towards his guests' interests. "We are mighty glad to hear it," he added.

"My chances are looking fine, thank you, sir," replied Plummer, proudly.

"You gentlemen are to have the same room you had before," said Mrs. Bailey, offering them more biscuits. "Mr. Cleveland has been occupying it, but I am going to put you together. I'm sure you won't mind, will you?"

"Not a bit, Mrs. Bailey," assured Plummer, glancing at Cleveland.

"Perhaps you and Mr. Cleveland will like to go hunting again while you are here," she proposed. "Mr. Parker says there are hundreds of chickens along the Sun River now. Our menfolks never go hunting. I bought these sage hens from a halfbreed."

"I'd enjoy it; especially if you will cook them like these, Mrs. Bailey. And there are ducks too, I noticed in the river, as I came in," smiled Plummer, turning to Bailey, who said, "Oh, yes, plenty of ducks, and a little later there will be geese—thousands of them; but don't forget about your campaign."

"I'd nearly forgotten it," declared Plummer, jokingly; and thus apparently reminded, he told them the story of the Lovejoys, describing the little old lady so vividly that his hearers loved and pitied her, and ascribing to the old gentlemen all the airs of a Kentucky colonel. They were all enchanted with the story, giving them, as it did, a touch of another world wherein there was culture and refinement. Old homes which, though at present unsettled in war, had to these people in the wilderness a deep flavor of permanence and peace. For all about them stretched primitive reaches of unclaimed land, peopled sparsely by roving Indian bands; and what there were of settlements were wild, unruly, and far apart.

Plummer's handsome young face had as usual shown but little feeling in recounting the story. His masterful calm had masked both tone and sentiment, if indeed he had felt sentiment. His inscrutable gray eyes had not lighted with any such feeling as his words had plainly professed. But he *had* voiced a sincere respect for gentlefolk and refinement that kindled in Elizabeth's heart a wish to make him admire *her*, and to express his admiration.

There was little in such a place that offered entertainment for young people, and she had been made to feel more deeply the loneliness of the ranch life by his picture of the aged couple, so that desire for excitement was keened to a point of daring adventure.

After supper she was required to help her aunt with the dishes for a short time. Assisting little Margaret from her chair at the table, she led the girl to the kitchen. Cleveland, getting his hat from the hall, went out to the barn with Mr. Bailey; and Plummer, thus left alone, strolled into the sitting room. He stopped a moment to listen, then crossed to the center table and, opening the album, hastily took out the picture of James Williams. With a quick glance towards the open door leading into the hallway, he stepped to the fireplace and, holding the daguerreotype close to the fire, bent over it, gently brushing its smooth surface with the slender fingers of his right hand. Then he slipped the picture into the breast pocket of his coat, starting a trifle at the figure of a black cat crossing the hallway. "Kitty, kitty, kitty," he called.

The cat came to the door blinking at the fire, and Plummer drew a white handkerchief from his pocket. "Come, kitty, kitty," he coaxed, trailing the handkerchief on the bare floor in the firelight.

Thus attracted, the cat ventured into the room and was still playing with the trailing handkerchief when Elizabeth entered. She bore a lighted candlestick, which as she advanced she held aloft a moment so that its light fell directly upon her before she set it upon the table near the album. It may be that as she came along the hall she had premeditated her entrance and had guessed the effect which the candlelight thus held would lend. If so, she was something of an artist, for she looked bewitching posed so in a pink dimity dress, the great width of which emphasized the daintiness of her slim waist but did not quite hide the toe of her little slipper as she stood poised with the candle above her. On her curls the light fell with a golden sheen, at the same time enhancing the soft whiteness of her lifted arm, from which the lace of her wide sleeve fell away.

As she set the candlestick down with a shy glance at Plummer, he stepped impulsively towards her, a dozen compliments on his lips. In confusion she stopped, picked up the kitten and began to whisper to it, laying her blushing cheek against the sleek blackness of its fur.

At this juncture Mr. Bailey and Cleveland returned from outside. Cleveland found no excuse to stay away from the sitting room, but Mr. Bailey, thinking perhaps that the young people would enjoy themselves more alone, went to the kitchen.

Elizabeth was still confused and also excited. Casting about for something to do, she picked up the album and, seating herself on the sofa, motioned Cleveland beside her and began to show him the pictures. It was only the random act of a confused mind; but Elizabeth saw that it had a desirable effect upon Plummer, and she talked all the more gaily to Cleveland.

How little she knew with whom she had to deal! All Plummer's fury towards Cleveland returned. He felt more anger, then fear that Elizabeth would discover Williams' picture missing. He sat sullenly watching them a moment, then rose abruptly and went outside.

Left alone, the two on the sofa fell silent. Elizabeth, quickly repentant, ceased finally to turn the album leaves, and her eyes looked unseeingly across at the open fire.

Cleveland was uncomfortable, and angry with Elizabeth. For he had already discovered what he might expect from Plummer if he continued his attention to her, and now he was left so that he appeared to be courting her. He cursed himself for a fool in ever coming here.

As for Elizabeth, she was chagrined and a bit frightened. She turned a few pages absently—came to the page from which James Williams' picture had been stolen. But she did not notice. "Perhaps he *is* angry," she said, closing the album. "I will go and see." And catching up a white shawl from the back of a chair, she slipped out of doors, a quick blush of embarrassment reddening her cheeks.

A full moon sailed high in the sky, picking out the dark ranch buildings and silvering the river. A crisp breeze came dancing down the stream, rippling the water in little quivering patches that scudded here and there as though at play between the grassy banks, while up the shore beneath the trees glimmered the fires of a few Indian lodges, their outlines dimmed by the shadowy branches and heavy, rough barked trunks. It was one of those northern autumn nights when it seems to be summer again, the more poignant because the trees are partially bare in the moonlight and one knows it is not summer.

Gathering her shawl about her shoulders, Elizabeth looked about uncertainly. She had acted upon impulse, and what her Aunt Jane might term her boldness shamed her. She was frightened, but she was determined to see and speak to Plummer—to make amends for her treatment of him. She had been rude to him—intentionally rude, she told herself, and now she would ask him to return with her to the house. This decided, she walked a little way. She felt that he might have gone to the barn and was looking towards it almost apprehensively when Badger, having heard her steps and discovered that she was alone, came padding up to her out of the shadows, nosing her hand for attention, which in her anxiety she denied him. "Where is he, Badger? Where is Mr. Plummer?" she whispered.

The hound wagged his tail, and as though to answer turned his head towards the river. Elizabeth looked, too, and discovered Henry Plummer perhaps a hundred yards below the ranch house, walking in the moonlight. He was walking away from her, but in a moment he turned and was coming back.

Elizabeth shivered. But still determined, she moved towards him, timidly, one hand on Badger's head, until she had come up with him face to face.

"Are you—are you angry?" she faltered with an attempt at lightness which she could not give her trembling voice.

"And if I *were?*" he muttered, as though to himself, his attention seemingly devoted to whittling a willow stick in the moonlight.

She hung her head. Her heart beat wildly. Badger, pressing close against her, looked into her face and whined. With fingers that shook she tightened her hold of the dog's collar, the blood surging to her face.

"Elizabeth!" Plummer's voice was husky with passion. He seized her impulsively, but as suddenly sprang backward, letting her go and raising his arms to shield his throat from the white fangs of the wolf-hound who had leapt upon him like a panther.

"Down! Badger, down!" gasped Elizabeth, her voice frozen with terror, her arms about his neck dragging him back. "There Badger, down!" She trembled as grudgingly the enraged animal turned from his attack. "Oh, did he hurt you?" she sobbed, covering her face with her hands. "Oh, oh!"

"Not the tiniest bit," Plummer assured her, his heart bounding with gladness. "I moved too quickly," he said, taking her hands down and gathering her gently in his arms. "He did not know I love you, Betty, and would not harm one of those pretty curls." He laid his cheek against them and whispered, "Betty, do you hear me? I love you!"

She did not struggle. Partly from joy, and partly because she feared that Badger might again spring at his throat, she was still—submissive in his arms—thrilled, but frightened by uncertainty. She knew so little of his world, where he moved as a hero and where men obeyed him—still she wanted him to love her. She was ashamed, joyful, frightened all in a breath.

"Might I have one kiss, Betty?" Plummer pleaded, pressing her close. "Just one, to tell me you love me, too?"

"I—I can't," she stammered, "not now. Oh, please don't! Now *now*. Let me go. We have—I must get back. Come, will you?" Confused, her heart fluttering, she freed herself and stood breathless, with her head bent. "Come," she whispered again, turning away. And he followed her, his thoughts flying to the future.

Jack Cleveland was playing with the cat when they entered. No one else was in the room. Plummer said cheerily, as he walked towards the fireplace with Elizabeth, "It's bright outside as day."

"Is it?" Cleveland asked, soberly, with a glance at the window.

Elizabeth, still confused and blushing, rubbed her hands together before the fire. "It's getting colder and colder," she shivered, drawing her pretty shoulders forward under the shawl. Then, as though to hide her embarrassment, she crossed to the organ and sat down there. "Let's sing 'Sherman's March to the Sea,'" she proposed, and not waiting began to play and sing.

Plummer and Cleveland both sang with her; and presently Seth and Jane Bailey came to stand behind her, pride and pleasure in their eyes; they also joined in the new song, so inspiring to Union folk.

When, with Seth Bailey's deep voice ringing, they finished the patriotic song, Elizabeth, without waiting for a suggestion, began "The Last Rose of Summer," so popular then. No voice accompanied hers. Perhaps she knew she would sing it alone. Her sweet soprano voice was softened, no doubt, by remembrance of the moments by the Sun River.

"Why, Betty Bryman!" Jane Bailey's voice was tremulous. "I never heard you sing like that. I'm just all needles and pins."

"I love that song," said Plummer, gently, his eyes on Elizabeth. "I shall never listen to it again without thinking of you."

20

"Bad news this morning," remarked Mr. Bailey, seating himself at the breakfast table.

"What is it, Uncle Seth?" asked Elizabeth, anxiously, her eyes meeting Plummer's uncertainly.

"Badger got caught in the bear trap that I set day before yesterday. His leg is broken. I shouldn't be mentioning it before breakfast, but I shall have to kill him."

"Oh, no! Uncle Seth. Please, please don't!" begged Elizabeth, her eyes filling with tears.

"I think I dislike the thought as much as you do, Betty, but his leg is beyond mending, and there is no other way to relieve his suffering than to shoot him, poor dog."

Elizabeth, white and trembling, left the table, and Bailey's eyes followed her. Little Margaret, not quite understanding, but quick with sympathy, climbed down from her chair. "Poh Betty," she whimpered, toddling after her.

113

"I knew it would upset the whole household," Bailey sighed. "Elizabeth loves that hound. We all do. I won't kill him, myself, and Parker declares *he* won't."

Mrs. Bailey slipped away from the table. Plummer could presently hear her talking soothingly to Elizabeth in her room. He was seized with a longing to go to her and he stirred nervously in his chair, his head turned towards the door of the sitting room through which Elizabeth had disappeared.

"But he must be killed," continued Mr. Bailey. "The bone of his leg is crushed, and he's in a terrible condition. You see," he explained, "a stick or a stone was thrown up by the jaws of the trap, and although they are offset the jaws must have caught the dog's leg between the obstacle and themselves. The trap would hardly have broken the leg under other circumstances, but it's broken bad, and I don't know how we'll manage his taking off. I can't do it."

"I'll kill him," said Cleveland suddenly.

Plummer turned in his chair. The steely cold of his eyes as he fastened them upon Cleveland's was that of unfathomed hatred. "You won't!" His words were velvety soft, but in them was that terrible challenge which the band of outlaws knew so well.

Cleveland's eyes fell to his plate, which he nervously pushed aside, and Plummer, turning to Mrs. Bailey, said, "Let me see the dog, please. Perhaps I can save him, Mr. Bailey."

Bailey had been so abstracted that if he had noticed what passed between the two young men it failed to impress him at the time. He now threw Plummer a hopeful glance, and, forgetting their breakfast, the three men rose and went to the barn where poor Badger was lying upon a bed of straw. The dog, seeing Mr. Bailey, began to wag his tail, and the kind-hearted ranchman turned away to hide his grief. "That's pretty tough," he said, with his back to the suffering animal.

Plummer knelt beside Badger and began to examine the mangled leg, the dog following his fingers with his muzzle as though warning him to be gentle. "It's a bad break, but I am going to try to save him," he said at last, adding that he would need some warm water and some cloth for bandages.

The ranchman hastened to the house to get them, and Plummer, selecting a board from a box in the barn, began to make splints.

"Henry, I believe I will saddle up and start for Bannack today," Cleveland said when the door had closed behind Bailey.

Plummer paused in his splint making, the knife in his hand deep in the edge of the board. The thought of ambush, of treachery, suggested itself to him, and his lips parted in a sneering smile of open accusal. "No, Jack," he said. "I crave your company. We will go together when we go. The trail is long and extremely dangerous when a man is—alone." He thought he caught the glimmer of guilt in Cleveland's eyes, and as he returned to his task his knife bit more deeply into the board. Cleveland went out of the barn without speaking again, and when Mr. Bailey returned with a basin of warm water and some cloth and strong string Plummer was kneeling beside the dog, speaking to him gently.

"Now, Mr. Bailey," he said, looking up, "will you use your good offices to prevent Badger from biting me, for the operation will be painful and he doesn't seem to care a great deal for me anyway, I'm afraid. I shall be as gentle as possible, but he may not understand that I am trying to help him."

However, Plummer was so gentle that only once, when the pain was too great to be borne in silence, did Badger snarl or attempt to harm him. Indeed no woman's hand was ever more tender or more skillful than his.

"I do believe you have succeeded, Mr. Plummer," declared Bailey, eagerly arising from his knees when the operation was completed. "Elizabeth will be so grateful, and I need not tell you how much I thank you. I never could have accomplished it myself."

"Badger's a noble dog," said Plummer, brushing the knees of his trousers. "I am afraid he's done with his wolf killing, however."

"I shan't care about that, if he gets well," replied the other, much relieved.

"You will know in about three days," said Plummer, stooping again to examine the bandages. "If the swelling recedes you will know he is doing well, but I would not remove the bandages nor allow him to tear them off. He may do that unless you watch him, especially if the bones begin to knit. The itching is almost unbearable in a human being, and I suppose it is the same in the case of a dog." Then he stood up and, resting a hand upon the ranchman's shoulder, said, not without an inward tremor: "Mr. Bailey, I am not well known to you, but I have fallen deeply in love with your niece, Miss Bryman, and I want you to know that my intentions toward her are honorable. I am taking this opportunity to tell you because we are alone here. Please let me give you the address of my people in Connecticut. You are at liberty to use it as you may see fit. I want *you* to use it. Will you permit me to court Elizabeth here at your home and wed her, if she is willing?"

Seth Bailey looked straight into Plummer's eyes. There was something about this young man that he could not like, try as he might—something he could not fathom, nor even name.

"Elizabeth is of age," he said at last. "I shan't interfere with her affairs unless I should feel that while she was at my house such interference was necessary. Have you spoken to her?"

"I have told her that I love her. It was last night. Perhaps that is why Badger dislikes me. He is jealous of Elizabeth's attention."

Bailey stooped to pick up a straw, thus relieving his shoulder of Plummer's hand. Then, straightening himself, he spoke in a monotone, and more to himself than to Plummer. "I like you. You are a strong man and you compel admiration; but I can't quite believe in you, somehow. I wish I could."

"That is because you do not know me sufficiently, Mr. Bailey."

"Perhaps it is. I hope it is," he said seriously.

"Oh, Seth!"

It was Mrs. Bailey's voice that called near the door.

"Yes, Jane."

"Someone wants to see you. Can you come to the house for just a few minutes?"

And Bailey, as though glad to leave the barn, hastened to join his wife outside.

Plummer, left alone, began to be tortured with fear. Perhaps the caller was Williams—the man whose picture was in his pocket. One had few callers in a place like this, and Williams had been here before. But Mrs. Bailey knew him. She would have mentioned his name in summoning her husband, surely. But it might be. Williams might know that he was a visitor there, and so be cunning. He tiptoed to the door, opened it a little way, and stood for several minutes with his eyes riveted upon the door of the ranch house. He saw a saddle horse cropping the dry grass near the porch, and panic seized him. What if Elizabeth knew? Were they telling her even now while he was there in the barn? It must be Williams who was in the house. He couldn't bear to see Elizabeth after she had learned his hideous secret. He wouldn't wait. He would mount the messenger's horse—Williams' horse, maybe—and flee. If they dared to follow, he would—Ah, how he wished they would follow him, damn them!

Then a door opened in the ranch house and a sudden thrill swept over him. It left him calm, cold and ready. Like a flash, his hand fell upon his gun and a lust to kill lighted his gray eyes. "Come on, Jim Williams!" he whispered. "Come on and get it! I'm waiting for you!" The door closed, and he heard the sound of quick steps upon the porch.

But it was not Williams who was coming. It was Elizabeth. Plummer, leaving the door, hastened to Badger's side and was kneeling there when she entered.

"Oh, Mr. Plummer!" she cried, "Uncle Seth says you have set Badger's leg. How good of you. I can never thank you enough!" She dropped on her knees beside the wolfhound and caressed him with her hands. "I was so afraid you would have to die Badger dear," she crooned. "I just couldn't have stood it. I know I couldn't." The dog's brown eyes worshipped her, and he sought to rise. "No, no, Badger; lie down," she urged. "You are sick and you must stay in bed like a nice dog. That's it," she said as Badger settled back under her hands.

"I feel sure the bone will knit," said Plummer, looking at her tenderly, almost swept over with relief at her manner. "I have done my best to save him for you, Betty."

"It was kind of you," she murmured, almost inaudibly, her face averted as she rose from her kneeling position.

Plummer patted the dog's head soothingly, and then stood up beside her deliberately. "Elizabeth—Betty, I love you," he said, taking her two hands gently in his. "Won't you love me? Won't you be my wife? If I am elected sheriff, won't you come to me at Bannack?" His voice trembled with consuming tenderness—a feeling he had never known until he met her, and which he marveled at, while he allowed it to master him. His eyes, which seldom showed passion, now burned with the light of tenderness and devotion. "Won't you, Betty? Won't you?" he whispered, his arms encircling her. He bent his head close to hers. "Betty, won't you speak to me?" he pleaded.

"I think I will, Henry," she whispered softly.

117

He raised her face and kissed her lips. "I'll come for you, Betty," he whispered. "And we'll be so happy, dear."

"I'm so terribly afraid—afraid of—something, Henry!" she whispered, clinging to him.

"What is it, Betty? Tell me." His own voice startled him with its sound of dread.

"I cannot tell you what it is I fear," she said, looking up at him with eyes that both appealed and searched. "I think it is the thought that they may kill you. That must be it. Yes, I am sure that must be it."

He laughed and drew her hand down on his shoulder. The dread her words had aroused was stilled and relief flooded over him like sunshine chasing clouds over a hill. "Have no fear of that, dear Betty. They are afraid of *me*. I do not wish to boast, even to you, little sweetheart, but I fear no man," he said.

"Oh, I know it, Henry. I have always known it. Even I am afraid of you."

"*You* are? Don't say that! Please don't," he begged. "I'll make a confession to you, Betty." He bent his lips to her ear and whispered, "You are the one person in the whole world that I fear—the only one!"

"How perfectly ridiculous!" she laughed, a little relieved. "I think everybody is—is just a teeny bit afraid of *you,* though, Henry; honestly, I do."

"I ought to make a good sheriff, then, oughtn't I?" he laughed gaily.

"Splendid! I know you will be elected, too."

"And it was you who put the idea into my head, Betty," he said, and kissed her again.

"Uncle Seth and Aunt Jane will be fearfully surprised," she blushed.

"No, I do not think so. I have told your uncle I love you."

She lifted her head. "You told him? What did he say, Henry? Was he angry?"

"No," he said, half-unconsciously counting truth a fortification this time and taking shelter behind it. "He said he liked me, but that he isn't sure he believes in me, that's all. He did say, however, that he would not meddle with your private affairs."

She was silent for a time. "Isn't it queer, Henry?" she said at length. "I liked you from the first moment I saw you, but for a long time there was—was—well, something like the thing that troubled Uncle Seth, I suppose, that kept tormenting me."

"Are you troubled now, dear?" he asked her gently, with his arm still about her.

"No. I am sure it was just that I was afraid of you, at first. I don't believe you would be afraid of an army, Henry. It is that feeling which is behind the other, I am sure."

"I have told you that I am afraid of you, Betty."

"Oh, but you are playing with me. You are afraid of nothing," she sighed.

"Nothing but a little woman with wonderful eyes and beautiful brown hair—a dear little lady who wouldn't harm a living thing, if she could help it," he declared ardently. And his words were true.

"Listen! They are coming," she whispered. Freeing herself from his arm, she dropped to Badger's side and knelt there, turning with exaggerated surprise to greet her aunt and uncle as they entered the barn. "Oh, Aunt Jane!" she cried, clasping her hands joyfully. "Badger is going to get well. I know he is. See how nicely his poor leg is bandaged?"

They gathered around their pet, and while his tail played a tattoo upon the straw his eyes thanked them for their love and kindness. Even Chief had stalked into the barn and with discerning muzzle smelled about his stricken companion, whining in sympathetic understanding.

"My horse, Mr. Bailey?" asked Plummer after a time. "Has he improved any since I left him here? I hadn't thought about him until now."

"Yes, he has; but he'd better stay where he is for the present, I guess."

"I must be going back to Bannack, and if he were, well I would take him with me."

"Better leave him here until spring. There's plenty of good pasture, and he isn't any trouble," assured the ranchman.

"I'd be glad to leave him, if he will not bother you, Mr. Bailey," said Plummer gratefully.

"When are you going?" Elizabeth wanted to know, looking up at him shyly.

Plummer consulted his watch. "We shall start directly, Mr. Cleveland and I. We can easily reach the Murray Stage Station by dark if we ride hard."

"And when may we hope to see you again?" she asked, dusting her hands with her handkerchief.

"The day after the votes for sheriff have been counted I shall come," he answered, and their eyes met for a moment in understanding.

"I'm so glad you have a good traveling companion, Mr. Plummer," said Mrs. Bailey, earnestly. "The roads are dangerous, they say."

"Yes, so am I," agreed Plummer. "The roads are not as safe as I wish they were. Mr. Cleveland and I are old friends and that will make the journey pleasant. I wonder where he is."

"He's in the house whittling a wooden doll for Margaret," said Mrs. Bailey, smiling at the remembrance of her child's pleasure. "He's such a good-hearted young fellow."

"I'll go and ask him if he is ready to start, and then we'll saddle up," Plummer said, and as he started towards the house, the rest followed.

Cleveland readily consented to an early departure and offered to saddle the horses himself. Meanwhile Plummer gave final instructions regarding Badger.

"We shall follow the doctor's orders," laughed Elizabeth. "We hope for his early return to see his patient," she added with a coquettish glance.

"He will come; never fear." And seeing Cleveland coming with the horses, he turned to shake hands. "Good-bye, Mrs. Bailey," he said. "Good-bye, Mr. Bailey." After which he stooped suddenly and kissed Elizabeth, who blushed rosy red with embarrassment. "She'll explain, Aunt Jane!" he called back gaily as he swung onto his horse and turned off beside Cleveland.

Mrs. Bailey looked at Elizabeth. "Oh, Aunt Jane!" sobbed that young lady, throwing her arms about her aunt's neck. "It—it doesn't need ex—explaining, does it?"

21

Plummer had declared to the people at the ranch on the Sun River that he and Jack Cleveland could easily reach the Murray Stage Station by dark, but when night came they had not yet arrived there. The wind waxed keener, and as the shadows of night gathered both young men fell silent. There had been no conversation between them, except for an occasional word. Each felt the strain of the growing feud between them, and each seemingly sought to put it down, so that when the darkness came it brought the silence with it. They were alert and watchful of each other's action, and the strain was growing tenser when far ahead a light glowed in the gloom.

"There's the station, and I'm glad to see it," said Cleveland with a sigh.

"It's been a tiresome journey," was Plummer's short rejoinder.

At the station the keeper greeted them eagerly. "Good evenin', gentlemen," he said, as they stopped in front of the door. "Git down an' come in. Hank! Hank! Take these hosses an' feed 'em," to a tousle-headed youth who was reading just within the door. "Nice night, ain't it?" he asked, leading the way inside.

"Yes, it is wonderfully fine, although it looks as though a storm were brewing. One feels the chill after a long ride," said Plummer, trailing his spurs towards the stove and spreading his hands.

The station keeper stirred the fire, opened the draughts a trifle, and then inquired, "Traveled fer?"

"Only from the government ranch on the Sun River, but we started late," replied Plummer, rubbing his hands.

"Supper'll be ready in jest a jiffy," promised the host. "Mag! Mag!" he called towards the kitchen, "git supper fer two! Jest write yer names on the register, will ye, gentlemen?"

"Henry Plummer an' John Cleveland, hey? Ain't the man that's running fer sheriff, be ye?" he queried, turning to Plummer.

"Yes, sir. I'm the candidate for sheriff," admitted Plummer, smiling.

"Well, well, I'm mighty glad to know ye, Mr. Plummer. My name's Simmons, Alf Simmons. I've heered a lot about ye, an' we're all hopin' ye git elected. Hev a little drink? What say?"

"We will, sir," agreed Plummer, "or at least *I* will."

"I'll join you," said Cleveland, turning from the stove.

The station keeper, opening a little box-like desk, drew out a small jug. "Come all the way from ol' Kentuck," he whispered, as he poured a liberal drink for each. "Awful murder the other day upon the Stinkin' Water," he added, as he stuck the cork back in the jug by striking it with the palm of his hand.

"Is that so?" inquired Plummer, holding his glass towards the candlelight.

"Yes—poor Dutchman found dead. A feller was shootin' grouse with a scatter gun an' a bird flew up near to him. Bang! went his gun, an' down fell the grouse. The feller went to pick it up an' there 'twas, a-layin' right on the heart of a dead man. That's how they found out."

"Found out what?" asked Plummer carelessly, his glass near his lips.

"Found out the man had been murdered."

"Do they know who killed him?" asked Cleveland.

"No, of course not—not yet, anyway, but I hope they will find out, an' hang him," said the station keeper earnestly.

"Yes, yes. So do I," agreed Plummer. "If I'm elected sheriff I shall try to put a stop to this wholesale murder."

"I bet you *will*. I can tell it jest by lookin' at ye. I've heered quite a lot about ye, an' now I believe every word of it, yes, sir, every word. Let's have one more little drink—what say?"

"No, thanks. No more for me," laughed Plummer.

"I've had enough, too," declared Cleveland. "But I could eat a whole beef this minute."

"I'll jest go an' punch up Mag. She's lazy as a pet mare. Hev to keep at her all the time." And the station keeper disappeared through the dining room into the kitchen, where he met with a warm reception, judging from the hurried way in which he came out.

"It'll be ready in jest a jiffy," he laughed. "She's a-doin' fine, fine," he chattered, brushing the back of his hand against his side. "She burnt me. Let's us three have another little drink—just us three an' no more—what say?"

"Well, make it a light one and I'll join you," laughed Plummer. And Cleveland permitted the landlord to pour another drink for him, as well. "Here's good luck to ye, Mr. Sheriff. I hope ye win," proposed that worthy host, and would have continued talking, but a shrill female voice cried "Supper!" cutting short further expressions of good will.

"There! I told ye she'd git a hustle on herse'f. I hev to keep at her every minute; lazy as a half-froze snake, that woman is. An' fighty. Why, she'd bite the nose off'n a grizzly bear. Come on in, while the grub's hot. I'll set down with ye while ye eat. I'm lonesomer than a hole in a hillside." Leading the way, the garrulous, simpleminded fellow motioned them to be seated and straddled a chair himself, his short legs grotesquely spread to make room for his round belly. Then folding his chubby arms on the chair's back, he sighed deeply, after which he asked, "Union men be ye?"

"Yes," said Plummer, glancing at him and thinking of Kentucky.

"Good. Gineral Grant's goin' to whip hell out of Lee. See if he don't. I come from pretty fer South, myse'f, but I'm Union."

Just then a horse galloped up to the door of the stage station and stopped. "There! jest as I git set down," grumbled the station keeper, "somebody comes. Oh, Hank! Hank!" But the boy, evidently engrossed in his book, did not answer and the landlord reviled him. "*Con*-demn that con-*demn* boy! He ain't worth bear bait notime. Excuse me, will ye? I'll hev to go an' see who 'tis." He rose grudgingly from the table and left the room; but evidently his ire was short-lived, for he greeted the stranger as cordially as he had welcomed them. "Git down an' come in!" they heard him say. "Come right on into the dinin' room. Got some friends here. What's your name? I'll introduce ye."

The stranger replied, "Lane," and Plummer's eyes met Cleveland's as though to warn him to be careful. It was Club-Foot George who clumped into the room with the host.

"Gentlemen," began the latter, "this is Mr. Lane, Mr.—what did ye say yer first name was, sir?"

"George," grinned the cripple.

"Oh, yes! Meet Mr. George Lane, Mr. Plummer and Mr. Cleveland."

The introduction politely acknowledged, "Where ye from, Mr. Lane?" continued the host, sitting down near Plummer.

"Virginia City. I'm a shoemaker. My bench is in Dance and Stuart's store there. I'm thirty-two, ain't married, and I've got a club-foot," said the new guest glancing amusedly at the others at the table, his yellow teeth baring in a clownish grin. He knew that by thus speaking he would stop the inquisitive questioning of his host, and at

123

the same time acquaint Henry Plummer, his chief, with the fact that he was firmly established in the store from which the stages left for Fort Benton and Salt Lake City. Plummer would then know that he, Club-Foot George, was now able to secure important information—information that would be of great value to the bandits.

"No, now, I didn't go fer to pry into yer private affairs," stammered the station keeper repentantly. "Tain't none of my business —jest wanted to be sociable—that's all. Lonesome—lonesome as a hell-diver in the middle of the Atlantic Ocean, I am. Let's us all hev one more little drink, what say?"

"Not for me," objected Plummer.

"Nor for me. I'm half through with my supper," said Cleveland.

"Then Mr. Lane and I'll take one, won't we, Mr. Lane?" urged the host, anxious to appease the newcomer, and at the same time avail himself of an opportunity to imbibe.

"I'll join you," agreed Club-Foot George, rising with alacrity.

When the two had left the room, Plummer turned and glanced towards the kitchen door. Every thought of reformation had left his mind, even his bitter hatred for Cleveland. His habit of leadership had its way, and already he was scheming to take advantage of the opportunity offered by Club-Foot George's position in Virginia City. So suddenly did the lust for plunder sweep over him that it annihilated any twinge of conscience or thought of Elizabeth. It was his master—when only a few hours before he had thought to turn it easily from him forever. He whispered, "George will be valuable now. Did you catch the meaning of his words?"

"Yes," returned Cleveland, relieved at Plummer's interest, as if it might reestablish friendship between them. "We must try to arrange to have a talk with him, Henry."

They were interrupted by a black-eyed woman who shoved open the kitchen door in answer to a shout from the office. "Well, what is it?" she demanded querulously.

"Supper for another gentleman!" shouted the landlord, and Mag disappeared, slamming the kitchen door behind her.

"I'll try to talk with George," whispered Plummer, hastily continuing. "I'll make some excuse, and when I do, you try to interest the station keeper."

"I'll do the best I can," Cleveland assured him eagerly. "I wonder where George is going?"

They had no further opportunity to talk privately, for the landlord and Lane now returned. But after supper Plummer began to pace up and down in the office, walking slowly and apparently in deep thought.

"Bothered about somethin'?" asked the landlord solicitously.

"I confess that I am," returned Plummer, continuing to pace the floor.

"Can I he'p ye any, do ye reckon?"

"Not unless you can read Spanish," mumbled Plummer, as though the chance were so remote that it was not worth a moment's thought.

"Spanish! Spanish!"

"Yes; I have a letter that is written in Spanish, and I know it must contain important news concerning my brother who is in Mexico. If he were well he would have written, himself, but as it is, I am afraid he is ill, or dead perhaps, and that this letter tells me of his condition."

"Excuse me, Mr. Plummer," offered Lane, "I read Spanish. Mebby I kin be a help to you."

Plummer came to a halt before him. "Mr. Lane," he said, "I will be grateful if you will read the letter; but as it may be of a private nature—you see, my brother is in the government service in Mexico, may I ask you to come into my room with me?"

"Sure," returned Lane, heartily. "I'd be glad to."

"Then, Mr. Landlord, will you please show me my room?" asked Plummer.

"Ain't that lucky?" demanded the worthy host of Cleveland, upon returning to the stove in the office. "Think of finding a man that can read Spanish right here handy, an' jest where ye needed him. I call that luck. I do hope that letter ain't loaded with bad news. Reckon 'tis?"

"I hope not," smiled Cleveland. "Mr. Plummer has been anxious about it for three days. How long have you been in this territory, Mr. ——— , Mr. ——— "

"Simmons," supplied the landlord. "My name is Alf Simmons." And thus afforded an opportunity, he launched himself into telling the story of his life, ever and anon returning to thoughts of the mysterious letter. "Gosh A'mighty, it's jest like totin' a snake around in yer pocket ye thought was dead, but mighn't be," he said. But Cleveland, playing his part, turned him back to his boyhood days.

125

"What are you doing here?" asked Plummer after he and Club-Foot George were left alone, with a candle to light the bare, cold room. His first impulse was to question George as his chief.

"I had to be away today," began Lane. "You see, Henry, Bummer Dan has sold his Alder Gulch claim. He left Virginia City this afternoon with his money an' gold. Bill Bunton, Bob Zachary and Frank Parish will take him in, 'long about Bill Bunton's ranch on the Rattlesnake. That's why I had to be away. The boys'll hold up the stage on the trail to Bannack; most likely at the Rattlesnake. I kin prove I was here if I ever have to. An' Henry, George Ives has killed a fellow—a Dutchman. I'm afraid he's talked too damn much. Tell him to stop drinkin' so much when you see him."

"How long have you had your shoemaker's bench in Dance and Stuart's store?" inquired Plummer.

"Nearly a month. I see an' hear all that's goin' on. I kin always send you an' the boys word when the coaches carry worthwhile freight."

"What are the chances of my election? I mean, what are the miners in Alder saying?" Even as he asked the question, Plummer remembered how he had resolved to keep away from his men. Well, he would finish with Club-Foot, and that would be all.

"They're all for you," Club-Foot said. "You'll be elected, an' then the whole game'll be ours. I'm worried about George Ives, though, Henry."

"Are you going back to Virginia City from here?" asked Plummer, paying no apparent attention to Lane's fear about Ives.

"Yes, I only wanted to be away from Virginia City an' off the trail to Bannack."

"There are only a few more days before election occurs," said Plummer. "Work hard for my success, and don't try to leave this place in our company in the morning. If you have any news of importance to communicate, send some stranger with a letter, but be sure of your messenger. We'd better join Cleveland and the station keeper now. We mustn't be overlong with the Spanish letter."

"Well, how was it?" the landlord wanted to know when Plummer and Lane joined them.

"Oh," laughed Plummer, "it was a prank of my brother's. He is well and hearty and has found a Spanish sweetheart. It was the lady who wrote the letter. There was nothing important about it, but I would have continued to worry over it, if it had not been for Mr. Lane."

"I'm glad, awful glad. Hev a little drink? What say?"

"No, thank you," refused Plummer. "I'm going to retire."

22

Never before in the world had a gulch been discovered which proved so rich in placer gold as Alder, and even to this day when there remains no new country, no undiscovered gulches, and the prospector has passed to return no more, its record of wealth in gold dust stands unexcelled.

Among the fortunate ones who reached it early was Bummer Dan, a careless wanderer who happened to stake one of the best claims in the gulch. He made money more rapidly than he could spend it, but tiring of the new camp in spite of his prosperity, he sold out his claim and prepared to leave the diggings. He knew the dangers of the road to those who traveled them with gold dust, and accordingly planned to hide his departure. He let no one in Virginia City know of his intentions to go away, save the clerk who booked passengers for travel on the daily coaches, and the crippled shoemaker whose workbench was located near the stage clerk's desk in Dance and Stuart's store, from which the coaches took their passengers and express. The clerk had sworn secrecy, and the simple shoemaker, pegging industriously at a miner's boot, had not raised his head when Bummer Dan whispered, "I'll be at Dempsey's ranch. Tell the driver to save a seat and pick me up there two trips from today, savvy? Two trips from today. An' here's a nugget fer keepin' yer mouth shet, young feller." Poor Bummer Dan. Fortune had picked him up but was soon to drop him once more into the ranks of the poor—all his toil and privation having gone to enrich a band of cutthroats.

Plummer and Cleveland, on their way to Bannack from the Sun River, left the Murray Stage Station early, and without seeing Club-Foot George. The morning was cold and blustering, a storm having begun soon after dark on the evening before. Even as they had reached the station, black clouds had been rolling towards them from the northwest; and now the weather was extremely disagreeable. It continued squally all the day, with flurries of dry snowflakes every now and then, and they were glad to put up a short day's ride from Bannack. They heard nothing further, however, of the intended stage robbery until they reached the mining camp itself.

There, having turned their horses over to the stableman, they went into the Pioneer Gambling House, and as they had expected found a crowd of men discussing the stage holdup. As he and Plummer entered, Cleveland saw Bob Zachary standing near the stove apparently listening to a conversation between two miners. He went towards him, but Plummer, halting by a group just within the door, asked, "What's the excitement?"

"The coach from Virginia City was held up and robbed almost within sight of town," replied one of the group, a miner named Cass Masterson, who owned a good claim on Grasshopper, and whom Plummer knew slightly.

"When?"

"This morning." Evidently not caring to discuss the affair in the hearing of others, Masterson nudged Plummer, who walked with him to a corner of the room. Masterson was older than most of the men in the diggings, slight of build, and gray about the temples. He appeared to have been used to gentler ways than many, and while he, like the others, had formed no friendships and even few acquaintances in Bannack, he had an air of respectability about him which found recognition. He had admired Plummer for his fearlessness in arresting Jack Horan, and since then had looked upon him as a friend of law if not of himself. In the corner he turned, his thin face serious with his suspicion. "It looks as though somebody in the inside of the stagecoach business must have been careless," he whispered. "Bummer Dan sold his claim in Alder and took the coach with a lot of dust and money on him. A fellow who was on the coach with him tells me he swears nobody knew of his departure from Virginia City except the clerk in Dance and Stuart's store. But he declares that when they held him up one of the road agents said, '*You* are the man we were after!' when they took his money and dust. You see, there were several other passengers—all with some dust, but none with as much as Dan. It looks queer, don't it?"

"Rather." Plummer was thinking of the shoemaker in Dance and Stuart's store. The clerk—would he suspect him?

"The fellow that runs the ranch on the Rattlesnake where they change horses acted mighty queer," Masterson went on, and Plummer's interest quickened. "His name's Bunton. He couldn't, or pretended he couldn't, locate the change of stock when the stage pulled in at the station there. Rumsey, the driver, had to stay all night at the ranch and then come on to Bannack with the same six horses, plumb worn out. This morning the fellow Bunton rode in on the coach and was, of course, held up with the others. But Rumsey believes he was in on the play and is sore as a wolf because the road agents made him disarm his own passengers. I believe Crawford must stand in with the gang, don't you?" he whispered, with a glance over his shoulder.

"He might." Suspicion of the sheriff as well, and Plummer would use it to his own advantage; but if Bunton was implicated he would have to be extremely careful. So far he had never been with Bill Bunton, and he would take care to keep away from him in the future. "Is the sheriff out with a posse?" he asked sarcastically.

"No, of course not. There he is drinking with the man that killed George Evans. I know him—everybody knows him. Even Crawford knows what he is."

Plummer glanced in the direction Masterson indicated and beheld Jack Cleveland in quiet conversation with the sheriff, their heads together. Quick suspicion of possible betrayal seized him. His smouldering hate, engendered by Cleveland's secret visit to the Bailey home, suddenly flamed with added fuel. His own safety, his success, were now in danger. He had often been seen with Jack Cleveland. Even now he was occupying the same cabin with him; and people, other than himself, knew him to be a murderer. What was Cleveland telling Crawford now with his head next to his? How long had he known him? Cleveland knew more about his own past life than any other living man.

"Did *he* kill George Evans?" he asked, his voice tuned to surprised incredulity, his cold eyes fixed upon the object of his increasing hate.

"Yes, that's well known now," said Masterson. "I—we have wondered if *you* knew it, Mr. Plummer?" he added.

"I? No, indeed!" lied Plummer. "George Evans was a friend of mine. It's news to me—news I won't forget or overlook." This last was true enough. His quick mind reaching for an excuse to take Cleveland's life, had found it.

"And that man killed my old friend," he murmured, "and I have sheltered him."

"Yes, Mr. Plummer, killed and robbed him. Everybody knows it. Won't you take a drink with me, sir?"

"Gladly," assented Plummer, himself leading the way to the bar where Jack Cleveland was again drinking with Crawford. While they drank he appeared to listen to Cass Masterson's confidences, meanwhile covertly watching Cleveland and Crawford and straining to catch what they were saying. He secretly thanked his luck for this excuse to kill Cleveland, thus satisfying his jealous hatred as well as turning away suspicion from himself.

Four men were leaning on the bar between him and Cleveland. Beyond them Cleveland was tapping it with a glass of liquor and saying, "I know every rascal on both sides of the range." Then, as the four men turned to leave, he pointed to one of them and said, "There's a man that owed me money—that fellow with the red beard. Know him?"

Plummer snatched the chance to provoke a quarrel which he knew would further excuse what he finally intended. Springing to Cleveland's side, he whispered, "Stop it! You are drinking and don't know what you are saying."

"I don't, hey?" Cleveland leered, straightening his body. "Who in hell do you think *you* are?"

Plummer sprang backward and aside, like a crouching cat. His gun flashed twice, the reports so nearly together that they seemed only one. Cleveland sank to his knees. Two bullets were in his breast.

There was a rush for the door. Men nearly tore it from its hinges in getting outside and away. Only Plummer and Crawford, who had dodged behind the bar, were left to hear Cleveland's hoarse pleading, "Don't—don't shoot me when I'm down!"

"I won't shoot you when you're down!" Plummer stepped backward with the certainty of a man who is about to put an end to a helpless, dying elk. "Get up and fight, if there's a fight in you," he sneered.

Cleveland, bleeding and blind with the shock of two mortal wounds, staggered to his feet. His hand fumbled desperately for his gun. "I'll—I'll fight," he faltered.

However, no man, even were he sound, could have won such a

fight with Plummer, who was the quickest man with a six-shooter ever known, and who depended for his very life upon his skill. Scarcely had Cleveland straightened his body when he fell again, a third bullet in his breast and a fourth in his head near his left eye.

Plummer, with his gun still in his hand, walked nearer and looked a moment without compassion on the upturned face of his old friend, after which he tucked his gun in the waistband of his trousers under his vest and strode out of doors, leaving him alone with Crawford. The men outside made way for him, stepping aside to let him pass through whirling snowflakes that were whitening the ground. They had been talking among themselves. He had killed the murderer of George Evans; and even if they wavered over the virtue of the deed, it was nevertheless a punishment of crime. Something had to be done to stop crime. Their miners' court had been unsuccessful. Here was a man who, single-handed, had arrested one murderer and killed another. Both deeds took on a light of justice in these men's eyes, furnished, no doubt, by a kind of helpless desperation. And it is little wonder.

So the men returned his greeting, half uncertainly but without hostility, and he went straight to his cabin sure that he had nothing to fear for killing Cleveland. But as he crossed the dark uneven street to his and Cleveland's cabin, it began to be borne in upon him that Cleveland might not yet be dead. If he was still alive and conscious he might talk to Crawford. He cursed himself for not making sure that Cleveland was dead before he left him. He made no light, but hurriedly felt his way to the window between the stools and the table and looked out across the street through the falling snow. They were bringing him out. Four men were carrying Cleveland out of the Pioneer Gambling House and towards Crawford's cabin, beyond the butcher shop. He must be alive.

With an oath Plummer turned away from the window and began to walk the floor, both hands clutching the brim of his hat. Crawford would learn of his connection with the gang of road agents. He would lose Elizabeth, the election—perhaps his life—because he had fumbled in killing Cleveland. Cleveland knew more about his past than any other man, and now he was going to expose him to Crawford. He must kill Crawford. There was no time to waste. A single minute might be fatal. He would do it. He would kill Crawford, election or no election. Resolved, he bolted for the door and as he snatched it open bumped against Bill Bunton coming in.

"You got him, Henry!" he said, his voice always patronizing, charged with wonder. "What did he do to you, damn him?"

"That's my affair," snapped Plummer. "He did enough. Hear me? He did enough!"

"I *bet* he did. Well, you got him all right."

"Is he dead?" Plummer's long fingers closed on Bunton's arm like a clamp of steel.

"No, not yit; but he'll die. He's —"

"That doesn't matter," Plummer cut him short. "Go at once and get somebody—some one of the boys—to stay right by his side till he dies. If he tries to talk, kill him."

Bunton turned to do his bidding. "Wait!" ordered Plummer. "Spread the story that I killed Cleveland for the murder of George Evans. Get it going fast. It's only four days to election. Hurry!"

Bunton went out of the cabin and Plummer lighted a candle, but blew it out again and began to pace the floor. He had intended to avoid Bunton. Now he had sent him on a mission. He was in a devil of a mess. He stopped before the window and looked out across the snow, and he could see a group of men around Crawford's open door. Some of them went in and after a minute or two came out again—satisfying a morbid curiosity—then tramped back down the street towards Goodrich's Saloon. He watched them intently to discover by their manner, if he could, whether Cleveland was alive or dead. They stopped nearly opposite his window, and in anxiety he pressed his face against the glass.

Their attention, however, was directed not on him or his cabin, but farther down the street, from which direction he now heard ribald singing. Then a wagon loaded with men and women came rattling up the frozen street, its iron shod wheels slewing in the light snow with erratic suddenness. To the amusement of the men across from his window, it sped past, the driver standing upon the seat and lashing the horses with the ends of his long reins while his drunken passengers screamed, cursed, or sang to express their various feelings. Just up the street the wild driver turned his team so sharply that the wheels cramped and tilted the wagon box dangerously high, and came racing back. An audience was what he most desired, both for his horsemanship and the talent in his wagon, and with a blood-curdling oath he stopped before the watching men so abruptly that he was pitched headlong on his team. "Whoah!" he shouted, slipping onto the wagon tongue and thence to the ground among the horses' dancing feet. No one moved to succor him, but the excited horses, understanding, no doubt, suffered him to extricate himself without running away, so gentle is chance with infants and inebriates.

Now a woman climbed down from the wagon to the snow-covered ground, and after pulling up her skirts, bowed with drunken stateliness to the watching men, after which she turned about to bow again, this time to the dark window of Plummer's cabin. Then she began to dance tipsily, until someone in the wagon cried, "Sing, Countess, sing!" She needed no urging, but began:

> *'Tis the las' ro-hose of sum-mah*
> *Left bloo-hmhing al-one,*
> *All her love-lay companions*
> *Are fa-ded an' go-an!*

The words were scarcely recognizable, but they stung Plummer like a lash. This drunken outcast was singing Elizabeth's song—the song which her sweet voice had sanctified—Elizabeth's song—Elizabeth, the girl he loved. In a flash there appeared to him a full realization of the difference between Elizabeth and himself. The gulf between him and his love was darkened to blackness and deepened beyond his ken by the sight before him. Although he forbade it his thoughts persistently picked up the thread of his own dissolute ways with women, and led him protesting bitterly to review his conquests, successes, and subsequent desertions of those whose love he had won and thrown aside. He ground his boot heel into the dirt floor.

Why should they torture him now—these women of other days? He had never before known a moment's remorse. If Elizabeth should learn—"God! It must not be," he groaned aloud, as again the words of her song came to him in the high-pitched voice of the poor wretch outside.

> *And from love's shi-ning cir-cle*
> *The gems drop a-way.*
> *And fond hearts lie with-ered*

And fond ones have flow-wn
Oh, who would in-hab-bit
This bleek world a-laon!

A muffled knock on the door recalled him. "Come in!" he cried.
"It's me," said Bill Bunton, in the darkness. "Cleveland's dead."
"Good. Did he talk any?"

"Not a word. Just said it's none of your business when Crawford asked him about you an' him."

"I've got to kill Crawford. Get word to him so that he will talk. Tell him I'm going to kill him—that he has got to fight me."

"But, Henry, the election?" protested Bunton.

"I know, I know," interrupted Plummer impatiently. "That is one reason why I want to kill him—to get him out of the race. Everybody knows that I have denounced him as sheriff and as a man. I believe it will help me if I kill him, after a quarrel."

"All right, kill him," agreed Bunton. "He ought to be killed, all right, but we got to be careful. What excuse'll we offer?"

Plummer began to pace the floor. "The stage holdup; his friendship for Jack Cleveland, the man who murdered Evans; his damned cowardice ever since he has been sheriff. There's plenty to say. Say it! I'll kill him. Go and tell him I intend to kill him. Tell him that I've said he is a low coward. Tell him—no, tell him anything that might make him fight," he finished with an oath. "Go now and start it. Why do you stand there?"

Bunton went out, wondering at the condition of his chief, whose former coolness had departed.

23

Bannack was astir at an early hour. Men had heard that Crawford the sheriff had quarrelled with Henry Plummer—had insulted him—and that Plummer had sworn to kill him on sight. Stories that hinted darkly of Crawford's intimacy with Cleveland and with those who had robbed the stagecoach were being freely circulated. Some even said that Crawford had been given a share of the plunder and was a member of the gang of outlaws. Everybody knew that Plummer had repeatedly denounced Crawford as a coward and remembered the arrest of Jack Horan, a task which had been generously assumed by Plummer when it had rightly belonged to the sheriff. Surely that arrest was a public service.

The morning sun quickly banished the snow from the few shingled roofs along the main street, leaving only patches of white on the dirt-topped cabins from which tails of smoke were curling. In the street before Goodrich's Saloon, whose square front of flimsy boards extended higher than its ridgepole to give it an appearance of greater size and importance, a group of miners stood or leaned against a hitching rack. Wherever men were gathered, there were one or more of Plummer's men to listen to their conversation, to encourage his supporters, to brand any who spoke against him for future punishment; and they were here.

"I tell you Crawford ain't no good on airth," declared a miner at the hitching rack. His black slouch hat was turned sharply up on front till the wide brim touched its crown. His pipe stuck smartly out, like a charred peg that seemed to fasten the mass of hair of his long, untrimmed moustache and beard to his face, giving him a half-wild and thoroughly unkempt look. "Plummer's a gentleman," he went on, hooking his thumbs in a leather belt which supported his heavy six-shooter. "A gentleman, Plummer is; an' he knows more in a holy minute than Crawford can think of in a lifetime. I heered last night that Crawford was tellin' around camp that Plummer was courtin' Catherine, the Squaw. That's what's made Plummer mad, *I'll* bet you. Plummer ain't that kind of a man. It's a lie, an' it's enough to make any man—There's Crawford now," he broke off, snatching the pipe from his mouth to point with its stem at the sheriff coming out of his cabin and starting down to Goodrich's Saloon.

A hush fell on the group. They watched Crawford open the door and enter the saloon. When it had closed behind him, a man in the group laughed nervously and said, "We don't want any more cowards for sheriff. I'll vote for Plummer."

"I wonder where he is?" put in another, restless under the belief that something was about to happen.

"He'll be along, don't you fret," said Bill Bunton, keeper of the Rattlesnake stage station, who had slipped in among the miners unnoticed. "I'll bet that Crawford's—Here's Plummer now."

Plummer *was* coming, his tall, erect figure as usual inspiring that indescribable feeling of awed worship which a small boy knows for his heroes, though they be buccaneers.

"Good morning, gentlemen," he greeted, pleasantly, as he passed.

"Good morning," they murmured with their eyes fixed upon him as though by some compelling force.

"By God, he's goin' in!" whispered a man in the group, as Plummer calmly opened the door of Goodrich's Saloon. "He's goin' in!"

The door shut behind him. But it opened suddenly, emitting a man who came out hurriedly, glanced nervously to the right and left as though undecided which way to go, and then walked rapidly out to the group of miners, as though glad of their company. "They're in there," he whispered. "Both of 'em's in there. Plummer just come in." But the others did not seem to hear him. Their eyes were on the door of Goodrich's Saloon.

Crawford had been standing near the stove with his back towards the door. But when Plummer entered the saloon, as though sensing the approach of his enemy, he turned to face him, nodding pleasantly.

Plummer offered no greeting. "Crawford, you have said that I am courting Catherine, the Squaw," he began, in a voice that was scarcely audible. "It's a lie, and I demand satisfaction. Come outside and fight me."

"Mr. Plummer," returned Crawford, "you have been misinformed. I have said nothing of the kind and I have no cause to fight you."

"You are a coward," breathed Plummer. "Come outside, if you dare."

"I neither know what cause there is for fighting you, nor why I should be afraid to go out of doors on your challenge."

"Come on then," said Plummer.

As he spoke he began urging Crawford towards the door, and the sheriff followed him, while the few men who had remained in the saloon, stared. "Now," said Plummer, having succeeded in getting him out of doors, "draw your gun."

"No, I will not. You know that you have the advantage of me."

"If you think so, I'll give you time to draw and cock your gun before I go after mine. Come, draw!"

"No!"

"Then I'll kill you."

"I'll give you all the chance in the world," said Crawford, and he turned his back and walked away.

Plummer dared not shoot. He had no scruples, but public opinion would have turned against him if he did. Inwardly raging at his failure to provoke a quarrel with Crawford, he walked back towards his cabin, passing the group of miners and nodding affably, with no trace of his anger or resentment on his handsome, well-controlled face.

"Crawford's a white-livered coward," growled Bill Bunton, still watching with the group of men. "He'll try to bushwack Plummer. See if he don't."

Crawford, as he walked rapidly away from Plummer with feigned indifference, had expected to be shot in the back. He maintained his show of calmness, however, until he reached his own cabin, where a number of his friends had gathered to encourage and counsel him. At sight of them, he threw himself upon his bed, sobbing hysterically. "He'll kill me! He'll surely kill me!"

"You've got to kill *him*," said a miner. "I've brought my new rifle for you. It's a double barrel an' the best gun in this camp."

"But I don't want to kill him," sobbed Crawford from the bed.

"Very well, then," scoffed another, who was a member of Plummer's gang. "Let him kill *you*. It's *your* affair," and he left the cabin in pretended disgust.

Skillfully played up, the news of Crawford's apparent cowardice made more friends for Plummer. Men who had believed in the sheriff now openly admitted him a coward; and Plummer's friends embellished every tale that was told concerning whatever Crawford had done, or had failed to do, as an officer. The camp was still divided, it is true, but even though some of the miners disapproved of the quarrel itself, they believed more and more that Crawford was not fit to be sheriff. His deputies had been powerless to stop lawlessness, and they knew Plummer was without fear and that he would act. He *had* acted; he had arrested Horan, and he had killed Cleveland for the murder of George Evans; he had spoken publicly of Crawford's unfitness for his office; he had declared that if he was elected he would put an end to the lawlessness in the mining camps.

After his unsuccessful attempt to provoke Crawford to quarrel,

Plummer had gone to his cabin and once inside had tossed his hat upon his bed and begun to pace the floor like a caged panther. He had made matters worse, for if Cleveland had talked to Crawford, the latter would now have a good reason for repeating anything the dying man might have said. He suspected that Cleveland *had* talked, notwithstanding that Bunton had insisted it was not so.

His rifle rested on two wooden pegs that had been driven into holes in the cabin logs, and as he walked his eyes were upon it. At last he turned to the wall and, reaching to take down the weapon, stopped with his arms extended. It was as though he had suddenly been challenged by an unspeakable terror. He glared at his own face in a small mirror which hung under the rifle. Those eyes that looked at him from the glass were his own; filled with hate, with fear, with loathing, they were yet his own. They held him, mocked him, accused him of what he knew too well—of what Elizabeth had not discovered—God! *Had* she discovered it? He turned his back to the mirror with a curse on his lips, ran to the bed, picked up his hat and put it on, pulling the brim down over his forehead. Thus reinforced, he took the rifle from its pegs, examined it carefully, and was putting new caps on the tubes when Bill Bunton came into the cabin, closing the door carefully.

"He's lookin' fer you with a rifle!" he cried.

"Who is looking for me with a rifle?" asked Plummer, glancing up.

"Crawford! He's got Cavan's double-barreled rifle."

Plummer smiled with satisfaction. "He prefers long range, does he? All right, he won't have long to look for me." And with his own rifle he went out of doors.

Bill Bunton, following, saw Crawford, who had evidently been watching for Plummer, come out of his cabin beyond the butcher shop with his rifle ready for instant use. He cried a warning to his chief, and Plummer stopped short, discovering Crawford across the street. A wagon was standing nearby and he moved toward it, placing a foot upon a spoke in the wheel and resting his elbow on his knee. Then he aimed at Crawford. But before he could fire, a bullet from the sheriff's rifle shattered the bone in his right arm. He dropped his gun and stood erect. "Fire away, you coward!" he cried, and another bullet clipped a piece from his hat brim. He laughed derisively, and being unable to use his own weapon, picked it up with his left hand

and walked back to his cabin while the citizens marvelled at his calmness. Friends rushed to assist him, and to run for the doctor at his request. His shattered arm was bleeding profusely.

Meanwhile Crawford had fled. His second shot at Plummer had so frightened him that in spite of appealing friends who sought to dissuade him, he rushed wildly to the livery stable where he kept his saddle horse and, mounting, rode away from Bannack forever. The news of his fight was received with jeers by Plummer's friends, and Crawford's loyal supporters now felt that their cause in opposition to Plummer was lost.

But, although he apparently had the field to himself, Plummer, with his arm in a sling, sick with the pain and fever he was suffering, was a busy man on the day before election. He feared that in a mass meeting the miners themselves might select a new rival for the office he was so anxious to gain. He had warned his emissaries in the camps outside of Bannack, so that they were active as he.

No such move as he dreaded was made in the camps in Alder Gulch, but secretly a miner's meeting had been held at night in Bannack, with the result that on the morning of election day Jeff Durly was put forward as a candidate. At midnight messengers had ridden away to Junction, Adobetown, Nevada City, Virginia City and Summit in an attempt to acquaint the miners there of Durly's candidacy. But the thousands of men who had gathered in those camps since the discovery of gold had been made in Alder Gulch could not be reached in so short a time.

One more effort there was, which though too mean for Plummer's notice, produced more of an effect than the projection of a new candidate. Before the first streak of the dawn of election day showed in the northeast, a wobbly wagon drawn by two boney horses came out of Virginia City and crept down the winding way of Alder Gulch. The wagon was cluttered with rickety household furniture, and the rattling pots and pans vied with the squeaking of the wheels and the creaking of the wagon box. On the seat were a man and a woman, and behind them, perched on a roll of tattered bedding, a boy and a little girl who gazed without interest through the rents in the torn canvas cover, the bows of which gaped here and there like the polished ribs of a half-devoured buffalo carcass on the plains. Joggling and bumping over the stony way, the wagon at length turned a bend in the road below Virginia City and stopped. The man stood up and looked behind, ahead, and across the gulch where a flickering light showed in a tent near some willows. He peered intently into the gloom as though expecting someone to come out of the dark.

"What is it, Jim?" asked the woman in a querulous voice.

"Shh! Never mind. Let me alone an' keep still," whispered the man, as he reached under the seat and, after fumbling a moment, drew out a tin cup. "Hold the lines," he said.

The woman obeyed, and the man climbed down with the tin cup in his hand. A large boulder was near the wagon wheel, and dipping his fingers into the cup, he smeared a spot on the smooth surface of the rock, then drew from his pocket a piece of paper and, laying it on the spot, rubbed it with his hand a moment.

"Whatever are you do——"

"Shh! Dammit, keep still!"

He climbed back into the wagon, took the lines and drove on. Five times in this manner he stopped between Virginia City and Junction, and pasted a paper upon rocks and trees near to the road. But the morning dawning, he dared do no more and, standing up in the wagon, he hurled the tin cup far out into a clump of willows on Alder Creek.

"I've got one more paper," he grumbled, "but I dasn't do no more. It's gittin' too light."

"Let me see it, can't you?" asked the woman.

The man handed her the paper. It was eight inches square and upon it was written:

WARNING!
Henry Plummer is just a rode ajunt an a mer-
derur. Look him up in Californy—also Idaho.
sined by
A man that knows him.

"Jim Bent, you're a crazy man," declared the woman, returning the paper.

"Mebby I be, but I'm a-goin' to keep a-goin' now till I git out of here—a damn long ways out, too. Anyhow, they've struck it again in Florence, I hear. Gitap, Pete! Joe!"

He tore the remaining paper into small bits, tossing a few scraps first on one side and then on the other, and watched the morning wind carry them away.

24

It was past two o'clock in the afternoon of the same day when, in the interests of Henry Plummer, Club-Foot George rode down Alder Gulch on his way to the camps below Virginia City, and seeing a group of miners gathered about a rock that had been adorned by Jim Bent, pulled up to read the warning. "Who did that?" he demanded angrily.

There was no answer. Men pressed about the boulder, but without even a glance at the horseman, went silently away. Club-Foot George got down from his horse and tore the paper from the rock. "It's a lie!" he cried. "A damned lie! I know Mr. Plummer, and he's a gentleman. Who did this thing?"

But the miners withdrew, one by one, and no man answered. No man knew who had posted the warning, but now that it was suggested to them, many, reviewing what they knew of Plummer, felt that its words were true; and if they had not already voted, they did not vote for Henry Plummer.

At Nevada City the warning had found supporters, and men were discussing it guardedly. But there was nothing that could now be done to really beat Plummer for sheriff; it was too late. Jeff Durly was without friends outside of Bannack, and even had the warning been posted sooner—even had the miners in Bannack taken earlier action—it is doubtful if their candidate could have won.

The day ended at last, and the hour came when the polls were closed. Before seven o'clock the vote of Nevada City, Adobetown, Junction and Summit was known in Virginia City. Even had Bannack revolted, it could not have changed the result. Henry Plummer was sheriff.

A wild revel broke out in the camps in Alder Gulch. Dance halls were crowded with cheering men, and horsemen rode through the streets firing guns and racing pell mell between tents in a mad game of *follow-the-leader*. Gaily decked wagons loaded with singing men and women from the dance halls drove up and down the gulch until morning came, when daylight ended the revel. The excitement was contagious, and men who had neither voted for Plummer nor believed in his fitness for the office of sheriff were impelled to join in the celebration by a spirit of recklessness that was master of the placer camps.

Soon after the votes were counted, Club-Foot George and Frank Parish saddled horses and started for Bannack with the tidings that all the camps in Alder had voted for Henry Plummer. It was morning when they arrived there and the town had already worn itself to fatigue with celebrating. Some made an attempt to renew the celebration but it commanded little interest. The revellers had worn out their enthusiasm for the time.

Plummer was closeted in his cabin with Boone Helm and Jack Gallagher when Club-Foot George and Frank Parish entered with their news from the camps in Alder Gulch. The five men began at once making plans for the future, and discussing the appointment of Plummer's deputy sheriffs in the different camps. It went without saying that these were to be made from the ranks of the road agents and from a number of citizens whom the outlaws believed to be as lawless and desperate as themselves but who had lived in the camps for a considerable period of time without having incurred the distrust of their fellows.

"And now," finished Plummer, as the first glint of sunlight touched the white mountaintops, "I want you to go away and keep away. Whenever you have anything of importance to communicate to me, send a messenger with a letter, or make an appointment for a meeting, if that is necessary. The minute one of you gets into trouble we shall all be implicated unless these precautions are carried out. We must not seem to be close friends. Drunk or sober, never speak to me as a friend. I am the sheriff—that's all. I shall be away from Bannack for the next few days, and when I return I will announce my appointments. They will be the men we have selected. Good night."

Thus dismissed, the four men went out of the cabin into the cold morning, and Plummer, left alone, blew out the candle and sat down on his bed. He had expected to feel elation, but now that he had won the prize it seemed but an empty thing. His triumphs had always been so. His only compensations had been in the conquests he had made—in overcoming the barriers which the struggles themselves had set in his way. The prizes he had gained were invariably of less worth than he would have believed before they were his own. And always, after the fire of enthusiasm for the chase had burned out, he found only the ashes of his desire to reward him. Suddenly he rose and began to pace the floor. Elizabeth—would it be different with Elizabeth? Surely he could not again be mistaken and find, after the conquest, that she too would lose her place in his heart. He loved her —wanted her more than he ever wanted anything, but now he was afraid. It was still dark in the cabin, for the sun had not yet pierced the gulch and there was a makeshift shade drawn across the window. He lighted a candle and, taking off his hat, walked deliberately across the room and looked into the mirror on the wall, forcing himself to study the face reflected there a moment. "Damn you," he hissed, as the candlelight grew stronger and his eyes made out his features in the tiny glass. "Damn you, I hate you!"

His spoken words seemed to rouse him and he turned guiltily to glance at the door. Then he blew out the light and resumed his pacing, for his arm was thumping with pain and he could not rest. He was wracked with pain and tortured with forebodings concerning Elizabeth. It was not so much that he imagined the hurt to her which the death of his love would mean, as that he dreaded to lose this most precious thing in his life, the love and trust of an innocent girl—just as men will dread to learn a truth because it might destroy their fondest illusions. He refused to believe that he would not love her to the end of his life.

Tap, tap, tap, there came a knock on the door.

"Come in!" he called.

It was Bill Bunton. "How's your arm, Henry?" he inquired.

"It's giving me a little pain, but I expected it. I have rested some, and don't feel at all bad. What time is it?"

"Nearly nine o'clock."

"Is that so?" Plummer feigned surprise. "I must have slept quite a while," he said.

"Shall I go over to the Chinaman's and get you some coffee, Henry?"

"Yes, I wish you would, Bill. Bring some ham and hot cakes, too. I'm as hungry as a bear."

Bunton went out for the breakfast and Plummer stretched himself upon his bed. It was growing light in the cabin when Bunton reentered with a tray. "I've brought you a surprise with your ham, Henry," he said, as he carefully set the tray upon the rude table.

"What is it, Bill, an egg?" laughed Plummer, sitting up on the bed.

"I hope to die if it ain't, Henry—a sure enough hen's egg."

"Where in the world has it been hidden so long, Bill?"

"It's fresh—fresh as a mountain daisy, Henry. I'll bet that the damned Chinaman has been holdin' out on us. Set up an' eat while it's hot."

Plummer ate with a relish which gave no hint to Bunton that he had spent the night in suffering. "Do you know if the Massey house is still for sale, Bill?" he asked after a while.

"Yep. Massey has gone to Summit. Why?"

"What does he want for the place?"

"Two thousand dollars, and it's a bargain."

"I think I'll buy it, Bill."

"Your share of the stage holdup will help a lot," chuckled Bunton. "I've got it here fer you." Fishing into a dirty pocket, he handed Plummer twelve hundred dollars in treasury notes. "What you want with the house?"

"I'm going to marry and settle down," Plummer told him quietly. "Who has the Massey place for sale?"

Bunton stared a moment, but being well trained, easily adjusted his thoughts. "Judson, down at the corner," he said. "It's a four room house an' well built. Shall I see to it fer you?"

"No, I'll attend to it myself, thanks. And Bill, after I am married—"

Perhaps fate herself, in terror lest her plans for Henry Plummer be altered, hurriedly interrupted, so subtle does she seem with moments —so infallibly does she appear to control men's destinies. Someone knocked on the door, and Bill Bunton never knew that Henry Plummer had intended to say that after he had married he would have nothing more to do with his old associates in a social way. "Come in!" called Plummer, and George Ives, sometimes called Gentleman George, entered the cabin.

"Congratulations, Mr. Sheriff!" he offered gallantly. "How's the arm?"

"Fine," laughed Plummer, rising.

The tenseness of a cat about to pounce upon its prey came to his good arm. He knew that Ives was jealous of him and that his reputation as a fighting man had made him many friends among the outlaws.

Ives lighted a cigar, his blue eyes glancing from Plummer to Bill Bunton craftily. "I'm glad your arm is better, Henry," he said, dropping the burned match to the floor.

"George," began Plummer evenly, "Club-Foot George has told me that you made a killing recently over on the Stinking Water. That Dutchman, you know, and Club-Foot is afraid there will be trouble over it. You are apt to be careless when you are drinking. I think you had better clear out for a while. They are talking, I hear."

"To hell with them," growled Ives. "Who are you going to appoint as deputy sheriff in Virginia City?"

"Jack Gallagher."

"Good," applauded Ives. "Jack is a splendid choice; and who will be deputy here?"

"Dillingham, for one; then I shall appoint Buck Stinson and Ned Ray," said Plummer.

"Ha, ha, ha!" laughed Ives. "Then you tell me to clear out for a time. Why?"

"Because I fear the miners. Remember what happened on the other side, and get out for a few months."

"No, sir, I'll stay here. They can't get *me*," boasted Ives. "Is Dillingham our kind of a man?"

"Not exactly, but I think it is a wise move to deputize him. He has been here for some time. We can handle the situation, even with him as a deputy."

"Yes, you bet we can. If Mr. Dillingham gets nosey, we can lose him in the willows. There are a lot of lost ones in the willows along the Stinking Water."

"How many of the boys are in Alder?" asked Plummer.

"Oh, almost twenty. Long John is camped in Daylight Gulch, and Alex Carter, Whiskey Bill, Dutch John and Hayes Lyons are at the Cold Springs. Besides, there are a bunch at the Daly ranch."

"Tell them to stay away from me," said Plummer. "I will let you know when there is anything worthwhile going on, and I want to be kept informed of what they are doing. But be careful not to arouse suspicion by crowding into Bannack or advertising the fact that I am a friend."

Ives started, but checked himself. "Your gun hand is pretty well used up, isn't it, Henry?" he suggested.

Plummer thought he caught a threat in the words. Quick as a cat springs, he whipped out a six-shooter and poked its muzzle against Ives' ribs. Startled, Ives sprang aside. "My, but you're touchy," he muttered.

"Well, be careful of your words. I am still chief, and mean to hold my position. One hand is as good as another," he said. He had been watching Ives and waiting for an opportunity to tame him, and crippled though he was, he had seized it to good advantage.

At length Ives laughed. "I believe you are quicker with your left hand than you were with your right," he conceded with feigned admiration.

"Long ago I taught my left hand to be useful when its mate was suffering," said Plummer. "It comes in handy now to be able to go back to it and find it able."

"Well, I'll be riding," said Ives. "I'm going to the Daly ranch," and he went out.

Without commenting on having drawn his gun on George Ives, Henry Plummer, turning to Bill Bunton, said, "I'm going to have a look at the Massey place, now. You had better not accompany me."

He found Massey's agent at Goodrich's Saloon, and after visiting the four-room well-built cabin, set on a bare knoll at the end of and a little back from the main street, he bought the place and paid for it. Then with his usual zeal, he began to furnish it as lavishly as he could. Before noon carpenters were at work building shelves and laying floors. And when they had finished the small jobs there, he set them to building a scaffold on which to hang Jack Horan, who had sometime since been condemned to death for the murder of Keeley. He was determined to execute Horan as quickly as possible. He believed that his prompt action in hanging the convicted man would establish him as a worthy official in the eyes of those who had selected Jeff Durly to run against him; and, even while part of his thoughts were employed with making a home for Elizabeth, he was planning to take Horan's life.

The next day he was again busy about the house. He forgot nothing. Even a clock, an article difficult to obtain, ticked cozily on a shelf in a clean little room of the new home. A Chinaman scrubbed and cleaned all day, and the yard was relieved of its litter, so that when dark came the place was ready for Elizabeth. But alone in his cabin that night he spent the hours as he had those of the night before, in pain and with misgivings, for he had come to distrust himself—most of all to fear that dread moment which might sometime come, with her so near him—when she would find him out.

When morning came he was gone, and not a soul knew where.

25

There is no doubt that Henry Plummer had intended to lead a clean life with Elizabeth Bryman. But even before he left Bannack to make her his wife, he had realized that he was too deeply entangled to completely extricate himself from the coils of his old associations. His encounter with George Ives had shown him very plainly that he must still be chief. In all probability, his pride would never have allowed him to yield his control over the gang. At any rate, it was clear that to attempt such a thing would mean his end. But he believed he could so manage his affairs that Elizabeth would not lose her regard for him. He would be careful. He would be as clean as he could. He would keep apart from his men. And she would not guess his duplicity.

His wound he could explain, and did. She pitied him, petted and pampered him under the belief that he had been a victim of lawlessness, and that his life had been spared to her by a miracle. That he had been elected sheriff by an overwhelming majority was a warrant for his good standing in the eyes of other men, and she became his wife with pride in her young heart. She was quick to see that other men showed deference for her husband, and did not guess that as time went on it was often a respect born of fear and distrust—an unpronounceable something about him which induced them to submit to his will. That strange thing, too, was upon herself—that feeling she had tried to explain in the barn where Badger the wolfhound had lain crippled. She could not name it. She was sure of his love, sure that she loved him, and yet she could not suppress a feeling which she called fear whenever he caressed her. It bothered her, this ghostly, unnameable thing, and no matter how bravely she strove to put it down—and at times succeeded—it persisted. "I'm silly," she told herself over and over again. "He's a perfectly splendid husband, and the handsomest man I know."

Henry Plummer himself was truly happy. Every minute of time he could spare he spent in the house with Elizabeth, and he had told her of his great happiness every day since they had left the Bailey home on the Sun River. He did not wish ever to be away from her, but there were many things to demand his attention. A week after they had settled in their home in Bannack, he spent an entire day at a ranch which he owned on the Rattlesnake. It was there he kept a swift saddle horse, and he went there from time to time to exercise him.

The snow had disappeared and, although the ground remained frozen, the days were clear and bright. The sun feigned the warmth of summer throughout the hours of daylight, and when the nights came they were keen and starlit until the approach of dawn.

This was Elizabeth's first day alone in her own home, and after doing her housework she sat by the sitting room window overlooking the rambling mining camp that stretched along the crooked way of Grasshopper Creek. She knew nothing of mining and little of the ways of miners. The unsightly heaps of tailings piled along the sluices, the idle claims that had been abandoned for the winter, seemed to her the debris of a deserted quarry, and yet she knew that in washing the gravel in the piles the miners had found gold. Down the street between the rows of cabins, store buildings and tents, men were going in and coming out of saloons, gambling houses and dance halls—always night and day she could hear the strains of dance music, loud and often very ugly. Stages came and went away, leaving men in Bannack or taking them to the other camps in Alder Gulch. She wondered how far away the famous diggings could be and if she would ever see them. All was bustle and stir in the street, but in the diggings where the miners had found the wherewithal to enable them to live through the coming winter, all was silent, mussy— a tumbling jumble of stone piles, sluice boxes, rockers, and empty tents. Beyond, the mountain peaks were whitened and their whiteness abruptly cut off a little way from their summits under the bluest sky in the wide world. Along Grasshopper Creek the quaking aspens were bare and she tried to picture how they would look in the spring with fresh green leaves. She and Henry would be watching them come out. A little flame of joy shot up through her.

At last her eyes wandered from the camp and the diggings and out along the road that led to Salt Lake City, whence much in the way of supplies came into Bannack. Suddenly she rose and shaded her eyes with her hand. A snakelike body seemed to be crawling along the winding road towards the camp. It was not a train of wagons. It must be a pack train, she thought. She went to the door that faced the valley below. A man down in the street ran into a saloon and then popped out again, followed by a dozen more. The man began to point excitedly at the moving pack train. A crowd gathered about him; and a cheer broke out at the sight of the oncoming, heavily laden animals, swinging strangely under their burdens of goods for Bannack merchants and miners. The street became packed with men, and the cheering was loud when into the camp there padded twenty loaded camels. Camels in Bannack! Elizabeth could not believe it. Camels from the desert of Sahara packing food to gold miners in Montana. Yet there they were before her.

"Excuse me, lady," said a voice beside her.

She started, frightened, and backed into the house as her eyes fell upon a coarse-looking man with a crippled foot.

"Oh, you startled me so!" she said in a voice that trembled.

"I—excuse me, but is Mr.—the sheriff at home?"

"No, sir. He is at his ranch on the Rattlesnake," she told him, partly closing the door.

"I'll see him this evenin' in town, no doubt," said the man, moving away.

Elizabeth closed the door and locked it. Then she tiptoed to the window and watched the man go down the hill to the street where the camels were being unpacked.

It was nearly dark when Plummer reached home. Elizabeth, in a frilled apron which her mother had made for her, was waiting, supper all prepared. She flew to unlock the door.

"Have you been lonesome, Betty dear?" he asked, kissing her.

"Yes, indeed I have, Henry. A man came to see you, an awful-looking man with a turned foot—and oh, what do you suppose came to town today? Guess!"

Plummer smiled. "I don't know," he said. "What was it, a band of Indians?"

"No. Camels! Camels! Real live camels, Henry."

"They are overdue, and had better be getting back to the country below Salt Lake before a bad storm comes. Our winters here wouldn't suit camels, do you think?"

"Overdue? Have camels ever been here before?" she asked, as though she had been robbed of a find.

"Yes, dear, once, anyhow. They used them in Nevada and in California, too, but they won't do. You were not frightened by the camels, were you, Betty?"

"No; but that man! Who was he, Henry?"

"His name is Lane, he told me. He rode over to the ranch. It's nothing but a horse stealing case, dear."

"Was he the thief?" she asked, pointing her finger at him.

"He declared not," laughed Plummer. "The coffee smells so good and you look so sweet, and I'm so hungry and happy," he finished, drawing her to him.

"Supper is ready, too, and you are late, Lord High Sheriff, and Lady Sheriff has been waiting ever so long. And do you know that you always wear your hat in the house, my dear?"

"Do I?"

"You do."

"It's a habit. I've been so much out of doors. In fact, I like to wear my hat, Betty, if you don't mind."

"How funny! But of course I don't mind—much."

He tossed the offending hat upon a chair and sat down at the table. She stooped to kiss him gratefully and brushed his hair back from his forehead.

"Please don't do that, dear!" he said, jerking his head away, and something in his voice startled her. She sat down at the table opposite him with her eyes bent upon the plate before her.

"How wonderfully you have cooked this meat, Betty," he said striving to hide his displeasure.

"I'm so glad you like it," she answered, but his rebuke had wounded her and he knew it. The words which had stung her had been wrenched from him by dread, and he would have given anything he possessed to be able to recall them. It was the man in the mirror who had spoken them, not Elizabeth's husband, her lover. He sought desperately for a way to placate her, to wipe away the hurt he had done her.

"I have bought for you the prettiest horse in the whole territory, Betty," he said finally, after the silence between them had been long.

"Have you?" she asked, trying to show interest.

"Yes. He is a blood bay single footer, gentle as a kitten, and with plenty of life. I hope you will like him. We will go riding together one of these days, before it gets too cold."

"Where is he, Henry?"

"At the ranch. You may have him any day. I will bring him here for your inspection the next time I go out there."

"May I go with you the next time?"

"Of course, if you want to go, dear. I wish I might help you do the dishes, but with one hand it wouldn't work, I'm afraid," he added, as they rose from the table.

Elizabeth began to gather up the dishes. Her cheeks were flushed and her pretty mouth drooped. Suddenly he seized her and held her almost roughly against his breast. "You *do* love me, Betty, don't you?" he begged.

Elizabeth, beginning to cry, flung her arms about his neck. "Oh, yes! Henry," she assured him. "I do!"

"Forever and ever, Betty?"

"Oh, yes," earnestly, "forever." And then they kissed each other.

Jack Horan was to be hanged in the morning. Plummer did not tell Elizabeth of this. He rose early and went directly to the jail where the condemned man was a prisoner. Summoning his deputies and a doctor, and followed by a motley crowd of people, he led Horan to the scaffold. He had everything planned. There was no delay—no hitch—and the trap was sprung by the sheriff himself. When the doctor pronounced Horan dead, Plummer ordered the body buried. The affair did not consume an hour, although it was the first legal execution in Bannack. Plummer had taken prompt steps to carry out the sentence of the miners' court, and the people felt reassured that at last they had elected a sheriff who would end the lawlessness in the territory. The scaffold would stand as a warning to evildoers—a monument to law and order in Bannack. There could be no question of that. The hanging of Jack Horan was acclaimed by honest men as proof that a law-and-order sheriff had at last been elected, and Plummer had foreseen this result clearly. The fact was that there had been need of hasty action to arrest suspicion, for Club-Foot George had sought Plummer on the day before because of trouble in Virginia City.

Dillingham, the newly appointed deputy sheriff, was dead—killed by members of Plummer's band because he had warned an acquaintance, a man named Washington Stapleton, that he had been marked for robbery on his way to Virginia City. Stapleton had in turn told the men who were to travel with him, and some one of their number had talked. Such confidences, when violated, travel fast and far, and several of Plummer's men had heard.

Meanwhile, Plummer, not aware that Dillingham's life was in danger from his own men, had sent him to Virginia City as deputy sheriff to recover some stolen horses which rumor said were there. Dillingham was quick to locate the missing horses, but needing assistance in taking them and not knowing that his brother deputies were members of the gang of road agents nor that he had been condemned to death by them for warning Stapleton, he sought their aid.

The miners' court was in session. Having concluded that his brother officers would be in attendance upon the court, Dillingham made his way to a rudely constructed lodge beside Alder Creek where Dr. Steele, a highly respected citizen, sat as judge, while by his side, acting as clerk of the court, was Charley Forbes, one of Plummer's bandits. Such was the true status of society at the time.

Pushing his way through the crowd of miners gathered there to listen to the court's proceedings, Dillingham beckoned to Buck Stinson and Jack Gallagher, both deputy sheriffs, both members of Plummer's gang, and both in close attendance upon the court. Stinson saw and answered the signal and, rising from his seat, crossed behind the judge to whisper to Charley Forbes, who with no excuse to the court followed Stinson outside, leaving Jack Gallagher in the lodge. They had sworn to hunt Dillingham down and kill him. Now they were saved the trouble of hunting. He had come to them.

Another of the gang, Hayes Lyons, who was in the crowd about the court, had seen Dillingham and was already with him when Stinson and Forbes came up. They did not wait nor parley. "Dillingham, we want to see you," said Hayes Lyons. "Come this way."

Thinking that Buck Stinson, his brother deputy, had something of importance to impart, Dillingham followed the three ruffians to a spot some twenty yards from the outskirts of the crowd, where Lyons suddenly turned upon him and said, "Take back what you said to Stapleton, damn you!"

"Why boys, I didn't mean—"

"Quick!" cried Stinson, stepping close to Dillingham. "Out with it."

Forbes called out, "Don't shoot!" and fired as he spoke, and Dillingham fell dead at the feet of the three outlaws and within fifty yards from the judge on his bench. The whole thing had been so quickly executed that eyewitnesses were scarcely aware of what had happened until, ordered by the court, Jack Gallagher hastened to arrest his brethren, assisted by miners appointed by the outraged court. Jack Gallagher, quick to see trouble for the gang ahead, rushed in and took Forbes' gun, secretly reloading it while he pretended to search the prisoner. There was great excitement and cries of "*hang them!*" But as Buck Stinson was a deputy sheriff and Charley Forbes clerk of the court, these cries were easily smothered out of deference to the position they held.

"Hold them safe until we learn the truth," ordered the court when the cries had subsided, and the crowd suffered the men to be hurried away by a guard and held in a half-finished log cabin that stood on a hill overlooking Daylight Gulch. Meanwhile witnesses were examined and the case tried before a jury that retired at dusk with the evidence.

The gang, of course, did not intend to leave the prisoners to the mercy of the court, so an attempt at rescue was made. Late at night the cry of a nighthawk was repeated again and again from the willows in the gulch below the cabin, and Charley Forbes began to sing. The guards became alarmed. Nighthawks had gone south for the winter.

"Stop that singing!" one of them ordered.

"I won't," declared Forbes and continued his song.

"Stop it this instant, or we'll tie and gag you," threatened the guard, entering the cabin with a rope.

Forbes ceased his singing and sullenly sought a corner where he sat down muttering. Reinforcements were sent for and the prisoners held until the next day, when the court reconvened.

"What is the verdict?" demanded the judge, rising from his seat.

"Guilty!" was the cry.

"But wait!" demanded a voice. "Charley Forbes' gun was loaded when it was taken away, and we heard him say, 'Don't shoot!' before the shot was fired. Let's not be too fast, men!"

The crowd murmured. Men with material already in their hands with which to erect a makeshift scaffold looked sheepishly at each other. Then somebody laughed aloud.

"Turn 'em loose!" called a man far back in the crowd, and the cry was taken up by dozens of voices until, swerved from wrath to mirth at its escape from taking human life with its community hands, it assented. "Turn 'em loose!" it cried.

So Plummer's men were free; but he saw the terrible threat in the crowd's action. He well knew that the winter months ahead were the most dangerous ones for him and his kind. They enforced idleness upon the brave spirits who in softer seasons sought to make new discoveries of gold among the uncharted hills and gulches, wandering far and wide under the urge of the wilderness in the mistaken belief that it was only the gold they wanted. Warned by the cruel weather, these men reluctantly abandoned the quest until again the pussy willows should show their silvery selves to the baby summer; and now they were gathered in the camps for shelter, and would form strange companionships that knew little of genuine esteem and nothing at all of real intimacy. Before their fires they could sit and wait and dream, build anew their filmy castles, and with unfound nuggets of virgin gold pave the streets of their undiscovered Eldorado. Moreover, the miners themselves could not work their claims in the camps, and, huddled in their cabins or tents with chance callers or acquaintances, might establish real friendships. Then confidence, the stranger, would visit them inevitably, suspicion might find voice, and suspicion was the dread spectre to Henry Plummer now.

26

How strange and unfathomable are the workings of fate, and how unexpectedly she rings up her curtain to expose agencies which she has set to serve her ends.

The morning sun had hardly climbed the Tobacco Root range of mountains far toward the east from Grasshopper Diggings, five days after the execution of Jack Horan, when a miner, on his way to the blacksmith shop with two dull picks across his shoulder, saw Doctor Glick come out of Cass Masterson's cabin and softly close the door behind him. There was something in his manner which caught the miner's attention, and he turned from his course in order to speak to the physician, whose kindly eyes had made him many friends in Bannack. Doctor Glick was not overly tall, and an inclination to stoutness, together with the full beard he wore, made him appear shorter than he actually was. Having taken a few steps from the little cabin, he was standing with bowed head and hands thrust deeply into his trousers' pockets. His thoughts were heavy, and no wonder. He was the unwilling confidant of murderers and highwaymen, and just now a piece of their handiwork had thoroughly stirred him. Where would it all end, he wondered angrily. The night before, just after he had fallen asleep, he had been wakened by a hard-ridden horse dashing up to his door. Urged by some premonition of danger, he had crawled from his bed to look out of the window. A horse stood in front of the cabin door with sides heaving, and the next moment its rider had sprung to the ground and the doctor heard him pounding loudly on his door.

"Hello!" he had called. "Who's there?"

"It's I, Henry Plummer, Doctor," a voice had answered promptly. "Will you come to the door?"

Without making a light he had opened the door and, recognizing Henry Plummer, had asked, "What's wrong, sheriff?"

"Can you come with me, Doctor?" Plummer had urged. "It's important, or I would not ask it at this hour of the night."

"Where do you want me to go?"

"Not far," Plummer had promised. "A man has been shot, and the wound needs attention at once. I will go with you, Doctor. I'll get a horse for you, and be back here in a few minutes. Will you go?"

"Yes, of course, if it is important; but first I must dress."

"I'll get the horse; but please hurry, Doctor," urged Plummer, and the doctor had hurried into some clothes. In a few minutes Plummer was back with an extra mount, and together they rode away towards the Rattlesnake. Plummer did not talk on the way. After they had ridden several miles through the sharp cold of the night, the doctor had broken the silence with, "Where are we going, Mr. Plummer?"

"Never mind, and follow me," Plummer had returned shortly. "We are almost there."

The curtness of the sheriff's answer had not escaped Doctor Glick, but he had continued to follow until, drawing up near a grove of cottonwood trees on the Rattlesnake, Henry Plummer swung down and tied his horse to a sapling. There he motioned the doctor to dismount, then ordered him to follow and led the way into a thicket.

Among the willows not far from the bank a carefully screened fire was burning. The doctor saw seven men about it, all with black handkerchiefs tied just under their eyes, or with blackened faces. Plummer, without speaking to any of them, walked to a blanket upon which a man was lying and, bending over him, motioned the doctor. "This is your patient," he said. His words were spoken in the tone he always used when under stress and the doctor, already aware of the danger of his surroundings, doubtfully approached the sufferer, who immediately drew the end of the blanket over his face, completely hiding it.

"Get at it, and see what you can do. It's the right leg, and it's a bad wound. Attend him and then we'll go back to Bannack," said Plummer.

Doctor Glick had obediently treated the wounded man, removing the bullet and bandaging the leg. During the operation no one spoke except when he asked for assistance. "Is that all you can do for him?" asked Plummer, when he had finished.

"That is all, Mr. Plummer," he had told him.

"Then we had better be going." And without a word to the patient or any of the men about the fire, Henry Plummer led the way back to the horses. There he suddenly wheeled and poked a gun under the doctor's nose. "Now you know all," he challenged. "Those are my men—some of my men. I am their chief. If you utter one word of what you have seen or know, I will kill you—kill you as I would a mad dog. That is all. Get on your horse, and let's get back to town."

Back in Bannack, Plummer had given him a handful of nuggets and ridden away to his own home.

And so the doctor knew that what he had guessed before was true. It was all a terrible business. Yet what could he do?

"Morning, Doctor," greeted the miner who had been watching him.

"Good morning," returned the doctor.

"What's wrong in there, Doctor? Is Cass sick?"

"He has been shot—mortally wounded. He can't live. He cleaned up the other day, and last night two men held him up. He went for his gun and they shot him—both of them. He won't live until night."

"Oh, my God! That's awful. Is he conscious?"

"Yes. Somebody must stay with him. I hoped that you would. You'll see that he's not left alone, poor fellow?"

"Of course, Doctor. Of course." And leaning his picks against the logs of the cabin, the miner brushed the soil from his shirt. "I'll go right in an' see him," he said. "He's a good man, Cass is."

"I'll come back in a few hours," promised the doctor. "I can do little for him. Don't let him talk much, and be careful who listens. If you know too much they'll get you, too. This is a terrible condition to live in, but we must make the best of it," said the doctor. Having given this advice, he hurried away to minister to other patients. He had not come to the mines to practice his profession, but he had found little time to look for gold.

The miner watched him ride away for a moment and then silently opened the cabin door and entered. At first he could not see his way in the dark interior. There was no window but, when his eyes had become accustomed to the dim light, his heavy boots began to move across the dirt floor towards the bunk in a far corner, where a man lay motionless. Bending low over the form on the bunk, the miner spoke softly.

"Hello, Cass, old boy. It's me, Bill—Bill Thompson. I saw the doctor, and he told me you'd been shot. Don't try to talk. I've come to camp with you, Cass, and to help you what I can. I'll build a little fire, I reckon. It'll be more cheerful." Going to the fireplace, he whittled shavings from a pine stick and struck a match, whistling softly as he watched the young flames spring into a bright blaze. The whistling was a strained effort to cheer the dying man, who could not know that salt tears were wetting the weather-roughened cheeks of the young whistler while he knelt at the fireplace, dreading to return to the bunk.

The wounded man stirred and moaned, mumbling words which

the miner did not catch. He hurried to the bunk, eager to be of real service. "What is it, Cass?" he whispered, bending over the sufferer, who was feeling under his soiled pillow as though searching for something here.

"I'll get it, Cass. I'll get it, boy," and the miner drew a leather wallet from beneath the pillow and handed it to his comrade. Masterson, fumbling with the strap, at last got it open. His fingers poked blindly among its contents and drew forth a tintype of a woman and a young girl of perhaps thirteen, which he held before his eyes a moment and laid upon his breast with a sigh. A second time his fingers searched the wallet, and again finding what they sought, handed a slip of paper to the miner. Thompson walked back to the firelight to read it. It was a receipt for dues in a Masonic lodge in the states. Bill Thompson whirled around, and grasping Cass Masterson's hand, pressed it as a brother Mason. "Why didn't you ever say so, Cass?" he whispered.

"Why didn't *you*, Bill?" with a sigh.

"I don't know, Cass. Seemed as though there couldn't be very many of us here, and so I never said anything to anybody. Are there any more of them that you know of, Cass?"

"No; but if there are enough, I want them to bury me, Bill."

"Who shot you, Cass?"

"I'm not sure, but I think it was Bill Bunton and George Ives. We're living in an awful country, Bill. There's no law, and we are strangers—all afraid of each other, that's the trouble. We should have found a way to get together—Masons, I mean."

"I'll find a way, Cass. Don't talk too much. Is this your wife and child?" he held up the picture.

"Yes. It will kill her. Take the wallet. You know my claim. See that they get a square deal. I'm getting blind. Give me a drink of water, Bill."

Thompson hurried for a cup of water and raised Masterson's head gently. "They got my cleanup," he gasped. "See to them—my wife and child—as I would for yours if—"

A bloody froth came to his lips. He choked and fought for breath a moment, and then lay still. Bill Thompson gently laid him down and wiped away the red froth from his whitened lips. "Oh, but you'll pay for this, you dogs," he groaned. "You'll pay, you'll pay, you dogs —you murderers!"

A burning log fell from its place in the fire; Thompson crossed the room to replace it. A thin cloud of blue smoke filled the cabin and he opened the door to let it out. Then he searched the room, gathered whatever he thought might be of use to the wife and child of Cass Masterson and, with the wallet in his pocket, sat down at the rude table and wrote:

NOTICE

All Master Masons are requested to meet at
Cass Masterson's cabin at one o'clock tomorrow
(Thursday) afternoon to bury him.

Signed,
A Master Mason.

When he had finished, he went out of the cabin and down to Goodrich's Saloon, where in a conspicuous place outside the door he tacked the paper, wondering what would be the result. He had walked but a short distance on his way back when a man called after him, "Oh, partner! Just a minute, please."

Bill Thompson stopped and waited.

"Did you post that notice?" asked the stranger, coming up.

"Yes; I did. What of it?"

"I'm a Mason," said the man, extending his hand.

"The deuce you are!" cried Thompson, grasping the man's proffered hand warmly. "Maybe you are. Come with me and prove it."

And together they went back to Cass Masterson's cabin, where throughout the night they watched their dead brother, strengthened in the thought that they had met and that there might be many more of the craft scattered through the camp.

Downtown a crowd soon gathered about the notice. Men looked into each other's eyes but spoke no word. They read the notice and turned away. Others took their places. But there was a strangeness about it all—something mysterious, and when morning came the paper was gone. Some hand, sensing trouble, perhaps, had torn it from its place in the dark of night while Bill Thompson and a brother Mason watched by the fire in Cass Masterson's cabin.

Morning came at last, and with it a knock on the door. Bill Thompson opened it. A man said, "I read the notice and I'm a Master Mason."

"Good. Come in and prove it," requested Bill. "Here's my receipt for my dues, and here's my friend's here, and here's poor old Cass Masterson's receipt, too. Look 'em over, and then if you are satisfied we'll begin on you."

The stranger satisfied Thompson that he was a Mason, and the three prepared to meet and examine any others who might come to the cabin. Before noon the room was crowded with Masons from nearly every state in the union. Each man was formally examined, and then, having posted guards about the cabin, Bill Thompson asked if there was a past Master present.

Four men held up their hands and one was chosen to preside. A lodge was opened, the first one in the territory. At the grave thirty Masons paid their last respects to Cass Masterson under the curious eyes of the uninitiated, some of whom rejoiced at the gathering which meant so much for law and order. When the Master had delivered his oration, the others, leaving two men to fill the grave, marched back to the Masterson cabin, where again guards were placed to keep off strangers while men bared their hearts and told of their fears. Names were freely used, for the mystic tie which bound them together made them strong in their determination to put a stop to the reign of terror that had so long made the mines a hell.

"We must find a leader," said Thompson. "I know the man for the place. He's not a Mason, but that don't make any difference to us nor to him. His name is Jim Williams. I know he's the man, for I saw him in action once.

"We were crossing the plains—fifty wagons of us. There was a bad man in the party—a man who was a killer, and a great bully besides. He was without fear and when he was drinking was a demon. We couldn't rid ourselves of him, but had to suffer him to do about as he pleased. One night in a small settlement he killed two men and boasted of it in a most heartless fashion, but there wasn't any law, and we were forced to go with the man in our company. His name was Slade—Joseph Slade—now over in Alder Gulch.

"Well, one night one of our wagon bosses died, and an election was proposed to select his successor. But Slade strides into the firelight and with a vile oath declares that there won't be any election—that he has elected himself to succeed the dead wagon boss, and that settled it. 'Get back to your own fires—all of you!' he roared, pulling a six-shooter.

"There was a rush to get away, and an hour afterwards the camp was quiet, cowed. Slade's fire was next to mine, and at daylight I was up and stirring. So was Slade, who began issuing orders as wagon boss. We had yoked our cattle when Jim Williams came to Slade's fire, alone. I saw and heard him speak.

"'Slade,' he says, leaning carelessly against a wagon wheel, 'I understand you have announced there would be no election to select a new wagon boss—that you were going to be wagon boss yourself.'

"'I have, by God!' defied Slade, springing towards him with a hand on his gun. 'I have, an' it goes. No —— —— —— —— can stop me!'

"I saw Jim Williams' eyes. I shan't ever forget the awfulness of the light that came into them. They weren't blue any longer—they flamed, and Slade seemed to wither under their fire.

"'There *will* be an election right *here* and *now,* and the man selected will act as wagon boss. Do you understand me, Slade?'

"It was all over with.

"'Yes, sir, I guess I do,' stammered the killer. He turned and walked away, beaten like a cur with those blue eyes.

"Let us go about our business quietly. I will tell Jim Williams there is a decent element in the diggings, and that it stands for law and order. Let every man here seek out our brethren. Be sure of your men and then tell them how we've got together, at last. Let's not talk. Let us keep still, but watch everybody. Let's remember names, and meet here again a week from today."

So they dispersed; and suddenly, as though the winds had borne a warning to wrongdoers, men ceased to brag of evil deeds. Fear had come to many who, knowing nothing about the Masonic fraternity, guessed wildly at the future and, whispering, discussed the burial of Cass Masterson with others of their ilk.

Henry Plummer, moving about the camp in his new role of sheriff, was deeply concerned. The Masonic meeting had startled him, for in it he recognized his own danger. Whenever men who because of mutual ties—even though they be merely of a social nature—gather together, a united front is apt to be formed in some common cause.

He pretended elation, however, and expressed it wherever his words would reach Masonic ears. He was glad of the meeting. It would help him to clean up the camp, men told each other. And at once there was less of rowdyism on the street and in saloons.

Two days after the burial of Cass Masterson, Henry Plummer, superbly mounted, met Bill Thompson just outside the town, and affecting interest in a pair of gloves which Thompson wore, stopped his horse to examine them. "By the way, Bill," he said, trying a glove on his left hand while his right in a sling held fast to the buckskin gauntlet, "I'm delighted over the gathering of Masons here." Then, dropping his voice and giving it a confidential tone and looking straight into Thompson's eyes, he said, "I've always wanted to become a Mason, myself." "How can I do it, Bill?"

"By petitioning a lodge, as we all do, Mr. Plummer," answered Thompson, who had heard nothing against Plummer's character. "Of course there isn't any lodge here," he added, "and we can't make a man a Mason; but I believe we'll have a lodge in Bannack soon."

Plummer reached and laid his hand on Thompson's arm. "When a lodge is finally instituted here, take my name to it, will you, Bill?" he asked, deeply serious. "I'll furnish the best of references from back in the States," he added as he gathered up his bridle reins.

"Of course," replied Thompson. "But it will be some time before we can hope to get a charter or even a dispensation. When we do, though, I'll let you know," he promised.

"Thank you," smiled Plummer. "And just look upon me as your friend, you Masons. Will you?"

"Surely." Turning in his own saddle, Bill Thompson watched Henry Plummer ride easily away.

27

Elizabeth was happy whenever her husband was with her at home. She hummed contentedly about her small household, finding delight in her cookery and in maintaining the neatness he so much admired. But there were long nights when he was away—called suddenly by duty, he told her—and their dreary loneliness had become a terror to her. They were telling on him, too, and she was quick to see that his face, naturally pale, and immobile because of the vigilance he kept over himself, had grown paler and thinner and more drawn, with the hardened look that wind and storm give to any human countenance set long against them. She had ventured to protest—to suggest that his deputies might take most of these disagreeable trips instead of him. He had only smiled and kissed her, thankful that she did not know his night rides were made to direct his gang in breaking the law he had been elected to uphold; for the gang had sent for him more and more frequently of late to direct especially difficult robberies.

The Lovejoys, to whom Elizabeth had secretly looked for friends when she should go to Bannack to live, had long since gone. Mrs. Lovejoy had fallen ill with the first cold weather and, much frightened, old Mr. Lovejoy had made arrangements to leave with a party who were going to Salt Lake City within a week. The rigor and privation of the mining camps had weakened even the spirit of vengeance, and Mr. Lovejoy had left with only the faint comfort that Plummer would undoubtedly be elected and that the lawless element would be punished.

There were few women in Bannack. Elizabeth had made no friends there. Her husband had not encouraged her to do so, and had even warned her against chance acquaintance in mining camps, so that for her there was no company save his own.

The winter was coming on. She had heard much of winter in the mountains, and each cloudy day left deeper snow on the mountaintops and an added feeling of loneliness in her heart, shut off as she was from other folk. Bannack frightened her with its strings of fragile dwellings and log cabins, among which few but roughly garbed men ever passed. There is no season so depressing as when winter seems to struggle for mastery over weakening autumn's days—when the brighter sunshine is fickle and every passing storm drags the snowline on the mountain sides down and nearer to the valleys. This dread of winter in the mountains, which had grown upon her like some embellished tale of torments told to frighten a child, and her husband's night rides, which she felt must be endured, weighed heavily upon her. On dark and cloudy nights, or when the sky was sprinkled with stars brighter than any she had ever seen, and he was away, she put out her light to sit by the uncurtained window and wait—wait, shivering in dread of her own loneliness on other such nights to come. An alarm at the door, the sight of a horseman at dusk, filled her with dismay, for always her husband went away, either with the caller, whom she never saw clearly, or very soon after he was gone. And always it was in the chill gray of morning when he returned, paler and more worn, but without a word of explanation to her of his night's adventures. Once when he had been gone longer than usual and her wild imaginings had been especially tortuous, he had returned in a dishevelled state. There was even blood on his shirt where a bullet had creased his shoulder, and a new terror arose to plague her when he left her there alone. He made light of his wound, laughing at "the clumsiness of some men with weapons," and led her to believe that his hurt had come from a gun in the hands of a careless friend. He still carried an arm in a sling, since Crawford's bullet was embedded deeply there, so that he seemed to her too weak and unfit for the arduous night rides.

One evening when the candles were lighted and they had settled down at a game of cribbage, someone rapped upon the door.

"There! Oh, don't go, Henry, please!" she begged. "Send a deputy. It's so dark and windy."

However, his hand felt swiftly for his gun, and rising he went to the door and opened it. She heard a voice whisper a few words in the darkness and saw her husband go outside and close the door. She was alone in the house.

There was no light in the kitchen and she hurried on tiptoe to its darkened window to look out. She saw her husband and a large man walking away from the light of the sitting room window and thanked heaven that the stranger was afoot. She thought it presaged good— that her husband would not go away. Ashamed of spying, she turned back into the lighted sitting room and picked up a stocking she was knitting.

When they had walked twenty yards from the house outside, Plummer turned to the visitor and asked, "What do you want, Boone?"

Even Henry Plummer never looked upon that face without thinking with disgust of the deeds which had marked it. Boone Helm was of all his men the wickedest, the most heartless and brutal. He was guilty of every crime—even of killing and eating a traveling companion.

"There's somethin' goin' on," whispered the brute out of one corner of his ugly mouth. "Somethin' queer over yonder on Yankee Flat. Men is goin' into the old Masterson cabin an' none's a-comin' out."

"How many have gone in, and who were they?" Plummer asked.

"'Bout a dozen so far, an' I don't know none of 'em. But it's mighty quiet in there—no carousin' ner noise, so it's a meetin', shore's hell's afire."

Plummer bit off the end of a cigar. "Go on back downtown, Boone," he said. "Keep away from Yankee Flat, or the dark-lantern gentry might get you. Don't talk about the meeting, and as you see them tell the boys not to hold up or harm a Mason if they know it."

"Are them that's in Cass Masterson's cabin all Masons, do ye reckon?" Boone Helm asked, anxiously.

"I don't know, but I'm going to find out. Good night, Boone."

Helm turned away and Plummer stood watching his huge figure until it was gone from sight down the dark slope. Then he went back into the house. "I'm going downtown, Betty dear," he said, in answer to her apprehensive, questioning look, and putting on his hat continued, "Leave the cards just as they are, for I'll be back soon. Now don't you go and look at my hand or the deck while I'm gone," he added playfully, kissing her.

But, although he had spoken to Elizabeth ever so lightly, the gathering on Yankee Flat was absorbing him even as he closed the door and went out. "Damn them," he muttered, buttoning his sack coat. "They'll continue to meet now, the dark-lantern devils."

There was a bright moon in the sky, across which jagged white clouds were flying in the keen wind from the mountains. Henry Plummer kept as far from cabins and tents as he could in his course towards Yankee Flat, now and then meeting a miner, however, in spite of his care, for it was not yet nine o'clock. He was anxiously curious to see what manner of men were going at night to the meeting, to make sure that they were Masons. If they were, then the Masons were becoming active—too active. He congratulated himself on his wisdom in publicly expressing his sanction of their gathering for the Masterson funeral and for what he had said to Bill Thompson. Thompson was sure to report the sheriff's words to his brethren, he thought, and they would look upon him as a friend. He still had hopes that they were too few to hold together and that some way might be found to stop the meetings. If not, then he would join the

Masons and become a power there. His luck, his ability, and his official position were sure, he believed, to make him a leader in the fraternity. At any rate, once a member he could and would find followers there who would be valuable to him. With all this, however, there was a feeling of fear which, in spite of his belief in himself, he could not entirely put down.

The Masterson cabin was apart from the others on Yankee Flat, and near it on the south side a pile of house logs had been skidded in readiness for builders. With a quick look around, Plummer stole swiftly behind these and hid himself in the shadow of the pile, where with nothing between him and the cabin he settled down to watch its door in the moonlight. Red sparks were leaping from the chimney and one thin dart of light pierced through a chink in the logs, stabbing the frozen ground. He could hear no sound of talking. The cabin, dark save for the red sparks and shaft of light, was as though unoccupied. He smiled grimly, and his eyes looked away to where, under the moon, wagons with long sway-backed canvas covers, cabins and tents, staked horses, roving mules, and ponderous oxen were scattered thickly. He counted the lights for want of employment—more than two hundred—and many tents and cabins were darkened. "Lots of people here," he thought, with a glance at the darkened door of the Masterson cabin, "and how many are Masons, I wonder?"

Not a man passed the door, either coming or going, although he held his position for more than an hour. His fears, multiplied by the silence of the meeting, began to take definite shape. One thing occurred to him. If anything began to happen, he would send Elizabeth away. There were his people—her people would be better.

At last three men came out of the cabin, passing close to the pile of logs. Then in another moment there were four—then four more, then three, and so on until fifteen had come out of the cabin, the last leaving it in darkness. He had recognized only two, Bill Thompson and Wilbur F. Sanders, a young lawyer. They had come out together and passed very near him. He had tried in vain to catch a word of their earnest conversation.

When they had all gone out of sight he stood up, his ears tingling with the cold, and started back to his home. He was sure that the same men who had attended the Masterson funeral had tonight been in the Masterson cabin, excepting Sanders. Sanders had lived on

Yankee Flat, but was not in Alder Gulch. If the Masons had gathered in Bannack, they might also meet in Virginia City. Sanders might gather them there, and Plummer had a fearsome regard for Wilbur Sanders.

Once, about three weeks previous, when Plummer had been about to go upon a secret mission of his own, somehow the story had got abroad that he was going out with others to locate some silver lodes. He had denied it, but the rumor had persisted, and Sanders had come to him asking if he might join his party. Plummer could not permit Sanders to go with him, for his errand was a robbery. To rid himself of his company and yet leave him friendly, he had told him that he was going to the ranch on the Rattlesnake to secure some horses there. "But," he had laughingly added, "if I should by any chance run across a silver lode in my travels, I'll promise to locate a claim for you as your agent."

But after Plummer had got away from Bannack without him, Sanders had convinced himself that he had been fooled and, securing a mount, had tried to trail him. What followed he knew from Bill Bunton, who, in high glee at what he had termed a joke on Gallagher, had told him the facts. Bunton had wondered how much Sanders had guessed, for upon his return to Bannack Plummer had learned that a young man named Tilton, who had been robbed with a party which he and his men had plundered on that excursion, lived with Wilbur Sanders and his wife on Yankee Flat—that he had in fact come out with them from the East. As soon as he had learned this, he had gone boldly to Tilton and as sheriff asked him if he had recognized any of the highway men who had robbed him. The young man had had the good sense to reply that he had not. Plummer was not even yet convinced of the truth of his statement, and he feared that Sanders, after his experience at the ranch on the Rattlesnake, might begin to put two and two together.

Sanders had ridden from Bannack on a mule, the only mount he had been able to obtain, and after a vain attempt to follow Plummer had come at last to the ranch on the Rattlesnake where he fully expected to find him, but instead he had found Red Yager who, because the night was stormy, had allowed him to stop there. Sanders, not suspecting that he was in the robbers' stronghold, had spread his blanket before the fire and gone promptly to sleep, his booted feet projecting "a couple a' feet beyond his blankets," for young Sanders was a tall man indeed. Later on, Red Yager had retired and sometime after he too was asleep, somebody had pounded on the door. Red, getting up in a hurry, had taken a candle and double-barrelled shotgun from behind the bar and gone to the door, which he unbarred after assuring himself of the identity of his night visitor.

It was Jack Gallagher. He was in an ugly mood, and tramping in and throwing his saddle on the floor, he demanded meat and plenty of whisky, which Red supplied. The food and drink did not smooth his temper, however, and he next insisted upon trading his jaded horse for a fresh one. Sanders, wakened by Gallagher's boisterous talking, became interested in the horse trade. Perhaps as he listened from his bed he had suddenly associated Gallagher with the secret party of silver hunters, which he believed more than ever (since Plummer was not at the ranch) to be out somewhere in the night. He was a stranger to both Red Yager and Gallagher; and, in his anxiety to share in the new discoveries of silver mines, he rose on his elbow and asked, "Where's Plummer?"

It had been like a coal of fire in a keg of powder. With a snarl of rage, Jack Gallagher had sprung to the bedside and levelled his cocked six-shooter at Sanders' head. The young lawyer had lain looking helplessly into the Irishman's eyes when, as though timed to save him, the bar leaning against the door fell with a crash. Startled at the sound, Gallagher had gone off guard enough to turn his head. Instantly, Sanders had leaped from his blanket, ducked behind the bar, and come up with the double-barrelled shotgun cocked and pointed at Gallagher.

"Shoot! damn you, you've got the drop," Gallagher had husked, slowly unbuttoning and holding wide a soldier's overcoat he wore.

But Sanders had not shot. "No," he said. "I don't want to shoot, but if there's to be any shooting done here I want the first shot."

"By God," said Gallagher, relieved, "have a drink with me." And Sanders had taken the drink.

All night long, after returning to his blankets, Sanders must have heard the coming and going of the men of Plummer's gang. And then there was the robbery of Tilton, who was living in Sanders' house.

Plummer, no longer lost in thought, realized that unless Tilton had recognized him and told Sanders, there was no cause to worry yet. He was sure that not one of the fifteen men he had seen come out of the Masterson cabin suspected him in the least. Yes, he decided, he would join the Masons. It was the best and safest thing to do.

He was whistling merrily when he opened the door of his house. As he stepped into the warm wood-sweet kitchen, Elizabeth was putting the coffee pot on the shining stove. She flew to him. "You came back!" she beamed.

She put her soft arms around him and looked up into his eyes. "I've been thinking," she began. "Whatever's become of Mr. Cleveland, Henry dear? I've been going to ask you every day, but I kept forgetting."

He had expected this. He had wondered at her silence regarding Cleveland's absence, and had long ago fashioned a story explaining, even excusing it. Sometimes a carefully rehearsed falsehood that has seemed exactly suited to a possible future requirement, and that has been embellished with due regard to detail, will suddenly in the face of its long-expected engagement fall flat and refuse to be presented. It was so now. Henry Plummer's lie would not come to his tongue.

His arm slipped about her and, drawing her to him, he said, "Betty, a man does not always know who he is chumming with in this wild country, and sudden discoveries often make enemies of friends. I—" He broke off suddenly, as though his mind had been cleared of a mist that dulled it, and raising her face looked steadily into her eyes. "Will you promise me now that you will never again mention his name to me or to any other living soul—man, woman or child, Betty dear?"

"Why—yes," she faltered, "if—if you want me not to—even to you."

There was wonder in her wide blue eyes, but also a little fear. She did not like it when he looked at her so. It was nicer when they did not talk about things.

He kissed her lips. "It's better that way, Betty dearest," he assured her, his eyes staring at vacancy, as though some picture were there. "I hope that you will believe me when I tell you it is much better for us both never to mention his name, Betty. Do you?"

"Yes, oh yes, Henry," she assured him earnestly, her gentle hand feeling tenderly of his wounded arm.

"Come then, little gambler," he said gaily, tossing his hat away, "let's finish our game of cribbage while the coffee is making. Great land! I wouldn't think of leaving a hand of cards lying about in anybody's presence but yours," he told her as he led her to the table and seated her with the courtesy he never once forgot.

He knew how slender was the thread of his happiness and hers. How he longed to strengthen it and keep her an innocent believer in him, her husband.

28

The weather, now boisterous, now calm and beautiful with bright blue skies in which a cloud the bigness of a man's hand would have seemed a scar, appeared reluctant to bring the winter to the mines, although mining itself had ceased for the season. There had been flurries of snow, and the valleys had been white more than once since the equinoctial storms, but these threats of winter had passed taking the snows with them, so that only the higher mountains remained white. Men did not know the seasons of the section—and, as though it would frighten the weak from its domains, the wilderness hinted of terrors it did not possess. The camps were overflowing with miners and those who preyed upon them. Money was plentiful, and everywhere. The stagecoaches, often robbed, were making their regular trips bearing the mails from home and new adventurers to the mines. Still, traveling on the roads was risky and growing more dangerous each day, so that travelers were few unless they were a large company and well armed.

On the afternoon of the third day after the meeting in the Masterson cabin on Yankee Flat, two horsemen were climbing up a gulch in the Tobacco Root Mountains eastward from Bannack. Below them the Ruby Valley was bare of snow and yellow with waving grasses. Far off the Trappers and the Bloody Dicks were white and seemed to sit like a picture of winter on the valley, through which the Grasshopper flowed, as though two seasons were touching Bannack and waiting for it to choose between them. There was no snow on the trail that followed along the gulch's northern side, but white patches had lasted down deep in the gulch beside the creek which was sheltered from the sun during the shortening hours of day. Blue grouse rose from sunny spots with their startling whir of wings, and bluejays and Clark-crows and camp robbers and magpies flew with grating calls across the gulch from side to side, their plumage flashing in the sun, as the horsemen passed.

At length the two reached a small meadow on the edge of a deep slide of sharp shale bordering a cliff that towered more than a thousand feet above it, and came upon a roan mare and three Spanish mules grazing. The mare, startled, pranced to the center of her domain where, with the mules crowding close to her, she surveyed the horsemen with astonishment until they had crossed the meadow and turned up the creek.

Here they soon arrived at an arastra, its hurdy-gurdy wheel trailing heavy stone drags over a bed of granite within its tub. The horsemen pulled up to watch the faithful wheel at its work churning the reddish water in the tub to frothy whorls as the drags crushed the gold ore beneath them on the stony bed.

"Clever," said one of the horsemen, pointing to a clacker so arranged that at every revolution of the wheel it proclaimed aloud that all was well with the whole machine.

The speaker was a tall man, young like the majority of men in the camps, and rather heavy for the horse he rode. A pair of light blue eyes that seemed ready to laugh at the least excuse made men call him friend wherever he went. It would have been difficult to imagine him in a serious mood. He was Tom Henderson, high in the affairs of the miners' court at Bannack.

As they sat watching the arastra, a water ouzel came swiftly zigzagging down the creek and, alighting on a black boulder in midstream, began to sing in the sunlight that was flooding the meadow from the western sky. Clear and bewitchingly sweet, the tiny bird's song rose over the roar of the creek and growling of the arastra.

The other man sat straight in his saddle, with his head bent far forward to listen to it. He, too, had blue eyes, and while they were not so laughingly genial as Henderson's, nor so friendly, his face was strikingly honest and belonged to a lover of the out-of-doors. He was a small man—spare, even. His right hand, gloved, was tucked into the breast of his tightly buttoned coat, giving an impression of a pose as he sat straight in his saddle with his head bent. But it was not a pose.

An honest nature never poses. It was merely the manifestation of a state of mind that was habitual with him—a determination to set or follow an example—as though looking ahead in secret he constantly saw himself confronted by an emergency and had quickly set himself to overcome it. This characteristic had occasioned his nicknames, used interchangeably, Sanctimonious Bill, or Honest Bill. There was that in his thin, bearded face that promised fidelity to an adopted cause—and he was even now proving that his face did not belie his character, for the man was Bill Thompson of Bannack in search of Jim Williams.

"This must be his arastra," he said at last, as though grudging to break a pleasant spell cast upon him, when the ouzel ceased his song and, curtsying, sped away down the creek like a leaden bullet. His voice was agreeable, deeper than could be expected from so slight a frame. "Come on," he added, "his cabin can't be far off."

Within perhaps a hundred yards they came upon a cabin hidden in a clump of firs. A bareheaded man with the sleeves of his California shirt rolled up to his elbows was daubing the cracks between its logs; a gold pan full of mud hugged against his waist. "Get down— get down an' come in," he called cheerily, slapping a handful of mud into a crack. He had not even spared his greeting until he should have appraised his visitors. They *were* visitors, that he knew.

"Hello, Jim!" cried Thompson joyfully, dismounting and running towards him, skipping like a schoolboy in spite of being "sanctimonious."

"Well, Bill Thompson! By jimminy! I'm as glad to see you as I would be to see my mother. Get down," he called again to Henderson, depositing the pan of mud on the ground before him and hastening to open his cabin door. "It's getting right chilly. I'll start a fire, boys. Come in, I've got the very last of my ore in the arastra, an' I'll clean up tomorrow." He seemed anxious to talk—to spill out his pent-up thoughts—to hear his own voice speaking to friends. "How have you been making it, Bill?" he asked, rubbing the mud from his fingers against the logs.

"Fairly well, Jim," replied Thompson, looking all around the cabin. "How are things with you?"

"I've got no complaint to make. I'm working a small vein of high grade gold ore and running it through an arastra. It's a one-man mine, but I'm doing pretty good, I think. I'll know more about it tomorrow night after I've cleaned up the machine, but I'm pretty sure the result will be all I expected." He opened the cabin door and listened. Clack-clack-clack, sounded the clacker, and he smiled. "Working all right," he said, "but it's pretty cold."

"Jim," said Thompson, thrusting his hand once more into the breast of his coat, "we have come here to talk to you about the lawlessness in the diggings at Bannack and Alder Gulch. Fifty decent men, Masons, got together to bury a man in Bannack the other day. It was the first time any one of us realized there was a law and order element there. We know of fifty more men now in Alder Gulch and in Bannack who will stand by any more that is made to enforce the law. We want a leader, Jim, and I have come here to ask you to take command. Let's see if we can't stop the wholesale robbery and murder here. We are anxious to aid the officers of the law in doing their duty, Jim. Won't you help us?"

Williams began filling his pipe with slow fingers, and after a time lighted it with a splinter from the fireplace. "Well," he began, "D'you know who's sheriff? D'you know who are his deputies?"

"We know Henry Plummer, and some of his deputies, yes," replied Thompson, sensing something dramatic.

"But likely you *don't* know that Plummer's chief of the road agents and is a red-handed murderer, do you?"

"No, Jim. Is that true? My God!"

"True as gospel, Bill—true as gospel. Sit down, you an' Tom. He was even tried for murder in California, that I know of, and his deputies are members of his band of outlaws. Club-Foot George, that has a shoemaker's bench in Dance and Stuart's store—he's a spy. He knows the goings and comings of passengers on the coaches—knows when gold is being transported, and lets the gang know so they can waylay 'em. Yes, Plummer was tried and acquitted of cold-blooded murder in California before he came here. They're a secret order and a hard nut to crack. If a move is made, it's got to be swift. There can't be any bungling. To start and fall down would mean death to a lot of men, with the bandits strong like they are and in power. How many good men can you muster?"

"A hundred."

"That's more'n enough, but we'd need the moral support of all of 'em, God knows."

"Will you organize us, Jim?" asked Thompson, eagerly.

Williams leaned his elbows on his knees and smoked. He seemed to withdraw into a moody silence, looking over Thompson's head and beyond. He loved his mine and cabin, the arastra and the little meadow, with his whole heart. They were his very own and he believed that he would find a fortune here. If he went away—took up the cause of law and order—he might never come back. He knew that his life would be in danger from the hour he turned his hand against the outlaws. What had they to do with him, apart and by himself in the mountains? Should he leave his cabin to seek trouble, anger, for others? Or should he tell them to fight their own battles? Slowly, and as a man who has carefully weighed his words, he gave his answer: "I'll meet you and twenty picked men in Virginia City a week from tonight."

"Good!" Thompson's face showed relief. His whole person seemed to grow lively with it. Tom Henderson leaned over to shake Jim Williams' hand.

"You've got to be mighty careful—mighty sure of your men, an' be quiet," Williams went on. "Henry Plummer knows that I know him. I saw him in Lewiston, and again in Deer Lodge. We can't work through our legal authorities. We'll have to organize a vigilance committee, if we act at all. It is the only way, and then—well then, we'll have the authorities against us. In the end we'll have to hang the authorities—most of 'em, if we are going to clean up the outlaws here, because the authorities are outlaws, and the sheriff's their chief. I'll feed your horses, and cook some supper. You can't go down the gulch tonight."

"If," he resumed after returning to the cabin after attending to his guests' horses, "you fellows are sure that fifty men can be trusted, we can end this outlawry." He seemed to be warming to the ordeal, as if, now that he had turned his face towards it, he felt stimulated by its demand upon his courage. "Half the number of good men is enough if they've got the support of the rest," he said. "Men are afraid of each other here. That's the reason for the mess we're in. A man whispers about his suspicions, and then he's missed. You can't blame men for keeping still. A lot must suspect that even their public officials are in cahoots with the road agents, and they know their spies are everywhere, but don't dare trust their companions because there's no real

174

friendship here. But fetch twenty good men and meet me in Virginia City a week from tonight."

With that Williams seemed to drop the subject, as men of few words will when they have said what seems to them sufficient. He took a lump of sugar from a tin cup on the table and opened the door of the cabin. "Oh, you're here, are you? Couldn't wait, could you?" he asked, with feigned disgust. A low nicker answered, as Kit the mare came close to the door and took the sugar lump from his fingers with her soft muzzle. "Now git, you beggar!" he said, closing the door to stand listening a moment to her receding steps. "Keeps her from straying off," he smiled in explanation of his show of fondness for the animal. "But she's an awful beggar," he added. "Smells sugar more'n a mile."

He lighted another candle, and, pouring some coffee into a buckskin poke, laid it on a cut of wood that served as a stool. Then with a round boulder the size of a man's fist he pounded the coffee beans in the sack until they were ground fine, their odor pervading the cabin. "Sourdough bread, venison and coffee! How's that suit you?" he asked, rising from his knees.

"Fine." Tom Henderson was examining a chunk of ore in the light of the candle on the table. "Out of your mine?" he asked.

"Yes. Wish it was all like that, but there's only an inch or two of it." Williams stopped on his way to the fireplace with the coffee to point out colors of gold on the chunk of ore which Henderson held. "A ton or two like that would just about fix me," he said, half to himself.

"Bet it shows up good in a pan," mused Henderson, turning the chunk.

"Yes—pans like a house afire." Williams blew out the extra candle and went to the fireplace where he prepared a meal, his broad redshirted back to the two men seated upon his bunk.

The single bunk proved to be their bed for the night.

"Reckon we can all sleep in one bed tonight, can't we, boys?" their host asked after supper.

"Fine," agreed Henderson.

"Of course," agreed Thompson.

"Then if you don't mind, let's all turn in. I've got a lot to do tomorrow and the days are getting short."

175

After his guests were in bed, Jim Williams blew out the candle and opened the cabin door. "I want to hear the clacker," he explained. "It's pretty cold to be grinding ore, but this here is the last of the run."

29

During most of the night Jim Williams, young and strong though he was, slept fitfully, turning over and over in his mind the problem of making successful war upon the organized band of road agents, for he saw himself the leader in the coming strife and already began to feel the burden. Twice since Alder was struck he had visited Virginia City. Once on his way back he had stopped overnight at Adobetown with a friend he had known in Nevada, and all night had listened to tales of murder and outrage. He knew many of the outlaws by sight, knew they hung out at Daly's ranch, and at Cold Springs on Wisconsin Creek, and at the ranch on the Beaverhead. Long after his bedfellows were asleep he got up and smoked his pipe, even holding a lighted candle to look at the sleeping men who shared his blankets. Both were younger than himself, not over twenty-eight, but he was satisfied with their faces, even in the repose of sleep. And at last he himself slept.

He awoke with the daylight, his ears catching the sound of the clacker with returning consciousness, and sitting upon the bed, he pulled on his boots. "All's well with old Mary Ann," he murmured to himself good-naturedly. He stood up and stretched himself. Smiling compassionately, he had turned to see if he had disturbed his sleeping guests, his fingers rumpling his long hair, when a sound outside attracted him. He glanced expectantly over his shoulder through the open door, tucked his red shirt into his trousers, tightened his belt, and crossed to the table to get a lump of sugar. Kit was coming up the trail from the tiny meadow, with the mules behind her.

"The little beggar," he murmured fondly, going outside. "Here, take this an' git! Couldn't wait for smoke to come out of the chimney, could you? Gettin' worse an' worse!"

After a final affectionate pat, he knelt by the creek and drank deeply of the cold water; then returned to the cabin, kindled a fire, and softly closed the door.

The change of temperature in the room wakened the sleepers.

"I have a proposition to make," offered Williams, as soon as he had bidden them good morning, and while he began preparation for making fresh coffee. "If you'll turn in an' help me clean up the arastra, I'll ride with you today. I've thought it over, and there's no good reason for waiting a week before we commence our work to better the conditions in the camps."

Thompson bounced off the bunk and dragged out his bedfellow. "Of course we'll help you, Jim," he said. "Tom here'll go out and re-stake our horses."

It took them longer to clean up the arastra bed than they had expected. It was past two o'clock when the work was done and the amalgam retorted. They would have to ride to Virginia City where Williams would leave his clean-up in safe hands, and, besides, the mules would have to be taken to the Daly ranch for winter pasture. It was too late to start with so many errands to do, so they quickly decided to wait until morning. In so doing, they did not guess that their whole course of future action had been changed, or that the stage where they would act first would be set and waiting for them almost within sight of the gulch's mouth as they rode into Nevada City the next day.

It was hardly light when they breakfasted. The sun had not yet shone over the snow-capped peaks above the cabin when they set out for the Daly ranch, although far across the Ruby and the Beaver-head the whitened Trappers and the Bloody Dicks were already revelling in its golden warmth. They hurried down the chilly gulch in the morning's shadows, and when they reached the plain, where in the bright sunshine the grass and the weeds and the sagebrush sparkled with crystal drops of water melted from the white frost which had silvered them in the night, they headed straight for the ranch where Williams, buying a saddle horse, regretfully left his mare and mules in winter pasture. It was noon before they could get away from Virginia City, leaving the clean-up in safe hands, and after two o'clock when, on their return trip down Alder on the way to Bannack, they came into Nevada City.

There, as they entered, they saw a crowd of men gathered about a wagon in the middle of the street, and everywhere miners coming out of dugouts, adobe houses, and tents to join them. Williams, who was slightly in advance of his companions, rode up to the wagon and looked into it. The body of a dead man was lying on the bare bottom of the wagon box, and there was an ugly bullet hole in his forehead. "What's wrong here?" asked Williams, dismounting. It was as if, feeling the obligation of the authority but lately placed upon him and seeing the crowd of men, he felt bound to speak.

No one answered as his blue eyes glanced over the men about him. "Come, speak up," he urged, climbing into the wagon. "Who brought this man's body here?"

"I did." A man elbowed his way towards the wagon. "I found it lying on Ramshorn Creek just about the Pete Daly's ranch," he explained.

"Men," began Williams from the wagon, "this is murder. You leave the gulches with your gold and you never know how far you'll go until some black-hearted murderer shoots you down. This man has been shot in the forehead and most likely was asleep in his blankets when his murderer crept up on him for dust. Only a little while ago another wagon stood here, and in it was the body of a man—a man whose dead hands had tufts of grass an' leaves in them. What did those things? What do the grass and leaves tell us boys? Them and the marks of a lariat around the murdered man's neck told us that he had been wounded and then dragged alive by a saddle horn to the spot where he was found, and there shot a second time by—WHO? Let's find out! Let us be *men,* and go out and get his murderer! After we get him an' hang him *high,* then let's get the others—all of them! We can clean this country like other countries have been cleaned if we're men. How many of you will follow me?"

A cheer broke out. Men crowded close about the wagon, anxious to enlist with Williams. Here and there he beckoned to a willing one whose eyes had withstood his own, until he had selected seventeen men. Then he got down from the wagon and led them away to a cabin. Placing a guard at the door, he turned to his new company. "There's twenty of us, and I know of a hundred more, if they're wanted," he said. "Now go arm yourselves at once and get your saddle horses and a blanket each and a lunch, and meet me here in one hour. If any man is inclined to weaken, let him say so now, for we've got real work to do." His glance once more swept their faces, but had made no mistake in his choosing.

"Captain," began one, "I know where the Dutchman's body was found, and I—"

Jim Williams cut him off. "We'll come to that later. Get your horse. We leave in one hour."

He was a miner no longer, but chief of a tribe at bitter war. His step was light, even springy, unlike his own, and now that he had talked to the crowd he was done with speeches. His words were few and to the point—sharp commands. Men who knew him and familiarly called him "Jim" now said "Captain Williams" in addressing him, for somehow they knew that their leader had no intimates in his command.

"Palmer!" he called when a number of the men had returned with their horses, and a strapping miner wearing a full beard followed him into the cabin.

Palmer had found the body of the man in whose dead hands had been grass and leaves, and for twenty minutes Williams questioned him, learning all he knew—even his suspicions. After him, the man who had found the body in the wagon was summoned, and finally two others whom he knew could help him learn the knowledge he needed.

It was growing dark when the twenty men rode out of Nevada City, their captain leading. No one of them had asked whither they were bound; not even Thompson or Henderson had been taken into the leader's confidence. It was evident to them that the whole course of action they had planned had been suddenly changed in Nevada City by the sight of the dead man in the wagon, although they did not know what was in the mind of Jim Williams. It was like him, they reflected, to plow straight ahead like this, beginning his task with whatever came his way first, once he had set himself a duty to perform. For four hours they rode silently and at a steady gait, then crossed Wisconsin Creek, their horses breaking through the ice on the stream and dissipating the stillness. Gaining the north bank, Williams turned up the creek and, after riding a little way, called a halt. "We'll wait for daylight. Wrap yourselves in your blankets and rest. I'll stand guard," he said.

Some of the men, used to exposure, slept by their horses. Others, wrapped in their blankets, tramped about to keep warm throughout the hours of the night. But Williams, walking up the creek still farther, stood guard until the dawn, when he returned and roused the sleepers. Then mounting, once more they all moved on—towards a camp built of brush, not far from the creek a mile up the stream from the road. As they neared it a dog barked.

Williams spurred his horse and rode rapidly into the camp, followed by the others. The men, wrapped in blankets, were sleeping about a dying fire. He sprang from his horse. "Lie still!" he ordered sharply. "The first man that moves'll get a quart of buckshot in him. Is Long John here?"

"Yes, sir," a voice answered in the gray light.

"Get up and come here, Long John," ordered Williams.

"What do you want?"

"I want *you*. Be quick!"

A tall man with a thin face and one eye that drooped rose from among those about the fire, letting fall his blanket. He came straight toward Williams, his face gray with sleep and cold and fear. Williams was quick to disarm him. "Men, keep your eyes on the others. If any move, shoot to kill," he ordered, leading Long John to a horse which belonged to one of his party. "Get on this horse, John," he commanded, handing the bridle reins to Bill Thompson, and turning to select three other men—one of whom was Palmer, the man who had found the body of the Dutchman, and who had offered information at the cabin in Nevada City. "You three mount your horses and join Thompson with the prisoner," he ordered. To the rest he said, "I'll be back within two hours. Keep these other men prisoners until then."

The five men rode out of the camp with Long John, leaving fifteen to guard the others. While they were recrossing Wisconsin Creek, Williams called Palmer up alongside of him. "I want you to lead us to the spot where you found the Dutchman's body, and as straight as you can go," he said.

So they rode on through the valley that lay gray and frozen in the early morning. At length Palmer stopped at a grove of trees on the Stinking Water. "This is the spot, Captain," he said, swinging from his horse.

Williams, turning to Long John, ordered him to get down with the others, and when he had obeyed, placed a hand upon his shoulder. "We've brought you here under arrest for the murder of Nicholas Tiebalt. What have you got to say?" he demanded.

Long John was trembling like a leaf. Twice he tried to speak, but his voice refused to function. And as though to act as a dumb witness against him, a mule came slowly into view through the willows, cracking the brush and gazing curiously. "Whose mule is that, Long John?" asked Williams.

"That's—that's the mule the Dutchman rode down here," answered the frightened man, dropping his eyes before those of his questioner. "But, so help me God, men, I didn't kill that man," he faltered.

"I guess we'll have to hang you, John," said Williams, taking hold of his arm.

"No, no!" begged the trembling man. "I didn't do it. I can clear myself. The man that killed the Dutchman is at the camp on Wisconsin Creek now."

"What's his name?"

"George Ives."

"Men," said Williams, "you stay here and guard Long John while I go back to the camp and arrest Ives."

Long John watched him ride away and a look of hope crossed his face. "I never killed that Dutchman," he said to Bill Thompson. "Can't I go about my business?"

"No. Sit down," Thompson ordered.

Long John sat down with his back against a willow bush. The Dutchman's mule, glad of company, came close to the group. But not one of the men spoke of the mule or gave it apparent notice. It was as though each man recognized the dumb brute's presence as a torture to his prisoner, and forebore.

Tom Henderson built a fire, and in searching out dry wood jumped a cottontail that ran blindly between Thompson and Long John. Both men instinctively grabbed at the rabbit, and Long John sprang to his feet as though he would chase it. But Thompson's "Sit down, John," recalled him. No one spoke of his move, although all of them had seen it and knew what had been in his mind.

The fire warmed them, and they built it up again and again, watching the river and the muskrats swimming from shore to shore until nearly noon. Then Jim Williams came up with the party. And he had not only George Ives as a prisoner, but Bob Zachary, Alex Carter, Whiskey Bill and John Cooper, as well.

They started for Nevada City at once. George Ives was the life of the party. If he felt any concern as to his fate, he kept it perfectly concealed. He joked and related anecdotes of scrub-horse races, embellishing them with such lively details that interest in the subject grew apparent, and he finally suggested a race.

Both captors and prisoners were young men with a zest for life and a love of contest. The road was level and Daly's Ranch only a few miles away. So they took up the suggestion. Then after two or three trials of speed had been made by the fleetest horses in the company, Ives bet an ounce of dust that his horse could beat the winner of the other races to Daly's. His offer was accepted, and the race began at once, to the amusement of the whole party.

Ives' horse was fast, and the other animal, having already run two short races, was no match for him. So Ives, once gaining a lead, had the advantage. He plied quirt and spur, and raced away like the wind.

Then Williams and the others saw through the ruse. Gentleman George was making his escape. They left a guard with the rest of the prisoners and gave chase. At first the fugitive was so far in advance that the pursuit seemed hopeless. Two horses, faster than the others, gained on Ives, but the distance to be lessened between them and him remained great. Then ahead, at the Daly ranch, a fresh horse was discovered, ready-saddled for use. Somebody who had been at the camp on Wisconsin Creek had ridden ahead and arranged for a fresh horse for Ives. The two horsemen seeing this urged their mounts to utmost efforts, and were successful in preventing Ives from dismounting and changing horses. He passed the ranch only two hundred yards ahead of his pursuers, who knowing that he could not long maintain his speed now, stopped at the ranch and took for themselves the fresh horse and a mule that was standing at a hitch rack there. Ives, realizing that he could not escape with his worn horse, turned up Ramshorn Creek and jumped from his saddle to hide in the willows. The two men were now, however, only a moment behind him, and they sprang from their own saddles and ran into the bushes after him. They found him hiding under a rock. "Come out of there!" one called, and Ives, laughing merrily, crawled forth.

"I thought I'd fool you, boys," he said, edging close to the smaller of the men.

The other, discerning his intent, cried, "Stop where you are! If you take another step I'll kill you."

"Well, well," laughed Ives. "You are a queer lot. I was only fooling."

Other members of the party now came up and, ordering Ives to remount, took his bridle reins and led him back to the road. He produced a flask of whiskey and treated all who would drink. Then he began again to tell stories, chatting and laughing, still carrying off the whole affair as a joke. But this time the men did not rise to his merriment. At sunset they rode into Nevada City and secured their prisoners for the night.

30

Startling news travels fast. Nevada City knew of the arrest of Ives and the others, and had even heard of the chase, two hours before Williams arrived there with his prisoners. The people remembered now that they had noted a foam-bespattered horse dashing up the gulch, the rider plying whip and spur, even before they had learned of the coming of Williams' men. And now, somehow, they believed that their news had come with that horseman. But nobody knew who he was—or, if they did, they would not tell.

Doubtless this mysterious horseman who left relays of horses was Club-Foot George, who not long after dusk rode through Nevada City on his way to bring Henry Plummer from Bannack, sure that Plummer would demand the prisoners in the name of the law. He rode desperately, even killing the last and best of the horses in his effort to reach Bannack in time. The horse fell dead a mile out of the camp. Leaving the poor, steaming brute in the road, Club-Foot George ran, as best he could, to Plummer's door.

It was almost daylight by then, and the sudden summons wakened the sheriff and his wife from a deep sleep. Plummer rose and began to dress, and Elizabeth sat up in bed, frightened by the continued pounding. The house was dark and Plummer made no light. Having hurried into his clothes as fast as his crippled arm would permit, he felt his way out into the living room. The pounding had ceased, but just as the bedroom door closed behind him a man's face was pressed against the window. Elizabeth, thoroughly frightened already, screamed in terror, for the face was that of the cripple who had startled her on the day the camels had appeared in Bannack.

Plummer rushed back into the bedroom, gun in hand. "What is it, Betty?" he asked sharply.

"There! There!" she trembled, pointing at the window where yet the face of Club-Foot George showed against the polished glass.

"Go away from there, damn you!" cried Plummer, leaping forward.

"Henry! Come out, quick!" begged the man. "I was afraid you were gone."

"It's all right, dear, don't be afraid," Plummer assured his wife, and kissing her trembling lips, he went outside to Club-Foot George. "What the devil do you mean by coming to my house in this manner, and at this hour?" he demanded angrily.

"When I tell you, you won't think I done wrong," panted the cripple. "Oh God, Henry, we're gettin' into it." And in a breathless, half-pleading way he recounted what he knew of Williams' speech from the wagon, of the formation of the posse of miners that had taken the prisoners, of the arrest of Ives and the others, of Ives' futile attempt at escape, and pleaded with his chief to get his horse and ride to Nevada City to save his men.

Henry Plummer listened.

"Is the leader's name *Jim* Williams?" he finally asked, evenly.

"Yes," said Club-Foot George, "it's *Jim* Williams."

"Wait a minute. I want to be sure," and Plummer, drawing a wallet from his pocket, took from it a tintype and held it before Club-Foot George. "Can you see?" he asked. "Is this the man?"

The cripple turned the picture towards the bedroom window through which a candle was now shedding its light. "Yes, yes, that's the man. That's Jim Williams, damn him," he gritted.

"I thought likely," murmured Plummer, calmly. "You go back and tell the boys I'll come as soon as I can get there. Don't wait for me. Go to the stable and take my spare horse, but use your own saddle. I am afraid George Ives has started things this time."

"You'll come?" asked Club-Foot George, starting down the hill. "You'll be sure to come, Henry?" as though he feared his chief would fail him in the pinch.

"Yes. Hurry back and say I am on my way," he answered impatiently.

Satisfied, the cripple went stumbling down the dark slope, and

Plummer, entering the house, lighted a candle in the kitchen and looked scrutinizingly into the face of Jim Williams upon the tintype he had filched from the album at the Bailey ranch. "Damn you," he muttered. "I wish I had the drop on you. I've been expecting you to cross my trail and—now you have."

"Henry!"

"Yes, Betty," hastily hiding the picture in his pocket. "What is it, dear?"

"That's just what I'm wondering, Henry. Come in here, won't you?"

"Well, what is it? Are you still frightened?" asked Plummer, sitting down on the bed beside her without looking directly at her.

"Yes, I am," declared Elizabeth, her face pale in the candlelight. "That man that looked in at the window is the same one that scared me so that other time. Oh, such an awful face! What could he want of you, Henry? Who is he?"

Plummer's mind was working fast. He knew the time had come when he must get Elizabeth away from Bannack or lose her confidence. "Betty, dear—" his words were soft and low, though there was nothing of the quality in them that men so dreaded. "Betty, he came to warn me that the Indians have taken the warpath. They are on the move towards this camp now, but they are two days' march from here and troops are being sent out from Salt Lake City to help us. There is no cause to be frightened, dear. Just stay, and I'll go and light the fire in the kitchen. Then I'll come back and tell you all about it." He spoke as he might have spoken to a little child, smiling as he left her warm in bed.

But when the kitchen door had shut between them he was like a man mad with grief. "Betty—Betty, I shall have to give you up," he groaned, his eyes staring at emptiness and the thin fingers of his left hand clinched in the silent agony of realization. He must act now—there was no time to waste. The one important thing was that she should not find out. Other crises he could face. He could not face that one. He began to pace the floor, forgetting where he was—forgetting the fire.

"Henry!"

He stopped suddenly, his blood leaping to his pale face. "Yes, dear," he answered in a level voice.

"What is it—what are you—"

"I hurt my arm. That's all. I was taking off the bandage."

He spoke without thought but now hastily unwrapped the bandage from his arm, hanging the sling on the back of a chair. He feared she might come into the kitchen. He moved the fingers of the hand so long out of use. The pain was sharp, and the bared hand swollen and blue.

Remembering his errand, he kindled the fire in the kitchen stove with a great clattering of lids and stood there waiting for it to burn up. Was he near his end? Could he keep her—keep Betty if he escaped? How much would she learn in spite of him if the whirlwind came?

"Henry!"

He went in and sat down beside her, and forcing his voice to the colorlessness of its custom, he said, "Betty, dear, I am going to send you home to your father and mother to stay until spring. I had intended to do it, anyhow, for the winters here are not pleasant, but I hated to have you leave me. You see, Betty, if we wait much longer the roads will be next to impassable, and so, considering the Indian scare which I really believe amounts to little, I think you had better go today. Could you get ready, dear?"

"Why, Henry Plummer, how strange!" She sat up to stare, looking like a frightened child in her high-necked nightgown.

"Not at all, Betty. The winter will be uncomfortable here, and then if the Indians should come, I would much rather you were safe and—"

"Leave you here alone?" she interrupted, amazed.

"Why, my dearest Betty, I could not leave. They would call me a coward if I ran away in the face of a mere rumor of coming danger. I am the sheriff, you must remember, and the people look for help from a sheriff."

She pleaded with him to go with her, or to allow her to remain with him, using all her feminine art, her little endearments which usually swept him off so easily, even her tears, but he gently insisted that she go, and go alone. The more he thought of it, the more terrified he was to let her remain in Bannack another day, lest some move on the part of the awakened people should acquaint her with his real character. Somehow he knew that the trouble in Nevada City would entangle him, and he feared that the visit of Club-Foot George had already aroused suspicion in Elizabeth's mind. To preserve her regard for him, he must send her away.

"Betty, I know you dislike the man who came here this morning," he said. "But for some reason of his own, he seems fond of me. It was kind of him to come and warn me of approaching trouble, and may I ask you not to mention the reason of your going away to anyone? There are good reasons for the request. One is that the people would think us foolish, and the other concerns the man who brought me the news."

By the last he bound her to secrecy, for there was mystery in the way he spoke the words, and, dreading the unknown in the world in which he moved as a man, the wondering, trusting girl assured him earnestly that she would not mention to anyone her reason for leaving Bannack. Tearfully, in the dim light she began to gather her things together, tucking them into a large carpetbag which he had brought to the bedroom. "I'll go and tell the clerk at the stage office to call for you, dear," he said. "Then we shall have time for our breakfast before the coach leaves."

It was a gloomy morning for Elizabeth, and as dark for Henry Plummer. A wolf will acknowledge but one master among men—one love. To take it from him leaves deeper pain because it is so. And perhaps the cold who love at last suffer more severely than those who come more easily to love. On the way to the stage office Henry Plummer's emotion choked him. He thought just then that he would rather die than part with Elizabeth, if only by dying he might hide his past from her and leave her forever believing in him.

During breakfast together they did not talk. Elizabeth cried softly to herself and Plummer was striving for mastery over his feelings. When the stage called for her, he was himself again. Tenderly, he helped her to a seat and kissed her lips. "It's just for a little time, dear Betty," he whispered. "Good-bye, my darling."

After all, when she was gone, a great load was lifted from him. Let trouble come if it must. He was ready for it now. She would ever be ahead of the news from Bannack, no matter what happened, and he sighed as he watched the coach moving rapidly away on the road towards Salt Lake City, bearing its most precious burden.

When it was out of sight, he turned away towards the livery

stable and, saddling his horse, started towards Alder Gulch, as he had promised Club-Foot George. But as he rode his mind began to work at the problem before him, and he saw the danger of interfering with the angry citizens of Nevada City. He would wait at Bunton's ranch on the Rattlesnake for news. Arriving there, however, he found that Bill Bunton had gone, and he turned back to Bannack, abandoning his men to their fate.

31

Even as Henry Plummer turned his horse back in the direction of Grasshopper Creek, the street in Nevada City was filled with men. Standing or moving about restlessly in the half-frozen mud of the road, two thousand miners watched the pacing guards, posted about the cabin where George Ives and the other prisoners were confined, and wondered at the daring of those who had arrested them. The morning was clear and bright and still, as though waiting an event. There was no snow and the sun shone with unusual warmth for that season of the year. But the men were tense, anxious, fearful that some tragedy was impending, and there was little talk among them. Small boys, delighted by the crowd and not guessing its terrible import, seized the opportunity to play, dodging with shrill cries and laughter in and out among the silent miners like wild colts in a field of clover. Emboldened by the excitement of a game of tag, they rudely bumped and jostled groups intent in whispered conversation, unmindful of frowns or warnings, until a red-headed urchin who had elected him-self 'it,' cried out. "Here comes a wag-on! Here comes a wag-on!" in shrill sing-songy tones.

Then there was a stir in the crowd—a mass movement—a parting as though in obedience to a command, and a wagon, pushed and drawn by men, was wheeled to a point two hundred yards from the jail. The crowd, having parted to give it room to pass, now closed in about it, anxious, fearful, but still curious. A man who had been pushing the wagon climbed into the box and held up his hand for silence. A murmur swept through the assembly like a gust of wind in the willows, and then silence fell upon it. Even the urchins were still—held by the spell of an unguessed thing that was in the air to frighten them.

"Men, we are about to try George Ives for the murder of Nicholas Tiebalt," said the man in the wagon, clearly. It was Jim Williams, with a double-barrelled shotgun in the hollow of his arm. His head was bare and his long hair reached nearly to his shoulders. His muscular arms, brown almost as a mulatto's, were naked to the elbow, the sleeves of his coarse homespun shirt rolled tightly up. His eyes, narrowed with the challenge of battle, swept the crowd from Alder Creek to the hillside, as he repeated clearly, "Men, we are about to try George Ives for the murder of Nicholas Tiebalt."

"Like hell you are!" retorted a voice from far out on the edge of the crowd, and men craned their necks to discover the speaker.

"Arrest him!" someone shouted.

"No, No! One at a time," another objected.

"You don't dare!" came from the other side of the wagon.

"Silence!" ordered Williams. "George Ives is to be tried for the murder of Nicholas Tiebalt, here and now. He shall have a fair trial before a jury, and the verdict of that jury shall stand and be carried out, because you will be the jury. Besides that, we shall appoint an advisory committee, consisting of twelve men from each of the mining districts, that shall first pass on the evidence shown. Wilbur F. Sanders will act as prosecuting attorney, and Messrs. Davis and Thurmond of Virginia City will appear for the prisoners. I shall read the names of the advisory committee, and as they are called, let them come to the wagon!"

As he commenced to read off the list, men began elbowing their way towards the wagon, until sixty armed committeemen had gathered between the wagon and the pressing crowd.

"Now," said Williams, "we shall proceed with the trial. Guards bring George Ives to the court."

"You dirty stranglin' pups!" someone cried, as the guards started promptly for the jail to bring the prisoner.

Williams cocked the double-barrelled shotgun which was charged with buckshot and stood erect, waiting for the guards to bring George Ives from the jail. The crowd watched him intently. How many among them belonged to the road agent band no man could tell. What would be the result of a verdict of guilty, in case the trial should proceed to an end unmolested, none could guess. Perhaps a majority of all the men present sympathized with the outlaws, but there was confidence in Jim Williams' voice as he cried, "Open a way for the prisoner and his guards, men!"

Instantly a lane through the assembled miners stretched from the wagon to the jail, and down between the long lines of anxious faces Gentleman George Ives, chained and shackled and escorted by armed men, walked smilingly to the wagon. He bowed gracefully to acquaintances here and there—but now men were afraid to know him. When, however, he was helped into the wagon and sat beside his attorney, he opened a brisk conversation with them, and his eyes coolly scanned the sea of faces about the wagon.

Several men, attorneys for Ives and for the prosecution, now climbed up into the box. One was destined to become a leader in Montana in after years—Wilbur F. Sanders, the young attorney for the prosecution of George Ives. Standing there that day when only the few dared to be known as enemies of organized lawlessness, men must have recognized in the tall young lawyer some of his greatness and thanked their God for such as he and Jim Williams. Taller than any in the wagon and younger than Williams, Sanders, spare of form yet broad-shouldered, with wide forehead and fearless poise, must have appeared even then as a pillar for the building of Montana as a state.

The trial began. Palmer, called to the witness stand, told how he had found the body of Tiebalt. "I was hunting grouse not far from the river," he told the jury. "A grouse flushed from a thicket and passing through a small open space in the bushes offered a chance shot. I fired and I saw the bird fall in the midst of another thick growth of willows. I made my way towards the spot and, after some time being spent in searching, I found it lying on the breast of a dead man."

"Did you recognize the dead man?" asked young Sanders.

"No, sir."

"What then did you do?"

"I went in search of Long John's camp that was not far away, and when I got there I told him and George Hilderman, who was with him, that there was a dead man in the bushes a little way up the stream from their camp. I asked them to help me load the body into my wagon, as I intended taking it to town to have it identified."

"Did Long John or Hilderman help you, Mr. Palmer?"

"No, sir. They said there were plenty of dead men lying around in the willows and that it was none of their business."

"You mean that they refused you any assistance?"

"Yes, sir."

"What then did you do?"

"I got the body into my wagon as best I could, and brought it here where it was easily identified."

"In what condition was the body when you found it, Mr. Palmer?"

"It was frozen, and the man had been murdered."

"Tell the jury what led you to believe that the man had met a violent death."

Palmer recounted what Williams had told from the wagon box on the day before.

"You say that it was evident the man had been dragged alive and that, in his desperate efforts to save himself, he had clutched at the grass and bushes?"

"Yes, sir."

Throughout Palmer's examination Ives' face did not show any fear. He even smiled at the witness as the latter seated himself on the edge of the wagon box near him. He had one hope. He felt certain that Plummer would come and put an end to the trial.

But it dragged on until nearly three days had been consumed. The patience of the miners, who had not quitted the camp, was at the breaking point when at last Long John was called by the prosecution and brought under guard from the jail to the wagon.

"Long John, how long have you known the defendant, George Ives?" questioned Sanders, rising and leaning near him.

"Five years. I knew him on the other side."

"Tell the jury what you know of the murder of Nicholas Tiebalt."

In a voice that trembled with fear, Long John began to speak, and a new stillness crept upon the crowd.

"George Ives told me he killed the Dutchman," he said.

Men pressed closer—a wave of sound ran through the throng, and "That's a damned lie!" was shouted across from the hillside.

"Go on, Long John," urged Sanders, ignoring the voice. "Tell the jury what George Ives told you."

"He said—he said he held up the Dutchman," faltered Long John, "and took his money from him. He told him he was going to kill him and the Dutchman wanted time to pray. Then—then George Ives told me that when the Dutchman knelt down and begun his prayer, he shot him."

Long John's testimony wrought a change in Ives. He sought to rise, but was held back by his guards. He quickly regained his composure, however, and smiled into the faces about the wagon, but the crowd realized the horror of the crime now, and it suddenly surged with the cry: "Give the case to the jury—give the case to the jury!"

The cold winter dusk had settled over Nevada City when the sixty men of the advisory committee withdrew to consider the testimony. The prisoner still showed no fear of the verdict.

As the committee returned, a clamor rose in the crowd, and Jim Williams waved his hand for silence. Beginning near the wagon, the sound of voices died away until silence had spread over the two thousand men in the darkening, muddy street.

"The verdict is guilty!" shouted Williams.

"Thank God for that!" cried many voices, though mingled with the acclamation, there were threats, cries and curses—howls of indignation and derision. "The murdering ruffians dare not hang him!" taunted a man near the wagon. But gun locks clicked and the voices of opposition faded. Men had at last learned that the roughs were not in the majority.

"I move that the report be received and the advisory committee be discharged," cried Jim Williams from the wagon.

"Second the motion," came from a dozen throats.

"As many as favor the motion say 'Aye.'"

"Aye!" thundered the crowd.

"Those opposed say 'No.'"

A scattering chorus of 'no's,' weak and uncertain, no match for the lusty throat of affirmation.

"The 'aye's' have it," declared Williams, "and the advisory committee is discharged."

Then Wilbur Sanders stood up beside Jim Williams, and said, "I move that George Ives be forthwith hanged by the neck until he is dead." Before the friends of Ives could grasp the situation, the motion was carried with a cheer, in spite of all efforts on the part of the attorneys for the defense to stay it.

Now at last George Ives realized his situation, and he began to beg piteously. "Wait! men. Oh, wait until tomorrow," he implored. "Men, give me time to write to my poor mother. Sanders! Sanders! Help me!" he begged.

"Ask him how much time he gave the poor Dutchman!" shouted a man with his foot upon the wagon wheel. "Make a scaffold—make a scaffold!" he cried.

Willing hands brought a log and laid it across the walls of an unfinished cabin. A large dry good box had been found and was placed under a noose fastened to the log, and George Ives was led to the spot. The moon had risen and the mud of the street was hardening under the bite of the frosty air. Ives was stood upon the box and the noose adjusted about his neck. Someone cried, "Look out! I'll kill some of these murdering devils," but the threat was unheeded. The worm had turned. A whole section, outraged and smarting under the hurt of countless crimes, had suddenly found itself the master, and its hand was heavy upon this first murderer to be delivered into its power. Hearts hardened to the task beat furiously in men's breasts when Jim Williams asked, "George Ives, have you anything to say?"

"I am innocent."

It was the password of the infamous gang, and a cry went up, "Banish him! Don't hang him!"

"Is that all, George?" asked Williams, stepping back.

"I didn't kill the Dutchman," said Ives foolishly. "Alex Carter killed him."

"Men, do your duty," ordered Sanders, and as the box was pulled from under the condemned man's feet, the clicking of gun locks was heard.

As though seized with a sudden realization of what it had done, the crowd surged backward from the scaffold. The body of George Ives swung in the night wind.

"He is dead," said Jim Williams. "His neck is broken."

32

When morning came in Nevada City, the street was deserted. Only the trampled mud, frozen hard, together with the log and the dry goods box, recalled what had transpired there on the night before. Smoke from the adobe chimneys of cabins along Alder Creek was proof that men were awake, but as yet not a soul was to be seen in the camp. A dog came round the corner of the cabin walls that supported the hangman's log, sniffing curiously at tracks in the frozen mud as though he read in them a story of unusual interest. Hearing a growl, he raised his head and met the challenging eyes of another of his kind. Evidently they were enemies of long standing, these two, for without a moment's preliminary, they fell to fighting there under the hangman's log. The noise of the battle penetrated the cabins and here and there a door opened to learn the cause of the disturbance. Men, glad of any excuse to talk to their neighbors, now came hurrying into the street and surrounded the fighting dogs. "They're at it, again, them two devils," said a big bareheaded miner. "Just you wait. I'll fix 'em," and he ran to fill his camp kettle at the creek. Returning, he dashed the cold water upon the fighters, and a laugh—a much-needed laugh went round, as the surprised dogs separated under the icy deluge.

"We don't allow lawlessness here any more," laughed a man, turning to the miner next to him.

"You bet we don't, brother," the other agreed.

And so they fell to talking and laughing, began to forget their fears for friendships formed under stress of necessity, and to look forward with gladness to the coming reign of peace and law and order there in Nevada City.

The cabin which had served as a jail was at present empty. No evidence that was deemed sufficient to warrant the execution of any save Ives had been offered as yet. Even Long John, because of his testimony against George Ives, had been allowed to go free, although men believed him to be equally desperate and deserving of death with the outlaw they had hanged.

The execution of George Ives had been an open challenge to the outlaws and their retaliation was expected by many citizens. That death would be the portion of all who had figured in the arrest and trial or execution, they did not doubt, but the growing friendship among them gave the men courage and hope. With a mixture of trust and apprehension, they awaited the next move. But they did not have long to wait.

Two horsemen, Bill Thompson and Tom Henderson, rode into Nevada City at noon and, going from cabin to cabin, spoke quietly to a man here and there. Then they rode away in the direction from which they had come. A little later the men with whom they had spoken saddled their horses and, singly or in pairs, followed them to Virginia City farther up Alder Gulch. What was going on? Nobody knew—not even the men who had so promptly answered the summons, or at least, they said they did not know. The departure of the men from Nevada City was a mystery, and the wondering miners gathered in groups to discuss it.

"I'm damned glad of it, anyway," said an old California miner. "I've seen such doin's before in my time, an' they always meant a lot of trouble for folks whose ways were crooked."

"I guess you are right, uncle," agreed a young man, standing near, "but why take so few when there are so many that are anxious to help? We're all ready to act, now that a start has been made."

The grizzled miner smiled. "Them was all mighty good men that they took, I noticed," he said. "It don't take many of that kind, lad. What we that's left behind must do is to stand back of 'em. Ah-ha!" he finished, as a horseman turned into the street and rode furiously past them on towards Virginia City. "Ah-ha!" laughed the old man, pointing a boney finger at the rider. "That's one of 'em. That's Club-Foot George. He's ridin' straight to hell, he is, as sure as there's gold in Alder. Go an' get it, you black-hearted devil, you! I've knowed you a long time. You got away once, but this time you'll hang, hang, hang!" He chanted the word as though it pleased him highly. Men had crowded close to hear him. It was so new, this feeling of trust, they wondered if their ears had heard aright, but the old miner had seen such times before and, nodding his gray head, he turned away to his cabin, leaving the others to ponder over the happenings of the night and the day.

Club-Foot George had passed but a little while when another horseman was seen galloping up the trail from the valley below. Abreast of the little knot of miners in the street. He drew rein and dismounted from his panting horse. "Men," he said, "Lloyd Magruder has been murdered."

"What's that?"

"Yes, murdered in the Bitterroot Mountains—him and his party, all of them—heads split open with an axe while they slept."

"My God!"

Lloyd Magruder was well known in the gulch. He was a candidate for Congress, and had recently left Virginia City for Elk City with a large sum of money and gold dust. One or two of the miners had seen him only a few days before. The news of the murder seemed unbelievable. As the awful details of the brutal slaughter of the five men were unfolded, the wrath of the miners of Nevada City grew to white heat.

"I'm going on to Virginia City," said the horseman, after telling what he knew. "Magruder had many friends there, and they will feel his loss."

The sad news spread like fire, and Lloyd Magruder's name was upon every tongue soon after the messenger reached Virginia City. It even found its way into a building where a secret meeting of men from Bannack, Nevada City, Junction and Summit was in progress. No one knew of the meeting save those who had been summoned to attend. Speech was guarded as well as windows and doors. But a late arrival had heard that Lloyd Magruder had been murdered, and he was appointed to go with one other, as a committee of two, to secure the details of the crime. Within less than an hour they were back with their report.

It seemed that Lloyd Magruder, after having disposed of his train of goods in Virginia City for nearly thirty thousand dollars in gold dust and treasury notes, besides seventy-five mules that he had accepted in lieu of money, had departed from the camp with a hired guard consisting of Doctor Howard, Chris Lowrey, John Romaine and his old and tried assistant, William Page. Shortly before the party left the gulch it had been joined by Charley Allen, two brothers whose name was Chalmer, and a man by the name of Phillips, the latter being about sixty-five years of age. Allen had recently sold his mining claim for twenty thousand dollars in gold dust, and had joined Magruder for protection and aid in getting safely out of the country with his money. The pack train, traveling light, was hurried down the gulch and out over the valley to Bannack with the seventy extra mules driven loose with the pack animals, for Magruder was fearful of snow which might make the mountains impassable. He had been obliged to spend three days at Bannack, but had at last started with his company for Elk City to join his wife. In the meantime, he had grown especially fond of Lowrey and spent much of his time on the trail in his company, telling him of his hopes and fears, and even acquainting him with the amount of money he had gained by his venture. He had not known Lowrey until he had hired him at Virginia City and of course did not suspect that he, along with Doctor Howard and Romaine, were members of Plummer's gang, or that the three had carefully planned to murder and rob him on the way. There were nine men in the party and Magruder felt secure from attack by either robbers or Indians.

One night, when they had made camp for the eighth time since leaving Bannack, they built their fire near the summit of the divide and not far from the point where the trail began to descend the mountains into Idaho. Magruder's heart was light, for no storm could stop him now and he would soon be with his wife in Elk City. While the mules were being unsaddled, Doctor Howard stepped close to the side of William Page and whispered, "When you drive the mules out of camp tonight, take them a full half mile away, and stay with them until I call you." His voice carried a deep threat to Page, who was not a strong character. There is no doubt that the weak-hearted man understood. "Your life will pay for any blunder," added Howard, quick to catch the fear in his eyes.

"All right, Doctor," replied Page, and took the horses and mules out of camp as bidden.

There were heavy snow clouds in the sky and the night came on early and was dark. The wind in the high mountains was sharp and bitter cold, but, used to hardships, the men warmed themselves by the fire for a while and then crawled into their blankets to wait for the daylight. Magruder, with no suspicion in his heart, sat by the fire with his friend Lowrey, who with an axe at hand conversed with him in low tones so they would not disturb the sleeping men lying in the shadows not far away. "It's almost ten o'clock," said Magruder, filling his pipe. "It will soon be morning now." He smiled and bent forward to secure a burning firebrand with which to light his tobacco. Lowrey, waiting for a chance to strike, chose this move as his opportunity. He raised his axe and clove the head of Magruder, who fell lifeless in the blaze of the fire.

Doctor Howard, watching from the shadows, ran to Lowrey's side and, snatching the axe, struck Magruder again, after which, with the rapidity of some supernatural demon, he split the heads of the Chalmer brothers in their bed. Allen, awakening, sat up to receive a charge of buck shot in the face, and Romaine, in bed with old man Phillips, drove a bowie knife into Phillips' heart.

It was over, and Page was summoned to help in clearing the camp. The equipage, saddles, bridles, ropes, and gear of all kinds were burned, the iron bits and rings scraped into sacks and the sacks tied fast. Then the bodies of the dead, wrapped in blankets, were carried to a cliff and dumped over it to fall to the bottom of a canyon eight hundred feet below, while the sacks containing the scraps that would not burn were thrown over after them. Not a portion of anything belonging to the equipage of the pack train was left to tell of the murders.

Then the storm came on—a heavy snowstorm, so that when daylight dawned there was nothing left to mark the camp or its tragedy. All was white, clean, and still under the straight-falling snowflakes and the murderers saddled the choicest horses and left the spot seemingly unable to tell any tales. But the mules and pack horses persisted in following, in spite of shots and shouts to drive them back. Used to following a leader, and anxious to leave so forbidding a place, they clung to the trail behind the murderers, trusting them to lead them out of the snow that was rapidly deepening over high mountains. Ninety horses and mules make a formidable show and not being able to shake them off, the murderers finally rounded them up and shot them down—all of them—and left them for the wolves. So there was nothing left of the outfit of Lloyd Magruder.

That was the story the committee told, and at midnight twenty-four men, well mounted and heavily armed, and more than ever determined, rode out of Virginia City. None but their captain, Jim Williams, knew whither they were bound.

So far, he possessed no proof that Henry Plummer was connected with the gang of road agents in Montana, although, as we have seen, he was sure that he was its chief. But Plummer was sheriff and therefore entrenched behind official position. To lay hands on him now without proof of his infamy here in Montana might turn the miners against the Vigilantes. Unless he acted quickly he feared that Plummer might escape. But he could not yet chance the arrest of the sheriff. He would have to wait. He would arrest the outlaws as fast as he could find them. Somewhere in this course of action he felt certain that he would find the proof of Plummer's connection with the gang. He had no idea where he might find Doctor Howard, Romaine, or Lowrey, who had murdered Lloyd Magruder, but he did know the whereabouts of two other members of the gang. And he was on his way to take them.

33

Close by a window of an unlighted room in his house in Bannack, Henry Plummer sat with his face towards the camp. News of the execution of George Ives had reached him in the afternoon. From the moment he heard it, each stranger seemed to him to be a spy. The miners had gathered in groups and conversed, and he had watched their faces to catch traces of suspicion concerning himself. More than once he thought he had read their thoughts, and that he was the subject of their guarded talking. Now he was brooding by the window, while outside the sky was clouding over as though a blizzard threatened. He knew men too well to believe in their keeping silent when they were fighting for their own lives, and he feared that he had been implicated, that his name had been used in the trial at Nevada City. The shadows had grown into night, and the night into the gray of morning; still he sat by the window thinking, now of Elizabeth, now of his own situation. Once he smiled grimly as he thought of Elizabeth's surprise when she should find a package containing ten thousand dollars in currency in her luggage. He had placed it there, knowing it would be far safer if she did not guess its presence. If anything should happen to him—

A hard-ridden horse stopped outside his door. Plummer bent his face to the glass and peered out into the dim light. A man dismounted and came hurriedly to the door. It was Jack Gallagher, his deputy sheriff, and Plummer hastened to admit him.

"They've hung George Ives, Henry. There's hell to pay."

"Yes, I know they have, Jack. Sit down."

"What are we going to do about it, Henry?"

"There is nothing we can do. We must not run away. We must stay and fight them. We could not get away if we would," replied Plummer in an even tone. "Have they implicated us—I mean have they implicated *me?*"

"Not that I've heard of, but Long John turned traitor and told that Ives killed the Dutchman, damn his black soul."

Plummer's face showed signs of relief. "We will kill Long John on sight," he said. "But so long as they do not suspect me, I believe we can stand them off. Where are you going from here, Jack?"

"I came here to tell you how things were going, and to ask you what I'd better do, Henry."

"Stay here—that is, go back to Virginia City as fast as you can go. You are deputy sheriff, remember," advised Plummer.

"I'll remember it, but don't *you* forget that you are sheriff, if I get into it myself. Are you going to stay here in Bannack?"

"Yes, of course."

He had half-planned to leave, but he did not hint of his plans to his troubled deputy. A general exodus of his men might make his own escape impossible. Let Gallagher take care of himself, he thought.

"Henry, the boys have killed Lloyd Magruder and five other men that were with him," added Gallagher after a silence. "They made a big haul. Magruder had a lot of gold and currency with him. So did Allen."

"I wish they hadn't done it," declared Plummer. "It's a bad time just now to be making killings. Who did the job?"

"Oh, you know, Doctor Howard, Lowrey and Romaine," said Gallagher. "They must have cleaned up at least fifty thousand dollars—one of the best jobs we ever did."

"I wish the spring were here," Plummer sighed, with no thought of the booty.

Jack Gallagher turned sharply towards his chief.

Plummer smiled. "Not that, Jack," he said, realizing he had gone off guard. "Not that. I'm lonesome now that my wife has gone away. Every hour is a day to me, and in the spring she will come back, or I will go to her. It is not fear of men that makes me wish for spring. It is the desire to have my wife with me, or to be near her."

Gallagher looked out of the window where in the camp a few lights now burned. He did not believe that Plummer could mean what he had said about his wife. He had caught what he had at first thought was fear in his chief's speech and manner. And it had startled him. Could it be fear, he wondered? No—Henry Plummer did not know the meaning of fear. But there was something wrong with him.

A flurry of snow brushed the window panes and he could feel the chill wind about the sash. "Well," he said, turning towards Plummer, "I'll go back to Virginia City now. If I hear of anything further I'll let you know, Henry. And I'll stay here as long as you stay." With a straight look at Plummer, he held out his hand, and Plummer shook it.

"Good-bye, Jack," he said.

He watched Gallagher mount his horse and ride away, and then sat down by the window again. It was snowing hard. A blizzard, sudden and violent, had come, and the light flakes were whirling blindly in a bitter wind from the north. A little clock on the shelf struck six. Its chimes reminded him of Elizabeth, and he counted the bells with a heavy heart. It was time to face another day in Bannack or to fly, and he could not determine which to do.

But fate was fast completing her plans for him. That same day the Vigilantes made a capture which changed their method of procedure so that they no longer felt obliged to wait for some crime to furnish evidence of their suspicions, but set out directly to capture and hang every member of Plummer's gang.

Just as the clock in his house told the hour of six, four men from a party of twenty-four were creeping towards a camp fire on the Rattlesnake. Cautiously and with heads bent against the storm to protect their faces from stinging snow, the four men finally reached a cottonwood tree that stood in the shadows near the fire. The howling wind whipped the blaze until it leaped high, widening the ring of light about it so that the four men crouched close to the cottonwood's giant trunk to hide, while their eyes searched the camp. Two beds of blankets were spread upon the ground and three men, not yet out of bed, were gazing sleepily at a companion who was industriously gathering wood. Presently, the busy one came to the fire and dropped a large stick upon it, spreading his hands to the blaze.

"Hands up, Red Yager!" came a voice from behind the tree.

The man's hands shot upward, his eyes searching the shadows about him. Not a soul was in sight, though against the rough bark of the cottonwood he could see the barrels of a shotgun levelled at his head.

"The rest of you lie still," ordered the voice. "Red, come here! We want you," and stepping from behind the tree with the levelled gun in his hands, a stranger stood before Red Yager. There was no mask covering his face.

"Good morning, friend," laughed Yager, with his hands still above his head, against the leaping glare of the fire. "You're an early bird. What do you want with me?"

"Come here."

Red walked obediently towards his captor, and before the other men in the camp realized it, he was gone. The shadows outside the fire ring had swallowed him.

"Where are you taking me, fellows?" he asked, as they ploughed through the drifted snow in unbroken silence.

For answer the leader ploughed a few steps farther and stopped at a tree to which Red could see three horses tied. "Get on this horse," he commanded.

Red mounted, but the bridle reins were kept in the hands of his captors. They disarmed him, and, as he was helpless, he suffered himself to be led onward. After a time, through the mist of whirling snow flakes he could see the forms of many horses, and when his captors joined them, the whole company moved away without a spoken word.

Red did not enjoy the silence.

"God! it's cold," he said, buttoning his coat and shoving his hands into his trousers pockets. "You boys must have wanted me mighty bad to come after me in weather like this," he observed to the horsemen nearest him.

The man rubbed his ear with his gloved hand, but made no answer, and Red bent his head to the blizzard.

At Dempsey's ranch there was a halt; two men dismounted and went into the ranch house, while an extra horse was made ready for use. In five minutes the two men returned and, between them, talking excitedly, was a small man known as George Brown. "What do you want with me? I am innocent," he whined, hanging back at the sight of the company of horsemen.

"Get on this horse," was the answer, and there was nothing to do but obey.

The company moved on again through the deepening snow and did not halt until they had reached Laurin's ranch on the Stinking Water. There they camped for the night. The snow was drifting about the ranch house, and the wind cut like a knife. Instead of lessening, the storm was increasing each hour. The night would be terrible to the unsheltered. The men, worn by fatigue and exposure, slept by the blazing fire, kept bright by Jim Williams and one other guard. Even Red Yager was asleep when, at ten o'clock, Williams called, "All hands."

"Come, Red," he said solemnly. "Your time has come."

Yager sat up with the others, staring sleepily at the snapping fire, shadowed by moving forms, and as though to taunt him the wind shrieked in the chimney top. "It'll be a cold job, won't it?" he said slowly, glancing around the room at the staring men.

No one answered. Jim Williams added fuel to the fire while the men buttoned their coats and gloved their hands.

"I know you're goin' to hang me, and I merited it years ago."

The men, who had kept their eyes averted, now turned them in surprise upon Red Yager, hardly believing their ears.

"You've treated me well," he went on, calmly, "and I'd die happy if only I could live to see the rest of 'em hanged first, because most of them are worse than me."

"Well, if you'll tell us who they are," proposed Williams, "I'll promise you, Red, that not one of them'll escape."

"I'll tell—I'll tell—and not to get off. I don't want to get off, boys!"

"Well, I'm listening," replied Williams, the shotgun across his arms.

"Henry Plummer is chief," began Yager. "Bill Bunton, stool pigeon and second in command, George Brown, secretary, Sam Benton, roadster, Cyrus Skinner, fence and roadster, George Shears and Frank Parish, roadsters, Hayes Lyons, telegraph man an' roadster, Ned Ray, council room keeper at Bannack, George Ives, Steve Marshland, Johnny Cooper, Mexican Frank, Dutch John, Alex Carter, Buck Stinson, Long John, Whiskey Bill, Bob Zachary, Boone Helm, Bill Terwiliger, Gad Moore and Jack Gallagher, roadsters, Club-Foot George, spy. There's a lot more but I can't remember them right now. The password is 'Innocent,' used in any way. Get Bill Hunter—I forgot Bill Hunter, men. Be sure you get him. He's the man that put me where I am tonight. Now hang me, for I'm not fit to live."

He had spoken hurriedly, as though he were afraid that his life might end before he could name the gang, willing to die, as he had said, provided he was sure they would die likewise. There was not a man there who did not feel stirred by his candor.

Williams opened the door. "I'll keep my word so far as I can, Red," he said. "None of 'em shall escape us. Come."

As the Captain stepped out into the bitter night with his men, Red Yager followed willingly, but Brown began to wail, "Oh, let me live for my wife and child! Let me go! I'll never come back here, if you will only let me go!"

"Brown," said Yager, disgusted, "if you'd thought of your wife and child before this, you wouldn't be putting these men to this trouble. It's a job to hang a man on a night like this. Shut up, and take your medicine like a man. The Vigilantes have got us and we're going to hang."

At daybreak in a single file through the blinding storm which had not abated, the Vigilantes rode away from the Stinking Water, leaving two bodies hanging as a warning to all evil doers. On one was a paper bearing the words, "Red—road agent and messenger." On the other a card, "Brown—corresponding secretary."

34

A just cause, although ripe and ready as tinder, must await the spark of leadership to set it blazing with proselytizing brilliance. The whispered story of the hanging of Red Yager and George Brown was now like the snow—everywhere. And everywhere men sought to lend their hands to break down the reign of terror in the camps. They were eager to join the Vigilantes, now that a start had been made, and impatient to tell what they secretly knew or guessed of the outlaws. Nobody, however, save Williams and his men, knew what Red Yager had told, or that the Vigilantes possessed the names of most of the band of road agents, or that Henry Plummer, the sheriff, was its chief. But every good man was now determined to be of use in bringing law and order to the camps, often at great cost of time and suffering by exposure to winter, until every one of the criminals was executed, or driven from the Northwest. They hanged sixty-odd, and a notice tacked upon the door of a cabin occupied by a man of bad character became sufficient warning for the occupant to fly, although the card bore only the cryptic figures 3—7—77.

Ploughing through the snowdrifts without meeting a soul on the way, the Vigilantes reached Nevada City at midday, where, as though waiting to goad attention, news of a fresh outrage met them. Moody's train had been attacked two days before at Red Rock.

Hidden in the cantinas on the saddles and in the packs of the mules had been eighty thousand dollars in gold dust and, in a wagon that accompanied the pack train, a carpetbag containing some fifteen hundred dollars in treasury notes. Notwithstanding the dangers that were now confronting him, Henry Plummer, having learned of the amount of the treasure to be transported, had evidently been too greatly tempted by a last chance to enrich himself before he should leave life in the mines forever, and had designated Dutch John and Steve Marshland to rob the train. But both the robbers had been wounded in their attempt to secure the booty. Moody himself had fired the shot which had found its mark in the shoulder of one of the bandits, and he was positive in declaring that the robber was Dutch John. The other thief, a stranger, had been shot in the breast by a man in the wagon who, when an opportunity offered, had fired through a hole in the wagon cover, though not until after the carpetbag containing the treasury notes had been taken. The packers had then followed the trail of blood left in the snow by the flying highwaymen, but crippled though they were, the robbers had escaped them. Dutch John, however, was a marked man, not only because of Red Yager's confession, but because of the wound in his shoulder, and a detachment of the Vigilantes was sent out at once to arrest him.

Meanwhile, two wagon trains had been forced by the fearful cold to camp in Beaver Canyon. A mile of drifted trail separated them, and, as the men were kept busy with fires which might save them from perishing, there was no visiting between the camps. Some of the freighters' hands and feet were already badly frozen and the ears and tails of more than half their oxen were frozen stiff.

As these stormbound men crowded about great fires built in cottonwood groves in Beaver Canyon, they discussed the execution of George Ives, Red Yager, and George Brown, for already they had learned of these hangings as well as the story of the attempted robbery of Moody's train. Not a man among them but felt himself strengthened by the bold action of the Vigilantes, and some of them burned now to take part in the war against the highwaymen, since such as they suffered most at their hands. Never before had they dared to talk even among themselves. Now they were talking, some boastfully. But there were only two men in both the camps in Beaver Canyon who had truly enlisted in the cause of the Vigilantes.

Near noon a white man and an Indian, riding up the canyon on their way to Salt Lake City, passed close to one of the fires. The white man stopped and asked for some tobacco.

"We are mighty short on tobacco," replied one of the freighters, crouched by the fire. "The outfit just above us is better fixed and can give you some. Try there."

"Oh, give the men some tobacco," broke in a freighter called Neil Howie, rising from the ground and handing a small supply of the weed to the fellow on the horse.

"Thank you, friend," said the latter, but his hands were so badly frozen that he could not take the offered gift and was obliged to call the Indian to receive it for him. Then, with a final glance at the others about the fire, he rode away with his red companion.

"Boys," said Neil Howie, going back to the fire, "that's Dutch John, the man that attempted to rob Moody's train. Let's go and get him."

But no one volunteered, so Howie, running up the road alone began calling, "Oh, partner—Oh, partner!"

The white man stopped and turned his mount to meet the oncoming freighter. He recognized him as the one who had given him the tobacco, but he was suspicious and swung his rifle barrel in line with Howie, poking his swollen trigger finger through the guard of the weapon. Howie saw and understood the move but, without hesitation, ran close. "Give me that gun, and get down!" he ordered, looking squarely into the white man's eyes.

For just a moment the fellow wavered, and then got down from his horse. The one man had found him, and his will was as nothing under the glance of his master's eyes. Meekly and in great fear, Dutch John went with Howie to the fire, where the men made room for him, some doubtful, others curious.

"You know why we've arrested you, John—for your attempt to hold up and rob Moody's train," said Howie, while Dutch John warmed himself by the blaze.

"I never had von ding to do mit Moody's train," denied the prisoner, squatting beside the fire.

206

"We can settle that question in a minute," said Howie promptly. "If you didn't have a thing to do with Moody's train there won't be any bullet wound in your shoulder. Take off your shirt. "I'd freese man," protested the prisoner. "I'd freese sthiff if I took off mine shirt."

"Bah, no, you won't freeze. Take it off this minute." And Dutch John began to bare his shoulders.

No sooner had the shirt been removed than a fresh wound showed itself. Realizing that he had made a mistake in refusing to remove his shirt, the frightened man began, "I got dot leddle vound py accident. I vas ashleep already over on de Peaferhead. Mine fire ketch de blanket an purn an purn till it purn my pistol holster. By an' by, Pang! I yomp! Got in Himmel! De fire purn de cap on my pistol. She vent off! Dot bullet vent indo mine shoulder. It's in dare dis minute—see? Feel!"

Howie smiled. "Let me show you that what you say is impossible of belief, John." And taking a cap from a box in his pocket, he put it on a stick of wood, then held the stick in the fire where the blaze was hottest. The cap withstood the heat until the stick was nearly consumed before it exploded. "You see, John," laughed Howie, "you would have burned to a crisp before the cap exploded. Then besides, I can't believe that a gun strapped at your side and pointed downward could possibly wound your shoulder. I guess you'll have to go with me to Bannack."

But, among the twenty men in the camp, Howie could find no one willing to help him take his prisoner to Bannack. They said it was a fool's trick—that they didn't know how many of Dutch John's friends might be close around. And so Howie left Dutch John with them to go in search of John Fetherstun whose outfit was a mile farther up the canyon, through drifted snow.

Fetherstun, who was of Howie's sort, promptly agreed to lend a hand, and the two men set out for Bannack with Dutch John, with the thermometer at thirty-five degrees below zero, and without any other provisions than the shank of a small ham.

This journey required three days of travel and two nights spent without shelter, but in spite of the dangers from Plummer's band of outlaws and the weather itself, Howie and Fetherstun arrived safely at Horse Prairie twelve miles from Bannack City.

Howie had no faith in the regularly constituted authorities and was therefore determined to hand Dutch John over to the Vigilantes if he could find them in Bannack. He possessed no knowledge of Plummer's duplicity but was anxious to avoid him because he feared that Plummer, jealous of his position as sheriff, might take his prisoner from him and then later on a cowardly jury might set Dutch John free. He would not take Dutch John into Bannack until he had first made sure it was safe to do so. Turning in his saddle, he proposed to Fetherstun, "John, you hold our prisoner here a while, and I'll ride into the camp to look things over a bit. I'm afraid there might be an attempt to take Dutch John away from us. We can't afford to lose him after the trouble we've had."

"All right, Neil," agreed Fetherstun, "I'll build a fire and wait a decent spell. Then, if I don't see you coming back as though the devil were after you, I'll come on in."

"Get down, John," he commanded, as Howie rode away.

Dutch John dismounted and helped his guard gather wood. They were hungry and stiff with cold, but, finding shelter in a small grove of quaking aspens, they built a fire against a fallen tree and, hovering over it, they conversed in friendly fashion, as if one were not captor and the other prisoner.

It was past three o'clock. The days were short, and Fetherstun was anxious to get into Bannack with his charge before dark. He decided not to wait long.

Meanwhile, Neil Howie was only a short time in reaching the camp, where, leaving his horse, he set out to visit the saloons and gambling houses. He loitered in each place sufficiently long to catch the drift of the talk in front of their bars and about the card tables, without realizing that nearly two hours had now elapsed since he had left Fetherstun. But when he came out of Goodrich's Saloon, he saw that the dusk was coming on, lights were being lighted, and, satisfied with the result of the reconnoiter, he turned towards his horse.

But a voice arrested him. "Hello, Mr. Howie."

Howie turned to face the man he had hoped to avoid.

"Hello, Mr. Plummer," he returned, and even as he spoke he saw Fetherstun and Dutch John enter Sears' Hotel across the street.

"When did you get in?" asked Plummer, glancing across the street to the door of the hotel, through which Fetherstun and Dutch John had just passed.

"Just a little while ago," answered Howie. "It's cold, isn't it?"

"Who were those men that just went into the hotel?" Plummer asked. "I've been looking for some fellows wanted for horse stealing," he added.

Howie knew he could not hide Dutch John now. He knew that Plummer would find his prisoner even if he had not already recognized him.

"One of them is Dutch John, Mr. Sheriff," he said boldly. "He's my prisoner, and—"

"*Your* prisoner?" sneered Plummer. "What has Dutch John been doing? What is the charge against him?"

"Attacking Moody's train."

Plummer whistled, as if in surprise.

"Well, is that so, Mr. Howie?" His manner had suddenly changed. He was courteous again, but patronizing. "I'm glad you've got him if that is the charge," he said. "I'll take good care of him, I assure you."

"No, thanks, Mr. Plummer," said Howie boldly. "I've had some trouble taking Dutch John, and I mean to keep him."

"Why, why, Howie!" Plummer assumed surprise. "You surely do not sanction these brutal hangings that have been going on. You certainly are willing to have your prisoner tried in a regular court."

"Not until I learn if the people want him," replied Howie doggedly. "I've got him safe, and I'm going to keep him until then."

Plummer turned abruptly and walked away, and Howie, suspecting that he had gone to find his deputies, hurried to the Sears' Hotel where Fetherstun and Dutch John were eating a lunch and warming themselves at the same time. Come on, Fetherstun!" he cried, beckoning him outside. "Come with me!"

He and Fetherstun took their prisoner to an empty cabin on Yankee Flat and prepared themselves for an attack, bolting the door, darkening the windows, and building up a good fire in the fireplace. Night came on. After a time the two watchers in the cabin heard the tramp of horses in the awful cold outside. Springing to their feet, they stood ready to hold the place against Plummer as long as they could.

"Hello, Howie!" hailed a voice outside.

"Hello, yourself! What do you want here?" returned Howie from within.

"You are holding Dutch John a prisoner, and we've come to relieve you of him. This is a committee of citizens, and not the men you expected."

They heard many sounds outside, as though a considerable number of horsemen had surrounded the cabin. Neil Howie cocked his rifle and went to the door.

"You'll have to prove that," he challenged. "Advance one to the door—and I warn you to send only one, for if there are two or more, we'll fire."

Voices were heard in low conversation. Then, "I'm coming, Neil. It's I—Bill Thompson."

Howie, with his eye to a crack in the cabin door, saw a form approaching through the deep snow. When the man tapped on the door, Howie opened it, and after admitting him shut and barred it. The man was in truth Bill Thompson.

"It's all right, Neil," he assured Howie, whipping his hands about his shoulders. "God, it's cold!" Then he bent and whispered into the other's ear.

"Take him," agreed Howie. And he unbarred the cabin door.

Bill Thompson stepped outside and whistled the notes of a meadowlark. Dark forms began to come from behind the cabin and from out of the night everywhere until the little room was filled with armed men. They crowded about the fireplace, and Fetherstun heaped wood upon the blaze. No one spoke for a time, but finally the leader moved from the fire, elbowing his way across the cabin to the corner where Dutch John was sitting on the floor.

"Dutch John, we have tried you for murder and highway robbery," he said. "Your sentence is death."

Dutch John was a giant in stature, but his coarse face went white at those words.

"Oh, men, let me live!" he begged. "Cripple me. Cut out my tongue and let me go, but don't take my life!"

"No, Dutch John," replied the leader firmly. "We are going to hang you."

Dutch John swallowed hard and made a great effort for self control.

"All right, den," he said, "if I can't talk you oud of it. Is dere a man here who can write de German language? My hands are so bad froze I can't use my fingers, and I want to write to my mother in Germany."

But since there was no man there who could do the favor for him, he was obliged to remove the rude bandages from his hands and write the letter himself. In it he recounted clumsily what had befallen him, and admitted its justice.

Half an hour later the little cabin on Yankee Flat was empty save for the lifeless body of Dutch John, which swung from a crossbeam in the dim light of the dying blaze in the fireplace.

35

Henry Plummer had no intention of taking Dutch John from Neil Howie when he turned and left him. Howie's declaration that he would hold his prisoner until he learned if "the people" wanted him had quickly turned him from the project, and he went directly to the livery stable where he saddled his horse. He did not go home, but rode out to his ranch on the Rattlesnake where he kept his spare horse in a pasture. It was nearly eight o'clock and dark. The storm had ceased, but the cold was intense. The sharp wind had driven the horses into the willows and quaking aspens along the stream, so that he had trouble in finally corralling the band. From it, he easily caught his fast horse, a beautiful strawberry roan, after which he let down the corral bars and allowed the others to go free. He fashioned a hackamore for the head of the high-spirited roan and, mounting his saddle horse, led him back to Bannack, stabling both animals there. Then he went home.

He made a light and kindled the fire in the kitchen stove. The water in the bucket was frozen hard, and the dishes of several hastily prepared meals stood unwashed in crooked piles. The house was cold and hollow. Its windows, frosted over since the blizzard, needed no shades to shut the light from chance passers by, but he pulled them down. Then he went outside and, filling the coffeepot with snow, hurried in to put it on the glowing stove.

For half an hour, twice adding snow to the coffeepot, Henry Plummer stood over the stove preparing his supper, his thoughts busier than his hands. He had made up his mind to fly. There was time. He was sure that he had not yet been implicated. But if Dutch John fell into the hands of the Vigilantes, it might be too late. Dutch

John might talk. He had never liked Dutch John. It had been Ives' fault that he had ever been admitted to the gang. What folly he had shown in permitting it. And Ives! He had brought the storm about their heads. Damn Ives! But there were no Vigilantes in Bannack. There was time, plenty of time, to get away. The Vigilantes could not reach Bannack before tomorrow. And tomorrow he would ride— ride the roan. They could not catch him—not if he were once on his roan. He smiled. With an even start they could never catch the roan horse, and he would ride him to death if he must.

As soon as he had eaten his supper he pulled off his boots and got into his bed. It was tumbled and uncomfortable. For a time the crackling fire in the kitchen stove gave him its company, but at length it went out and the cold crept in. He tucked the blankets about him. He would take two of the best of them with him tomorrow. He must get some sleep. There could be no knowing when his next chance would come. The thought angered him. He was nervous and scorned his condition. His arm pained him, and he turned over to relieve the pain. But he could not sleep, and at last got up, lit a candle, and rekindled the fire. He was chilled, and reaching for a heavier coat, loosened Elizabeth's gingham apron from the nail beside it. It fell to the floor, and he stooped to pick it up, holding it reverently in his hand. He would go to Salt Lake and then send for Elizabeth. She would come to him. All would yet be right. Why should he worry? He was still a young man. His luck had never failed him. Elizabeth would come to him, and then they would go far away from any who knew him. He would begin a new life with her. She would never know—never if once he got to Salt Lake City.

It was past two o'clock before he finally returned to his bed to sleep fitfully.

In Alder Gulch, seventy-five miles away, a miner opened the door of his cabin and threw a pan of dishwater upon the snow, pausing in the doorway a moment to wonder at the stillness and stinging cold of the night. Suddenly his eyes caught the shadow-like form of a man moving upon a hilltop above the gulch. Still holding the dishpan with both hands, he stepped out into the snow to get a better view of the moving form. In a moment it disappeared over the hilltop, but then there came another, and yet another, until at regular intervals fifty men had passed over the hill under the sparkling stars.

The miner rushed back into his cabin. "Bill! Bill!" he cried, "The Vigilantes! The Vigilantes! The hills are full of 'em. Run! Run, man! run for your life. Here, take this blanket—quick! Bill, for God's sake!"

Bill Hunter, for it was he whom the miner had warned, rose from a bunk in the cabin, and hastily prepared himself for an awful night. "Git into the drain ditch, Bill," implored the miner, excitedly. "Git down an' crawl clean to the end of the ditch. Hurry!"

Bill Hunter dropped into the deep drain ditch and upon his hands and knees crept through the snow until he reached the drain's end. Then he ran for his life—but though he saved it for a few weeks, they caught and hanged him at last.

Slowly and with great caution, a cordon of men was forming around Virginia City. Along either side of the gulch and across it, above and below the town, they stretched in a line, each man fifty feet from the other; then they waited in the cold, watching the lights from the tents and dance halls glance and play upon the snow. The wild music of the hurdy-gurdy places seemed but a few yards away, so close were they to the town, and the shrill cries of the caller for some bawdy quadrille, above the discordant chorus of drunken voices, rose towards them clearly in the sharp mountain air. The gambling houses were jammed with men and women with gold to lose at the games there, and the saloons and dance halls were crowded to utmost capacity. The long, crooked rows of lighted tents and cabins seemed to be bursting with life and excitement under the eyes of the silent watchers.

Down in the town, four men engaged in a game of poker sat at a table in a corner of the Gold Dust Gambling House and, with the deep interest of professional gamblers, played steadily without a word of conversation among them, until, in a moment of apparent abstraction, the eyes of one of the players wandered out over the crowds about the faro layouts, as though expecting to find a familiar face there.

"Ante, Jack," said the man across the table from him.

The player addressed suddenly threw his cards upon the table with an oath and moved his chair away.

"What's wrong, Jack?" asked the fellow, puzzled.

"I've got a hunch that while we sit here and get out money, those

213

damned stranglin' Vigilantes are condemning us to death. That's what's wrong, if you want to know, Boone."

"Oh, hell, ante," laughed Boone Helm. "Are you afraid of a few pinheaded Vigilantes, Jack?"

"I've played all I'm going to," said Gallagher. "I wish I had lit out when I was in Bannack. I think we'd better scatter, we four. I've got a hunch," and he walked out of the place.

Lights in the cabins and tents where miners slept were few now, but the public places were still bright—would be bright as long as the night lasted, for there was a harvest to reap from the spendthrift miners and newcomers in the camp. But the crowds within them were thinning somewhat and here and there the music had ceased altogether, telling of a lack of customers, a dearth of pretty women, or a grouchy proprietor.

A wolf howled out on the hills just back of the line of men, and the echoes awoke and tossed the voice of the night prowler back and forth among the cliffs and canyons until it grew faint and was lost.

Fighting to keep their blood from freezing, the men tramped to and fro, slapping their hands and stamping their benumbed feet in the snow throughout the long hours of the bitter night. At last, when the day was coming and Virginia City was nearly asleep, fifty armed men marched up the street to arrest every member of Plummer's gang found in the camp, and within an hour Jack Gallagher, Boone Helm, Frank Parish, Hayes Lyons and Club-Foot George were in their hands. "Bill Hunter is gone," said the leader, after a thorough search had been made, "but we'll get him, no matter where he goes. Tell the men on the hills to come in."

Glad of relief from their long vigil, the men came into the camp from the hills, and, as though they knew just what to do, surrounded a partly finished store building on a corner, well up the main street. From a crossbeam that rested upon the log walls, five ropes were tied and their dangling nooses hung directly over five large dry goods boxes to which extra ropes had been fastened.

A crowd was gathering despite the early hour, so the prisoners were conducted to the place under a strong guard. The people were held from the store building by the men who had watched throughout the night. They were in no temper to permit any disregard for the command to stand back.

"You have each been tried by the committee for murder and high-way robbery," began the leader, addressing the prisoners within the walls of the building, his face showing the marks of weather and fatigue. "Your sentence is death."

"I am innocent!" The cry came almost in unison from the lips of the condemned men, as they were led to the boxes under the cross-beam.

"Judge Dance, will you pray with me?" suddenly asked Club-Foot George, holding back.

"Willingly, George." And the judge, in whose store the villain had plied his trade, knelt beside the road agent, while silence fell upon the watchers.

But they did not get far with their prayer, for Boone Helm, who had mashed a finger in attempting to escape, interrupted. "Oh, for God's sake, if you're going to hang us, do it!" he cried. "I'm sick of this damned palaver. Either hang us or bandage my finger. It hurts like hell."

Judge Dance added an "Amen," and rose with Club-Foot George, advancing towards the boxes. When the nooses were adjusted many hands laid hold of the ropes that were to pull the boxes from under the prisoners' feet.

"If you have anything to say," said the captain, "you may say it now."

Frank Parish, Hayes Lyons and Club-Foot George did not open their mouths. Their faces were pale but resolute. But Jack Gallagher, with an oath, said, "Gimme a drink of whisky."

The drink was brought and handed to him.

"Slack off that rope, you dirty murderer," he cried, "and let a man take a parting drink. Boys, how do I look with a rope around my neck, hey?"

Then, turning to the crowd behind him, "I hope God Almighty will curse every damned mother's son of you, and that I'll meet you all in hell!"

While the curse was still on his lips, the box was jerked from under him, and as he fell, struggling at the rope's end, Boone Helm, who was standing on the box next to him, cried, "There goes one! Kick away, old Jack, I'll be in hell with you in five minutes. Hurrah for Jeff Davis! Let her rip."

A few hours afterward the bodies of the five murderers were buried on Cemetery Hill.

36

After the hanging of Red Yager and Brown, Bill Thompson had left the party of Vigilantes at the Laurin Ranch and, riding into Bannack after nightfall, visited many cabins where there lived men he knew and trusted. He did not tarry long at any door but, whispering his message, hastened on. So while the cordon of Vigilantes was closing in on Virginia City in Alder Gulch, a detachment of them was riding hard towards Grasshopper Creek where men were gathering in Cass Masterson's cabin on Yankee Flat.

There was no light nor fire in the cabin, but at its door, part open, Bill Thompson watched, admitting the armed men as they came with an admonition to silence. Each new arrival, anxious to know who besides himself had been summoned, peered curiously into the silent bearded faces about him and in the cold darkness sometimes ventured a whispered, "That you, John!" as he huddled with the others near the bunk in the corner or leaned against the log walls.

At last Thompson closed the cabin door. "That's all," he whispered. "Make a light, one of you, and tell me the time."

A miner on the bunk struck a sulphur match. Its blaze, spluttering blue, gave a savage look to his untrimmed black beard. "Five minutes to twelve," he said, closing his watch with a click. The match went out, and an acrid odor of burnt sulphur pervaded the room.

Bill Thompson breathed upon his numb fingers and softly re-opened the door. A whorl of dry snow dusted the door- sill.

"They're coming," he whispered, stepping outside in the shadow of the building.

Those within heard the tramp of approaching horses and then men dismounting near the cabin. In a few minutes Jim Williams and ten men filed in.

"Bill," said Williams immediately, "take four men and arrest Ned Ray and Buck Stinson. You know their cabin. Act quickly. Shoot if you must."

Thompson picked his men and with them left the cabin. Outside, he stopped for a moment to give his directions, after which the five men proceeded directly to the cabin occupied by Stinson and Ray. They broke in the door, seized the sleeping men, and disarmed them before either could resist.

Buck Stinson pretended wrath. "What do you mean by such doings?" he fiercely demanded, struggling. "I'm deputy sheriff here, an' you'll—"

"That's enough, Stinson," said Thompson shortly. "Keep quiet, or—well, you keep still, understand? Now come along quietly."

Stinson remained quiet as far as the cabin, but immediately upon seeing Williams demanded, "What's all this damned horseplay about? I'm innocent of any crime."

Jim Williams made no reply. Turning to Tom Henderson, who was beside him, he said, "Tom, make a fire. We'll wait the daylight for the other job, and the boys are cold."

By the other job he meant Henry Plummer.

Plummer had been up with the first gray of dawn. He knew nothing of what was happening in Virginia City. He did not know that Buck Stinson and Ned Ray were prisoners not three hundred yards from his own house, or that the Vigilantes had grown into an organization of several hundred men. But he had decided to fly, and his sleep had been filled with dreams. Now that the day was at hand, however, the dreams had vanished before it. He built a fire in the stove and then, while he waited for water to heat, sat down on the couch and read a letter from Elizabeth which the coach had brought in the mail of the evening before. It had been written in Salt Lake City—a hurried but loving note. He had read it many times, and each reading had increased his longing to be near her.

"I'll come, little girl," he whispered. "I'll start today—in an hour. Then I'll send for you. I'll leave this cursed country forever, Elizabeth, and no matter what may happen I will never send you away from me again—never!"

He sat still, staring into space, seeing her pretty curls, her big trusting eyes, her sweet mouth, her young rounded figure, her little coquetries, the things she liked and disliked. A flood of tender, protecting love filled his heart, the more tender because she still believed in him who was not worthy.

He had not quite finished his dressing. His coat was on the back

217

of the chair near his bed. His arm, no longer in a sling, was rapidly mending and he could use his hand again to some extent. He got up and poured some water from the teakettle into a washbasin and, as he soaped his hands, there came a splintering crash.

He whirled and sprang for his coat in which was his gun. "*Stop!*" cried a voice, and Henry Plummer stood still, for Jim Williams' blue eyes were upon him from the broken door.

"I want you, Henry Plummer," said the owner of those eyes, and his words were unrelenting.

"All right, Mr. Williams," Plummer answered without a tremor in his voice.

But startle was in his eyes, and they left Williams' face, glad of respite. "I'll just slip on my coat and then we'll—"

"Stop! I've got a man here to wait on you, Plummer. He'll get your coat. Stand fast or I'll kill you." And Williams stepped across the broken door into the room.

Plummer's eyes shifted craftily from his coat to his captor, his lithe body bent as though determined to spring for the garment. His hands clinched, opened and clinched again convulsively, and the muscles of his neck were tense and rigid.

Then suddenly the blood left his face white as death. For a moment calmness was gone. The strange power which he had possessed and which he had made his fellows feel deserted him. Perhaps because its chief prop, which fate now took away from him, had been the speed with which he could draw and use his gun. The dread spectre had come—Elizabeth would know. The thought wrung a groan from his whitened lips. "Oh, God!" he faltered, "Don't take my life. Let me live for my wife who believes in me—*trusts* me. I am too wicked to die. Let me live for my wife. Have you no pity for her?"

The shotgun in Williams' hand was steady as the sun. He did not answer Plummer, and there was no sympathy in his eyes. "Now, Bill," he said, without turning his head.

Thompson stepped from behind him and moved softly across the room. He took the coat from the chair, removing the six-shooter and a knife from its pockets. Then he handed the garment to Plummer, who took it and, as though ashamed of his show of weakness, smiled into Williams' eyes. "You have ruined that door," he said lightly, and put on his hat.

Williams' expression did not change. "Come, Henry Plummer," he said, "your sentence is death."

A tiny clock on the shelf struck eight. Plummer glanced at its dial and his eyes lingered, but Williams' hand was upon his arm. He sighed, and with a last look about the little house, followed across its broken door to the scaffold which he, himself, had built to hang Jack Horan in those first days of his great happiness.

The Vigilantes with their prisoners, Stinson and Ray, had gathered about the rude gallows to wait. The news of Plummer's arrest had somehow penetrated the miners' cabins, and now men could be seen seated upon the snow-covered roofs on the hillsides. The blizzard had spent itself hours ago, and the morning sun had flooded Bannack with an almost unearthly brilliance. Tom Henderson's breath was white in the keen of the cold as, looking anxiously towards Henry Plummer's house, he said, "They've got him. They're coming, boys. Close up, close up!" and the snow creaked as men shifted their positions. Back of them curious miners and boys crowded close.

The men on the cabins stood up, knee-deep in snow. As though obeying a signal, each shielded his eyes from the blinding light of the morning sun to look towards the hill down which three men in single file were trudging through the snow.

"It's him," they murmured. "It's Plummer. They've got him." Their short, half-spoken sentences were full of wonder, even fear.

"What in God's name *is* this?" panted a young man, scrambling up beside a bearded miner from California, whose collarless red flannel shirt, open at the neck, exposed his hairy breast in defiance of the cold. He appeared not to hear and, still shading his eyes with both hands, stood motionless, the mountain wind rumpling the long yellow hair about his bronzed neck.

"Vigilantes, young 'un," he muttered, at last. "Vigilantes holdin' a necktie party. If ye're honest, there's nothin' to be afeared of. If ye ain't, ye'd best make tracks." Then lower, to himself, "Now ye'll git yer neddin's, Mister Henry Plummer, of San Francisco."

The three men, Bill Thompson, Henry Plummer and Jim Williams, filed past the cabin, Thompson's knees tossing up fluffs of dry snow. His eyes were straight ahead, and in his right hand he carried a navy six-shooter. Plummer with head erect, coat open, stepped lightly in Thompson's tracks, and knowing that a gun's length behind him Jim Williams strode with a double-barrelled shotgun across his arm, looked neither to the right nor left. The crowd about the scaffold parted to admit them, and then quickly closed behind the broad back of Jim Williams.

The young man, impulsively, slid from the roof. He had tended Plummer's horse at the livery stable—had even done chores about his house. Plummer had been kind to him—had even given him the coat he wore—the finest coat he had ever had. There was some mistake here—some terrible mistake. He ran breathless to the very foot of the scaffold, hoping to help—to prevent, if possible any harm from coming to the sheriff. But there among the grim-faced men he was as one suddenly stricken dumb. His throat contracted with terror, and, wild-eyed, he heard Jim Williams' voice as though far away.

"Bring up Ned Ray," it said.

A Vigilante took hold of his arm. "Move back a little, Charley," he whispered kindly. "You're in the way."

He shrank from the touch of the man's friendly hand, stepping backward obediently, as Ned Ray, struggling and cursing his captors, was dragged to the scaffold and hanged. He did not know if an hour had passed or only a minute when Buck Stinson's body had taken the place of Ned Ray's, and Williams' voice was saying, "Bring up Henry Plummer!"

Now no man stirred. The others were common criminals, but there was something about this man that commanded respect, even while men knew he merited death. Tall, handsome, intelligent, Henry Plummer knew what was in their minds. A smile, almost of pity, was on his thin lips as, folding his arms, he met their glances defiantly. But he was suffering intensely. Under the last of his will his glance turned to Jim Williams standing in the brilliant sunlight, a leader, a master of men. And he was in his power. What was more—far worse—his past was in his power. Not long now until he would be telling Elizabeth what manner of man she had married. He bent his head in the agony of losing her love. When he raised it again and looked out upon the sun-dazzled, snowy hills, he was suddenly glad he would not live to bear that loss. If he lived longer—lived now to see her again, some day the time would come when—

"Bring him up here!" called Williams.

A man approached and laid his hands upon him. "Come," he said. And without a word of protest, Henry Plummer followed to the scaffold and allowed Williams to adjust the noose about his neck.

"Henry Plummer, is there anything you wish to say before you die?"

He turned to Williams, whose face was stern with resolution, and the old light of calm fearlessness came into his gray eyes, but only for a second, for the rope was about his neck and its prickle brought hopelessness. His eyes shifted to the upturned faces.

Suddenly, as though determined to bare a secret, dreaded truth, he tossed his hat into the crowd. Men dodged as though it were a deadly missile. But he did not notice. His quick, slender fingers brushed the long hair from his forehead, drew his palm slowly across his brow. "See," he cried. "See! The Almighty God made me a murderer when He in His wisdom fashioned my skull. Do you, in your righteousness, blame the wolf or the tiger for their ways that were determined by their Creator? Did not the same hand make them which fashioned the tiny bird and the snake that devours it, even as it sings its songs of praise to its Maker?" He paused and a cynical smile curled his lips. "It's all a riddle, men," he almost whispered—"all a riddle and guess as we will, we cannot know its answer."

A man near the scaffold cleared his throat uncomfortably. Plummer's smile deepened. Unconsciously, he brushed the long hair back over his forehead and turned to Jim Williams. "You will take my life," he said evenly, "but in doing it, I beg you to give me a good drop. That is all."

He looked critically up at the gallows and stepped backward. At that moment he caught in a glance the frightened face of the young man who had tended his horse. "Wait," he said, as Jim Williams reached to pinion his arms.

Snatching off his necktie, he tossed it lightly to the youth.

"Good morning, Charley," he said pleasantly. "Keep that to remember me by."

Then he died.